RUBY FLAMES

SHATTERED LIGHT

1

RUBY FLAMES

Richard Knaak

POCKET BOOKS
New York London Toronto Sydney Tokyo Singapore

An *Original* Publication of POCKET BOOKS

POCKET BOOKS, a division of Simon & Schuster Inc.
1230 Avenue of the Americas, New York, NY 10020

ISBN: 0-671-03266-6

First Pocket Books printing March 1999

10 9 8 7 6 5 4 3 2 1

Cover art by David A. Cherry

Printed in the U.S.A.

Prologue

THE KINGDOM OF FUEGO LAY IN BURNING ruins. The shrieks of those caught in the flames vied with those of the people seeking escape from the living fury that followed in the firestorm's wake. No hiding place proved secure; the invaders ferreted out their prey, giving quarter to none they uncovered.

An impossible array of monstrous warriors stalked the once-gleaming streets. Lizcanth, those emerald-scaled, savage reptilian warriors, led the way, brandishing tremendous long swords or wicked, clawed weapons. Some nearly eight feet tall and twice as wide as a human, the Lizcanth were clearly commanders of this unholy horde. Under their hissed orders, ax-wielding ogres covered in fur and grotesque, bent kobolds with clubs battered down any and all resistance. Wide-eyed, huge, lemurlike Yngling, mostly blue-furred, hunted among the ruins for anyone the ogres and kobolds had missed, especially the mercenary reavers, among the few humans to have launched any useful defense against the horde. Barely held back by their leashes, scruffy, twin-headed scevan also searched, sniffing the ground and now and then raising their lupine heads to check the air for the scent of humans.

Above, the great dragons circled, waiting for their next opportunity to strike. Their colors were dominated by blue, for among dragons blue despised the fire mages most. Whatever color, though, be it red, green purple, or another, their presence took all hope from those still alive. The behemoths added to the toll simply by flying, their incredible wings stretched so wide that they could not help but batter the few remaining spired towers, once the crowning achievements of the city's builders.

The grand, imperial palace lay as a vast pile of rubble, the emperor either crushed beneath it or slaughtered by ghoulish warriors, the walking dead, swarming over its remains. Some wore ragged armor, some were missing limbs. While a few looked simply like pale warriors, others had no faces left—flesh and sinew torn away by the claws of Yngling or the jaws of a scevan. Whatever their condition, they hunted and fought without mercy, unmindful that they often killed friends. Once they had been the defenders of this kingdom, but the power that controlled this holocaust had turned them on their own kind after death. Unless burned, the bodies of the dead immediately joined the ranks of evil, there to wreak a havoc more gruesome and soul-shattering than even the dragons.

A few bursts of magic here and there attested to a fire mage or a mentor still standing his or her ground, but even Fuego's most stalwart champions dwindled in number as the seconds passed. One of the feline mrem, allies to the humans, fell, the last of his kind in this region. The furred warriors had fought as bravely as the rest, ever the mortal enemy of the Liz-

canth, but against such terrible might, they, too, could only die.

The red sun dominated and from it the horde seemed to draw strength. This was their time, their moment to triumph . . . and all the inhabitants of Fuego, kingdom of the fire mages, could do was pray that their end would be swift and relatively merciful. . . .

Gasping, Menthusalan pulled himself free of the sorcerous image of destruction he had summoned. Gray, narrow eyes blinked, trying to adjust to the shift in lighting. Sweat poured over the flat, oval features that marked his ancestry as coming from the once mighty clans to the south, warriors of legend long civilized. Like most of his kind, he grew no facial hair, enabling any onlooker to readily study the many age lines cutting across his once smooth skin.

The mentor pursed thin, dry lips and ran a hand over close-cropped, gray hair, trying not to immediately return his gaze to the sphere and the display within. Fuego in ruins! Monsters, with almost as much hatred for one another as they had for humans and mrem, actually working in concert! Menthusalan could not imagine a scenario more incredible and more frightening.

He looked around his dimly-lit chamber, suddenly very nervous even about the shadows in the corners. The serene order and cleanliness of Menthusalan's surroundings did nothing to assuage his fear. Impeccable and exacting among spellcasters, the mentor's study reflected in every way his personality, and generally helped him keep his thoughts in order . . . until now. The bookshelves that lined the walls of his study were filled with an orderly and quite comprehensive selection of texts and scrolls, a collection even his good friend Prymias, most honored of the fire mages save for the emperor himself, readily admired. A case to the far side of the room contained alphabetized, jarred samples of the various chemicals, flora, and other items he found of use in his experiments. Atop the case, neatly polished, were half a dozen artifacts of different sorts ranging back even to the last days of technology. Menthusalan had collected and carefully catalogued these and countless other prizes, learning what he could from each in order to better understand the workings of his world. Now, though, all the arcane knowledge the mentor had gathered over his six decades of service seemed not enough to console him.

Menthusalan stared briefly at the sphere, for the moment banishing the fearsome image that had so shook the elder sorcerer. He had begun this search simply because of an interest in history, especially that of some of the mage wars in eras past. The second and third ages since the fall of man had lasted roughly two thousand years, but very little knowledge about them remained. So many people during those ages had simply sought to survive, hoping for the day when humanity could reclaim the world of Delos from the monsters brought into existence by the stirring of the Laria.

To think that once men without magic flew through the sky or even dared to sail beneath the sea . . . Technology had ruled then, but in their hubris its engineers had sought to control the ultimate sources of power, make anything possible. It was said that they had tried to tap into the power that enabled the world and the stars above to exist, although Menthusalan thought that unlikely. What he did know, nearly for certain, was that by utilizing devices capable of astonishing feats, these engineers had reached out to their lone moon and used it to tap into forces that made even the mighty mentor shiver.

Unfortunately, they had tried to control too much. No longer under their control, the tap showered Delos with sorcerous energy. The sun literally split, becoming the blue, green, and red orbs that left the world with no concept of true night. Lands changed and many of the laws of nature, so long accepted, suddenly altered, leaving the world in turmoil. Mountains sank and seas rose. Continents were torn asunder, leaving but a fraction of the land once available for humanity. Thousands perished, even millions, if the tales could be trusted as to the number of humans living at that time.

Then, when things at last began to settle down and the survivors finally thought they might be able to rebuild their world with the magic now available to them, they discovered that with it had come a darker horror that made even the carnage before seem, in some ways, so insignificant.

The Laria had woken.

From the records he had unearthed over the years, Menthusalan knew that the Laria had existed for millennia, but had been kept imprisoned or under some spell of sleep for most of that time. However, the magical storms that had buffeted Delos had broken the spell keeping the Laria in check and, having been kept prisoner for so long, the demonic creature struck back at those around it with a vengeance.

What the Laria looked like, no scholar could agree. Most simply saw it as a darkness so black as to be able to suck a man's soul from his body if he happened to glance at it. What they, and now Menthusalan, knew was that the Laria personified all that was potentially evil in magic. If a thing could be corrupted by use of power, the Laria would corrupt it. Worse, the Laria had also been able to see into the minds and hearts of the tiny mortals around it and had used that power to bring to life the fears—the things that scared humans from birth on. Vampires, ghosts, and ghouls were but a few of the monsters suddenly rising from the mass graves of the cataclysm. Experiments left over from the age of technology enabled the Laria to create even more horrific creatures, such as the marauding Lizcanth or the ungodly floaters, who had an especially avid taste for mentors.

"And yet we have always fought back," Menthusalan muttered. "Even when we were fighting each other." At times, mankind had nearly freed itself from the darkness, but always there had been those who had thrust the race back into the lair of the Laria. Unfortunately, it had been mostly the work of wizards which led to the continuous downfall of humans. Sometimes the mentor wondered why the Laria even bothered;

men were just as capable of destroying themselves with or without its help.

He shivered, forcing himself to return to the subject at hand. During his research he had come across vague rumors of some monstrous horde slowly gathering strength in the mountains to the north. Such rumors ever abounded, the nightmares of every generation of humanity, but this time there appeared to be some credence to them. Menthusalan had searched, found only a few more vague snippets of information. He had contacted the city of his birth, Dismas, but, as usual, they replied with statements that could be taken for nothing as much as something.

The mentor touched the medallion resting against his elegant but simple sable robe, stroking the black pearl in the center. One reason he had agreed to be one of Dismas's representatives to Fuego so many years ago was because he could not stand his own homeland. Evasive, untrustworthy, and prone to carelessness were the words he thought best described the kingdom of Dismas. The mentors there used the raw power of magic as opposed to fire, earth, air, or even the fourth forgotten element, water, and too often many cared little about the consequences of their dangerous work. At least in Fuego they monitored all up and coming mages with special tests and quests to qualify them for rank. In Dismas anyone with some ability who had a pearl to wield could call himself a mentor.

Still, I would defend you, too, Dismas, if you were so threatened. Yet Dismas did not seem in any danger . . . yet. Each time Menthusalan cast the spell, the image always returned to Fuego. This horde, if it existed, would surely attempt to sweep over all the human and mrem lands, but Fuego seemed to be of particular interest to it.

He needed to discover more before he approached Prymias. The other fire mages distrusted the slim, much too polite mentor, so unlike what they expected of someone from Dismas. Prymias would listen, though, listen and then warn him if this matter had to be dealt with in a different manner than what Menthusalan desired. He might even tell the regal mentor that his part had been completed, that now this matter required the work of the fire mages. If so, Menthusalan would not be offended. He trusted Prymias to see things through to the end.

The mentor concentrated on the large pearl in the medallion, but his eyes were on the sphere. This time, he would not hesitate. In order to discover the truth, Menthusalan would have to delve deeper than the vision; he needed to see the motivating force behind it, discover any and all roots. Then and only then would he have enough with which to go to Prymias.

An image formed in the sphere, but not the carnage overtaking his adopted home. Now Menthusalan scanned the vast mountain range north of Fuego. In some areas, the chain existed only as numerous hills while in others, a veritable forest of jagged, snow-topped leviathans loomed over everything. The elder mentor began his search in the lower regions, seeking with his magic any disturbing presence.

The candles surrounding the small, weathered

oak table at which he worked shrank low and yet Menthusalan still found no clue. He expanded his search to cover the peaks to the northeast, areas often shunned even by the monsters themselves. The Laria did not live there, but other dark powers had abused that land over the centuries, making it inhospitable to all, save for a few savage creatures.

Still nothing—no—a faint something. It seemed to lead away at first, putting him on a trail to the northwest, but then, almost as if someone had slapped the mentor in the face, the trail returned to the northeast, heading deeper and deeper into one particularly godforsaken region.

Menthusalan suddenly had a great desire to abandon his quest, although for what reason he could not yet say. The nearer and nearer his search took him to this place, the more anxious he grew. Now the senior mentor began to wonder if perhaps the Laria did indeed live there and had been stirred to action by the human's search. Menthusalan grasped the pearl and tried to end the scrying spell, but something prevented him.

A castle with five craggy spires materialized in the sphere, a bone-white castle perched in the side of a scarred mountain. As the image grew in size, Menthusalan realized that the castle had been ravaged by war itself, that a third of it had been ripped away in some conflagration far in the past. Scorch marks draped most of the stone walls. Some of the towers barely remained attached. In one area near what had likely been the great hall, an immense balcony with stone rails carved into the shape of roaring lions still stood, but part of its side had been torn away. To all appearances the entire structure appeared long abandoned, yet Menthusalan could not shake the feeling that the answer to his quest lurked within.

But did he dare enter?

What is this place? the mentor wondered, gray eyes narrowed so thin that one might have thought him almost asleep. Perhaps a fire mage might have recognized this castle, but Menthusalan could only hazard a guess. The abode of some wizard? Very possible. Some of the more powerful dared to have their own domains beyond the safety of the kingdoms. Had its master suffered the fate now intended for Fuego?

Curiosity overriding caution, Menthusalan leaned forward. Perhaps he had found his clue. . . .

Then a flash of flame so dark as to be black seemed to burst free of the magical sphere, strikingt the stunned mentor. Menthusalan barely had time to shield himself and those shields buckled under the onslaught. He felt the heat sear his face and the flame lick his cropped hair. The mentor flung up his hands, trying to add a physical shield to the magical ones quickly failing him. From his mouth erupted what should have been a cry of anguish but instead transformed into a single word.

"Ebonyr!"

The intense black flames immediately vanished, sucked back into the scorched sphere, which then shattered. Menthusalan collapsed onto the floor, his last thoughts as he lost consciousness still concerning his search and, most of all, the name that he had uttered, one which, until that moment, the mentor had never heard before.

Ebonyr. . . .

Chapter 1

FERYLN BEGAN TO WONDER AT THE FOOLishness of his secret hunt. Only a month before his official rite of passage and he had decided to go out and hunt a scevan by himself. The elders always preached against anxiousness, especially when it involved a hunt, but Feryln had been too nervous, too needful to prove himself to himself before he had to do the same for the entire village. Because of that, he had snuck out after his family had gone to sleep and went to hunt one of the lupine horrors, intending to bring back one of its two heads as proof. Scevan were dangerous, but they were also stupid, despite the old adage about two heads. The mrem had calculated exactly how he would hunt one down, even to the killing stroke. Of course, that meant finding one, which was where his plan had first begun to fall apart.

Scevan constantly haunted this part of the mountain forest, either alone or in packs. At least once a week hunters brought back the carcass of such a beast. Stories said that magic had created the scevan from another creature long since vanished, which would explain the twin heads. One had to know just how to outwit a creature that could look two directions at once. At the very least, if a lone hunter could not find a scevan, the scevan should have found him. Not so this night, for so far Feryln's lance and sword remained unbloodied. The nearest he had come to a hunt had been when he surprised a rabbit, a trophy that would have earned him ridicule, not honor.

Nose and whiskers twitching, the tall, sleek mrem sniffed the air. Attentive, brown, feline eyes searched the dark forest, seeing details that the cursed Lizcanth or the clumsy ogres would have missed completely. A small creature leapt from one tree branch to another. Feryln's pointed ears rose as a bird called in the distance. The green sun stood high in the sky, its emerald light casting a calming touch over the lush, sloping forest and adding an interesting touch to the mrem's short, golden brown body fur. The gentle winds rustled his loose, shoulder-length hair, which had darkened this last year almost to the color of his brown leather kilt. Although most of the catlike mrem slept during the green shift, Feryln had always enjoyed it the most.

Still no scevan. Feryln extended his claws in frustration as he lithely but cautiously wended his way along the uneven mountain terrain. By now, he stood a very good chance of having been discovered gone by some member of his family. If he returned empty-handed, his shame would be double. A slight growl escaped; that would never do, not if he hoped to impress a potential mate someday soon. While his broad features, prominent cheek bones, strong, healthy teeth, and even the streak of black fur along his right ear gave him some advantage in attracting a future mate, his lack of showing as a hunter would work against him. Even being of one of the most prominent bloodlines in the village, that of Brouka the Keen-Eyed, who it had been said could throw a killing strike at an animal from twice the distance as any other hunter, would not erase Feryln's shame . . . or at least, so he believed.

Gripping the lance tight, the young mrem continued on, eyeing the mighty trees and rising, rocky slopes for signs of acceptable prey. Feryln's whiskers twitched again as scents reached him, but all were faint and none originated from anything more dangerous than an owl. *I should turn back. Maybe no one has discovered me missing. I could try another night. The village is only a little more than an hour's journey back if I maintain a swift pace. I could make it before—*

A sound from the direction of the village made him pause. While he could not identify it, it unsettled him for some reason. Again Feryln thought about returning to his home. He had failed to locate, much less kill, a scevan and if he returned now, perhaps he could forget about this night. Many young mrem made their first adult kill at the rites; he would just have to be one of them.

With a hiss of frustration, Feryln turned back, picking up his pace. Despite his decision to return, though, he still had an uneasy feeling, as if he were now the hunted and not the hunter. The mrem paused once to sniff the air, but sensed nothing. Around him the leafy branches of the trees and bushes shook, but only because of the wind, the young hunter decided, not any lurking beast. He wrinkled his nose in frustration and peered in the direction of the village.

In the distance, plumes of smoke began to rise above the trees.

Feryln bared his fangs, a hiss of horror escaping the mrem. He blinked, wishing away the smoke, but still it remained, growing by the second. Not even the largest bonfire in his village could cause so great a cloud. He could only think of one terrible reason for such a great fire.

His family, his people, were under attack.

Feryln started forward . . . only to fall the next moment as a massive, stench-ridden form dropped upon him from his left, snarling and snapping at him.

One set of fangs clamped hard into his shoulder, causing the golden-furred mrem to scream. Another lupine face thrust itself toward his throat and only by sheer luck did Feryln succeed in holding the jaws back with his free hand. He then extended his claws, thrusting them into the beast's own throat. The monster howled and blood splattered the desperate warrior on both the face and body, even staining the clan crest, a silhouetted mrem in battle stance, on the front of his kilt.

His attacker pulled back momentarily, revealing the twin, savage faces of a nearly full-grown scevan, this one a particularly ugly beast with matted, brown and black fur and two muzzles that looked as if someone had kicked them several times. The lupine horror pawed at the earth with curved, sharp claws. One head turned downward, hacking up blood. The other glared back at him through heavy-browed, yellow orbs. Feryln slowly reached for his sword, knowing he stood a much better chance of surviving with it. His counterattack had proven a fortuitous one, but the scevan still outweighed him and its wounds would only make it more furious. If he could pull the blade free, he could kill the monstrous beast.

The scevan, though, did not choose to wait, leaping even as the mrem pulled his sword. Feryln abandoned his grip on the hilt, knowing that he could never fully draw the weapon in time. Extending claws on both hands, he met the lupine horror's assault full on. The pair rolled over and over, at last crashing against the thick trunk of an oak. Feryln's entire body vibrated from shock, but it was the scevan who took the brunt of the blow. That gave the young warrior a moment's respite, time he used to strike at the most vulnerable spot in easy reach—the eyes of the uninjured head.

Claws raked across the furious scevan's orbs. The howl that followed nearly deafened Feryln, but he nonetheless completed the attack. Blood splattered him again, nearly causing him to vomit, yet he managed a second, albeit shorter, strike back.

The scevan lashed out blindly, the yellow, encrusted fangs coming within an inch of Feryln's nose. Claws tore at his flank, leaving an array of ragged, bleeding wounds there. The injured mrem gritted his teeth. If he surrendered to the pain, the beast would take him.

At last Feryln managed to free a hand long enough to reach for his sword. The blinded head snapped wildly, the one with the throat injury settled for trying to claw him. The young mrem's hopes rose slightly. If the scevan remained disoriented much longer, he would be able to kill it.

However, his own growing weakness began to hinder him. Although Feryln freed the sword, the effort left him unable to bring it up. He gasped, trying to draw enough breath so that he could push himself on. So close, Feryln dared not surrender now.

The heads of the scevan paused. The one that could see glared at Feryln and although it did not strike, the other suddenly acted. The beast had recovered its wits and now both heads worked in concert. Fangs grazed Feryln's upper chest, drawing blood. Already weak, the new wound nearly made the mrem faint.

Mustering what effort he could, Feryln brought the blade up. He could not thrust it directly into the scevan's chest, but hoped to catch the beast in the side. The animal noticed his attempt and tried to bat away the oncoming blade with one paw. Feryln almost lost his grip again.

He had to do it now. If he did not kill the scevan with this strike, he would die. His family, his village, needed him.

Roaring, Feryln mustered his strength and

thrust. His cry startled the bleeding monster, giving the injured young warrior the chance to plunge the sword into the scevan's rib cage as hard as he could.

Both heads howled high and long. The mrem's grip at last faltered. The claws of his bestial adversary tore at his chest and arms. The scevan whined, then pitched forward just as Feryln's legs gave way.

The wounded beast's heavy weight crushed the air from Feryln's lungs, causing the weary mrem to black out, his last thought the certainty that he had become the scevan's meal.

Feryln awoke to pain and a foul smell that caused him to briefly slip back into unconsciousness. He stirred again, this time fighting both the pain and the stench, determined to survive. A heavy weight pinned him to the ground and only after several minutes did he realize the weight to be the bloody corpse of the scevan. Feryln wrinkled his nose in disgust. The beast might be dead, but if the mrem remained in this position much longer, its foul odor would soon finish the task its claws and fangs had begun.

Still in much pain, Feryln managed to push the massive corpse over a little. With effort, he dragged himself free, then succeeded in rising to a sitting position, but that was as much as he could do for a time.

Blood matted his fur. Feryln started to clean himself, then thought better of licking fur tainted by so much of the scevan. He sniffed the air. Yes, some body of water did lay nearby, most likely a stream. He simply had to drag himself to it . . . if he had the strength.

Then he recalled the village.

Gazing up, the mrem could no longer see any smoke. Hours had passed, though, precious hours that might mean anything. Perhaps the village had turned back the attackers, sent them fleeing back into the mountains. That had to be what happened; Feryln could not bring himself to imagine any other outcome, although uncertainties nagged at him constantly.

His concern for his family urging him on, Feryln made it to water; a trickling, clear creek, just as he had thought. The creek had to be an offshoot of the raging river passing just east of his village, a river that was the source of much of the fish devoured by his people. The cool liquid soothed him and aided the mrem in his efforts to clean his fur and his wounds. His stomach growled, but Feryln wasted no time on food. He would find something either on the way back or when he reached the village. Most likely his mother had already prepared a meal for him. Cold, yes, and one accompanied by a lecture, but certainly she would have a meal ready. She would.

Shivering, the gold and brown mrem rose as best he could and stumbled toward home.

The blue sun had already begun to descend, a terrible sign of just how long he had lain unconscious. Feryln picked up his pace as best he could. Some traces of smoke tickled his nose, but they were old. His ears twitched as he waited for the familiar sounds of village life, but despite moving ever nearer to his destination, the mrem heard nothing. Even the wildlife seemed subdued; the only birds he heard were the raucous crows. In fact, the nearer he got to the village, the more animated the black birds grew. The hair on the back of his neck rose.

Ahead of him, several trees lay shattered, as if one or more of the armored swegles, the great horned beasts, had charged through. Swegles were not often found in this region, though, preferring as they did the low, flat lands. Besides, other trees still standing bore different marks, as if some mad mrem had tried to beat them down with a club.

What has happened here? Nervous, Feryln clutched his sword, which he had earlier recovered from the body of the scevan. The lance had been lost to him, but the sword gave him some small comfort. The sharp weapon had been bloodied; from here on it would guide his hand true, so Feryln had been taught by his father.

His father. . . .

He ran the last few yards, already fearing, perhaps even knowing, what he would find. Despite that, when the young mrem entered the village that had been his entire world, the sight that greeted him caught Feryln completely off-guard. The sword fell from his limp grip and his mouth hung open as he stared almost vacantly at the carnage before him.

Once the village, while not the largest, had been one of the cleanest, the best-kept. Circular in design with a high wooden fence surrounding it, the village had supported several dozen families and other individuals. In addition to the buildings, both within and without the walls there had been small tracts of land used for farming, the greater fields on the outside, of course. Even before he entered the village itself, Feryln could see that nothing remained of those outer fields, the nearly ripe crops torn asunder or devoured by whatever had passed through here.

Most homes within the fenced area were simple huts with wooden roofs and three rooms, one for activities and the other two for the sleeping quarters of parents and children. Feryln's family, of some importance, had built on to the basic structure, adding rooms for his eldest brother and himself, the next in line to reach adulthood.

In the center of the village stood the one tall building, the common meeting place where all joined during poor weather or certain feasts. Nearly twice the height of any other structure, the common house stretched almost the entire diameter of the village, giving quick and easy access to all. In happier, warmer times, areas in the roof could be slid open to allow the sun in, if desired. Wooden benches and tables within offered enough seating even for the occasional guests from far-off villages. Feryln's own ceremony of adulthood would have taken place in the common house, it being the village's greatest symbol of stability and strength. Unlike the simple wood huts, it had been constructed almost entirely from carefully chosen stone, guaranteeing that at least one building would survive more or less intact even in the event of a forest fire.

It had not survived, although clearly fire could not be blamed in this case.

Every structure including the common building had been torn asunder. Even the wooden fence surrounding the village lay splintered in many places, as if that same herd of armored swegles had passed through, then passed through again. Feryln might have believed them the cause of so much devastation if not for the fire and its precision. Many homes had been purposely set ablaze and, he realized from the frightful stench, their inhabitants with them. Yet, the destruction of every building remained a distant horror compared to the ravaged forms lying everywhere in the open. Males, females, adults, and children . . . none had been spared. An arm that had been bitten off lay not that far from the stunned Feryln. A young maiden, her head crushed in, stared sightlessly at the clear heavens. Beyond, two warriors had been ripped in half and their remains scattered far apart.

Feryln dropped to his knees and retched. How long he stayed in that position, he did not know and, in truth, he did not care. Nothing registered at all until his thoughts finally twisted back toward his own family.

His family. . . . Forcing himself up, Feryln hurried toward his home. Perhaps by some miracle his parents, his siblings, still lived. Perhaps—

No! Please, no! The young mrem stumbled to a halt. A blackened pile of ash marked the place where he had been born. Even from a distance, a dismayed Feryln could smell the already familiar odor of burnt flesh. It almost made him vomit again, but for his family's sake he fought the feeling back. Gingerly he made his way to the charred ruins, forcing himself to seek the truth. Feryln quickly but regretfully ascertained that there were at least three corpses present, one adult and two younger mrem.

"Seren . . . Laius . . . Hegra . . ." Feryln hissed out his new pain. He knew now the fate of his mother, and his brother and sister. That left but his father and his older brother, both respected warriors. Might they still be alive?

The answer to one of those questions came swiftly. His father, Feryln the Elder, he found not far from the home of, Gristlo, his mother's sire. Both males had been battered almost to a pulp and only because of the streak of black near Gristlo's ear, the same streak that the distraught mrem had inherited, had Feryln been able to identify the elder. Feryln identified his father by the left hand, which missed two fingers. According to his father, years ago a Lizcanth had taken those fingers just before the warrior had taken the reptile's head. Feryln the Elder had proudly worn the teeth of that Lizcanth around his throat for many years.

Lizcanth . . . this had to be the work of Lizcanth despite there being no bodies, no traces. Only they hated mrem so much that they would dare attack a village as strong as this . . . and yet no great force of the reptiles had been noted in the region since Feryln's father had been a young warrior. Mrem from villages spread across several days' journey had banded together to push the lizards out of the area, eradicate them if possible. How could they have returned in such numbers?

Too soon, he found his brother as well. Herrick lay in one piece, but his stomach had been torn out by some jagged weapon, his life fluids now puddled around him. They had once looked much alike despite the difference in years, with Herrick being taller and minus the black streak. But now the little that remained barely even resembled a mrem. Feryln fell to one knee, honoring his brother as he had the rest of his family. Guilt overwhelmed him. He should have been here; perhaps he could have saved at least one.

Of course, it would have been more likely that Feryln would have perished with the rest.

A slight sound caused his ears to perk up. To his astonishment, Herrick still lived. How that could be possible, Feryln did not know, but immediately he worked to aid the older mrem. He began trying to dab the wound, finding some way of creating order from the terrible chaos. In some remote part of his mind, Feryln marveled that he could do as much without collapsing again.

"Fer . . ." Herrick's eyes were open, although one stared off.

"I am here! I am sorry for being away, Herrick!" Tears started down the younger brother's grimy, blood-soaked face, "I should have been here—"

"Be . . . dead . . . like me. . . ." Feryln's brother hacked. "Run. Go far . . . warn . . . any . . ."

"You must be still—"

Herrick coughed up blood, nearly choking. "Feryln . . . Lizcanth were—"

The younger mrem interrupted, the single word confirming his fears. "Lizcanth. . . . I thought so, Herrick! Do not worry! When you are well we will warn about the Lizcanth!"

"Lizcanth . . . og . . . ogres . . . kobolds . . . more . . . Feryln . . . all of them . . . they . . . together. . . ."

Together? What did his brother mean? It sounded as if Herrick claimed that the reptiles had fought alongside other monsters such as the ogres and kobolds, but that could not be. Ogres despised kobolds and kobolds despised ogres. The Lizcanth had use for neither. Clearly Herrick suffered from delirium.

The other mrem must have read his expression. "Truth, Feryln! Lizcanth . . . ogres . . . more . . . all together. . . ."

Herrick fell back, gasping. Feryln immediately went back to work on the wound, trying to bind the stomach area back together. He would save his brother, then, when Herrick had recovered, the two of them would avenge the village somehow. They would.

"Feryln . . ." Herrick put a weak hand on his brother's own . . . and died.

The overwhelmed mrem howled in anguish. With his brother dead, he had no family nor even a village. His life had been taken from him almost as if he, too, had died here. Perhaps that would have been better. If he had died here, the shame he felt for having run off would not weigh him down. Briefly Feryln contemplated joining his family; they could hunt through the ethereal fields together, forever dining on fat deer and other delicacies.

Yet, he truly did not want to die and knew that his family would not have expected it of him. No, rather than surrender, Feryln realized that what he had to do was what he would have done if Herrick had lived. Find the ones who had slaughtered his people and destroy them.

That he might be alone in this venture did not deter Feryln. If he had to hunt the murderers down one by one, he would do so. The young mrem rose. First he would bury his kin, and the others if possible. As the sole survivor, he saw it as his duty.

A gnawing in his stomach warned him that first he had to think of himself. Feryln would be useful to no one if he could not rummage up some food. Whoever the marauders had been, even if they were this unbelievable horde Herrick had spoken of, they had to have missed something edible.

After several minutes of searching, he began to wonder if he was wrong. What had not been destroyed had been taken, including the stores set aside for the poorer times of year. However, in one crushed house he found a few pieces of fruit that had been covered by the collapsed roof. Giving thanks to the absent owner, who Feryln knew must be among the victims, the mrem began to eat.

Midway through the last piece, he heard someone approaching. At first his hopes rose that perhaps there was another survivor, but then he heard the low, raspy breathing. Suspicious, Feryln put down the bit of fruit, then carefully drew his sword. He waited behind the wall, watching through a crack for sign of the newcomer.

A flash of green scale caused his eyes to widen. Feryln gripped his sword and tried not to panic as he caught sight of a huge, two-legged reptile with a maw full of sharp, tearing teeth and hands with talons almost twice as long as the mrem's own. The abomination scanned the devastated village with slitted red and black orbs that darted here and there constantly. His massive tail swung back and forth, adding further damage as the creature moved along. A tiny row of leathery plates stretched from the back of the monstrous warrior's head down to the very tip of his tail. The savage invader wore a tattered kilt that once had belonged to a mrem and carried several small pouches on his belt. Strapped to his back was some sort of weapon harness, although from his vantage point Feryln had not been able to identify what that weapon might be.

Lizcanth! It could only be one of the deadly creatures of which his father and other elders had spoken. The devastation made terrible sense now. The Lizcanth so hated mrem. Somehow, they had recouped and come to this region of the mountains again, catching his people by surprise. Now one of the marauders had returned to the village . . . but why?

Feryln recalled his howls of anguish. Fool that he had been, he had not thought the murderers might still be close enough to hear him. At least one of them, though, had come back to investigate.

But one I can take, he insisted to himself. I am a mrem hunter! I have slain a scevan! I can slay one Lizcanth!

His mind made up, Feryln tried to follow the reptile's path. If the Lizcanth continued straight, he would leave his back exposed to the mrem. While not the most honorable plan, Feryln reminded himself that the Lizcanth had attacked his village while most slept. Honor and the reptiles did not go together.

Luck held with him. The lone Lizcanth moved directly on. Feryln saw that the monstrous lizard wielded a peculiar weapon with jagged edges that resembled the creature's own vicious claws, only larger and sharper. The weapon required both hands, much like a war ax. The jagged edges were stained with recent blood.

Mrem blood.

Ears flattened, Feryln started forward. He had only killed a scevan, but after what this creature and his ilk had done, he had no fears, no hesitation, about striking him down.

Despite his silent steps, something alerted the Lizcanth. The monstrous warrior turned, forcing Feryln to pick up speed. The reptile hissed when he saw what attacked and raised his weapon in defense. Fortunately for Feryln, the reptile moved too slowly. The mrem roared, then thrust as hard as he could for the Lizcanth's throat.

The blade sank deep, cutting off the lizard's cry. The clawed weapon fell from the Lizcanth's massive hands, the creature quickly following suit. Feryln barely had time to withdraw the blade before it could be crushed under the reptile's dead weight.

The mrem shivered. While he did not regret what he had done, killing the Lizcanth still affected him. Yet, had there been a second attacker, Feryln would not have hesitated to repeat the act. The marauders deserved no sympathy, no quarter at all—

He barely heard the attack in time. Feryln stumbled back as a weapon identical to the one his victim had wielded nearly decapitated him. The mrem found himself staring into the eyes of a second, larger Lizcanth.

"Mrem . . ." the reptilian warrior rumbled. "Fresh meat . . ."

Feryln deflected a second attack, but the force of the green reptile's blow set his entire body shaking. The mrem backed up to give himself more time, then saw that another invader sought to join the efforts of his adversary. Only . . .what approached proved to be no Lizcanth, but rather a huge, shaggy creature with sharp teeth, massive ears, and a face that could best be described as a parody of mrem features at best. Taller even than the Lizcanth, it lumbered toward the combat with evil intent in its bestial eyes. In one hand it held a club nearly as large as Feryln.

His brother had spoken the truth. Ogres fought alongside Lizcanth. Mortal enemies had come together to obliterate the village.

"Mine!" the Lizcanth hissed. "Mine!"

The ogre slowed. Yet another phenomenon. An

ogre who obeyed the dictates of one of the reptiles. How was that possible?

Feryln hesitated. If the ogre did not interfere, perhaps the young mrem stood a chance against the second Lizcanth. Then, Feryln's ancestors willing, he might even defeat the ogre. Powerful the shaggy giant might be, but his reflexes were much slower than that of a young mrem . . . or so Feryln hoped.

The Lizcanth approached, bloodlust in his eyes. Feryln kept his sword at the ready. One foolish mistake on his part could end it all. The reptile, though, moved with less grace than a mrem warrior. Feryln could defeat him if he could but bide his time.

Then the third Lizcanth entered the village, followed almost immediately by a macabre creature with hands and feet much too large for its body and a head so wide one wondered how its owner could hold it up. Whereas the ogre had seemed a parody of a mrem, this dirty brown creature in turn appeared a parody of the ogre. It could only be a kobold, yet another creature said to have been run off a generation ago by Feryln's father and others. The kobold gave him a toothsome grin, as if anticipating what the mrem's flesh would taste like. In one hand it carried a weapon akin to a mace, a weapon fresh with blood.

A horde of monsters . . . all with a hatred of mrem . . .

Feryln held his ground for a moment more, then realized the folly of his situation. To stay would mean to die, to see that the village remained unavenged. In truth, faced by so many monsters from the stories of his childhood, Ferlyn's fear also played a significant hand. The Lizcanth were the horrors of his early nightmares, followed closely by ogres and the like. To face them alone so soon after witnessing the depths of their evil proved too much.

Shame besetting him, Feryln turned and fled into the nearest woods.

A cry rose up behind him, the Lizcanth and their unlikely allies giving pursuit. Feryln ran, darting around the trees with the ease of one born and raised in the wooded region. He did not know exactly which direction he ran, only that he ran from the monstrous foes. Each moment the young mrem expected to feel a set of claws in his back or a heavy, bone-crushing club against his skull.

Something massive flew overhead, moving so swiftly that by the time Feryln looked up, it had already vanished. The mrem's breath grew ragged. He could hear his pursuers behind him, more of them, it seemed to Feryln, than the few he had confronted.

Again something flew by, this time so near and with such speed that a veritable gale grew in its wake, one that flung the hapless mrem forward. Briefly he caught sight of a leathery wing, but nothing more. Unfortunately, Feryln crashed against a tree, losing his sword in the process. Stunned, he could not immediately rise.

A roaring filled his ears, but not the roaring of an animal. Feryln sniffed the air, realized that he stood a short distance from the river. Of all the directions he could have fled, this one would have been the least of his choices. The mrem had never had a need to build any sort of bridge spanning the wild river, for much farther upstream nature had taken its own steps, creating an overhang of rock that allowed those on foot to readily cross. Unfortunately, to head in that direction would put Feryln too near those now hunting him.

He ran the remaining distance to the river and looked over the area. During certain times of the year, the waters were calm enough for mrem to swim across, but one glance informed Feryln that this was not the case today. The water moved with savage abandon, frothing and jumping everywhere. Tree limbs and other flotsam rode helplessly downstream to the mysterious lowlands Feryln and his people knew about only from stories. Demons and creatures like swegles roamed there. Good mrem stayed in their villages and avoided such places.

He glanced behind him. Shapes moving among the trees revealed how little time the young warrior had left. Feryln looked north, where the mountains rose higher, then south, where the land sloped ever downward—except where it ended at sudden ravines—but could not choose a path. His mind no longer seemed to function. All he could think about was that he stood at the river's edge, unarmed and seemingly awaiting his death.

A Lizcanth, perhaps the same Lizcanth the weary mrem had confronted earlier, burst through the foliage. The scaly warrior raised the clawed weapon and hissed gleefully in his direction. "Mrrrem meat . . ."

Feryln quickly looked around, but found no weapon with which to defend himself. He glanced at the river again, saw to the north a tangle of tree limbs rolling about. Desperation convinced him to try what sanity would have rejected instantly.

The mrem leaped into the river.

Behind him, Feryln heard the Lizcanth hiss in frustration as his prey escaped. Then the mrem forgot his pursuers as he fought simply to survive the horrible current. Water assailed him from everywhere. The limbs he sought Feryln could not at first find and he suddenly feared that they had passed by already. Then the tangle rolled on top of him, nearly drowning the mrem in the process. Feryln struggled for air, trying to maintain a grip of some sort on what turned out not to be simply limbs, but the entire upper half of a young, uprooted tree.

He managed to wrap himself up enough in the tree to keep his head more or less above water at all times, but that proved to be the limit to Feryln's already wracked system. The bedraggled mrem took one last glance back, but both the spot from which he had leapt and his pursuers there had dwindled away thanks to the river's swift run.

Exhausted, Feryln lowered his head onto the tree and let the river take him to whatever fate it chose.

Chapter 2

VOICES STIRRED FERYLN FROM HIS EXhausted slumber. He found himself still tangled in the tree, which had washed up on the side of a much more subdued region of the great river. The weary, injured mrem forced his eyes open, trying to quickly identify his surroundings. Through blurred vision he managed to make out trees and a landscape much flatter than he had ever known, but other than that Feryln had no idea where he was.

Again the voices rose, this time louder and nearer. Memories of the hunters stirred the mrem to action. He struggled his way out of the broken limbs and crawled toward shore. If he could make it to the safety of the trees, then he could study the newcomers in secret. They might not be Lizcanth or ogres . . . but then again they might be something else allied with this unholy horde.

Unfortunately, after only half a dozen ragged steps, Feryln collapsed, unable to go any further. The injured and water-logged mrem lay face down in the dirt, barely conscious. He extended his claws, determined at least to strike out if one of the oncoming hunters decided to turn him over for a look.

The voices quieted. Feryln waited, but when they did not rise again, he breathed a sigh of relief. However, the breath faltered when he heard footsteps approaching.

"A mrem!" came the harsh voice. No Lizcanth, but not one of Feryln's kind, either. The battered mountain mrem remained still, waiting. He needed but one good strike, some blow that in at least a tiny way could avenge his family.

Someone touched his shoulder. "I think he's still alive, Rowlen! Hold on while I make certain!"

I must be ready! Every muscle in Feryln's body went taut.

Suddenly a second voice shouted, "Master Jarric! Stand away!"

The hand withdrew, but the mrem had already committed himself. He rolled over onto his back and, claws fully extended, swiped at where he estimated the hunter's throat would be.

He missed completely. Worse, strong hands seized his wrists in grips of iron, effectively ending any hope of escape. Feryln spat at his captor and tried to kick free. He would not be taken so simply; he could not let that happen—

"Easy, young one!" the second voice purred. "Easy! I am no foe!"

Gradually it dawned on Feryln that the voice he heard came from a fellow mrem. The haze of fear and desperation parted, allowing him to focus on the tall figure holding him prisoner. A tawny, scarred warrior with the tip of one ear missing and a snout much thicker than Feryln's. Gray had begun to spread through the stranger's coat and the green eyes held wisdom that only years of struggle could have gathered. The strange mrem wore his hair cut shorter, almost cropped. Instead of the kilts favored in the mountains, Feryln's captor stood clad in jerkin and pants, the latter designed with a mrem's tail in mind . . . and even wore boots, something no villager would have done. Only a few of the rare, seasonal travelers had ever been noted wearing the peculiar footgear. Mountain mrem generally either used sandals or simply went barefoot.

Differences aside, though, a mrem was still a mrem and the knowledge that he had reached his own kind nearly made the exhausted villager faint again, this time in relief.

"Easy, young one!" The other mrem helped him.

"Let me help you, Rowlen!" came the original voice.

At first Feryln looked forward to the extra aid, but when the other drew near, his eyes widened. What manner of beast was this?

Not quite as tall as a mrem, but slightly wider and utterly tailless, the outlandish creature reached toward Feryln. Its features were drawn out, much more than that of mrem, but not quite as much as an ogre, which it most resembled. Round, so very round, light blue eyes with too much white and too little pupil stared back at him, the nearest hair above them a pair of thin, almost nonexistent brows the color of flame. Below the eyes perched a narrow, somewhat pointed nose of little possible use for detecting scents. There were no whiskers, just a faint sprinkling of fur almost invisible above the mouth. The almost cheerful, full-lipped mouth opened, revealing even, blunt teeth, but this did nothing to assuage Feryln's rising fear. Swegles had blunt teeth, but still one did not stand in front of them when they chose to charge.

The hair atop the creature's head, hair which flowed down in back just below the shoulder, stirred the embers of the mrem's horror more, for it, too, matched well the color of fire, now so great a reminder of what had happened to Feryln's village. Yet, despite the long growth on top, what parts of the body that were not covered by the black and crimson robe with the fire pattern insignia on the breast were nearly devoid of any hair, almost as if this beast had chosen to shave his body.

Whether ogre, kobold, or some mix he could not imagine, Feryln wanted nothing of the creature's touch. He renewed his struggles, surprising Rowlen, who nearly lost his grip.

"What is with you now, young one? Master Jarric means you no harm!"

"What . . . what is he?"

"What is he?" Rowlen's expression shifted from confusion to amusement. "Aaah, now I see! You would be from the highlands, would you not, young one? Never seen a human before, have you?"

The nearly hairless creature frowned. "How could he have not seen a—"

The older mrem spoke again to Feryln, cutting off the other's protest. "You have never seen a human before. They would not have had much desire to journey to your high regions, young one." He made Feryln look at the fire-crested figure. "They are like us in many ways. More important, they are allies and, sometimes, friends." Rowlen leaned close. "Friends, young one. The humans are friends."

"Friends?" He could scarcely believe a mrem would ally itself with any creature, much less one so bizarre.

"Say the word. Say 'human.' "

"Human."

"Good! Now, if I let you go, do you promise not to run away or, more foolish, attack?"

Feryln eyed the pair. Rowlen he trusted and if Rowlen believed in this creature, then so would Feryln. Besides, the more he saw of it, the less dangerous the human seemed to be. With such blunt teeth and tiny claws, no more than stubs that looked like they could not even retract, what harm could it really do to him?

"My name's Jarric," the human said, extending one hand. He lowered the hand when Feryln simply stared at it. "I didn't mean to frighten you."

"I was not frightened!" the injured mrem snapped, embarrassed by his earlier reaction.

Jarric gave a slight bow. "My mistake."

Uncertain as to how to read a human's reactions, Feryln took the comment for honest apology. The possible confrontation now a thing of the past, his body again began to give out on him. When Jarric moved to help, Feryln did not protest.

"You look like you have rolled down the mountains, young one," Rowlen growled after a survey of Feryln's wounds. "But some of these were not made by falls. Did a beast attack you?"

A beast and more, but Feryln did not have the strength to answer him. Rowlen and his strange companion realized the depths of his injuries and began to administer aid. Jarric brought water for him to sip while the other mrem bound the worst wounds. After a time, Feryln recovered enough to relate his incredible story, which left both newcomers in almost as much shock as he still was.

"The emperor's council should be informed," Jarric stated flatly, ignorant of the fact that Feryln had no idea of whom he was speaking. The human shook his head. "The village, the scevan, the hunters, and then all the way down the river . . . some power watches over you, Feryln." He looked at Rowlen. "Master Prymias should certainly hear his tale."

"As you wish, Master Jarric."

Feryln had gradually noticed how Rowlen treated the human with some deference, an act which disturbed him a little, for Jarric appeared little older than the villager. Of course, Jarric treated the older mrem well, too, respecting his suggestions. The human seemed in control, but only by virtue of some status that Feryln could as yet only guess. It had something to do with the elaborate robes.

"Can you walk?" Rowlen asked him.

"Walk?" Feryln had to think and thinking still hurt. Finally, "Yes, I think I can walk."

"But slowly, I know. All right, young one. You will walk with me. That will ensure that you will not fall."

"Where—where do we go?" Feryln had lost his village, his world, and now these two strangers wanted to take him even beyond the edge of the mountains.

"To Fuego, of course," the robed figure, the human, responded. When he noticed the young mrem's blank expression, he added, "Home of those like myself, fire mages."

Mages? Feryln knew that word well enough, even if there had been no such people in his village. Mages cast spells, toyed with the elements. Feryln's folk, living in harmony with their environment, found such abilities disturbing. Tales said that mages had been responsible for catastrophes in the past which had forever marred Delos. Now Rowlen and Jarric intended to take him to a land where an entire group of spellcasters worshiping fire lived!

Of course, had there been such folk in his village, perhaps Feryln's family and friends would not have been slaughtered. . . .

"Master Jarric," Rowlen interjected. "Perhaps you could gather the things we dropped?"

Still eyeing Feryln, the human nodded. When they were alone, Rowlen leaned toward his counterpart. "Listen close, young one. Fuego stands as one of the great strongholds against the darkness which claimed your village. Humans rule there, but mrem interests lie in their success. You will see many strange and, no doubt, unsettling things in the kingdom of the fire mages. Know, though, that there stands the best chance you have of seeing your family and friends avenged."

The best chance to avenge my people. Fuego sounded indeed like the destination for him . . . yet, to walk into a kingdom ruled by fire mages—could he do that? Feryln eyed the human, the only fire mage he had so far ever seen. Jarric hardly seemed frightening. "Is he . . . is he really a caster of spells?"

"Young Master Jarric? A little erratic, but, yes. He is much like you from what I can see. Trying to strive to attain a place for himself, yet uncertain if he can surmount the final goal. That was why you sought the scevan—"

"And failed my family!"

"But lived to fight another day. Fuego will give you the chance to strike back, young Feryln. Will you take it?"

What choice did he truly have? Feryln nodded, grateful for Rowlen's reassurance. With such creatures as Jarric, Fuego had to be strange, indeed, but any place that would aid him in garnering the strength he needed to complete his oath to his village would be well worth the visit . . . he hoped.

"Are we ready?" the human called. In his hands he held two travel sacks and a staff, the latter evidently his.

Pain jolted Feryln's side as he tried to rise. He

stared at the path the pair seemed to be following, trying to imagine that the trek to this fabled kingdom would be gentle, and failing in the attempt. He would have to prepare himself for much discomfort. It would all be worth it, though, once he reached Fuego.

At least, Feryln hoped so.

Jarric studied the new mrem surreptitiously as the trio started off. Feryln's tale of tragedy had touched the mage. If it had been up to him, he would have led an expedition to the north to do combat with the fiends who had destroyed the village. Of course, not having even attained full rank yet, the young fire mage could not yet lead anything. That would change soon, though. When they reached Fuego, he would see his sponsor and receive his quest. Once he completed that, then Jarric could begin trying in earnest to help Feryln. In the meantime, the mountain mrem could rely on Master Prymias, who would surely not let a disaster such as this escape justice. Master Prymias would take care of everything.

The ambitious young spellcaster nodded to himself. Yes, once they reached Fuego, the matter of Feryln's people would be in good hands . . . of that Jarric had the utmost faith.

How could they all live so packed together?

The question repeated in Feryln's mind again and again as the trio neared the immense walls. For five days they had walked together and for five days Rowlen and Jarric had tried to prepare

Ferlyn for his first sight of a city, but the villager had secretly scoffed at their tales of spired towers rising like small peaks and walls so massive that they could block out any glimpse of the land around. When his rescuers had told him about the many people, he had found that even more unbelievable; Feryln had imagined a village some ten times the size of his own and thought that remarkable. Now he realized how limited his vision had been.

The great walls of Fuego stood twenty, thirty, perhaps even forty feet high; the young mrem could not say. He saw no brick, no mortar. The entire structure had a reddish glaze over it, as if the surrounding walls had all been baked together in some tremendous kiln. Recalling who it was who lived here, Feryln wondered if he weren't far from the truth.

Even before they reached the walls, he had counted more people, both mrem and, too often, humans, than he had ever imagined existed. They traveled to and from the city, some clearly on important journeys, others moving at less frantic pace, as if they cared not at all when they arrived at their destinations. If these samplings were small ones, as Jarric continually indicated, how many people inhabited Fuego itself?

Above the walls, the tall, gleaming spires gave mute testament to the skills of human and mrem achievements. Rowlen explained that while much of the kingdom's appearance had been designed by its human inhabitants, the cat people had left their mark, too. The elder warrior pointed out structures with more curve, more sleekness, that only a mrem could have conceived. Too often it seemed that human structures were short and squat or long and narrow, with little other difference. Mrem designs followed the natural slopes of the world, a sign of his people's nearness to Delos.

Through the high, iron gates they walked, gates creating a doorway so huge that Feryln wondered if giants, too, lived here. As they entered, the young mrem nearly leaped back outside, so very claustrophobic did he suddenly become. The people! The crowding! His nose twitched. The smells.

Rowlen chuckled, a sound that reminded Feryln that mrem survived . . . no, thrived here and if they could, so could he. All the battle-worn villager had to do was watch and learn. He would not let his simpler life dictate matters. Feryln would follow Rowlen's lead and through the warrior's example, the other mrem would grow strong enough to fulfill his oath.

Even despite the wonders surrounding him, Feryln's mind ever returned to the tragic scenes of his home. With such walls as Fuego had, his family would have lived. With so great numbers as inhabited this astonishing realm, the Lizcanth and their monstrous allies never would have dared to attack. Such thoughts haunted him, making even the pleasure of the sights and sounds around him a muted one at best.

They journeyed through a marketplace larger than three or four villages put together, where humans, who seemed to come in more varieties and shades than mrem, argued, harangued, and cajoled one another simply to make a deal. Tall, muscular humans wearing various outfits mostly consisting of leather and metal—uniforms, Rowlen called them—marched stolidly through the throngs, clearly intent on missions of which only they were privy. Watching them, Feryln decided not to take humans as so easy a target. Many might be like Jarric in form, a little soft, a little round in the features, but many others moved like predators, ready to strike a foe with but a wrong glance.

There were mrem, too, but while they varied less than humans, still they came in shapes and forms Feryln would not have believed. Plump, even fat, mrem sauntered among the humans, behaving almost exactly like them. Both males and females of his race abounded, many of them clad in flowing, colorful garments unsuitable for survival in the mountains. A few glanced at his own tattered clothes with what almost seemed disdain, but some, especially younger females, looked at Feryln with expressions that made him turn away in embarrassment.

Once he imagined he saw his brother. Feryln nearly started toward the golden brown form conversing with a human merchant, but a moment later the young mrem realized that the one he stared at stood taller and broader, his fur marked by white stripes at the shoulders. The face that turned, finally sensing his staring, belonged to a bored, pinched-looking warrior with one scar across his muzzle. Feryln quickly looked away, both ashamed of the mistake and regretful that it had not been Herrick after all.

There were even some dwarf mrem among the inhabitants, creatures identical in all matters to other mrem save size. The village elders had spoken about them but Feryln had still not believed they actually existed until now. He stared at them with such interest that one finally hissed at him and extended his claws, which might have seemed comical save that the claws looked to be quite serviceable, not to mention at least as long as his own.

As the trio forced their way through the ever-increasing crowds, other mrem who initially resembled many of those from Feryln's village materialized and disappeared again, each time leaving in their wake renewed pain in the weary survivor's heart and mind. After a point, Feryln began to steel himself against such things. If he did not, he would surely go mad.

The other sights of Fuego did help some to alleviate the agony. At times, the mountain mrem could even put aside some of his pain and enjoy himself. Jarric glanced at him at one point, grinning in that manner that still made Feryln want to bare his own teeth in response to a combat challenge. The mrem realized that his mouth had been hanging open and he quickly clamped it shut. The fur on the nape of his neck bristled as he imagined the picture he made. Small wonder so many looked at him with amusement and disdain. If he hoped to survive here, he had to learn to hide his ignorance.

Except where wood dominated, most of the more elaborate buildings had that same unsettling glaze. Fuego had more than its share of towering structures—anything above two levels was towering to the mountain mrem. Many bore crests near the doorways, sometimes the same crest repeating for several buildings in a row. During their travels Jarric and Rowlen had endeavored to explain how five or six great clans, called Houses here, controlled virtually everything. No one who remained long in Fuego went around without affiliation to one of the Houses. Among those of highest rank in each of the powerful clans were generally the fire mages.

Feryln eyed Jarric, who now concentrated on the crowded path ahead. Only once had the human revealed any hint of his supposed power and that had been when he had lit a campfire for them . . . or at least had tried to do so. Clutching a tiny ruby in his hands, the human had muttered some words. A breath later, the three of them had been hard at work stamping out what could have become a forest-ravaging conflagration. Several apologies later, a sheepish Jarric had promised not to attempt any further spells until they reached Fuego.

Rowlen had worn a look of sympathy then, later explaining to the other mrem that Jarric had great power, but his nervousness as they neared Fuego threatened even his slightest spells. Jarric, it seemed, had returned to his home to receive a quest, the final step before achieving full status as a fire mage. If he succeeded, the doors to power would be flung open for him, an eventual seat on the emperor's council even a possibility. If he failed, the young fire mage would not receive a second chance for seven more years.

Knowing how anxious he had grown before his own rite of passage, Feryln sympathized with the young human. That knowledge, in fact, had enabled him to develop a budding friendship with Jarric, although neither were aware of it yet.

Beyond the market they passed various businesses, then homes of some of the more affluent inhabitants of Fuego. While impressive with their high, sculpted fences, gilded entranceways and immaculate, if somewhat stunted, gardens, Feryln paid only passing attention to most of the latter, concerned now with where the three would eventually stop. Rowlen had spoken of the great Houses and that Jarric belonged to one called Gaius. Rowlen, too, had some connection with the house, but only in terms of his service to the young mage. Gaius had a reputation for breeding exceptional fire mages, and Jarric bore the weight of many generations upon his shoulders. The younger mrem assumed Jarric would at least be stopping at House Gaius, but when Rowlen broached the subject, both were surprised when the human declined.

"The guild has chambers for journeying members. I'll sleep there rather than bother anyone."

From Rowlen's expression, Feryln gathered this would not be considered normal. Nonetheless, the tawny mrem made no comment, only nodded.

Jarric had earlier suggested that they head immediately to the building housing the chambers of the emperor's council in the hopes of speaking with his sponsor, the eminent Prymias of the Ruby Eye. Jarric could not promise that such an audience would be granted so quickly, but at least they could leave word with one of those who worked for the master fire mage. Someone, he insisted, had to be told about Feryln's misfortunes. With nowhere of his own to go, Feryln agreed with the plan. The sooner steps could be taken toward avenging his people, the better it suited him.

Then at last they reached the citadel of the emperor's council.

The immense crimson structure did not stand very tall in comparison to other buildings, but its width stunned Feryln. His entire village could have fit inside, many times over and that was just on the ground floor. Three stories high and with windows wherever he looked, the council building resembled nothing he had witnessed so far. Shaped somewhat like half an egg lying on its side, Feryln wondered if perhaps one of his own had designed it. Four tiny towers jutted up on the left and right side of the edifice, each containing a watchful figure clad in mage robes. Humans in dark uniforms of a similar pattern to that which Jarric wore lined every gate, every entrance—warriors, not spellcasters. Mrem guardians also prowled the grounds, their simpler clothing bearing the same colors and markings. The power wielded by those within surely had to be great if outer appearances were any indication. Clearly the council did not simply advise the emperor of Fuego, they ruled his kingdom for him.

A mrem and a human met them at the main gate and after some conversation with Jarric, they let the trio through. Once inside, new sentries questioned the mage again, finally letting the three pass. Feryln and his companions continued on, at last climbing a huge set of steps leading up to the entrance of the building itself. Again, Feryln could not help gaping. Columns twice his height greeted them at the entrance, which itself consisted of two astonishing bronze doors decorated with elaborate patterns and creatures both living and mythic.

Human sentries opened the doors, ushering them in with stern glances. A figure clad in red greeted them solemnly once they entered.

"I am Colos," the cadaverous figure announced as the bronze doors clanged shut behind them. "How may I direct you?"

"Master Colos," Jarric began, stepping forward at the same time. "I am—"

"I know who you are, young Jarric." The narrow human slid his hand over his hairless pate. "Come for your quest, I'd take it."

"That . . . and something possibly more urgent. I must speak with my sponsor, Master Prymias."

The human in red had a very avian look to him, Feryln decided, one that increased as he looked down at the young fire mage. "His most senior member of the council is very busy at the moment. You know the correct procedures, Jarric. File a request with my office and I will see to it that it is passed on to the office of the council. They'll, in turn, pass it on to the acolyte in charge of requests for individual members, who will, if he deems it significant enough, pass it to the chief officer of Master Prymias's majordomo, who'll pass it on to her in order of priority. Then, if Castlana Dumarcus deems it of value, she will bring it before Prymias at the next meeting."

Feryln heard Rowlen growl low. Jarric wore an expression of extreme frustration on his face. Colos simply stood before them, fingers steepled and expression bland. This human did not like the younger mage for some reason.

"House Medici . . ." the other mrem muttered. "No friend of Gaius. . . ."

"Master Colos, you don't understand. This mrem here—"

"I only follow the rules as they've been dictated, young Jarric," Colos interrupted calmly.

"Master—"

"Thank you, Master Colos, but I will take it from here. There is to be an exception to the guidelines this once." The voice, rich, vibrant, and commanding, made the gaunt man stiffen and Jarric's face turn slightly crimson.

A female human clad in an elegant yet simple jacketed uniform approached from a side hall. As with the sentries outside, the jacket and pants matched the colors worn by Jarric, the former also accented by a yellow fireburst emblem sewn onto the right breast. Unlike the sentries and the fire mage, the uniform did little to hide the curved form of the newcomer. Even without the knee-length, leather boots she would have stood as tall as Colos.

Unlike most of the females of her race, the new arrival wore her hair short, almost wrapped around her head. Traces of silver accented her hair, darker in general than Jarric's but still the red predominant in Fuego. She had emerald, almond-shaped eyes, almost mremlike, a tiny but proud nose, and a curve to her full human lips which also reminded him of a creature more feline. Prominent cheek bones and a slight cleft in her chin, features which normally might have added masculinity to her looks, instead gave the newcomer a uniquely feminine appearance that at the same time warned that this woman should not be taken lightly. In contrast to most of the other humans he had so far observed, the imposing woman moved more like one of his own people, so much so that Feryln felt a slight flush in his cheeks. Had she been one of his own kind, he did not doubt he would have found her very attractive despite the decade and more difference in their ages. Judging by Jarric's reaction, the young mage already suffered such a predicament.

He expected some protest from Colos, but the unsettling human simply nodded, then retreated into some shadowy corridor.

The uniformed woman confronted them, arresting eyes swiftly taking the measure of each. In particular she studied the young, golden brown mrem, clearly noting the feline features that were broader than those of Rowlen, the odd black stripe in the fur near his one ear, the kilt that contrasted with the clothes of city mrem, and even possibly the sense of loss in the dark brown eyes. To Feryln, the only one who did not to recognize her, she said, "I am Castlana Dumarcus, majordomo for his eminence Master Prymias of the Ruby Eye." She glanced at Jarric, who tried too hard not to show that she unsettled him. A hint of something, possibly amusement, accented her every word. "Your apprenticeship has seasoned you well, Jarric. I'd hardly recognize you as the same person Prymias sent out."

"Thank you, Mistress Dumarcus," was all that the mage could manage.

Hands slim and tapering, yet firmly muscled, came together, almost as if she prayed. The one side of her mouth slightly curled upward, possibly a mannerism that kept any who met her constantly wondering what secrets of theirs she knew. From what little he had already seen of this female, Feryln did not doubt that if those secrets proved not to her liking, she would have the means to deal with the one trying to hide them. "Naturally, as your sponsor, Master Prymias knew of your arrival in Fuego the moment you reached the city. He has kept himself apprised of your progress and is already at work devising your quest. You should know within a fortnight."

Jarric nodded his gratitude. "I'm grateful, Mistress Dumarcus, but I didn't come here for myself. I've come for another, possibly urgent matter that—"

She silenced him with a glance. "Master Prymias knows why you've come, Jarric, which is the reason I came to head off that cretin Colos before he sent you away. His eminence wishes to speak with you immediately. You're to come with me now."

Castlana Dumarcus turned and without waiting, started off. Jarric and Rowlen followed immediately, but Feryln remained still, uncertain.

The young mrem swallowed. He had only just arrived in this overwhelming place. Surely this Master Prymias did not expect him, too. He could not even know that Feryln existed.

The female abruptly halted, then turned. Mremlike eyes seized his own. "Perhaps I didn't make myself clear. He wishes to speak with all of you."

"Surely not—" Feryln began.

Castlana Dumarcus cut him off. "Oh, yes, Feryln. Master Prymias desires to speak with you at length." What most resembled a predator's smile momentarily graced her human features. "Most especially you."

Chapter 3

BASKILLUS SAT IN THE TENT THAT WAS HIS by right as both lord and commander of the infernal legions, observing the mrem prisoner. The tent stood twice as tall and four times as wide as any other, and all accommodations the Lizcanth could fit into it had been added. A table stood in the center, a well-crafted one upon which lay the maps and charts the ambitious warlord pored over each day in anticipation of the beginning of the grand conquest. To the left, near the rear of the tent, cushions and blankets formed a sleeping area that might have been considered soft by some, but which Baskillus thought appropriate to his elevated station. A constant supply of food, some of it fruit but more often raw or slightly singed meat, sat in golden bowls nearby. A flask of wine, stolen off the body of a daring but foolish mrem merchant, sat next to the food awaiting his later pleasure.

The tent also gave him refuge from the madness that sometimes swept over the expanding force outside. The encampment had now grown to cover much of the serviceable areas of the sloping, winding landscape and if they did not march soon, Baskillus did not know where he would put the newcomers. Already the various factions and creatures fought for position, outbreaks occurring every day. If not for the power behind him, the Lizcanth warlord would have been hardpressed to keep matters under control and, as it was, he more than felt he deserved a few luxuries for the trial he faced.

Before he could enjoy himself today, though, Lord Baskillus had to deal with the prisoner. Not the young female he would have preferred, they being the easier to drive to panic in his opinion, but the Lizcanth leader knew he had to be satisfied with this older male. Besides, in another minute or two, it would not matter, for the hated feline would be, for all practical purposes, dead.

The emerald green warlord rose to his full height, towering over both the two guards and the prisoner, who had been pushed to his knees. Even for a Lizcanth, Baskillus stood tall, nearly eight feet. His towering form and accompanying strength had earned him much of his position, but his ability to keep his warriors under control even under the most dire circumstances had been what kept him there.

It had also, not long ago, brought him to the attention of that other. So far, that pact had worked well for the Lizcanth, but Baskillus acted as much out of fear as he did for profit in this great effort. No one denied the black one, not even Azur.

Not even, perhaps, the Laria.

"Two choicesss you have, mrem," he hissed. "A quick death or ssservice to the lord of all."

The wounded warrior tried his best to keep a brave face, but the lizard could read the fear hidden behind. Baskillus savored that fear, worked on it. The dark one desired a few mrem for other plans, commanding the Lizcanth lord to save one or two from each village ravaged. They had to be sent into a panic first, though, in order for Baskillus's master to use them. Young mrem, preferably female but also at times male, were the best choices. Older ones too often were set in their ways, unwilling to see the inevitable. They sometimes simply died.

Baskillus had no use for his people's hereditary foes. When the last mrem breathed no more, the Lizcanth would rejoice. However, until the dark one no longer required their services, the few chosen had to be tolerated.

Tail whipping behind him, Baskillus moved closer. His lip curled back a little, the Lizcanth smile. The mrem shivered, feline eyes as wide as possible. Blood and sweat matted what had once been sleek, brown fur and the smells stirred within Baskillus a great temptation to ignore his master's commands and simply bite the head off this prey.

"To ssserve isss all that remains for you, cat. Give yourssself and you sssave yourssself."

He saw a slight glimmer in the mrem's eyes, the sudden and quite predictable notion that perhaps these Lizcanth could be fooled. The prisoner no doubt believed, like many before him, that he could simply swear an oath, then escape at first opportunity. Baskillus almost laughed. It had not been so for him, why should this one think he would be so fortunate?

Fear and gullibility. He had the mrem where he wanted him. Now came the time. From a pouch hanging from his weapon belt, the Lizcanth leader removed a small object which he kept concealed. All the while Baskillus kept the prisoner's gaze snared with his own, the crimson, slitted orbs demanding the mrem's full attention. He had to do this the correct way, lest the dark one punish him.

"Your life yoursss, but oursss to command." Not quite the truth, but it would open up the prisoner's mind a little, make him more pliable before the final moment. "Do it you will, warmblood, will you not? The only way it isss that you might sssurvive."

One of the ogres who had captured the mrem—nearly battering him to a pulp in the process—had broken several of the feline's teeth in the process, but still the mrem managed to speak well enough. "I . . . do as you . . . want."

"All then you mussst do isss look here . . . look clossse . . ."

Baskillus lifted his jaw, revealing the folds of his throat and a tiny, blood-colored gem, a ruby, in the center. The mrem gasped and even the two other Lizcanth hissed. The guards knew what the gem meant and that alone kept them very, very obedient.

"Look. . . ."

The ruby flared bright. Prepared, the other Lizcanth had looked away. The prisoner, caught by surprise, cried out as the light blinded him.

With admittedly some pleasure, Baskillus took his free hand and, claws fully extended, ripped the mrem's throat open.

Blood splattered both. The prisoner gasped, choked, and would have died almost immediately if the Lizcanth lord had not acted again. He raised his other hand and, still concealing the object within, pressed the palm against the dripping, open wound.

The mrem shivered, then his eyes glazed. Blood immediately ceased flowing from the slashed area. Baskillus removed his hand, revealing a tiny ruby lodged within the prisoner's throat. Now this one glowed and as it did, an ominous thing happened. Flame engulfed the mrem's body, black flame that did not burn and yet, as Baskillus knew very well, hurt nonetheless. The wound at the prisoner's throat slowly healed, the skin tightening around the ruby. The mrem shivered throughout the process, seeming to want to scream but unable to do so.

At last the black flames died down, the glare from the ruby fading with it. The mrem slumped. Baskillus, who had suffered the same so very long ago, felt just enough sympathy to give the hapless prisoner a minute. Then, impatient, he had one of the guards throw water on the mrem.

"You know now," he hissed. "You know he who controlsss your very exissstence. He will command and you will obey . . . whatever he asssks of you."

The mrem swallowed and a few tears trickled

down his face. As time passed, less and less of the prisoner's mind would remain, but the body would still function.

The mrem nodded. *He knows better now,* Baskillus thought. There would be no escape, no subterfuge. No one betrayed the master.

No one who now lived, that is.

"An interesting tale you tell, young Feryln."

"It is no tale I tell. It is the death of my entire village."

That he could speak with such audacity toward the figure seated before him startled Feryln, but despite his uneasiness, he would not have the terrible tragedy relegated to some distant story. The deaths would haunt him forever, even if he did manage to avenge them. They might mean little to this human, but they meant everything to the mrem.

"I, of course, meant no slighting of your terrible disaster," Master Prymias of the Ruby Eye soothed.

Feryln had wondered why they called the human by such a title, at first imagining the mage to actually have such an orb of his own. Yet, despite his imposing presence, Prymias seemed as normal in his own way as Jarric. Of course, any other comparison of the two failed, for even Feryln, who knew nothing about magic, could sense the power of the massive figure.

It would have taken two Ferylns, maybe three, to make up the girth of Master Prymias, but none of that girth included fat. The eminent human resembled more a warrior than a scholar, although when he spoke his tone reminded the mrem of his old tutors. Prymias also proved to be the most hirsute of any of the humans Feryln had yet seen, even the burly sentries without. His mane, brown with flakes of silver, flowed down nearly to his hips and the graying beard, neatly trimmed, ended just below his throat. He wore robes not of black and red, but rather white and gold, evidently the colors of the emperor's council.

As for the ruby eye, it lay on the mage's sturdy chest, a gold chain keeping it in place. The ruby eye proved to be a true ruby, which Feryln learned all fire mages utilized for their spells. The gem did indeed resemble an orb, so much so that at times the mrem felt as if it, too, watched him.

"I did not mean that you—"

Prymias shifted forward, his movements as well as his features reminding the villager of a great bear. The master mage sat behind a tall desk covered with scrolls and books. Feryln had never seen the latter before and marveled that so much writing existed in this one chamber. Behind the robed figure more books and scrolls, all neatly placed, lined shelves in the wall. Curiously, though, despite those, Feryln noticed hardly any other trappings he might have associated with a magic user. In fact, there were few items other than the books and scrolls. The more he thought about it, the more the mrem realized that Master Prymias did not remind him so much of practitioner of the magic arts as he did one of the village headmen. "You meant what you meant. I take no offense, young Feryln. Do be seated again."

He had not even realized that he had risen. Feryln returned to the stool that had been provided for him. Born with tails, neither Rowlen nor Feryln could sit in normal human chairs without some discomfort. However, Prymias had made certain that two wide stools were waiting for the pair of mrem. It seemed that Jarric's sponsor knew everything about him, which at first had caused Feryln to wonder why he had to relate what happened to his village at all. Surely Prymias already knew.

He had not, but what he did know and how he had learned it unnerved Feryln more. Apparently the master mage saw nothing wrong with spying on his own kind, for the moment he had sensed Jarric in the region, Prymias had evidently linked his ruby to one of those the younger human carried, enabling the elder to watch and listen as the trio had journeyed on.

"You must understand, that with so many dangers lurking in the wild regions of Delos, we must take special precautions," Prymias had explained. "Although it looked and felt like dear Jarric, I had to be certain it was he and by the time I satisfied myself, I had already learned much of interest about you. Enough that I chose to keep listening. You do see, I hope."

Jarric and Rowlen nodded dutifully and in the end Feryln joined them. Nonetheless, despite his respect for the immense human, Feryln determined to keep on his guard with this one.

"Most interesting," Prymias repeated. He

glanced at Castlana, who had remained silent and emotionless throughout the retelling of events. She shook her head at some unspoken question, then returned to her neutral stance, the corner of her mouth still curled upward slightly. Feryln could recall no warriors from his village with such patience and precision. Despite her not only being human, but also female, he doubted that even Rowlen could have taken her should they for some reason have come to blows.

"As I thought," Prymias commented, his attention on the trio again. "No such activities have been reported in the past. Tell me, young Feryln, you saw the ogre and kobold with these Lizcanth only that once?"

"Yes, Eminence." Once had been too much.

"Then you don't know how many there might have been with them? You don't know if perhaps they were slave soldiers for the lizards? It wouldn't be the first time. The Lizcanth, for all they despise other races, are intelligent enough to know the strength and uses of ogres, kobolds, and others. Perhaps these were the only ones among their ranks."

"My brother—"

The bear stroked his beard. "Yes, he did mention them, too. Perhaps, though, he only saw the same ones that you did. A reasonable mistake and when you spoke to him he had been mortally wounded."

"He said that there were more. . . ." *Had he, though?* Now Feryln could not even say for certain how his brother had phrased it. More and more those events blurred together, growing no less horrible, however. The mrem tried to recall details and found himself beginning to second-guess. Perhaps Master Prymias had the truth of it after all.

"Still, we cannot let such a possibility, however improbable, go without more research. If, for reasons unfathomable, Lizcanth and others have joined forces, the potential for catastrophe would be unimaginable. Castlana." The majordomo snapped to attention. "You will make this a priority. I've faith you'll turn up the truth."

"As you wish, Eminence."

The senior fire mage met Feryln's gaze. "Be assured, good mrem, that rampaging Lizcanth are enough to stir matters up. You seek to avenge your family and friends; you could have chosen no better course than to come to me. I'll bring up this matter before the council, nay, before the emperor, as needs be. Even if the mrem alone are threatened, they are our friends," Prymias nodded at Rowlen, who nodded in turn. "And we protect our friends. Yes, we do."

Not knowing what else to say, Feryln settled for, "Thank you, Master Prymias."

"Think nothing of it." The huge, robed figure leaned back again. "Now, then. Until matters progress in that area, you must need find a place to stay—"

"If I may, Eminence," interrupted Rowlen.

"Proceed. I think I know what you intend."

"Master Prymias, Feryln has no family, no friends in the lowlands. From his tale, which I hold to be very true, he has striven against great odds for one so young. That being the case, I would request that he be assigned quarters with my detachment, so that, if nothing comes of matters, he will be able to earn a place as one such as myself." The elder mrem looked at Feryln. "If he, of course, desires such, that is."

In truth, Feryln had wondered some over his eventual fate. Vengeance might take years and, even then, the training that Rowlen had gotten would come into good use at other times. Rowlen, he suspected, would have been more than a match for any warrior of the village. Through him, Feryln might learn much. Besides, among his own kind he might at last feel a little comfort, something lacking since his escape from the hunters. "I would wish to join."

Rowlen and Jarric both looked relieved. Prymias clasped his heavy hands together. "Splendid! This will also enable me to readily find you should further facts come to light about this supposed horde, young Feryln. I see no difficulty entering him into your ranks, Rowlen. Castlana, see that it's done today."

"Yes, Eminence."

"As for you, Jarric," the elder mage smiled as his young counterpart stiffened to attention. "Relax, lad, relax. You've shown a good head for your part in this, something not every fire mage does. You must know how proud I am of you. I think of you like my own son at times, don't I, Castlana?"

The majordomo's gaze briefly shifted from her master to Jarric, then back again. The glance proved enough to make Jarric's cheeks redden slightly, but only Feryln seemed to notice.

"He shows much promise. You've always said so, Eminence."

"Exactly." Prymias stroked the ruby in the medallion. "By the end of the coming fortnight, I will have your quest ready. Prove yourself worthy and not only will you join our ranks, but I'll have a position of some importance for you on my staff."

Jarric barely remembered to keep his mouth from gaping open. "You honor me, Master Prymias."

"Not at all. I recognize talent." Prymias sighed. "Well, then. This has been an interesting meeting. Rowlen, your services to House Gaius have been, as ever, exemplary. No questor and certainly no reaver could serve so loyally."

"Through your house, my clan, my family, prospers, Eminence."

"Thank you. Will you see to these two young ones now, then? I know I can always trust your efforts."

"As you command."

Jarric and the older mrem suddenly rose. Feryln followed suit, bowing just as they did to the great mage. He still had some reservations concerning Master Prymias of the Ruby Eye, but could not deny the human's efforts so far. More important, Rowlen trusted him and Feryln trusted Rowlen.

The majordomo summoned an apprentice who led them out. Feryln found himself walking beside Jarric. Trying to at least for a time forget his own tribulations, the mrem studied the human. From what Feryln had witnessed, Jarric should have been quite happy about the outcome of the encounter with Master Prymias. The senior mage had done nothing but praise the younger and Prymias did not strike Feryln as one who wasted such words. Despite all that, however, the fire mage seemed to be buried under a great deal of thought, not even noticing the mrem until Feryln finally decided to speak.

"He will do as he said, Jarric?"

"Do? You mean about your village?" The human focused his thoughts. "Of course. Master Prymias always keeps his word."

The tone in which Jarric spoke indicated to the mrem that he would do better not to question the infallibility of the great mage. Determined not to offend Jarric any further, Feryln instead asked what he had first intended to. "You think about your quest?"

"Yes. You heard Master Prymias back there. I'd always felt honored that he chose to sponsor me as an apprentice, but I never understood that he had so much hope for me. The honor of working with him after the quest is one that any fire mage, even one from House Medici, who hate Gaius, would gladly welcome!"

"Then what is it that you fear?"

Jarric grimaced. "Is it that obvious? Master Prymias has high hopes for me. If he intends to take me on, it'll only be after a quest that proves me not only worthy of the ranks of the fire mages, but worthy of him."

Feryln now realized what so disturbed his companion. "And so you worry about how dangerous a quest he might send you upon." The mrem tried to think what might be expected of a fire mage during such a quest. His imagination, flavored by the trials he himself had suffered, brought forth terrible visions. "You are afraid that he might send you into something against which you cannot succeed."

Jarric nodded, morose at the prospect of what his sponsor might arrange. "Wouldn't you?"

"What do you think?"

Prymias of the Ruby Eye stirred from his contemplations. Castlana had gone to fulfill the orders he had given her and none of the rest of those who served him would have dared enter unannounced. Only one other had tacit permission, one whom the fire mage had expected, but, deep in thought, had momentarily forgotten. "I think that Fuego . . . perhaps all of Delos . . . might very well be in extreme, extreme danger."

"I would say that you were being redundant if I did not agree with you, my friend."

Prymias turned his chair in order to face the speaker. "You heard everything, then, Menthusalan?"

From out of a shadowed corner, the mentor emerged. That he had not been there earlier did not disturb the fire mage. Prymias frowned a little when he saw the thinner man's face. Menthusalan had dark circles under his eyes, circles that had grown since that fateful night several days ago. He also did not seem quite himself at times, as if he expected to find someone lurking behind him in the very shadow from which he had arrived. The fire mage did not bother trying to offer a chair; Menthusalan had rejected such a luxury earlier. The mentor could not even sit still.

"Yes, your ruby gave me complete access to the conversation. I heard and saw everything except at one point when you leaned forward, but by then I had heard enough."

"It sounds too much like your vision, old friend."

"My vision . . . I do not like to call it that. I would have nothing to do with it if I could." The mentor shivered. "Ogres and Lizcanth and kobolds and who knows what else. The youth mentioned nothing of dragons."

"Then perhaps there're none involved."

Menthusalan frowned. "I would prefer not to think that they are, but I would be a fool to ignore the possibility."

"I'll follow your lead. Tell me now, how did you know about the young mrem? I wouldn't have paid attention to his presence if you had not come to me and told me to see him immediately. A fortunate thing he accompanied young Jarric or I wouldn't have had any excuse to invite him in. The mrem don't like reavers dragging one of their own off without good, clear reasons and that would have just about been my only other choice. He certainly wouldn't have come here on his own."

"My apologies for the inconvenience, my friend. In truth, the thought that you should see him came to me in the same way the name Ebonyr did, completely from the shadows. . . ." Even acknowledging such a fact seemed to disturb

Menthusalan. The fire mage could not blame his old friend. Prescience had always been a rare and very unpredictable ability and neither had ever experienced it before the mentor's search.

"Ebonyr. . . ." Master Prymias stroked his beard. "Unfamiliar and yet not. . . ." He paused upon noticing something in the standing figure's eyes. "What is it?"

"I have . . . made a discovery . . . in the records you loaned to me. The ones from shortly after the founding of Fuego."

"Have you?" The bear nearly rose from his seat. "You know what this Ebonyr means? You should've told me!"

"There was no time. I only discovered it just before the mrem became known to me."

"How fortuitous."

"I hide nothing more from you than you hide from me, my friend," the sable-clad mentor retorted. "And in this case, I had no opportunity to do so. It was while reading the passages I had so long sought that I first realized the presence of the young villager. I do not like such timely surprises nor do I wish them upon anyone else, but if you doubt my veracity—"

Prymias waved the man's protest away. "No, no, friend Menthusalan! Forgive me and please go on. Who, what, or where is Ebonyr?"

"It was the sanctum of one of the earliest fire mages, the self-proclaimed Lord of the Black Flame, Ganth Kazarian."

"Ganth Kazarian?" Startled, Prymias fell back into his chair. "*The* Ganth Kazarian? No wonder Ebonyr stirred hints of some memory! Hadn't studied Ganth Kazarian since I was young Jarric's age."

"Nor I. Even we of Dismas recorded the depravities of Ganth of the Black Flame. He nearly turned the Four Cities into three."

"And would've then begun on Dismas, Terris, or Astra once he'd solidified his power. All Ganth cared about was his own existence, Menthusalan. Some called him the Laria in human form." The master mage considered this. "But Ganth is long dead, Ebonyr a scorched ruin, thanks to what later became the first emperor's council. Even he could not stand up to more than a dozen of Fuego's greatest, although I recall that nearly half of them died tearing apart his citadel."

"Perhaps, then, someone has gone to claim his legacy, another rogue fire mage."

Now Prymias of the Ruby Eye looked offended. "We try long and hard to cull such from the ranks. Ganth Kazarian can be thanked for that, at least."

A shrug. "Yet if your rate of success is as good as that in Dismas, then there would have been others, yes?"

"Damn you, yes. But no one of late. Pradix Gester was the last and the council had him executed in public. Yet . . . with so much hint of flame involved, if your vision holds true, then it would seem some fire mage has turned against his own! Who, though?"

Suddenly, the sable-clad mentor teetered. He looked around quickly for the nearest chair, then collapsed into it. Prymias, moving with great ease for one of his bulk, came around his desk to offer aid, but Menthusalan shook his head. "I am sufficient. Forgive my lapse; I have slept little and perhaps it is finally catching up with me . . . else why would such wild notions suddenly seem so reasonable to me?"

"What do you mean? What wild notion?"

The dark rings had grown even darker. Prymias worried about his friend's health. If Menthusalan could not continue at his duties, the next representative from Dismas might not be so reasonable a man with which to deal.

"You said they called Ganth of the Black Flame the Laria in human form."

"An expression, nothing else."

"Perhaps." The other exhaled. "Perhaps. . . . But what if there is some link of truth. Not that Ganth was the Laria, but that perhaps he made some pact before his death, some deal to save himself."

The councillor's knuckles whitened as his hands twisted into tight fists. "You're not suggesting . . . that would be impossible!"

"With the Laria, is anything impossible?"

"But . . . that would mean . . . would mean . . ." Prymias brought one fist down hard on his desk, actually cracking the wood slightly. "No! There must be another explanation! The Laria couldn't have brought Ganth back from the dead!"

"Then one of your own now betrays you. Someone who dares to delve into the secrets of Ebonyr."

The two sat in silence for some time, Prymias

trying to come up with any option that might be more reasonable than the two the mentor had suggested. While fire mages were not above vying for position, he knew of none who would go so far as gathering a horde together in what Menthusalan suggested would become an attempt to tear down the walls of Fuego. Yet, to take the other suggestion to heart meant accepting a foe even more monstrous. . . .

"Ganth is dead," the senior fire mage muttered. "Even the Laria couldn't put his ashes back together."

"There is a way of perhaps proving this one way or another," Menthusalan murmured, as if almost afraid to mention it.

"And what might that be? I would welcome anything that would disprove your insane suggestion, old friend."

The mentor rubbed his temples as if abruptly struck by an intense pain. Still, despite his suffering, he continued. "Ganth Kazarian, according to the texts, became obsessed with an object, so much so that he planned the destruction of Fuego simply to attain it."

"I don't recall that part anywhere, but go on. What is it and how do we make the best use of the knowledge?"

The mentor ceased rubbing his temples. A faraway look crossed his features, almost as if he stared back into time itself. "It concerns a legend about a great ruby shard fallen from the sky during the collapse. . . ."

Chapter 4

FERYLN FELL ONTO THE COT, NEARLY AS exhausted as he had been after that terrible flight from the hunters. The mrem unit of which he was now a part trained—hard, harder than even the village warriors had. Every muscle, including those in his tail, ached. He scarcely felt able to breathe, much less walk.

Outside of the plain, stone longhouse that served as the unit's home, he could hear several of the veterans using the scratching wall. Despite all their exertion, their definition of relaxation included yet more physical activity. True, it kept their claws strong and sharp, but how they retained enough strength to use the wall after training, he did not know.

For nearly two weeks Feryln had lived among these strange mrem, learning their ways and, in the process, learning about Fuego. The ways of humans were myriad and often bizarre and the mrem who lived here often seemed almost as odd. Fortunately, Rowlen had proven a helpful tutor, guiding the younger warrior around pitfalls that might have otherwise swallowed him whole.

The mrem unit held a position strange to him. Apparently it hired itself out to one of the great human Houses, although Rowlen had been quick to point out that he and the others were not to be confused with reavers. Reavers were mercenaries, warriors with more interest in profit than honor, and mostly human. The mrem here were all of one clan, Leonus, and they chose their masters based on many criteria, especially trust and integrity. Leonus had served House Gaius for several generations, bringing back to their clan much wealth, influence, and honor.

No one questioned the honor of the humans even though Feryln felt certain that it could not, for the most part, stand up to that of his people. He liked Jarric well enough, but most of the other humans Feryln had met left him just a little uncertain. Rowlen suggested that he needed more time to become used to them and perhaps there was some truth in that. Feryln would just have to wait and see.

He shifted on the cot, uncomfortable in the city clothes, the uniform, that he now had to wear. The jerkin fit loose enough, but the peculiar pants, although designed to accommodate a mrem tail, still felt too tight. The boots, too, made his feet ache. He had a great desire to chop off the fronts so that his toes could breathe. How a mrem could go more than a few steps in them he still could not understand and yet he did, pushing through each day's exercises despite all the handicaps, boots included.

He pushed himself because he still remained haunted by the memories of his village, his people. Awake or sleeping, the images remained burned in his mind, the faces of everyone who had died forever haunting his every moment. Feryln tried to hide it from Rowlen and the others, and knew that he only partly succeeded. Some of those in the unit found him moody, others mysterious. A few tried to draw him out and sometimes he pretended to respond, but each time it took effort.

"Well, well, young one, taking a nap? You should have stretched those muscles first, they might tighten up later."

Feryln rolled over. "I do not have the strength left, Rowlen."

The older mrem's ears twitched, the clipped one moving with less control. Feryln had finally learned that an ogre had bitten the one part off, then nearly torn the rest from Rowlen's bleeding head. The veteran warrior had prevented that by driving his sword up to the hilt into the ogre's gut. "And here I thought the young had all the energy. You should really go to the scratching wall, Feryln. Besides keeping your claws sharp, it will relieve some of the tensions bottled up within you. You bear too many burdens, young one."

Feryln began cleaning his arms, trying not to be drawn into any conversation about his burdens. He could never escape his anxieties and bitterness. Each day he hoped for something that would give him at least a hint that the day of vengeance would soon be at hand and each day he went to sleep disappointed. Master Prymias had not even bothered to summon him back. When Jarric visited, something that happened every two or three days, he could provide little hope. Jarric had promised that he would try to speak with his sponsor when he had the chance, but so far he, too, had been left waiting. Prymias had still not presented the young fire mage with a quest, which made the human as anxious as his mrem friend.

"So the scratching wall is not for you, eh?" Rowlen sat down on the cot beside him. "Perhaps some companionship would be better. Not an old cat like me nor a human like Master Jarric. I have seen both Pureesha and Alevi looking at you with interest, young one."

Feryln knew them both, especially Pureesha, who trained along as part of the unit. Lithe, silver and gray with a tiny nose and eyes so very gold, no one could mistake her for a male despite her being a warrior. A few summers older than him, but not so many as to make the match unlikely. In contrast, Alevi, whose brother also trained, was younger than Feryln by one summer. Softer by far than Pureesha, her tan form bore curves that he had more than once glanced at surreptitiously.

He liked both females and perhaps one day there might be something with one of them, but for now Feryln could not bother himself with other entanglements. He had to keep himself focused on only one thing: finding those who had slaughtered his people and seeing to it that they paid. As hopeless as that sometimes appeared,

Feryln could not give up. To do so would have gone against both his sense of honor and his secret shame for not having been with his family in the first place.

"All right. Even the females cannot entice you today. You leave me with but one option." Rowlen reached forward and before Feryln knew what he intended, the muscular mrem had pulled his younger counterpart to his feet by his jerkin. "You will come with me and we will walk the city a little."

"Rowlen, I have not got the strength—"

"No, but you have the nervousness. That will drive you for some time. You have spent almost your entire stay in here. If you are to live in Fuego, you should walk Fuego."

With that, he pulled Feryln toward the door and, minutes later, the pair found themselves among the inhabitants of the vast city. Despite his earlier attitude, Feryln had to admit being among so many active and colorful folk eased some of his tensions. Fuego bustled with activity at all hours, but especially during the height of day. Humans and mrem scurried here and there on what appeared to be important missions, even if all they sought were fruit in the market place. Something about the city just made one want to pick up his pace.

They passed one of the great Houses, but not that which Rowlen served. The black building reminded Feryln of a jagged mountain that had once erupted in the time of his grandfather. Although it no longer even smoked, the upper edge still bore the crown of spikes where once its rounded top had been. The spires of the building did so in a similar manner. A tall glazed wall with iron spikes on top surrounded the house and its land. Trees grew within the grounds, but stunted ones compared to those in the mountain forests.

Feryln heard the older warrior growl under his breath as two nearly black mrem clad in jerkins bearing a sun crest eyed them from the entrance of the looming structure. The mountain mrem said nothing as they passed the sentries, but once out of sight he glanced at Rowlen.

"House Medici and clan Panthren. A very appropriate match, young one. Try to stay clear of both." Rowlen would say no more and soon Feryln became engrossed in other sights.

Now and then a woman or man wearing the robes of a fire mage crossed their paths. In general these humans were older and less interested in their surroundings. They were invariably accompanied by others, those in pale red robes that Feryln had learned were apprentices, younger humans in less elaborate mage robes who had to be assistants, and, of course, several guards. It amused Feryln in some ways that beings as powerful as fire mages would need so many warriors around them, but he supposed the warriors served at least two purposes. The first would be so that the mage could concentrate on other matters than his safety. Even they could not always be wary. The second purpose Feryln had gleaned from the self-important expressions most of the spellcasters wore; the guards were a sign of status. The more there were, the more influential the mage must be.

Among the guards the mrem noticed a type he had come across a few times in the past. They seemed to have no set affiliation; protecting those of rival houses without any sign of contradiction. Most wore simple uniforms, generally dark leather trousers, shirts, and brown jackets. Others wore clothing indistinguishable from that of those common folk milling past them. All seemed of a similar sort despite dissimilar forms, humans who knew the way of the warrior and yet did not look to always abide by it.

Again Rowlen provided the answer. "Reavers. The mercenaries I spoke of, young one. Mostly humans, but a few younger mrem these days. Money is their honor and anyone with it may buy their sword . . . but he who buys had better pray that someone does not later come with a better offer."

Feryln would have avoided the reavers as he did the dark mrem save that two apparently unattached warriors chose shortly after to stumble into their path . . . quite literally.

The reavers, one a balding, scarred man with a hook nose, and the other young, mustached, and wearing a perpetual sneer underneath his aristocratic nose, had clearly had too much of some strong liquid. When Rowlen tried to steer Feryln to the side, the pair of humans shifted to block their way again.

"Cats," spit the scarred reaver. "I hate cats."

"We are simply passing by—" Rowlen began, but the younger reaver cut him off.

"Look here, Otak! This one's so fresh out of the litter he's probably still not sure which end of the sword to use!"

If they hoped to provoke a reaction from Ferlyn, they failed. He knew drunkenness and the tendencies it could bring about; there had been those in the village who fell victim to it from time to time. Words from such as these were not meant to be taken seriously. They revealed more the failings of the speaker than his target.

Again, Rowlen tried to play peacemaker. "Honored sirs, we have no quarrel—"

"You take the work of humans," Otak growled. "That's quarrel enough!"

Feryln doubted that House Gaius would have hired such as these, but that clearly did not matter to the two reavers. In fact, without any prompting on the mrem's parts, the humans quickly grew more and more agitated about the work they had supposedly lost to Rowlen and Feryln in particular.

"Four months of traipsing around behind that fat merchant while you sit in comfort licking your fur clean!"

"Maybe their masters like to watch their pets wash themselves, Otak!"

Beside him, Feryln sensed Rowlen finally begin to lose some of his reserve. He, too, felt the heat rise within. The foursome were but seconds from a fight that might leave someone dead.

Then a deep, calm yet somehow threatening voice cut through the reavers' taunts. "I warned you two."

Otak and his companion quieted. Feryln only barely held his place, not having heard the newcomer at all. With movements so silent even a mrem could envy them, a well-groomed figure almost a foot taller than Rowlen stalked past the two mrem and confronted the reavers. Long, black hair fell in great locks down past his shoulders and a clipped, equally dark beard covered angular features that the mrem guessed females of the species would find quite attractive. Under heavy brows a pair of eyes winter blue froze the two other humans in place.

Only belatedly did Feryln notice that the newcomer wore an outfit similar to the pair. However, this reaver kept his clothing as well-groomed as himself, making for a remarkable contrast to the seedy figures he now threatened. "No one with any sense'd hire the pair of you, Beloq. You're just as likely to slit their throats in the night, no matter how good they pay."

"Lies, Kain!" The younger reaver's hand slid toward his sword. Clearly this conversation had come up before between the trio.

Making no attempt to reach for his own blade, the one called Kain looked down his strong, angled nose at the duo and continued, "Is it, Beloq? I've heard a few things about you and Otak here, things I'd believe you both perfectly capable of."

"As opposed to his high and mightiness, the great Theron Kain?" Otak grunted. His right hand already rested on the hilt of a knife in his belt. He looked ready to draw it at any moment.

"You've had your share of dead masters before, so I've heard around."

"Only when they've betrayed a contract. You two know all about betraying contracts, don't you? Such as the one you made with that merchant you just spoke of."

"The Laria take you, Kain!" Unable to hold back any longer, Beloq drew his sword. At the same time, Otak pulled his knife free.

Rowlen and Feryln both prepared to defend the unarmed man, but the swiftness with which the lone human reacted left the two mrem warriors stunned. Seemingly from nowhere Theron Kain produced twin daggers whose jeweled hilts gleamed in the sun. One he brought around into the upper arm of the mustached attacker, the other Kain buried in the knife hand of Otak.

The screams were nearly simultaneous. Beloq clutched his sword arm, trying to stem the flow of blood. The hand that had held the sword went into spasms, opening and closing as if some muscle or nerve in particular had been severed or damaged by the strike. His companion, meanwhile, struggled to pull Kain's dagger free from the back of his other hand. The lone reaver had plunged the blade completely through, the point coming out of the center of Otak's palm.

Theron Kain wiped the one dagger off on Beloq's shirt, then, with a single tug, pulled the second free from Otak. Despite their wounds, the two immediately scurried off without a single glance back.

After cleaning the second dagger, Kain put the twin weapons back into his belt.

Rowlen extended his hand in the manner of humans. "You have our gratitude for—"

"I take money, not gratitude," the tall reaver commented, barely looking at the two mrem. Then a grim smile appeared. "But in the case of those two, I owe you. Even reavers must have standards and those two do more to damage our chances for work than a thousand trained mrem."

"Nonetheless, Master—"

A chilly look silenced Rowlen, something Feryln would not have thought possible. Theron Kain looked both mrem over. "I'm no master. I serve masters. . . . And I care little more for mrem than Beloq and Otak. We're competitors, though, not adversaries."

With that said, the human abruptly turned and left, leaving Feryln to puzzle out his words while Rowlen simply stared.

"So that is Theron Kain," the older mrem finally whispered.

"Who is Theron Kain?"

"Once a knight, I have been told, until claims came that he sold his lord out for money. Yet his skill is said to be so good that any will hire him even now. Among humans . . . and I should add mrem . . . he is considered the best warrior in all of Fuego, knights and paladin questors included."

Recalling the speed with which Kain had moved, Feryln could well believe that. Yet, how could any trust a warrior who had betrayed his lord? Again, the ways of this kingdom battled the notions with which he had grown up. Honor here seemed so malleable a thing; would any here have been as determined as Feryln to live up to the oath he had sworn? Rowlen, perhaps, but would any human?

He was still contemplating this question a few minutes later when they came across the one human in whom perhaps the young mrem could believe such things. Jarric, mage staff in hand and an unfamiliar medallion hanging around his neck, called out to them, then hurried to meet the pair. Feryln suppressed the urge to meet him halfway, noting that Rowlen maintained a dignified pace. Feryln suspected that Jarric should have likewise maintained his dignity, but, despite his status as a rising mage, he, like the younger mrem, had still not learned the patience of experience.

"Master Jarric." Rowlen bowed, with Feryln following suit. "You look pleased. May I assume that you have spoken with your sponsor?"

"I have!" Jarric paused to adjust the cowl of his robe, which, in his haste to reach them, had twisted around to cover the left side of his head. "Master Prymias summoned me only this morning. I'll admit I was nervous, Rowlen. You know what he said; if I succeed with this quest, he has a place for me already set aside."

The warrior nodded. "I remember, Master Jarric. A greater honor one could not ask."

"And a greater burden one could not ask, either." Nerves clearly still on edge, the fire mage clutched the medallion, which Feryln saw contained a small ruby. On the journey, Jarric had carried the ruby in a pouch, but some time since their meeting with Master Prymias, the younger mage had decided to emulate his sponsor. While Jarric's ruby could not match the eye of Prymias's own medallion, it looked very impressive indeed.

"If I may be so bold, Master Jarric," Rowlen finally said after the human failed to continue, "might we know the nature of your quest . . . or is it perhaps not for our ears?"

"I'm sorry! You of all should know, since I hope you'll be accompanying me. Master Prymias has recently had word of a possible artifact dug up by some villagers near the site of what might have been a place of learning during the Second Millennium after the collapse. He wants me to go there and ascertain whether the artifact is real. If so, I'm to bring it back to the emperor's council!"

While history among his own folk had always been passed down through verbal stories, Feryln had learned a little about the recorded past since arriving in Fuego and knew just enough to understand Jarric. The collapse the human spoke about concerned a fabled time when a different sort of magic—technology—had brought about great changes in the world. After many disasters, technology had faded away and magic as Delos now knew it had appeared. Several great civilizations had risen and fallen over the estimated five thousand years since that time and artifacts from them were occasionally discovered, some still useful. Even mountain mrem had sometimes come across these items, although they rarely touched them, preferring such magic to remain dormant. Humans, on the other hand, tried to make use of everything regardless of the risk.

Feryln thought this a monumental quest, one of great importance, but Rowlen did not display such awe. "You must journey to this village, retrieve the artifact, and bring it back if it is real?"

"Yes!" Beaming, Jarric did not notice the older mrem's lackluster response. "Won't it be a grand quest?"

"I am certain that it will." Rowlen smiled, erasing any visible trace of uncertainty. "And I will be happy to accompany you, Master Jarric, if that is what you wish."

"I'd hoped you would!" He looked at Feryln, who had remained respectfully silent. "What about you? Do you want to come too? I've got to take the lead, but they won't hold it against me if I've got two mrem along."

Feryln's pulse raced. To be out of the city again, moving among the trees, across the grasses, over rivers and streams. . . . Would he want to go too? The human clearly did not understand him well enough not to already know the answer. "I would be honored."

"Splendid!" In a fit of exuberance, the fire mage, staff in one hand, hugged each of them. Rowlen took it with good grace, Feryln a bit more stiffly. "We leave in two days! Rowlen will show you how to pack and where to meet me! I've got to go gather the maps and locate a few items! Rowlen, you know how to contact me if you need anything!"

"Yes, Master Jarric."

"Think of it! A few weeks from now, I'll be a

fire mage of full rank, every door open to me!" Almost leaping with joy, the red-headed spellcaster bounded away, drawing the eye of more than one amused onlooker.

Feryln could not suppress a smile and even Rowlen chuckled slightly. When at last the human had vanished into the crowd, the older mrem sighed, then indicated that the pair should return to the barracks. As they walked, though, Feryln saw that something distracted his companion. Unable to contain himself any longer, he finally asked.

"Nothing, young one," Rowlen replied. "Just always amazed at the ways of the fire mages. Master Prymias must want nothing to prolong Master Jarric's joining him. A journey to a distant village to simply verify an artifact and, if real, bring it back. I have heard of simpler quests, but not many." He sighed again. "Well, the journey should at least be a pleasant one and it will do you some good, I think." The warrior squinted. "Did he say what this artifact was? I cannot recall."

Feryln searched his memory, found nothing. "I do not think he mentioned it."

"No matter," Rowlen returned with a shrug. "If it were anything of importance, they would be sending more than one young fire mage. . . ."

Jarric of House Gaius continued to nearly float through the crowds. He knew, as he suspected Rowlen did, that his quest could have been of a much more difficult nature and while that bothered him a little, he had decided that Master

Prymias must want him so badly that the senior sorcerer had tweaked things a little in Jarric's favor. The young mage did not find himself bothered by that; he would more than prove himself working with the legendary figure. His fear of shaming House Gaius would at last be erased.

Since his apprenticeship had begun, Jarric had always lived in fear of shaming the great house. Gaius had continued to raise him in comfort after the loss of first his mother, who died in childbirth, and then his mage father, who perished fighting off a marauding band of ogres. Prymias had been most instrumental in his upbringing, becoming a foster father in many senses. To Jarric, House Gaius and Master Prymias were one and the same, and he lived to serve both to the fullest of his abilities, if only because he owed them so much.

So simple a task Master Prymias had set him. All Jarric had to do was travel to a village some two weeks distant and verify if this artifact was indeed the ruby shard the senior mage had heard it might be. Verify it, bring the shard back if necessary, and in return receive the mantle of a fully-vested fire mage.

So simple.

Alone in his chamber, Prymias of the Ruby Eye summoned forth a melon-size ball of bright flame. The flame crackled mere inches above his left hand, but he felt no pain, no heat. Touching his ruby with his other hand, Prymias whispered a few words.

Menthusalan's countenance materialized within the ball.

"It's done, old friend."

"The quest has been set? The young man will go?"

"Of course he will! I set him this quest and he's eager to do as I command! Good lad, that Jarric, even if a bit too trusting at times. Everyone knows I favor him, which only made him the perfect one for this mission."

Menthusalan nodded agreement. He had seen enough of Jarric to know the truth of Prymias's words. "He will go alone?"

"Likely Rowlen of the mrem will go with him. An excellent guiding force for Jarric. They should have no trouble reaching their destination." The massive fire mage leaned back. "Of course, they'll find nothing when they get there, but I won't hold that against the lad when he returns. He'll be a good addition to my forces and quite loyal, especially if I place him near Castlana." Prymias chuckled. "You should see the look on his face when she's around, not that I blame—"

"There is a more important matter at hand," the mentor cut in, his voice surprisingly sharp.

Disgruntled, Prymias nodded. Menthusalan had been more relaxed in the past. Since these visions had started coming to him, he had grown less and less tolerant of any matter that did not deal with them. "You're right, of course, old friend."

"Two weeks for them to journey there," The sable-clad figure mused. "Enough time to see that others learn of the legend of the ruby shard and the fact that there are those traveling to retrieve it."

"I still fail to see how this'll prove anything. Even if somehow this force that may be working out of Ebonyr hears of the rumor, who's to say that they'll do anything about it? They'll probably even suspect a trap!"

"If it is someone other than Ganth of the Black Flame, they may do nothing . . . although we both know how covetous a lot we spellcasters are, Prymias. Any ambitious fire mage would desire to study, if not use, such a ruby shard, for its potential outweighs a hundred perfect rubies, I would think."

"Yes." The councillor himself had already contemplated what he would do if such an item was his to use. Sometimes the bickering of the council and the inane proclamations of the emperor seemed too much to tolerate. One strong force, one strong, intelligent force, such as him, could do so much more. "Yes, they would not be able to resist making a move . . . and then we would know who they are."

"And, if it is Ganth, if Ebonyr's master lives again, he will be unable to resist the lure regardless of whether or not it might be a trap."

"It cannot be Ganth! Ganth is dead! Centuries dead! I don't know why I keep accepting this notion of yours—"

Menthusalan's narrow orbs narrowed further. "Because with one who may have trafficked with the Laria, death may not have been sufficient to put an end to his trepidations."

"Yes . . . you're correct, of course."

"I know I am, much to my dismay. And have you considered what might happen when Ganth or even simply some ambitious fire mage seeks the shard and finds only air? Have you considered what that one might do to those nearest, those sent on a mission to retrieve it?"

Prymias had considered it, long and hard he had considered it. In the end, that had not altered his decision. "If we send out an armed force, trumpets blaring, the trap would seem obvious. Sending a small party, yet one with some significant link to my august personage, makes it appear as if I'm trying not to draw too much attention to their task. At the same time, it hints that perhaps there would be merit in investigating on the off-chance the rumors are true. Regardless, the question is now moot. Jarric and Rowlen will do what they have to do. What must be done must be done, Menthusalan."

"You are certain?"

"Of course . . . and if to save Fuego I must sacrifice a loyal mrem and a lad dear to me, then so be it." The master mage stared into the flames, seeing not his friend, but another countenance, one formed from his thoughts. "I know Jarric would understand. . . ."

Chapter 5

FROM A DISTANCE THE FACE OF THE MOUNTAIN looked exactly like that, a face, a skull, actually, overlooking the sheer drop below. The eyes, the nose, and, especially, the great mouth were all major caverns, in some way connected deeper within. Some who saw the face believed it the home of the Laria, for surely such a creature would live in so ominous an abode. However, those who believed this would have been wrong . . . but not by far. The caverns were inhabited and in vast numbers by gargoyles.

A flutter of wings announced the scout's arrival. The dusky gray gargoyles at the entrance to the cavern that served as the mouth eyed the newcomer, but did nothing. This one had been sent out on a mission and if he had returned, it could only mean news of import. Their king would brook no delay, even from the guardians.

The scout stood on short, squat legs, leathery wings folding a moment after landing. Smaller than many of his kind, he was otherwise identical to them in face and form, including the twin horns sprouting from his forehead and the beak-like mouth in which row upon row of sharp teeth now gnashed in nervousness. Blood red orbs under a heavy brow ridge eyed the cavern with trepidation. The gargoyle scout scratched his scaly hide with talons worthy of any Lizcanth, then, knowing he could delay no longer, stalked inside, serpentine tail twitching all the while.

No light of any sort illuminated the inner recesses of the cavern, but the gargoyle did not need it to guide him. He had been born in this place, born serving the one he still served now. Around him, he could see or sense others of his kind perched on the ceiling, on the walls, against stalactites and stalagmites, wherever could be found a good foothold. Gargoyles were communal creatures, even more so than pack animals such as scevan. With numbers came strength and there were few other than dragons who would willingly face the winged furies.

The first chamber of the cavern also stood as the largest, enabling hundreds of gargoyles to gather here. Others swarmed in the lesser chambers, creating a vast force at the command of their infernal monarch. Although tightly packed together in some places, none dared leave their perches until given the word. To dare independent action meant to risk the ire of their king, something all feared with just cause.

None dared greet the new arrival, knowing that his mission required a swift return to their lord. The scout focused on the path ahead, hoping he had not already dawdled too long. Deeper and deeper he went, passing from chamber to chamber. Some denizens flapped their wings slightly, their only attempt at greeting. Most simply watched.

Near the last juncture, the scout briefly paused. A dim light, originating from farther on, illuminated the path ahead just enough for him to make out the grisly features within. Although already very familiar with this horrific place, he still found the final trek an unnerving one. From the walls, from the ceiling, from nearly every outcropping of rock, faces with all varieties of expression stared out at him. They were, in fact, of the rock, macabre visages carved into it wherever possible by a sculptor both brilliant and sinister. That alone would not have frightened the scout, but he knew that each face, whether human, mrem, ogre, or even gargoyle had been patterned after someone who had entered this realm . . . and never left. The lord of the gargoyles considered this his artistic accomplishment and all he summoned here were to admire it and remember that they could be added at any time.

With relief he pushed on past the watching faces, at last entering the place from which the faint illumination originated. A small glowing pool of clear golden water rested in the center of the chamber and perched before it on what might have once been a throne of rock awaited his lord, a winged giant much larger than any of the others in the cavern, even the guardians. Gargoyle orbs, not red but black as coal, surveyed the small scout, demanding he speak.

"Party leaves the kingdom of the fire mages,"

the scout quickly announced in a scratchy voice. "Young fire mage. Two of the cat folk. They travel in direction of village called Tresden." The scout hesitated, then added, "Might stop elsewhere, but thought that this party could be—"

In contrast to the scout, the larger gargoyle spoke in deep, smooth, almost singsong tones. "Could be the one I commanded you to watch for, yes. Aaah . . . wonderful, wonderful! This should prove most interesting, don't you think so?"

The scout, clever for a gargoyle but not so clever as his king, nodded slowly.

"These will be the ones, I am certain of that, the ones who seek this ruby shard! No great party would they send, no army! He, on the other hand, will send legions of fearful hunters to do his bidding!" The gargoyle king clasped thick, leathery paws together and spread his expansive wings. "We must watch these three, I think. . . . Yes, we must watch these three! It will be of much interest and enjoyment, I am certain, to see how they react in Tresden."

He laughed, a sound which made the scout cringe. Never was the gargoyles' lord more deadly than when his mood turned merry. The smaller gargoyle almost pitied the three creatures journeying to the village, unmindful of their possible fates. Then he ceased pitying them when he realized that his lord now stared again at him.

"You have some place to be, do you not, my little friend? Some place I would desire you to be . . . now?"

Shivering, the scout quickly bowed, then immediately scrambled out of the chamber, wings already spread for flight. Darting through the darkened cavern, the smaller gargoyle breathed a sigh of relief. He had lived through the audience and fulfilled the first part of his mission. Now he had to complete the second. Then and only then might his lord permit him to live. All gargoyles served their king under such dire threats and all thanked him constantly for the honor. As he exited the mouth of the cavern and fluttered off into the sky, the scout felt especially honored . . . and especially frightened.

And in the cavern chamber, the gargoyle king turned to contemplate the golden pool. Within the pool rippled an image, that of a castle, a ruined castle, perched on another far, far away peak. The battered yet ominous structure drew his gaze.

"Aaah, and what will you do about this, dear Ebonyr?" he whispered. "What will you do?"

He could hardly wait to find out.

Jarric traveled in high spirits. They had only been on the road for three days, but already he felt as if he had completed his quest, returning to Fuego with an ancient and revered artifact that would win him the acclaim of all those in the ranks. Master Prymias would greet Jarric, then reward him with a position the envy of all those who had told the young spellcaster that he would never rise above a journeyman practitioner. Perhaps he might even be groomed some day to become the master's successor.

First you must return, some tiny portion of his

mind suddenly reminded him. Annoyed, Jarric tried to recover the sense of euphoria, but once disturbed, it had abandoned him. His mood remained high, though, even with the knowledge that something, say bandits or maybe a scevan, could still interfere with their progress. However, between his spells and the skills of his mrem companions, the mage felt little concern.

"There is a village but two more hours travel from here, slightly off the trail," Rowlen informed him. "Sqwent, I believe it is called." The older mrem had consulted the maps earlier that day and seemed to be able to retain the minutest details for hours after. If he said a village existed two hours ahead, then two hours from now they would put foot in it. Rowlen could be that precise. It was one of many reasons that Jarric felt most comfortable traveling with this particular mrem. With Rowlen around, Jarric could concentrate on other matters, specifically their final destination, Tresden, still more than ten days distant.

He had never heard of the remote village, but then, he had never heard of many places other than the Four Cities. It sometimes astonished him that any place could exist outside of Fuego and its counterparts, so deadly could living be beyond the walls. Oh, traveling on occasion rarely proved that dangerous, but constantly living without the protection of the mages or the armies seemed foolhardy at best . . . and yet there were so many who did.

Of course, nearly all the mrem lived like that, but then, they were mrem. Feryln might have come from one of the more obscure villages, but his lifestyle had hardly been unusual. Mrem were hardier, though, more in tune with the wild. That did not make them more primitive, just different.

Jarric liked Feryln, thought that in many ways they were much alike. He hoped that the younger mrem would stay in Fuego rather than someday running off on his suicidal quest for vengeance. If the mrem would just be patient, Master Prymias would certainly find some information that would help. Master Prymias would discover the truth about this amazing horde gathering in the north and he and the emperor's council would set things right. Jarric had great faith in his sponsor.

Two hours passed and, sure enough, Rowlen's prediction proved accurate. After some cautious questioning, the villagers of Sqwent accepted them inside their primitive wooden enclosure. Sqwent consisted of twenty or so structures, mostly homes, but also a meeting house and a storage building. The homes were functional, but with little personal touches, such as flowers or bushes, accenting each. In the center of town, near the meeting house, a small fountain bubbled, the source of the village's water supply. Despite the simplicity of their surroundings, the inhabitants seemed quite cheerful. The fare they offered proved fair at best, but the trio appreciated anything after their three day trek. Rowlen gathered information while Jarric entertained. Few fire mages came this way and even a young one made for a spectacle. He did not feel he cheapened his art by performing, considering it good will that would favor Fuego in the future.

He kept the tricks simple. A few words, a touch of the ruby, and a warm wind lifted him up two or three feet in the air. Another touch brought him back down. He created a tiny sphere of fire in one palm, created a second and third, then juggled a little, finishing with tossing them high in the air and swallowing each as it fell. In truth, Jarric did not swallow them, dousing the spells as they neared his lips, but the effect worked. The villagers clambered around him, congratulating the friendly youth and offering him everything from food and drink to what might have been a marriage contract with one villager's daughter.

Fortunately, before he could say anything wrong, Rowlen pulled him aside. "Master Jarric, it would be good if you would get some rest. We have far to go and from what I have gathered, the path will be a little rougher for some time."

"Any dangers?"

"Nothing reported any greater than a nest of nits, but things could change. The scevan tend to come down the mountains this time of year."

Scevan did not bother the fire mage as much as the pesky nits did. Resembling tiny, mindless versions of the deadly Lizcanth, they often attacked in great force with sharp objects. Being only a couple of feet tall, they were often overlooked by most as nothing more than annoyances, but waking up with one perched on top of one's chest, as Jarric had done, could change that perspective. An armed, toothy nit looks very deadly from such close range. Granted, they had fled the moment he and Rowlen counterattacked, but the memory lingered.

Jarric swore that at the first sign of a nit nest he would burn the entire area down . . . hopefully without taking the rest of the forest with it.

It took some time to find Feryln, who sat alone near one edge of the village. To the human's surprise, the young mrem looked downcast, barely acknowledging their presence at first.

"Are you all right?" Jarric finally asked.

"Feryln—" Rowlen began.

"My village was like this one in many ways," the mountain mrem whispered. "So very much like it. Not just the enclosure or the way the homes are set. The people . . . they may be humans, but they laugh, cry, live, just as my village once did." Feryln looked up and to Jarric's surprise, there were tears in the feline warrior's eyes. "They lived . . . and then they died . . . died. . . ."

"I'm—" The fire mage had to force the words out, so taken aback was he by the deep emotions. "I'm sorry, Feryln. I didn't think—"

Rowlen put a hand on the other mrem's shoulder. "I think it best you get some rest, young one. You will feel better afterward."

"I do not think that I can sleep now."

"You will, young one. Trust me, you will." Rowlen sighed and added, "They would want you to go on for them. You can do nothing for them if you do not get rest."

At first Jarric thought Feryln would ignore the

advice, but then, slowly, he rose to his feet. "Perhaps you are correct. I think, though, that I wish to walk around a little first." A brief, sad smile graced the mrem's features. "The sounds, the sights, they are still comforting even if not my own people. I will not be long, I promise."

"As you wish, young one."

Feryln left them. Jarric watched him disappear, then muttered to Rowlen, "Should we leave him alone?"

"He is never alone," the older mrem returned. "His family and friends are always with him." He blinked. "Now come, Master Jarric, we, too, should get some desperately needed rest."

He accompanied Rowlen back to the quarters the villagers had given them, the one building that tried best to pass for an inn. There were only two extra rooms, one below the other, and only the upper room had what could properly be called a bed. Rowlen insisted the bed belonged to Jarric, who felt guilty but accepted it. Mrem did not in general enjoy human beds as much, preferring more natural comfort. As the other room had a cot and serviceable blankets, Rowlen insisted that those would do.

Although the older mrem had spoken true when he had suggested that Jarric needed the rest, the young, fire-tressed mage still found it impossible to sleep at first. It actually had little to do with Feryln's dark mood. Rather, casting spells for the villagers had reminded him of what he had once hoped to do. So many people distrusted spellcasters and for no good reason that he knew. Certainly, there had been those in the past who had used their gifts to enslave or murder others, but they were a rare handful. Most mages could be trusted implicitly—Master Prymias, for example. Besides, the worst mages had lived in times past, existing now only as legends and characters in children's stories. The only evil magic lay in the essence of the Laria—a force which all sorcerers, whatever their city, fought against together.

He still lay contemplating this when he heard a slight scratching from above. Jarric had been given the topmost room, which had angled walls but still managed to be roomy enough. He held his breath, waiting for the sound to repeat itself, which it did. The fire mage tried to convince himself that the scratching was just some animal or bird scrambling over the roof, but, if so, it had to be a fairly large one.

More scratching, this from another part of the roof. Now there were at least two of the creatures. Nits did not fly, but other things did. Jarric rose quietly, grabbing his robe. The medallion he did not have to search for, having left it hanging around his neck. Dressed, the mage peered at the ceiling and waited.

The scratching halted for a time, then picked up again. Jarric grimaced. It sounded as if at least three large creatures padded around above his head. He tried to think what they might be but although his imagination conjured up many things, none of them fit.

Then the noise ceased again. A moment later, something began to slowly but precisely tear at the outside roof.

Jarric could wait no longer. Whatever lurked outside wanted in and he doubted that it would be to his benefit to let it do so. Holding the mage's staff high and clutching the ruby in his other hand, Jarric stared at where he heard the noise and muttered.

The room grew warm. Encouraged, Jarric pushed harder. He repeated the words he had been taught, emphasizing them in just the correct way to achieve maximum effect. The temperature in the room increased dramatically, but as warm as Jarric felt, he knew that in another breath or two those on the roof would be feeling much, much warmer.

From outside he suddenly heard raspy squawks and snarls. The tearing ceased, followed by a commotion of great, flapping wings.

There existed but one window in the room, a low, shuttered one that would have been useless for seeing what lurked above but now might serve to observe what fled. He had kept it closed tight beforehand, the better to keep the room as dark as possible, and now regretted at least not unlatching it. Jarric hurriedly reached for the window, recalling just in time to bespell his hands so that they would not burn. He flung the shutters aside and, thrusting his head out, searched the sky for anything out of the ordinary.

The red sun shone down and in the moment it took his eyes to adjust to the light, the briefly-glimpsed flying forms vanished. He could tell only that they were fairly man-sized, but, other than the fact that such knowledge only ruled out monsters like dragons, Jarric learned nothing.

Someone began battering the door. He heard Rowlen calling his name. Jarric hurried to the door, well aware that if he took too long the powerful mrem would come bursting through it, lock or no lock.

"Master Jarric! We heard cries from above and when Feryln went to the window, he nearly burned his hands. I knew then that you must be defending yourself from attack."

The younger mrem stood but a step behind Rowlen, breathing hard. Jarric glanced at Feryln's hands, saw that the injuries were minor. Nonetheless, he felt guilty for causing his friends any distress. He had only wanted to heat the roof and room, but the spell had covered the entire building. The fire mage hoped no one else had happened to touch a window or outer door.

"My apologies to you both. I heard something on the roof, several things, in fact, and when they started tearing their way in, I acted quickly." A look of chagrin crossed over his face. "I overdid it a little, again."

Rowlen peered at the ceiling. "I see nothing within." He eyed the window. "Master Jarric. If you could remove the spell?"

"Oh, certainly!" Clutching the ruby, he spoke a few short words. Immediately the temperature dropped to a more normal level.

"Thank you," Rowlen went to the window, then darted out of it, climbing toward the roof.

Knowing the warrior's thoroughness, Jarric had not been surprised by the act. Rowlen would investigate the roof for any signs of damage and clues to the identities of the mysterious creatures. The mrem took his duties very seriously.

The fire mage turned back to Feryln "I'm sorry about your hands."

"The pain has already passed." The younger mrem's gaze continued to drift to the window. "Did you see what it was?"

"No. Only that they were about the size of a mrem or human and that they could fly very swiftly when they wanted to."

Feline eyes narrowed in thought. "Gargoyles."

Gargoyles? Jarric had to agree that gargoyles would fit the description, but he doubted that they could be the ones. "Maybe, but gargoyles don't like coming down this low. The texts say that they prefer the mountain caverns and valleys, sometimes old ruins if they're massive enough. Trees don't offer them the best protection. Besides, what would they want here? Certainly not us! They could find a lot easier prey. The village has livestock, after all."

Feryln seemed to accept his response readily enough, although clearly the mrem had not entirely discarded the notion. However, any attempt by Jarric to further press his point ended as Rowlen suddenly slipped back through the window. The warrior looked slightly perturbed. "Very curious. You must have caught them just as they started, Master Jarric. I found many scratches, indicating at least three creatures of some great proportion, but the only true damage I found consisted of one bit of roof that one of the creatures had pulled back a few inches."

"I cast the spell the moment I heard the tearing, Rowlen. They woke me earlier with their trampling about."

"Yes, I saw that. From the signs, they look to have run back and forth several times for what seems no reason . . . almost as if they were trying to make certain you heard them." Rowlen shrugged. "But that, of course, would make no sense."

"Did you find out what they were?" Feryln asked.

"I would have said that they were gargoyles, but such creatures rarely venture to regions such as this. One would more likely find them where you came from, young one."

His opinion justified by the veteran warrior, Jarric smiled. Feryln looked more subdued and yet, at the same time, somewhat relieved. "My father always said that gargoyles can be deadlier than Lizcanth."

"That they can be, young one. Still, whatever else it was that came this night, Master Jarric sent the creatures well on their way. We need not worry any more about them, although this does remind us that there are always good reasons to remain on guard." Rowlen yawned. "Come, we should return to our slumber so that we can make the best of the journey tomorrow. Master Jarric. . . ."

Jarric bid the two mrem goodbye, then returned to his own bed, feeling great pride in himself. He could now claim some danger on this quest, the better to prove himself capable enough to garner full mage status. Without meaning to, the young spellcaster began to embellish the event in his thoughts, choosing now to even take Feryln's suggestion that they might have been gargoyles. Rowlen had even hinted as such. He imagined that they had come to keep him from the ruby shard, having somehow, however improbable, heard of its discovery and the value the fire mages placed upon it.

He fell asleep, already dreaming of Master Prymias's proud, fatherly visage and Castlana Dumarcus's admiring glances as he finished relating his epic tale before an audience of hundreds. . . .

"Gargoylesss . . ." the Lizcanth hissed. "Gargoylesss. . . ."

"Ssstrike?" asked a second, slightly smaller one.

"Maybe." The first Lizcanth returned. "Maybe." The mottled green reptile glanced around, looking for the third member of their party. "Mussst wait to sssee."

They lurked some distance from the village where the two cursed mrem and the human mage rested, a tiny scouting mission sent originally with one purpose. The discovery of the three gargoyles, however, had changed that. While the two Lizcanth had garnered some amusement at the flying creatures' sudden antics on the roof, likely from some spell the human had cast, their simply being here had stretched the mental capacities of the pair beyond hope. No, they had to wait for the third member, the one who spoke for Lord Baskillus . . . and the dark one.

"A very, very wise decision," came a more fluid, rolling voice.

The two Lizcanth hissed, caught between hatred and fear. The larger finally knelt, responding, "We ssserve. We ssserve. Fled have the gargoylesss, their perch too hot it ssseemed."

"The mage, no doubt. He is the one to watch. He must be allowed to locate the prize so that he can verify its reality. I cannot do that. More important, he may be needed to carry it back. We may not be able to touch it and I cannot risk losing it because of impatience."

"And the two mrem?" Much hesitation preceded this question, for where once the answer always would have been death, now the pair might even be left alone so long as it suited the purposes of Lord Baskillus's dark master.

"Captured if simple to do, killed if necessary."

Both Lizcanth hissed. The possibility of mrem blood enticed them.

"Enough. Killed if necessary. They may have uses, too."

Subdued, the reptiles hastily nodded. This one spoke with the voice that even Lord Baskillus obeyed. They died slowly and horribly, those who defied that voice.

"Now, come. We must return to the others." The leader indicated that they should proceed him. The Lizcanth skulked past, trying not to look at the mrem who, but a few days before, had been brought as a helpless and beaten figure to their lord. Both had been there to hear the screams and both had known what those screams meant. None in the growing horde, be they reptiles, ogres, kobolds, even some of the undead creatures summoned, desired to join this mrem in his fate.

As for the mrem, he cared little what the stinking Lizcanth thought or did, so long as it served the greater purpose. He cared little because little remained of his previous existence. Now he served because all he could do was serve.

In the light of the red sun, the ruby embedded in his throat glistened.

Chapter 6

"THIS CAN'T BE TRESDEN."

Feryln had expected a place at least as large as his own village and from Jarric's protest, so, apparently, had the human. Rowlen, too, seemed a little hesitant, but he had read the maps and so of all of them could vouch for this being their ultimate destination. He had done so twice already, both times to the fire mage's dismay.

Sqwent, which lay twelve days behind them, seemed now a vibrant metropolis compared to Tresden. Even Feryln's own village, primitive as it had seemed, shone in comparison to this, their ultimate destination. Had not the younger mrem also studied the maps, he, too, would have at first refused to believe this was the place where the ruby shard supposedly had been discovered.

Tresden could barely be called a village. It could barely be called a settlement. Feryln counted perhaps five or six structures passing for houses and all of them in some disrepair. Feryln and the others had been given to believe that Tresden was a thriving outpost of humanity, but nothing thrived here save the mud. For once Ferlyn found himself yearning for the enclosing walls of Fuego.

The houses were more like huts, huts put together in haste and then left to the elements. Thatched roofs were in dire need of patching, one even open to the sky in places. The wood used to build the structures seemed to be half-rotten or cracked. Windows were not covered with glass but with rags which looked as if they had been dragged through the endless mud first.

Astonishingly enough, there were people to go along with the houses, people who eyed them with distrust and disrespect. Grimy and certainly unbathed, their unique fragrances affected not only the mrem's sensitive nostrils, but clearly the fire mage's as well. Most scurried out of sight, treating the newcomers like plague. Only one chose to speak to the trio, and he seemed as unlike his fellow inhabitants as Tresden itself was to any place one could actually call home.

"I am . . . Master Vahn." He announced this as if it should strike the others as terribly significant. Tall, gaunt, terribly immaculate, and with more animation to him than even a mrem cub just learning to crawl, the gray-haired figure announced himself a scholar of the ancients who had come out to Tresden in search of ruins. He had been the one who first alerted Fuego of the find—the most monumental find in the history of the Four Cities, or so he constantly claimed.

"But we were told that the villagers had dug up the shard in a field," Jarric countered, understandably confused. "Master Prymias said—"

"The illustrious Prymias of the Ruby Eye? Aaah, my young mage, the news must have filtered to him from apprentices with little knack for detail! No, some of the villagers may have aided in my efforts, but I assure you, the true credit for what you will see belongs to me! There would be no shard for the fire mages of Fuego otherwise!" He gave them a beatific smile.

Something about this human made Feryln's fur stand on end, but neither Jarric nor Rowlen appeared to notice it. It had nothing to do with Master Vahn's appearance, although his dark, almost black eyes and large beak of a nose did set the young mrem off for some reason. Neither did the scholar's manner of speech, ofttimes a bit too condescending for him, make Feryln so nervous. Even the overabundance and size of the human's teeth when he smiled did not shake the mrem, although it did put him in mind of a hungry scevan. The only thing that perhaps explained the sensation Feryln experienced had to do with the few other inhabitants of Tresden. Young or old, male or female, they all treated Master Vahn with a respect that seemed to edge toward anxiety—almost as if they were afraid of him.

Again, not even Rowlen noticed this and so eventually Feryln put the thought aside. Still, he could not bring himself to stand too near the scholar.

Despite Jarric's eagerness to see the shard and ascertain its authenticity, Master Vahn brought them first to his own unlikely abode, a cave mouth he said stood very near the site, and, over food, regaled them with the story of his research.

The area had once been an outpost of one of the previous great cities, buried after a cataclysm. Everyone else had assumed it never existed, but Vahn, ever Vahn, had persevered, searching and searching. The ruins in which he had discovered the shard had been hewed out of rock and the scholar believed an entire town, nay, a city, still remained to be found underneath. Of course, the artifact alone already proved reward enough for his efforts, for it showed that he and only he could have come so far in his efforts. He had turned legends into reality. "So many said that such a shard existed only in tales, but such short-sighted fools could never sway me! Few have as much foresight and perseverance as myself, I must humbly say!"

Feryln listened with the rest, gingerly pushing his meal around until he could work up the appetite to eat it. Vahn claimed living off the land a normal part of his work and his offering seemed to emphasize that. It was not that Feryln did not like lizard; his village had often used them to supplement their stores of food, but this one seemed too raw even for his tastes. Rowlen ate with less delicacy, probably having had to force down much less savory fare over the course of his life, but Jarric, too, seemed disinclined to touch much of his food, although in his case it might have had to do with his impatience.

At last, the fire mage could wait no longer. "Master Vahn. Forgive me, but if it's at all possible I must see the shard now! Master Prymias of the Ruby Eye has asked me to verify its existence and, if it is truly what you say, return it to the safety of Fuego—"

"You doubt me?" Vahn seemed to find this most amusing. "Of course, then, young mage, you shall see the fabled ruby shard immediately! Come!"

The scholar leapt from his seat, but, rather than march out of the cave, he headed farther inside. After their initial shock, the trio followed. Feryln squinted, eyes adjusting as rapidly as possible to the true dark. However, he wondered at the scholar's ability to make the trek in the increasing blackness. Humans did not see too well in such dark, Jarric had already stumbled many times despite the aid of his staff.

"One moment, Master Vahn," the fire mage finally called. "I think I need to create some light, if you don't mind."

"Light?" The tall man blinked, his eyes almost seeming like black pits in the gloom. "Yes, you are indeed correct, my young friend. Please do so. I would hate to slip and fall down some shaft."

Feryln doubted that Master Vahn would have had any such problem, but Jarric himself could take no chance. The fire mage clutched his ruby, muttered words, and suddenly a small ball of flame floated before him.

"How entertaining," Vahn remarked before proceeding on.

"How deep must we go?" Feryln whispered. It seemed as if they kept descending with each step. He had assumed that the shard would be somewhere within easy reach.

"I don't know," Jarric whispered back. For the first time, he sounded uncertain. "Master Prymias said nothing about Master Vahn or that the shard would be—"

"Just ahead!" the scholar shouted. "Just ahead to a wonder no fire mage could ever resist! A legend come to life, a treasure of power sought after by heroes and villains alike! I left it where it was, for I wanted you to see it in all its glory!"

The fur on the nape of Feryln's neck rose again. Perhaps the uncertainty he felt about Master Vahn had to do with the scholar's questionable sanity.

Yet, before he could bring up such questions to Jarric or Rowlen, a faint glow, somewhat red, somewhat purple, rose from a chamber just beyond. The nearer the party got, the greater the glow became.

"Come, come!" urged Vahn. "A few steps more."

Almost entranced, Jarric obeyed. Feryln and Rowlen kept a pace behind him and for the first time the younger mrem noticed that the older's claws were fully extended. Rowlen took no chances, although what the veteran warrior thought might happen, Feryln could not imagine.

"Now," came Vahn's silky voice. "Can you tell me that what you see before you is anything but what you seek?"

The ruby shard, aglow with a soft inner light that colored all around it rested in a tiny alcove carved into one wall of the chamber. Small enough to fit into the palm of one's hand, it resembled in form a thick knife blade, almost as if someone had carved it that way. The glittering artifact looked so very fragile, yet clearly it had survived countless centuries of strife and destruction. Even Feryln could not find words to describe what he felt in its presence. He wanted to pick it up, to hold it, but it was not his place to do so. The mrem glanced at his human companion, waiting for him to fulfill his duty. Jarric took a step forward, but then a step back as if afraid even that would cause the object of their search to vanish.

"Well, young mage? Will you not touch it? You can hardly take it back to Fuego if you will not touch it."

Urged on by the scholar, Jarric again stepped toward the alcove. With trembling hands, he gently, hesitantly, cupped the ruby shard. The artifact glowed brighter in his grip, almost as if greeting him. Feryln felt a tremendous urge to join the human so that he, too, could touch the crystal. He imagined what he could do with this artifact if he, like Jarric, was trained as a fire mage. With it, Feryln could sweep down upon the ravagers of his home, sending a storm of fire or some great creature of flame to destroy all of them. In one fell swoop, the mrem could avenge his people and, hopefully, cleanse the nightmares of their deaths from his mind.

Unfortunately, the truth was, in his hands, the shard would just be another pretty piece of crystal. Only Jarric could wield it and Feryln could certainly not ask him to do such things.

"It must be real, must it not?" Master Vahn whispered.

Jarric nodded mutely. He turned around so that the others could get a better look. "Beautiful . . . isn't it beautiful, Rowlen? Feryln?"

"Very beautiful, Master Jarric," the older mrem finally responded. Feryln simply nodded.

"Master Prymias will be so pleased." Jarric suddenly blinked, as if regaining some control of himself. Much to Feryln's disappointment, the fire mage opened a thick pouch hanging from his belt and cautiously placed the crystal inside. However, even then the mrem thought he could discern a faint glow through the leather.

Jarric turned to the scholar. "Thank you, Master Vahn, for all you've done. I'm sure that Master Prymias and the emperor's council will make certain that you receive your due once I return."

"Your having come here so swiftly to retrieve it is all I could ever have asked," Vahn returned, smiling at all of them.

Again Feryln's hair rose, but again he could not say why. So far, Master Vahn had been an obliging, if talkative, host. Still, he could not help wanting to extend his claws a bit.

"We should start back immediately—" Jarric began.

"Start back? By all means no. No, my young friend! You should stay long enough to rest!" The dark, so very dark eyes met each gaze. "By this time you must all be very, very tired . . . "

While Feryln would have liked to leave Tresden behind as soon as possible, he did see merit in the scholar's words. Rowlen and Jarric, too, looked agreeable. The party had walked quite some distance this day simply to get here; they would not get very far even if they left immediately. No, Master Vahn had the right of it. If they rested a few hours, they could cover much more ground when they began the journey back to Fuego.

The decision was Jarric's, but fortunately the fire mage saw things as Feryln did. "You're absolutely right, Master Vahn. We should get some sleep. Master Prymias would have my hide if something happened to the shard because my wits weren't at their best."

"Excellent, then!" The tall human put a companionable arm around Jarric, leading him and the others in the direction of the entrance. "You will stay with me! The cave is warmer and far more clean than those ramshackle little huts, I promise you that! You will sleep as you have never slept, you have my humble word on that!"

Swept up by his overwhelming manner, they could not refuse and, indeed, Feryln soon had to agree that the cave mouth made for a much better refuge than the decrepit homes of the village. The floor was dry, the cave remarkably free of bats, something the mountain mrem had never seen before, and the temperature moderate. It did not take the trio long to settle down, their bedrolls a simple matter to prepare.

All the time, Master Vahn watched over them, saw that they wanted for nothing. He even made certain that Jarric had a safe place for the ruby shard, a small hole near where the fire mage would sleep. A flat rock made the bag impossible to see and also would prevent Jarric from accidentally knocking the artifact when he rolled over.

Feryln found himself amazed at the swiftness with which sleep sought to overtake them all. Rowlen began to snore the moment he settled in. Jarric went to sleep immediately after checking the safety of the shard one last time. Feryln struggled longest, trying to sort some matters out. Everything so far had proceeded very easily, something that should have pleased him. Yet, he could not forget how peaceful and satisfied his own village had been just prior to its devastation. Did that explain why the mrem still felt some anxiety now? The situations could hardly be compared.

At last, unable to struggle against the inevitable any longer, he fell asleep . . . fearing, just a little in those final moments of consciousness, that he might not wake up.

Yet, Feryln did wake and to nothing extraordinary at all. Rowlen already stirred, moving about in preparation of a meal which, fortunately, proved to be something other than one of Master Vahn's very rare delicacies. Jarric woke a few minutes later, immediately reaching for the rock. The flame-tressed mage sighed in relief the moment he held the pouch, its contents clearly intact. He secured the pouch to his belt, then went to join the two mrem.

"Where's Master Vahn?"

"The scholar was nowhere to be found when I awoke, Master Jarric," Rowlen replied, handing some food to him. Rowlen had scrounged what little remained of the supplies that they had purchased from the previous village, a much more enticing location than Tresden. "I saw no reason to search for him. If he has not returned by the time we have finished, then, if you desire, we will look."

Ferlyn ceased his morning cleaning, taking the food Rowlen now passed to him. "Perhaps he is deeper in the cave."

"I do not think so, but it may be. The cave is a large one."

They finished their food, gathered up their things, and yet the scholar still had not returned. Jarric hated the thought of leaving without thanking Master Vahn again.

"Perhaps he is in the village," Ferlyn suggested.

"If he isn't, I supposed we'll just have to move on afterwards. We can't wait much longer."

They made their way to Tresden, only to find the inhabitants even less sociable than before. When Jarric sought to speak with one of them about the scholar, the villager muttered something about Vahn not being around, then disappeared behind the door of his meager hut. Two more attempts garnered even less success.

"A pleasant place, this Tresden," Rowlen muttered. The older mrem gazed around. "One would think that they fear something. I do not like that."

"What can they fear?"

"I would not care to find out."

Jarric returned to them. "Well, we can't wait any longer. Master Vahn will have to understand." The fire mage's eyes widened. "Master

Prymias! I should at least contact him before we leave! He'll want to know!"

"We are very far from Fuego, Master Jarric."

"I know, Rowlen, but I can try."

Feryln, unaware that the human could contact his sponsor from any distance at all, watched as Jarric handed his staff to Rowlen, then took the medallion with the ruby in both hands. He held the gem toward the blue sun, which now stood high in the sky, and whispered. At first the young mrem thought Jarric had already contacted the elder mage, but then he saw a tiny sphere of fire, much like the one used to illuminate the cave, form in the air before his companion. However, this one grew larger and as it did, the center of the fireball changed, becoming clear.

The mrem hissed, his ears flattening. A familiar countenance formed in the clear region, the countenance of Prymias of the Ruby Eye.

"Jarric? Is that you, lad?" Feryln thought Master Prymias looked a little perturbed about something.

The young spellcaster eyed the image. "Yes, Master Prymias, it's me. I—"

The image flickered away for a moment, then returned. The face within looked concerned. "Jarric, I can barely see you, much less hear you! Where—" The voice faded. "—you?"

Sweat had begun to form on the younger human's forehead. To the two mrem he quickly explained, "The distance is great! I've never tried from so far away, but I didn't think it would be much different!"

"Jarric?" came the other mage's fainter voice.

"Master Prymias," Jarric interrupted. "I'll be short, if you don't mind! I simply wanted to tell you that I've got the ruby shard—" The image faded again, returning, somewhat hazy, a moment later. "—from Master Vahn and it's real! I'll be—"

"Jarric!" Although distorted now, Feryln and the others could still hear the urgency in the councillor's voice. "The ruby shard . . . said you have it?"

"I'm losing the spell!" Indeed he was, the astonishing fireball sputtering and shrinking. "Master Prymias! Yes! Master Vahn, the scholar, gave the shard to me! It's real and I'll be bringing it back as soon as—"

With what sounded like a gasp, the ball of flame ceased to be. A wisp of smoke floated off, leaving in its wake only a sweating, exhausted sorcerer.

Jarric nearly collapsed. Rowlen quickly went to his side. "Master Jarric! Are you all right?"

"F-fine. I just need a few minutes to . . . to recover."

Feryln aided the other mrem in helping Jarric to a sitting position. Despite the human's hardships, Feryln marveled at his power. To even contact someone, however tenuously, from so great a distance surely had to indicate astounding abilities. The mrem recalled how some of the mage's other spells had not exactly gone awry, but had succeeded too well. Jarric had only meant to create a campfire and had nearly set the area ablaze. Not only had he managed to make the roof in

Sqwent so hot it drove off the winged stalkers, but had also heated the rest of the building as well. No, Jarric did not lack for ability; he only had to learn to control it better.

After several minutes, Jarric finally rose. "I'm better now. I think most of my message got through. Master Prymias certainly looked surprised."

"He did at that," Rowlen agreed.

"I think we should go now. Master Vahn still hasn't appeared and now that Master Prymias knows about the shard, he'll be anxious to see it."

"Are you certain you are ready? The spell took much out of you, M—" The warrior paused, ears high, nostrils sniffing the air.

Feryln, too, smelled the faint scent, but his ears flattened, already recognizing it.

The human, with his lesser senses, glanced at the two mrem, whispering, "What is it?"

Neither mrem bothered to answer, for, indeed, there no longer seemed any reason to do so. The sources of the scent . . . scents, now . . . came bursting from the nearest foliage, their numbers giving good reason why they did not fear two cat warriors and one young fire mage. There were ogres, at least four, each brandishing huge clubs. Two grotesque kobolds vied to be first to reach the trio, monstrous hands dragging on the ground. Emerging from the back came three, then four lemurlike monsters with huge, round, yellowish orbs and thick fur either dark or light blue. Yngling—creatures rarely seen even by their victims.

And with this terrible tide came a legion of Lizcanth, who seemed to be masters here.

Jarric steadied himself with his staff. "They're everywhere! All around us!"

Feryln hissed. He, at least, had no doubt that the horde he had wanted to find had now found him instead. Why here, though? Why now?

The tallest of the Lizcanth raised his weapon, one of the savage, clawed terrors Feryln had battled against before. The other monstrous warriors halted. In rasping tones, the reptile demanded, "The ruby shard, human. . . .the shard for your livesss. . . ."

The fire mage's hand went to the pouch. "No!"

The Lizcanth laughed, a cruel sound. "Then . . . take it we will from your torn, bloody bodiesss."

He waved the weapon and the circle that had formed around the trio tightened.

"Jarric!"

Prymias pounded on the desk, trying to summon back the image of the young mage. Nothing. Not surprising, though. He had known that the lad had potential, but did not Jarric realize that it took two spellcasters, sometimes more, to create a communication spell that strong over such vast distances? Prymias himself could not have done it without at least an apprentice to aid him, but to do so he needed far too much time . . . and time no longer seemed a commodity he had.

"He found the ruby shard? He found the damned thing! It shouldn't even exist! We made no fake! All we wanted to see was if anyone would follow the scent—and who in the name of Gaius is Master Vahn?"

"Something amiss, Your Eminence?" Castlana Dumarcus stood at the doorway, having evidently entered with that feline stealth the councillor generally admired . . . but not this time.

Prymias almost snapped at her, then thought better of it. He did not go out of his way to offend his majordomo. Castlana had become too valuable, often more capable of planning for certain situations than he himself. Trying to calm himself, the master mage took a deep breath. It only partially worked. "When Jarric . . . when Jarric departed on his quest, did you make the other arrangements I requested of you?"

A slight, crooked smile broke through the mask of indifference. "They were made before you requested them, Eminence."

He sighed. Some relief, if not enough. "Thank you, Castlana. You're dismissed for now."

"As you desire, Eminence."

Alone again, he contemplated the sudden change in events. A ruby shard that should have been nothing more than smoke and a man who should have been little more than that. This Master Vahn should not have existed and he certainly should not have been hunting for the shard! Where had they come from and what link did they have to his plans? Had the one Prymias sought turned the trap around, created something that would come back to haunt Fuego and him?

The master mage opened his left hand palm up. A fireball formed there, created with much more ease than Jarric's, but with far less strength. Prymias did not seek to contact someone so far away.

A moment later, the mentor's brooding image formed in the center of the flames. He looked as if he had not slept in days. "Prymias. Why have you—"

"Listen to me carefully," the fire mage interrupted. "We may have a very large problem on our hands. . . ."

Chapter 7

JARRIC CLUTCHED HIS MEDALLION, MAKing certain that his fingers touched the ruby in the center. With his staff, he drew a line in front of him and muttered the words he had been taught.

A cloud of bees, hundreds of them, appeared from nowhere, drawn by the spell. The fire mage muttered another word and the cloud moved with swift purpose toward the nearest of the attackers, striking wherever possible. The ogres grunted in surprise and annoyance and the kobolds tried to swat the swarm with their huge hands. They suffered the worst. With their thick fur, the Yngling were less in danger and the Lizcanth hides were so tough that Jarric quickly realized the bees were not much more than a visual pest to them.

The lead Lizcanth laughed at his consternation. "Fool of a mage you are! Take you we will if ssurrender you will not! Live you will, mage, but wish to live you will not, not as sservant of the dark one!"

Rowlen and Feryln had their swords out already. At the edge of his vision, Jarric noticed the younger mrem barely able to restrain himself from leaping into the attacking horde. These had to be part of the same group who had slaughtered his family, which made the mrem's ability to hold his position that much more remarkable. Of course, outnumbered as they were, Jarric feared that one way or another he and his friends would lose this battle.

Still, his tutors had always taught him that confidence remained a mage's best weapon. *Believe in your victory and your spells will succeed.* The young spellcaster tried to do just that. This time when he drew a line with the staff, he muttered different, more powerful words of magic.

An arc of fire formed before the nearest attackers, an arc that Jarric immediately stretched into a circle, momentarily cutting off the horde. Beyond, the Lizcanth hissed in frustration while the ogres and the others continued to swat away the last of his swarm.

"I don't know how long that'll hold them! We have to think of some way to escape from here!"

Rowlen studied the frenzied creatures. "Perhaps if Feryln and I guard your sides, you might create a wedge of fire to daunt them. Then we might find a way to flee from them while they regather. Feryln—"

The other mrem did not respond at first, still eyeing those beyond the fiery barrier. Jarric watched his gaze and thought that perhaps his companion tried to identify individual foes as those who might have personally murdered his family and friends. A futile task, but the mage could well understand Feryln's desperate need. Still, they all had to keep their heads if they hoped to come out of this alive.

"Feryln! Young one!" Rowlen repeated, this time catching the other's attention.

"I am sorry, Rowlen." Feryln looked chagrined.

"We must be ready. Look, already they force their way through the flames."

Sure enough, despite the fire, the Lizcanth were trying to reach them. Jarric had forgotten that the reptiles were creatures of heat, distantly related, some scholars claimed, to the great dragons. True, the Lizcanth burned, but not enough, thanks to their thick, scaly hides.

The first burst through, to be met by Rowlen's swift sword. The Lizcanth slumped to the ground, chest cut open by the mrem. However, a second and third beat their way through, requiring both mrem to act. Jarric wished that mages could use swords in times of crisis, weapons other than knives and staffs were generally forbidden to those of his calling, then cursed himself for not better using the weapon ever available to him. He had been trained to excel in magic, therefore Jarric had to depend on that and not keep wishing for that which he could not use.

I need something more certain, something that strikes with the deadliness of a blade! He had such spells, had learned them well, but to actually cast them . . . "If I don't," he muttered to himself, "nothing can save us!"

He dropped the staff, knowing the spell he had

chosen would work best if he directed it. The words came easy to him even though he knew what they would do. Jarric had killed before, but he had only killed nits, creatures scarcely more than animals. The Lizcanth and ogres, monstrous though they might be, were still intelligent creatures . . . who would slaughter his friends if he hesitated much longer.

Brow furrowed, Jarric spoke the words while pointing.

One, two, three, four missiles of pure flame shot from his finger. With each one the fire mage felt as if he had been slapped. Nonetheless, his spell worked well. Two of the missiles caught their targets directly in the chest, sending a Lizcanth and a kobold down. A third struck the Lizcanth fighting Feryln in the shoulder, causing the reptile to drop his weapon. Feryln finished his adversary a moment later. The last missile missed its intended target, the Lizcanth who appeared to be the leader. He dodged, having realized what was happening. However, in doing so, he left one of the Yngling open and the missile struck the furry monster in the stomach. Although it survived the strike, the Yngling could not douse the magical flames. It screamed and tried to run, almost setting one of its brethren afire. At last it collapsed and grew silent.

Still there were too many. Jarric had no idea how many spells he could complete. The ball of fire he had used to communicate with Master Prymias had drained him far more than he had expected and the missiles took a lot out of him. Still, Jarric could try . . . hope and try.

Again he said the words. However, the horde had become more wary. An ogre and another Lizcanth perished, but the other two missiles failed, one barely grazing a kobold who quickly smothered the smoking tuft of fur on his shoulder.

Jarric nearly collapsed. Beside him, the two mrem continued to combat other Lizcanth who had forced their way through the rapidly diminishing wall of flame. Too many of the savage lizards had broken through for Rowlen and Feryln to take unless the spellcaster could help them once more.

He grabbed the staff. Perhaps . . . perhaps if he dared to use the shard. From his studies, Jarric knew that such an artifact should be capable of many wonders. It could absorb more power or maybe magnify the spells he did cast, making them far more deadly. The shard seemed the only hope they had.

However, as Jarric fumbled with the ties of the pouch, a sudden, intense wind rose up. With the astonishing wind flew dust and debris, more and more with each breath. The horde halted and even the trio had to cease their efforts. The dust became so thick, the wind so violent, that it grew difficult to see. A Lizcanth swung blindly at Ferlyn, who did not even notice the blade that passed two feet to his left.

"What happensss?" came the voice of the lead Lizcanth. "What happensss?"

To Jarric's surprise, a voice he had not yet heard, one that sounded almost like a mrem, called, "Seize them now! Before it is too late! The winged ones come!"

Coughing, the mage wondered what the strange voice meant. *The winged ones? Before it was too late? Why would it be—*

Taloned hands gripped his shoulders, hands with startling strength. Jarric barely had time to register what was happening before the hands lifted him high, higher, into the air. Huge wings flapped rapidly, gaining altitude at an astonishing rate. He wondered at first whether a dragon had seized him, but realized that his rescuer—or captor—could not be much larger than him.

Then a rising form, or rather two rising forms, caught his eye. The one beneath looked to be Feryln, who hung limply, sword still in his hand. Staring long at what carried the mrem, Jarric wondered if Feryln would be pleased to know that he had been correct. Gargoyles did come this far from the mountains. That is, a few of them had.

A moment later, a third creature carrying Rowlen, who seemed to be taking the flight with incredible calm, materialized in the sky. The mage noticed that none of their attackers had likewise been carried off, which meant that the gargoyles had specifically come for the trio. Why, though? Surely, if anything, the leathery creatures had to be part of the same horde. Why steal away the three from the rest?

He twisted his head back in order to try to converse with the gargoyle, but a single glare from the horned monstrosity warned him off.

Unwilling to trust his spells at this height, Jarric tried to relax and wait, all the while wondering where they were being taken and hoping that his shoulders would survive the journey.

Mountains. Of course the gargoyles would take them to the mountains. Eyeing the fearsome peaks, Jarric wondered which they would fly toward. After some searching, he found one riddled with caves, almost creating a death's head appearance. Surely that had to be the monsters' home.

The gargoyles steered toward it, heading toward the mouth of the skull. Despite his shoulders feeling as if they were about to tear off, the human prayed for his captor to slow down. However, the gargoyle's speed instead increased, almost as if the creature could sense his fear and fed from it.

The peak proved even greater than Jarric had first supposed. There turned out to be a fairly large plateau before the eye, one that even had foliage. He thought that the gargoyles would land there, but then they banked, turning directly into the mouth of the cavern.

Day became dark, but the blackness did nothing to soothe the mage's fears. Even though he could not see them, he could hear, not to mention smell, that other gargoyles perched around him, watching as he and the two mrem were carried deeper into the system. Suddenly the knowledge that so many gargoyles lived here made Jarric wonder if the trio were headed for some chilling larder. Did the monsters eat their meals wriggling and screaming? He started to concentrate on a major spell, hoping he had enough to bring down the cavern on all of them. Better killed in a cave-in than fed alive to these creatures.

Suddenly his feet touched rocky earth. The fire mage fell to his knees, but the gargoyle lifted him back to his feet with very little effort. Nearby he heard Feryln and Rowlen land, the two mrem grunting as they struck the hard floor of the cavern.

"Gentle, gentle with my friends," a mocking voice commanded. "You were not commanded to bring them to me simply to batter them against the rocks, were you?"

The fearsome gargoyle who had carried Jarric suddenly transformed into a groveling servant. "Most sorry! Most sorry!"

"Send them forth," the voice commanded, ignoring the plea.

With much more gentle persuasion, Jarric's captor led him forward. A faint glow from a chamber up ahead allowed the human to at last make out some features. The area where they now stood seemed natural for the most part, but here and there he thought he saw the handiwork of some astonishing artisan, perhaps human, perhaps not. Faces had been carved into the rock, faces in varying displays of emotion. The artisan seemed to have carved them at random, picking outcroppings that could best be turned into the fanciful visages. The faces seemed to belong to every race and none. They looked vaguely human, vaguely mrem, even vaguely like gargoyles.

Then Jarric and the others were thrust into the last chamber, one clearly carved out partially by hand. The illumination he had noticed earlier proved to originate from a pool of some golden liquid. Jarric stared at the pool, awestruck. He could sense the aura of magic emanating from it, knew that it had been created by a very old, very powerful force.

"It calls you, does it not? It calls you and you would like to answer, would you not?" The questions were followed by a mocking chuckle.

Beyond the pool, perched upon a crude throne chiseled from rock, a gargoyle of monumental proportions watched the three, especially focusing on the human. Gargantuan wings stretched, the tips nearly reaching the sides of the chamber. Taloned hands capable of encompassing Jarric's head clutched the throne. A toothy, beaked maw curled up in a condescending smile.

The fire mage tried to meet the gargoyle's stare, but the black pits unnerved him too much and he had to look away almost immediately, which brought another chuckle from their inhuman host.

"So much squawk over so little a chip." One leathery paw opened. "Bring it to me."

"No!" Jarric tried to stop his guard, but the latter squeezed hard on his already sore shoulder. Jarric grunted in pain and while he stood helpless, the gargoyle removed the pouch and tossed it to its master.

The sinister creature opened the pouch with astonishing delicacy, removing the shard gently. The pale glow of the artifact vied with that of the golden pool. Raising the shard high, the gargoyle admired it, his monstrous features further distorted when seen through the shard. "A work of art, would you not say?"

"It won't do you any good," Jarric retorted. "Only a fire mage can truly tap its abilities!"

The creature laughed. It seemed to find much amusing, although certainly Jarric could see no humor in the situation. "So defiant a young one! Little mage, do you have any idea who I am?"

"You are the gargoyle king," Feryln rasped from behind the mage.

"Yes, mountain mrem, you would know me, would you not? Your dreams as a cub no doubt also held nightmares of my making, yes?"

The younger mrem made no reply. The gargoyle king chuckled again, then returned his attention to the shard and Jarric. "I daresay I know more about the shard than you, my dear young Jarric of House Gaius. I know its history and the blood which has been spilled for it. I know who covets it, who would tear Delos apart even against the will of the Laria if need be . . . all to obtain this most legendary bit of rock!"

"I don't know what you're talking about."

The great creature cocked his head to the side. The black pits bore into Jarric's very soul. "No . . . they never bothered to tell you that part, did they? Never bothered to tell you that others followed, others watched, coveting the shard and waiting to see if you found it, if you verified its magic! The moment you did, Jarric of House Gaius, you condemned yourself . . . and your masters turned their backs on your fate."

The spellcaster vehemently shook his head, trying to deny what the monster insinuated. According to the winged demon, Master Prymias and others had sent him on a quest as some sort of decoy, knowing that others would come to claim the crystal. Yet, that did not entirely make sense. Why possibly lose the ruby shard to this dark power, the one that evidently ruled the monstrous horde, much less risk Jarric's life? No, the gargoyle king had to be lying. "I don't believe you. You'd say anything. Anything!"

"I might and I might not, my dear Jarric; that is up to you to decide. Whether I lie, though, does not change what is. Aah, no it does not! You are pursued by Lizcanth and others under the command of Lord Baskillus, who, in turn, obeys the dark one who would place us all under his unyielding power simply for his own purposes." No humor tinted the scaly monarch's words now. "I am master here, not him! I will not bow to any other save the Laria! Let the lich go his own path, but he will not cross mine!"

Lich? Jarric prayed that he heard the gargoyle wrong. Such abominations only existed in tales even in the darkest regions of Delos. Undead did exist; vampires, ghouls, and animated skeletons raised by wizards, but when wizards themselves died, they stayed dead. They never came back except in nightmares and stories. Liches did not exist!

The gargoyle king must have read his growing anxiety. "Aah, I am sorry, dear, dear Jarric, but, yes, there are such things in the world, things, dare I say, more disturbing than myself?" He gently replaced the ruby shard in the pouch, securing the ties. Then, the gargoyle king carefully tossed the pouch back to the fire mage, who managed to catch it, then stared confusedly at their monstrous host. "I have no desire to claim the shard. Guard it well if that is what you desire, but always ask yourself if it is worth the risk."

"It is," Jarric returned, trying to sound determined.

"That will, of course, remain to be seen." The gargoyle king smiled, revealing far too many teeth. "I have come to like you, Jarric of House Gaius, you and your mrem, Rowlen of Leonus, and Feryln of the mountains, and so I give you fair warning that far too many know your quest. There are legions against you, legions led by the dark one, whose symbol is fire black as the hole where his soul once was." He turned his shadowy gaze to Feryln. "Young mountain mrem, you would do best to remember Lord Baskillus, I think. You have a destiny with him, a debt you seek paid."

Jarric glanced back, saw Feryln stiffen, then snarl. The mrem's ears folded back, as if he saw the Lizcanth in question before him. The gargoyle king had offered the name of the one who must be responsible for the slaughter of Feryln's village, but for what reason? Did he truly expect a lone mrem to successfully kill the reptilian leader?

"Many know of your quest, dear Jarric," the winged ruler declared again, returning to the mage. "Too many. Most working for the lich, and I do not desire the lich to have his prize, for then what would I be but his servant? Therefore, I will give you passage to safety, you and your friends, and in return, you will keep the shard from he who seeks it."

Silence filled the chamber as Jarric struggled with all the gargoyle king had told him. He understood only some, but enough to see that it would be to the leathery creature's benefit if the shard remained in the young mage's hands until Jarric could reach Fuego. There, Master Prymias . . . or some other senior fire mage . . . could utilize its abilities for the safety of the kingdom and—

Utilize its abilities? His eyes widened and only with effort did he keep his mouth from falling open. If only a fire mage could manipulate the ruby shard to its full potential, then did that mean that the lich . . . the lich . . .

He had to ask. "Great monarch . . ." The gargoyle's smile grew toothier at the politeness of Jarric's speech, but the weary spellcaster had no time for his mocking ways. "Great monarch . . . is this . . . is this lich . . . he's one of my kind? One of my calling?"

The question made the gargoyle king laugh so loud that the sound echoed throughout the caverns for several minutes. Even before it had faded, though, the shadowy-eyed lord of the air replied, "Oh, yes, dear, dear Jarric, he is . . . was . . . one of you! Watch ever for those under the banner of the flames black, and know, always know, that he who they call lord was once the fire mage, Ganth Kazarian . . . now back from death to reclaim the prize that was ever his obsession." The gargoyle pointed at the pouch he had returned to Jarric. "Your ruby shard."

The winds howled through Ebonyr, howled through the halls where once knights in onyx armor stood at attention, where once courtiers who had seen the power of his cause awaited his word. Some of their bones remained yet in those halls, most buried under the rubble that had been much of the roof. The winds howled, perhaps mourning those lost, mourning the moment of distraction when the combined forces of so many mages from young Fuego had turned the tide, sent a ball of flame from the heavens so massive that it had melted rock and left forever the remnants of the castle scorched. Then the warriors, human and the so-cursed mrem, had poured in to take the survivors.

The mrem. . . .

Fragments of the once beautiful mosaic pattern on the floor still remained, a pattern once forming the black fire crest that had been his banner. To the side, at last shunted out of the way, the shattered remains of a vast chandelier, a magical, crystalline delight, lay forever dark, the sorcerous energy that once illuminated the grand chamber long drained away. Now, only a few torches, widely scattered, gave the room light.

The winds howled and the ghosts around him howled more, but the figure on the crumbling, marble throne paid little mind to them these days. There could be no time to dwell on the past, not when the future threatened. It had taken him so long to revive himself, so long to gather his strength and begin again, only to find that he had been tricked. Despite his having escaped the death that had been planned for him centuries before, he now faced imminent threat of extinction . . . unless he worked to save himself.

Long, tapering fingers held together now only by scraps of skin, folded slowly into fists. Sockets that had once held eyes now burned with an almost charcoal flame fueled by vengeance and need. The once sun-yellow robe, almost gray from the ages, fluttered in the wind its wearer could not even feel. The cowl of the robe remained up, all but obscuring the tarnished, pointed crown and the fleshless face beneath. He could no longer smile or frown and even the loss of those simple actions added to the fire within.

Ganth Kazarian . . . Ganth of the Black Flame . . . rose slowly from the throne that would have once served for the emperor of all Delos had he succeeded. Beyond, the Lizcanth who guarded the shattered hall, there more for show than because he needed them, shivered and fell to one knee. They could sense his fury even if his countenance could no longer express it.

His cowl shifted, revealing more of the battered crown and the strings which had once been a flowing mass of scarlet hair. From out of the shadows emerged a vampire maiden, one he had chosen long ago when mortal desires had still been a part of his existence. Raven tresses obscuring much of her beautiful, moon-white face, she hurried to his side, reached up, and adjusted the errant cowl, being careful not to disturb the black scarf wrapped tightly around his throat. That done, she disappeared back into the shadows, secretly hoping not to be needed again for days to come.

The lich's mouth opened and although little remained of his tongue, still the power within enabled Ganth to speak, if in a grating, horrific voice. "The . . . ruby shard . . . my . . . ruby shard. . . ."

Even before his death, he had sought it, coveted it, knowing that in the end only it could do for him what he needed. He had found a replacement, yes, with the aid of the Laria, but the foul creature had tricked him, too, in the end, just as his once friends of Fuego had.

The armies grew larger every day as those who saw his might decided their best hopes of survival lay in serving him, yet now Ganth did not care if the Lizcanth, ogres, and the rest puzzled over his hesitation. He had planned for them to march on Fuego after eliminating the mountain clans of the damned mrem, the cat folk who still haunted his memories. Now, though, much of his forces had been turned to this new effort. If Fuego did not have the ruby shard, if it had truly been discovered elsewhere as his scrying had revealed when catching the words of the fire mages, then the city could await its day of death a bit longer.

The ruby shard would have already been his, but the gargoyles had dared defy him once more. The novice mage and the two cats had been flown off by the foul creatures. More valuable time lost. Yes, the gargoyles, too, would pay . . . and very soon.

He moved almost by gliding to the vast balcony beyond the great hall. It had been here where, long ago, the mrem had poured over the edge and entered his citadel. He had not thought that they would risk scaling the dangerous heights below and that had proved a most fatal blunder. Still overwhelmed by the shock waves of the fireball's strike, his own warriors had fallen quick and even their master had found himself hard pressed. The memories still burned and would burn until the last mrem died.

Pushing aside the past, Ganth of the Black Flame raised his left hand. A perpetual dark cloud covered much of the sky above Ebonyr, but now it shifted, broke apart, as Ganth called out in the tongue of magic. Three times he repeated the words and with each time, the gap grew greater.

Raising now his right hand as well, the horrific mage shouted out. "Azur! Your master summons! Obey or die!"

From beyond the veil of clouds came a roar that echoed through the heavens.

A titan flew through the gap he had created, a shimmering blue form dwarfing any other creature on Delos. Its wings were nearly as wide as Ganth's vast sanctum. The jaws opened, unleashing a second, ear-shattering roar. Such jaws could swallow a man, nay, four men, whole. A row of great spikes flowed from the back of the monstrous creature's head all the way down its incredibly long, serpentine tail.

The lich backed away just enough to give the giant room to land on the vast but precarious balcony. The gargantuan blue figure landed with surprising care, possibly knowing that what had been built so strong the ages had well begun to tear away.

"I am here," rumbled the tremendous dragon. "I obey . . . even if I would rather eat you and be done with it."

"But you cannot, Azur," Ganth mocked. "You are mine, mine as much as any of the others."

Azur, the great blue dragon, raised his head to hiss his displeasure at this spoken truth, revealing to Ganth the chain that ever bound the beast to the wizard. Buried within the folds of the neck was a small ruby, the link by which Ganth kept Azur pliant.

"Very well, then, oh, Master," responded the dragon. "What will you have of me?"

"There is a young fire mage—"

Crimson, draconian orbs brightened. "I may eat him?"

"At a cost worse than death, lizard! This mage. I will give you the image that one of my walking shells projected to me. You will seek him out where I say and you will bring him, alive and unharmed, to me!"

"Another I cannot eat? This is too much! First you, now this useless one!"

Ganth would have smiled had what little skin and muscle that remained enabled him. "But you shall be allowed to eat him . . . only after I am done, though."

The dragon spread his wings, much more

eager now. "Then let me be gone, the sooner to finish this! Already my appetite is whetted!"

"Wait!" The lich concentrated ever so slightly on the ruby in the dragon's throat. He had to conserve power, although Azur did not have to know that. "One task before you search for the young mage."

"Another task? How many—"

"Until I am satisfied." With that, Ganth sent a reminder through the ruby.

The dragon roared with sudden pain, almost slipping backward off the broken edge. Ganth cut the pain immediately, but the reminder worked. Azur looked much more subdued.

"Another task, then . . . Master."

"Yes, one that you may accomplish simultaneously." The fires through which the lich saw burned with increased fury. "The human is at present inside a mountain, a mountain populated with gargoyles . . . and they must be taught respect. . . ."

Chapter 8

CASTLANA DUMARCUS TOOK HER POSITION as Prymias's majordomo very seriously, putting into it a dedication that went perhaps beyond the limits the senior mage expected. At times, fulfilling her duties required her to delve into regions of which he would not approve . . . if he knew. Castlana considered this a necessary evil of her position, one that, deep down, Prymias surely understood. In the end, he desired her to keep things moving smoothly for him and that was what she did.

Now, though, some questions had surfaced that she found a bit too disturbing, questions which forced her to flow over her master's many scrolls and manuscripts, verifying or easing her suspicions. Castlana had perused several dozen already, her ability to scan pages rapidly and retain their information now proving most valuable. However, so far she had found nothing, which forced her closer and closer toward a conclusion the crimson-haired woman did not like.

While she continued to search, another portion

of her mind dealt with other problems, specifically Jarric. Although Castlana had not approved of Prymias's entire plot, she had, of course, coordinated it as smoothly as possible. Nothing should have gone awry, but everything had, up to and including this actual shard that had materialized from the ether and the attack on Jarric and the mrem. At present, the majordomo had no idea where the hapless mage might be, but certain resources set in motion since the beginning might soon alter that. Castlana hoped nothing terrible had happened to the younger man; he had always been likable and she did not find his embarrassment around her entirely without attraction. Most important, she had decided long before her master that Jarric would prove an invaluable asset to both Prymias's organization and, peripherally, to her own within.

The reaver captain should have reported back by now, though. She paid well for his services and so far he had not let her down. However, there were limits to what a mercenary would do, even for the money she offered. Perhaps something had come up that had forced him to abandon the matter. However, until she heard from him, Castlana preferred to believe that he still followed her instructions. If not . . .

She sighed, emerald eyes burning into the book before her. Another ancient volume perused and still nothing. The majordomo leaned back for a moment, stretching her neck and back muscles, running her hands through her trimmed hair. Yet more weight toward the supposition she favored least. Prymias's complete collection lay open to her, including the works that the mentor Menthusalan had borrowed before this entire debacle had begun. Especially the works the mentor had borrowed.

Castlana Dumarcus could say nothing yet to her master, not until she had learned more . . . and even then she might have to take matters in hand herself, presenting Prymias with the facts afterward and awaiting either his reward or punishment. A crooked smiled with little humor briefly graced her sculpted features. Such had often been the nature of her work, yet she would not have had it any other way.

The majordomo pulled the next manuscript toward her and continued reading.

The gargoyles took flight again, this time bearing their passengers along with much more gentleness. The notion of being borne through the sky still filled Feryln with much anxiety, but he tried to keep it hidden, not wanting to shame Rowlen and Jarric. The older mrem took the new trip stoically, as he took so much. Rowlen seemed content to survey the landscape below, which changed from high mountains to sloping, forested land, then a mix of both. As for Jarric, he, too, saw the flight differently than Feryln, especially now that he trusted, to a point, the gargoyle king. Glancing at the human, Feryln could see the fire mage actually enjoying the wind in his face and marveling at the world far below. Never mind that to the young mrem that world seemed too far below and that with one slip by the gargoyle it might suddenly come too close too fast.

Their leathery companions said nothing to them. The gargoyles seemed to want to get this task done so they could return to the security and darkness of their cavern. Feryln understood that they only tolerated the trio because the creatures' fearsome monarch had commanded his subjects to perform this deed. Otherwise, the two mrem and the human might already be lying far below, dashed upon the mountainside.

But one thing kept Feryln from completely falling prey to this fear of heights, and that concerned the name he had been given by the gargoyle king. Somewhere the horde of Ganth Kazarian gathered and somewhere in that horde the mrem would find Baskillus, the Lizcanth lord the gargoyle claimed responsible for the deaths of those dearest to Feryln. He had no reason to disbelieve the claim, having seen the Lizcanth warriors in his village. Baskillus. The young mrem warrior repeated the name over and over in his mind. Baskillus. Feryln would somehow find the reptile and, even at the cost of his own life, tear the monster's throat out.

He blinked, noticing that Rowlen had begun to shift. Had the heights at last gotten to the veteran? It did not appear so, for Rowlen looked more suspicious than frightened, as if he had just made some discovery. Feryln glanced at Jarric to see if he, too, had noticed Rowlen's behavior, but the human had his eyes closed, again savoring the wind.

Rowlen began to gesture, pointing to his right.

He looked up and shouted something to the monster carrying him, who completely ignored his protest.

Feryln looked in the direction he had pointed, trying to decipher Rowlen's protest. Did the older mrem want them to go that direction? Feryln studied it, then glanced in the general direction of the sun. Were they going more and more northeast? This high up, he had not paid much mind to directions, simply wanting the flight to end, but now it seemed that at some point the gargoyles had turned from Fuego and were instead heading deeper and deeper into the mountains where it had been said Ganth Kazarian lurked. That could hardly be correct. Yet, if the gargoyles had altered their course, perhaps they had done it simply to avoid an obstacle, after which they would turn south once more.

Somehow, Feryln found it impossible to believe his own suggestion. The winged creatures were up to something.

Now Feryln struggled, trying to get Jarric's attention. He shouted out, but his words were lost in the wind. Fortunately, the human happened to look down at Rowlen. He saw the older mrem's protest, then quickly turned to Feryln. Feryln tried to indicate the change in direction, but Jarric shook his head, uncertain as to what his companion indicated.

Frustrated, Feryln glanced up at the gargoyle carrying him. "Why do we head northeast? Where are we going?"

The gargoyle kept his stony expression, fearsome eyes staring straight ahead.

The mrem repeated his question with no better results. He looked at Jarric, who had likewise been protesting with his creature. Had the gargoyle king lied to them? Did he actually intend to deliver them to the lich as some sort of peace offering?

As he pondered this, a shadow momentarily blotted out the sun. Feryln ignored it until the shadow returned, this time from an entirely different direction. The mrem tensed, knowing that clouds did not move in so mad a manner.

Suddenly the gargoyles banked and dove, dropping hundreds of feet in seconds. Feryln let out a yelp, fearing that they intended to drop the trio, but, if anything, the one clutching him squeezed tighter, almost burying his claws in the mrem's already sore shoulders.

Again the shadow passed overhead . . . and this time Feryln heard the terrible roar.

He looked up and saw the great blue leviathan diving down toward the small party, impossibly huge maw opened wide as if to swallow all of them. The gargoyles dove lower and lower, taking different directions so as to confuse their much larger adversary as much as possible. However, the target that most seemed to interest the dragon proved to be Jarric, for whenever possible the giant twisted to pursue the mage. Less and less the beast appeared interested in the two mrem and Feryln could only guess that it had been sent from Ebonyr. Ebonyr meant Ganth Kazarian. The lich had even mastered one of the great dragons. Feryln shivered. That the black mage could control such a colossus spoke ill for the trio's hopes of escape. How could they combat such power?

Suddenly the tops of trees grazed the mrem's feet. Alert, Feryln noticed that his gargoyle continued to lose altitude, as if it planned to land and hide among the trees. While Feryln could not deny the sense of hiding from the dragon, he did not like abandoning his friends. He opened his mouth to protest, certain that they could at least act as distractions for Jarric, when the gray creature released its grip, sending him plummeting into the foliage.

Howling, Feryln tumbled into one of the trees, crashing through several branches before finally becoming tangled on two. He looked skyward, trying to understand what was happening while at the same time catching his breath. A tiny speck above looked to be the same gargoyle who had abandoned him. The winged fury rose higher and higher, heading in the direction Feryln had last seen the others.

The monster had abandoned him so that it could better serve its brethren. Feryln appreciated that, but wished that somehow he could have helped. Now he hung from a tree in a mountain forest who knew how far from the others . . . assuming they had met similar fates. Rowlen, he suspected, had been abandoned somewhere, but Jarric, who seemed the true prize so long as he carried the ruby, likely stood the greatest risk.

With effort, the mrem clawed his way up as best he could, trying to find some sign of the aerial battle. In the distance he could see the blue dragon trying to snap at something, but whether it had been Jarric or one of the unencumbered gargoyles, Feryln could not tell. The battle shifted farther and farther away as the seconds passed until at last not even dots remained in the sky.

Feryln tensed. He had been abandoned, possibly never to see his companions again. Yet, to give up hope went against mrem teachings. No warrior gave in to the enemy, especially when that enemy might be one's own fears and doubts. He had been taught, most recently by Rowlen, that a good warrior went on, regardless.

He would go on. Feryln would find Rowlen and, if possible, Jarric, too. He would try.

With the grace of his feline ancestors, he journeyed to the ground. The land rose on a slant to the east and in that direction even from the forest floor he could see the towering peaks. Keeping them to his right, Feryln headed north, assuming that to be the best direction in which to start looking for Rowlen. Considering how haphazardly the younger warrior had been abandoned, the other mrem might be in desperate need of his help. The gargoyles had clearly seen the pair as expendable once the mage had been threatened.

Feryln wended his way through the wooded region, listening for either the roar of the dragon or the call of one of his companions. However, for a long time the only sounds he heard were those of the forest, and even those seemed muted, as if the wildlife did not wish to draw attention to itself. Not so surprising if they lived under the shadow of Ganth.

On and on Feryln moved, certain that he had chosen the best direction yet finding no trace of either Rowlen or the human. Feryln found himself growing unused to being so alone; he had become close to the pair, especially the guiding force of the veteran warrior. For a second time he had been torn from those nearest him. The mrem extended his claws in frustration; had the fates condemned him to such an existence because of some failing? Feryln wished that he could find a Lizcanth, some foe, so that he could prove himself somehow.

The twin howls shattered his thoughts but a moment later.

Scevan. He knew the sound well. It might only be one beast, but he had to assume at least two as a precaution. They could not be all that far from him. He estimated the direction. Northwest likely. If he stayed on his own path, Feryln and the beasts would probably not collide with one another.

Then it occurred to him that the scevan might have found Rowlen.

Feryln drew his sword, which he fortunately had kept sheathed during the flight. He could not avoid the scevan after all, not until he knew if it had the scent of one of his companions. True, the beast might only be hunting some other animal, but the mrem could not chance that.

Another howl shattered the calm. The scevan actually sounded nearer. Feryln tightened his grip on the sword. He no longer doubted that he could kill one of the beasts, but if there were more . . .

Several minutes passed as he warily made his way toward the scevan. He heard no new howl during all that time and started to wonder whether the foul beast had run off in some different direction. Then twin throats called out again, so close Feryln quickly looked around, certain that the scevan must be in sight by now.

To his left he spotted a dark but indistinct form. It moved on four legs just like a scevan and appeared to be following some trail. Feryln hid behind a tree, then peered out, watching the beast as it drew near. It acted quite strange as it pushed through the foliage, almost as if moving forward took much strain. The mrem's eyes narrowed and he sniffed the air. The scevan's scent he noted readily enough. Few things smelled as strong as one of the dirty, lupine horrors, but did he smell something else as well?

One of the heads of the scevan twisted to snap at a branch caught behind its neck . . . a branch which Feryln realized looked far too long to be natural. He shifted, daring discovery in order to better see. The thing no longer looked like a branch, but rather a vine or—

A leash. Someone had put the scevan on a leash of sorts. Feryln followed the direction of the leash and finally saw the figure crashing through the trees far behind the beast. An ogre had control of the scevan, a very unhappy ogre. Feryln quietly hissed, startled that he had not noticed the huge creature before this, yet . . . who would have expected to find a scevan being used in such a manner, especially by an ogre?

The lupine monster paused, both heads high,

four ears perked up. The mrem cursed himself for a fool. Whatever he might think of the beasts, they had excellent hearing. It had sensed his hiss.

He judged the size and swiftness of the ogre. Feryln could take both adversaries, especially if he could separate them. The ogre clearly did not like his task, which would also mean that his concentration would not be the best. Ogres could batter things, but it took much effort for them to think beyond mayhem.

Feeling more confident, Feryln slipped around the other side of the tree, intending to catch the scevan and handler from behind. However, the mrem warrior froze a breath later, all his plans shattered. Beyond the first pair, a second scevan, likely also with a handler, searched a different piece of the forest. Even as he watched, a third beast materialized, no doubt also accompanied.

A search party . . . most likely searching for Feryln and the others.

Uncertain how extensive the search might be, Feryln debated his chances. If he headed north, he might run into more of the hunters. If he headed south, he might lose his chance to find the others, but at least the search party would probably pass him by. Then he could resume the trek north.

The second option more palatable, Feryln shifted to a tree farther south. So far he still only counted three scevan with three handlers, two ogres and one large, ugly Lizcanth. Perhaps these were the only three or perhaps the rest were indeed north of him. He doubted that, though.

Sure enough, a fourth beast, this one also controlled by one of the reptiles, materialized in the foliage. Unfortunately, it appeared to the south of Feryln's position, effectively cutting off his route. The mrem silently cursed, flattening himself against the tree. The hunters moved swiftly along, the scevan checking the scents in the air and on the ground simultaneously. Feryln checked the wind direction. The ones now directly north should not be able to pick up his scent, but the two guided by Lizcanth might.

The third passed his position, leaving only the last. Feryln readied his blade. If the scevan picked up his scent, he would leap at it. Surprise would give him enough time to do the beast in and still give Feryln hope of catching the Lizcanth off-guard.

Still luck seemed with him, for the fourth scevan continued on past his hiding place, the two heads more interested in something they smelled among some bushes. Their reptilian handler swore at them, urging the pair on with a whip. One head snapped at him, further taking the Lizcanth's attention. Feryln started to move around, the better to catch the reptile from behind, if necessary.

The handler's whip caught on a tree branch. As the reptile tugged on it, his gaze shifted by chance directly to where the mrem stood.

Feryln dove at the Lizcanth. Encumbered by both the struggling scevan and the tangled whip, the lizard could not defend himself in time. The mrem's blade sank into the Lizcanth's throat, cutting off the scream.

The scevan, though, turned on Feryln just as

he withdrew the blade. Feryln slashed at the nearest head, scored a direct strike that sent the scevan back, yelping. Unfortunately, the others heard the noise. A Lizcanth called out. Another shout rose somewhere to the west.

Again the scevan harassed Feryln. Desperate to end the struggle quickly, the mrem thrust hard at the area where the two necks joined. One head snapped at his blade, but missed. The tip of the sword sank in.

Howling, the wounded beast tore away from the conflict. Feryln waited for it to turn again, but the scevan had lost its taste for battle. It fled into the forest, the leash trailing behind.

Other figures materialized among the trees. More Lizcanth, weapons at the ready. An ogre, bashing his way through the foliage with just his fists. Scevan on leashes. Even . . . even a thing flying through the air, a round, repulsive, leathery ball of flesh with no discernible mouth or eyes, but a multitude of sinewy, monstrous tentacles squirming underneath it. Feryln could not make out any more detail, but the elders had warned the young about floaters, abominations created by the old magic. However, they were said to have only two tentacles, not the ten or twenty this monstrosity had.

With the image of the repulsive beast still burning in his mind, Feryln quickly headed south, the only direction still open to him. The mrem had sought either his friends or revenge, but he knew when a situation turned too deadly. Feryln could do nothing for anyone if captured or killed.

Behind him, scevan howled and Lizcanth hissed. Whether they had seen him remained a moot point; once they found the dead reptile, they would know that someone lurked in the area.

Feryln moved from tree to tree, seeking some refuge that the hunters would overlook. So far, none of his pursuers had noticed him, but he could not hide behind trunks forever. If the mrem could find some cover, perhaps he could wait them out.

A small ridge he had passed earlier caught his attention. Perhaps a little obvious, but worth at least reaching. His pursuers seemed more intent on the north. They might have already passed this way, in which case Feryln could at least rest.

The mrem moved cautiously away from the tree trunk. No hunter lurked within sight or hearing. Feryln breathed a little easier. Maybe he had slipped past them. Increasing his pace slightly, he neared the high side of the ridge. Once around the other side Feryln could—

Something snaredhis wrists, chest, and throat. They tightened, threatening to choke Feryln where he stood. He caught glimpses of leathery appendages like serpents, and something grotesque just beyond focus. It drifted a short distance above his head, trying to draw him up to it.

Another floater. The mrem had been so intent on watching for warriors he had forgotten to look up, not thinking that there would be more than one of these creatures. Now that mistake would likely cost him his life.

The blade slipped from Feryln's hand. Desperate, the mrem extended his claws and snapped with his fangs. He caught one tentacle, tore it in half with his teeth, then quickly spat out the dark ichor that poured forth from the wound. The floater responded by tightening its grip on his throat, slowly suffocating him. Like the one he had sighted earlier, this floater had more limbs than the legends insisted. Feryln knew that even if he managed to sever another of the monster's grasping tentacles, it would still retain enough to kill him.

Unable to breathe properly, his struggles lessened. He had failed his village, his friends, and himself. The wizard Ganth would add him to the scores of victims already claimed. Jarric and Rowlen were probably already dead as well. Perhaps it would be better if Feryln died now . . .

Hot ichor rained down on him, startling the mrem back to full consciousness. The tendrils securing him loosened, some of them flapping loose. Suddenly he could breathe again. Gasping, Feryln staggered forward, the floater doing little to hold him. The mrem fell to his knees, unable to do more than try to breathe.

Behind him, he heard a sound like a heavy ax chopping into an overripe melon. A faint sprinkle of fluid splattered him, some of it burning. Someone, no Lizcanth by his voice, quietly cursed.

Strong hands took him by the shoulders. "Afraid you'll have to breathe while you're on the move, mrem. That's not the only creature around this area."

Feryln rose, pausing only long enough to glance at his rescuer. His eyes widened and he started to speak, but the other urged him forward. Around them, a dozen or so other armed figures scurried for the safety of cover.

He had been rescued by reavers, Feryln realized, reavers who had to have come here with the express purpose of finding the mrem and his companions. Feryln felt certain of that, for how else to explain the presence of the leader, a human he had already met?

How else to explain the timely arrival of none other than Theron Kain?

Chapter 9

THE GARGOYLE DEPOSITED ROWLEN IN A tree which, at first glance, might have appeared sturdy, but which the mrem found out too late was actually very fragile, the victim of some blight. Rowlen only had perhaps a second or two to get his bearings before the branches gave way, sending him plummeting toward the distant ground. Only his long-trained reflexes had saved him from a broken neck or spine.

His first concern upon reaching the earth had been to locate the others, most notably Jarric. Whatever his concerns for Feryln, Rowlen's first duty concerned House Gaius. In addition, of the pair he suspected that the mountain mrem had a far better chance of survival than the city-born mage. Besides, Feryln had not been pursued by a dragon.

The feelings of mistrust that had briefly touched Rowlen when first hearing of the human's quest returned now in full force. The simple quest had turned into a calamity of gargantuan proportions. Every dark creature seemed interested in Jarric and the shard, and all of them seemed to have been privy to the knowledge of its existence far too quickly, almost as if someone had announced the discovery.

The warrior shoved aside such thoughts, understanding that if he followed them to their conclusion he might accuse one whom he had always respected highly. Instead, Rowlen pushed on. Jarric needed him, needed someone to save him. And the warrior was the only one around to do that.

He wished he had time to search for Feryln. The young one's aid would be well appreciated now and it would also relieve some of Rowlen's guilt. While he hoped that Feryln might return to Fuego and warn them of the debacle, he knew it more likely that the young warrior would do exactly as he was . . . search for his companions.

It did not take Rowlen long to discover that he did not walk alone in this area. He came across the first Lizcanth and scevan minutes after beginning his trek. Straining at the leash, the scevan searched the ground and air, seeking any scent. Fortunately, the hunting pair passed too far north, but their presence put Rowlen more on guard. He had thought the horde farther west or north, but now realized that the gargoyle had dropped him nearly in their midst.

He wondered if Jarric might already be their captive, but the gargoyles had moved with astonishing speed and dexterity, easily outmaneuvering the immense dragon. Rowlen clung to the hope that Jarric remained free in some other region of the forest, gradually finding his way back to the warrior. A bit wishful, perhaps, but the mrem would not think otherwise. If the black wizard's minions had captured the human or, worse, the great blue dragon had finally caught up—

Another figure, little more than a shadow at this point, moved through the woods far ahead. Rowlen planted himself close to the nearest tree, sniffing the air. Too far away for a scent. The figure moved nearer, as silent as the mrem. Certainly not a Lizcanth and especially not a kobold or an ogre.

Rowlen's ears flickered. The shape had defined enough that it looked possibly human. His hopes rose. Perhaps he had found Jarric after all!

Then the mrem saw that the figure moving so stealthily through the forest did not wear robes as the mages did. In fact, it moved more like a warrior . . . like a mrem warrior. Puzzled, Rowlen squinted, trying to make the stranger out.

A mrem! Could it be Feryln? He had thought the young one lost farther south, but perhaps the gargoyle's mad flight had turned the older warrior around too much, making him misjudge directions. Despite his hopes, Rowlen held his position, wanting to make certain.

The mrem moved yet closer . . . and proved to be a stranger. While the realization disappointed Rowlen, it still raised some hope. If there were other mrem in the region, he would have aid after all. He carefully studied the newcomer, gauging his strength and condition. Clearly the other warrior had recently been through a terrible struggle; one side of his face still suffered scars and damage. Cloth bandages covered neck and shoulder Yet, overall the newcomer looked strong, very strong.

Rowlen could not risk letting this opportunity pass. He needed any help he could get. It might take some time to convince the other of the importance of his duty, but Rowlen would convince him.

Stepping from behind the tree, he quietly called, "Warrior!"

The other mrem paused, very calm. He looked Rowlen over from head to foot before replying, "Hail, warrior."

"I am Rowlen of clan Leonus, in dire need of your aid."

"I am Tef of clan Madrac, and you are in woods with few friends."

"How well I know." Rowlen approached, sheathing his sword to show his good will. "I have already seen Lizcanth and I know there must be other monsters about."

Tef nodded cautiously. The bandages around his neck had been secured tight, indicating more than a slight wound. "The lord of Ebonyr, he who has been called Ganth of the Black Flame, has brought together many unlikely allies to create a vast horde. With it, he hopes to take Fuego first, then all of Delos."

"You know this?" Rowlen felt foolish after he asked the question. Living here, surrounded by foes, of course Tef's people would have garnered such knowledge.

"You said you needed my aid." Tef glanced

left and right, as if to assure that they would not be disturbed. "Are you alone?"

"Aye. That is my great concern. I seek my two companions, including a mage in my charge. He is a human. They look—"

"I know humans."

"Forgive me. He carries with him something of great value, something the lord of Ebonyr desires. I must find him and bring him back to his city, where the object may be protected by those who have the ability to do so."

Tef considered this for some time, finally nodding. "Yes, it would be good to find this human . . . and you would be the best hope of that at this point."

A peculiar way of putting it, Rowlen thought, but accurate. "Can you help me?"

"Yes." Tef smiled slightly, which revealed a jaw once broken. "We will find the mage, but first some preparations must be made."

"Preparations? We have little time and with so many of the dark one's horde about—"

The other mrem rubbed the back of one hand against his throat. "Have no fear, Rowlen of Leonus. Rest assured that once I have prepared you, you need not concern yourself about the legions of Ganth." The smile grew, which only served to make it even more jarring. "Not at all. . . ."

Jarric pinned himself against the side of the cave. The trees and foliage covering the entrance served to protect him from the eyes of the great blue leviathan, but it still had not given up. The dragon flew above the area, sniffing for the mage. Jarric recalled texts that had hinted that dragons might be able to actually smell magic. If so, the beast still might find him regardless of the human's luck in finding this place.

Well, perhaps it had not all been luck. The gargoyle who had carried him flew very near this location, almost as if knowing that here it would best be able to secrete its passenger. Then it flew to join its brethren in harassing the dragon, trying to draw it away. The plan had only partly worked. One gargoyle, Jarric could not tell which, had been swallowed whole by the dragon. The others had confused the blue, but not made him abandon the hunt. Even now they still fluttered above, but slower and with much less enthusiasm. Jarric suspected that they would flee soon or else they, too, might become snacks.

For all his training as a fire mage, the weary human wondered if any of his spells would be sufficient in at least deterring the blue dragon. It had been said that dragons were magic incarnate. True, there were a few tales of mages besting the creatures, but how many of those tales were true, Jarric did not know.

His hand came to rest on the pouch and the fabled shard within. Could he use the artifact to increase his chances? Would it be enough to destroy or at least deter the dragon?

Jarric could not bring himself to use it. If he failed, the shard would be lost to Fuego, who needed it now more than ever with the black mage Ganth returning from the dead. No, more experienced hands were needed to manipulate the abilities of the artifact. He would have to find another answer.

But I can't stay here forever! Yet, where could he go? If he left the shelter of the cave, the dragon would surely sense him.

Jarric peered deeper into the cave. Not a vast place, not when compared to the caverns of the gargoyles. Still, perhaps he might find another exit, one that would take him farther from the gargantuan creature above. A small hope, but the only one he had.

As he stumbled deeper into the cave, Jarric thought wistfully of his wizard's staff, which he had lost in the last few minutes of the furious flight. However ineffectual it might have been against the dragon, at least he could have used it to balance himself. The ground in here seemed strewn with rubble, as if at one time the cave had suffered a collapse. That thought did little to encourage Jarric, but the alternative remained stepping out into the open where the monster might spot him.

Some dim illumination still played, enabling him to slowly find his way. He would have liked to cast a spell, but feared that if the tales turned out to be true, doing so would attract the dragon's attention. For now he had to satisfy himself with trudging along.

To Jarric's surprise, instead of growing more cramped as it descended, the cave instead widened. He also noticed that the walls appeared extremely smooth, as if someone had once carved them so. Of course, the smoothness also could have been the result of extreme underground flooding after the snow on the peaks had melted at some point, but Jarric tried hard not to think of that. Besides, he thought the walls too regular for that. There even appeared to be edges, as if words or images had been carved into the rock.

When at last it grew too dark for him to continue, the fire mage finally decided to dare a spell. It took but a breath to create the tiny, floating fireball, but much longer for Jarric to ascertain that his spell had not, after all, attracted the blue leviathan. Perhaps the rock shielded him. The point became moot, though, as his eyes became accustomed to the illumination and he discovered that what he had thought were words or images proved to be just that.

The script looked like none that Jarric had ever studied, so smooth, flowing, and completely undecipherable. An image of a figure, possibly human, possibly not, seemed to point farther down the cave system. Jarric grimaced, then proceeded on in the direction indicated. He suspected that what he had believed a shallow cave instead extended into a complex system of tunnels, perhaps even some underground dwelling. Of course, with so many catastrophic shifts over the centuries, it was possible that the entire area had once been nearer to the surface. Some researchers had indicated that the mountains of this area had once been flat plains. With so much change even now, Jarric found himself willing to believe all of that.

Deeper and deeper he descended, the cave widening all the while. Where once Jarric could not have walked side-by-side with another traveler, now a good half dozen knights in full armor could have marched shoulder-to-shoulder. The floor remained strewn with rubble and on occasion some rocks still fell, but the more open space erased some of the claustrophobia the mage had experienced earlier.

"But where am I going?" he whispered. The whisper echoed down the cave, seeming to mock him.

Then, just when he thought he might descend to the center of Delos, the corridor leveled out and, a few yards later, opened up into a huge chamber.

Once, this had been a fairly large settlement. Even though many of the areas lay buried under tons of rubble, Jarric could make out separate buildings, not all of them simply of rock. Timbers preserved by the cool depths retained some strength, holding up doorways and roofs. Each of the buildings had a natural look to it, as if the creators had not wanted to offend the elements any more than necessary when designing them. While in some ways the designs reminded Jarric of mrem patterns, overall they had a more sweeping, grander sense of curve and line, almost as if someone had tried to sculpt works of art rather than homes. The fire mage thought it a shame that so little remained, but even the fragments touched him. Artistic patterns around the entrances resembled a variety of flora and fauna, all tastefully done. Few of the homes overshadowed others, as if the builders had been very aware of the sensitivities of their neighbors.

The same puzzling script appeared here and there, indicating who knew what.

In the ancient legends of Delos, it had been said that beings called elves and dwarves had once existed, disappearing many, many centuries ago. Some claimed now and then to have discovered their ruins, but few, if any, items had proved to be other than human artifacts in the end. Standing here, though, Jarric could not think his surroundings anything but one of the homes of such an ancient race. Although dwarves were said to be the ones who dwelt in mountains, the buildings were too tall. Either they had expected many taller visitors or perhaps elves had actually built this. Jarric did not know and doubted he ever would.

Captivated, he stumbled along, trying to investigate everything. Little of value truly remained; when the inhabitants left, they evidently had time to clear their belongings out. Generations of spider webs blanketed much, but fortunately few of the creatures Jarric spotted were any larger than his thumbnail. He found a few shattered statuettes that hinted at elfin features and one or two scrolls in the same script, scrolls which then proceeded to crumble to dust in his hands, but not much more.

Not much more, that is, until he entered the central structure.

Taller than the rest, the two-story oval building had flowering script on each side of the entrance. Once it might have been blue in color; some faded traces hinted of that. There were no windows, only the single doorway, which lay partially demolished. With time on his hands, Jarric removed some of the rubble, then crawled inside.

An emerald glow greeted him.

He stumbled back, certain that he had come upon some sinister spell in the making. Then, when no monster or spell struck, the young mage forced himself forward. To reach the source of the glow he had to shove aside a second battered door, which he did with more enthusiasm. If some magical device had survived this long, perhaps it might be something he could use.

Blazing emerald light briefly blinded him. Jarric raised his arm to shield his eyes. When his sight finally returned, he dared a peek.

He stared at an impossibility. The building which he had entered had barely been twice his height and yet he now stood in a vast chamber large enough to hold the blue dragon. The design reminded him of an amphitheater, with seats of stone carved into the far wall from floor to ceiling. To his left and right, sculpted, life-size figures of stern-visaged elders in elaborate robes, most quite eroded, looked down upon him from niches. If these were elves, which the ears seemed to indicate, they had been a tall, dour group.

In the center, the focus of both the seats and the imposing statues, stood a glittering platform made of what seemed to be gems of every type. Diamonds, emeralds, and, yes, even rubies had been used to construct it and the power that illuminated the artifact came from within those stones, not from some source without. Even from where he stood, Jarric could feel its magic, undrained by the passage of time. The spectacular platform had three sides, each with steps rising to the top. At the top itself stood what looked like an open doorway carved from pure white marble, one tall enough for even an ogre to walk through. Yet, if a doorway, that made no sense, for what purpose did it serve one to walk through it to the other side . . . unless . . .

Even the simplest children's tale spoke of the magic wielded by elves. They could do anything, go anywhere. The latter most interested Jarric. Here stood what appeared a doorway. Could it be exactly that?

With an eagerness borne of desperation, Jarric rushed to the gleaming platform and up the steps. He saw no controls, but if he had designed it, he would have made it so that the user simply had to think of his destination, then enter. Surely the elves would have done something similar.

Picturing Fuego proved no difficulty, especially the sanctum of Master Prymias. Jarric had some qualms about his sponsor now, questions that had arisen after the gargoyle king's comments, but he could not let that deter him from turning to the senior mage for help. Only Master Prymias might help him find Rowlen and Feryln, then put an end to the threat of Ganth.

The image well in place, Jarric walked through the doorway.

Laughter from somewhere above echoed through the vast chamber, mocking the fire mage who now stood on the other side of the marble frame. Jarric's disappointment gave way to a chill as he sought the one watching him. Had some elf remained behind all this time?

Another laughed. Two elves?

"Jump through again, jump through again!"

"Hopped like a toad, hopped like a toad!"

They were and were not the same voice. Jarric turned in a circle, but still he did not see the speakers. Then, movement near the entrance caught his attention. The fire mage readied himself, wondering if his recently-learned skills would avail him against something so old as elves.

From behind a giant stone figure guarding the inner side of the entrance, a scevan materialized. Jarric looked past the beast, awaiting its masters, when suddenly one of the heads pulled up and, instead of howling, laughed.

"Cannot open the door like that, not like that!" the second head mocked.

Scevan did not speak. Scevan were animals, however misshaped by magic. They might be more intelligent than some beasts, but beasts they still were.

With, evidently, the exception of this one.

"So very long, so very long," uttered the first head.

"So very long since so amused, so amused," added the second.

As the scevan moved nearer, Jarric noticed a few differences in it from the ones he had studied. This creature had a smoother, cleaner coat and ears longer and more tapered than the rest of its kind. Its fur had a darker tinge to it, too, almost black in many places. When the scevan moved, it also moved with more grace and cunning than its brethren.

The heads, too, held differences. The muzzles of this one were longer, narrower, with teeth not so irregular but definitely as sharp. As for the eyes . . . had they not been placed in the savage countenances of a scevan, the glittering blue orbs would have been perfect as the eyes Jarric would have expected on an elf.

"So very long since any visitors, any visitors," declared the first, its voice slightly deeper than the other.

"Save her, save her," amended the second, slightly less patient.

"Save her, yes, save her."

If an intelligent scevan, then perhaps Jarric could reason with it. Of course, reason did not work with Lizcanth or gargoyles, it seemed, but perhaps now . . . "I mean no harm!"

The heads laughed.

"Means no harm, no harm?" mocked the first.

"Cannot harm, no, cannot harm," corrected the second, a dangerous glitter in its all too intelligent eyes.

Did they insinuate that he could not hurt them? Were they so protected by magic that even his spells would have no effect? Jarric tried to decide whether or not the heads were lying.

"The door is not open, not open," informed the first.

"Cannot open without both keys, without both keys," added the second, just a bit slyly.

"Keys?" Jarric's eyes widened. "Where're the keys?"

The first head laughed. The second shook back and forth. They had no intention of telling Jarric these things.

What could he do? Could he trick the scevan? Judging by the intelligence he saw within those unsettling eyes, that would be no easy task. Jarric pondered. For now he could go nowhere, but perhaps he could at least gain some other information. Somewhere along the way, he might even discover a fact or two about these keys of which the monster spoke.

"Well, then," he began, walking to the edge of the platform. "Can you at least tell me how you know all this?"

The twin heads glanced at one another. After a brief, silent dialogue, the scevan stalked closer. Jarric readied himself in case it decided to leap up the steps and attack, but the scevan paused at the base. Four fearsome eyes gazed at the mage. "Told by the golden ones," the pair intoned. "Told by the golden ones."

The golden ones? Jarric shifted to the side. The scevan followed suit, remaining directly below him. The mage pointed at one of the statues. "Is that one of them?"

Both heads dipped in confirmation.

"Did they create you?"

Again the heads confirmed his theory. Small wonder why they did not quite resemble other scevan. These unknown people had created this beast countless centuries before, possibly even before the rise of the Four Cities. Perhaps the dark mentor Scevan, for whom the animals had been named, had uncovered the elves' spellwork before he had magicked his own.

"Where are the golden ones now?" He had a suspicion that he knew the answer already.

Both heads chuckled. The first responded, "Through the door now locked, the door now locked."

As he had thought. Likely they had taken the keys with them, . . . but why had they left the scevan behind? "Why did you not go with them?"

The moment Jarric asked the question, he wished he had not. The ensorcelled beast's four eyes narrowed and a look of long-nurtured hatred passed between the twin heads. Jarric had not thought about the fact that for whatever reason the elves had chosen to leave the creature, it might have resented being here so very long.

"We . . ." For the first time the heads shifted their mode of speech, almost becoming a different entity. ". . . were chosen to be the guardians . . . and we will guard until all of Delos falls beneath the sea."

Every word dripped with bitterness from a task set upon the scevan by masters so long fled from this world. Jarric might have pitied the heads if he did not distrust them as well. He tried a different tact. "And you make mighty guardians!"

Some of the bitterness and hatred dwindled away, to be replaced by pride. Condemned to forever guard this portal, the scevan still took its task seriously. Of course, that meant that the heads likely did not want to help the mage in any way. Jarric sighed; he had come here for nothing.

Still, perhaps the lupine horror could aid him after all. "Very well. I wouldn't want to disturb you from your task. Can you at least tell me, is there another way out of this place?"

The heads conferred silently again, coming to some mutual decision. They peered up at the mage, the second nodding and saying, "A way out, yes, a way out. If you come down, if you come down."

The scevan turned away, going to the entrance. Once there, the beast turned and sat, tongues lolling, eyes expectant.

With some hesitation, the fire mage went to the nearest set of steps. While the scevan had mocked him, so far it had offered no harm. The distance up the steps would have taken it but a moment to cross and if, as it said, he could not harm it, the monster would have attacked by now.

Silently preparing a spell, Jarric took a step. The scevan watched patiently.

He had just prepared to take a second step when a voice Jarric could only imagine as music given speech called out from beyond the chamber, "Go no farther, so handsome fire mage, unless you would truly desire them to tear you into tiny little pieces . . . which they will be happy to do!"

Foot still in the air, the young spellcaster fell back onto the platform. At the entrance he heard both heads of the scevan snarl in frustration, their treachery unmasked.

"To be eaten, to be eaten!" insisted the first.

"To defend the portal, defend the portal!" roared the second. The first took up that cry, the scevan now taking offense that someone would prevent it from performing the task for which it had been created.

"Oh, hush, my little ones, my sweet darlings . . ."

Looking properly chastised, the heads of the scevan lowered. Straightening, Jarric peered into the gloom beyond the entrance, trying to make out the one who had warned him.

"Naughty darlings! They know you didn't realize that they can't touch the platform; their masters didn't want them to follow, you see. They thought they'd have some fun with you, then when you stepped down, they'd tear you apart!"

Jarric glanced at the scevan, saw the truth of the words in the beast's eyes. "I owe you my thanks then, whoever you are. I'd come to you, but, as you said—"

The laugh reminded him of bells. "Oh, they wouldn't harm you with me around! They know I might not speak to them ever again if they did!" She laughed once more. "But if you're afraid I'm another trap, I'll come out first . . . then you'll see that you're perfectly safe!"

The fire mage's eyes widened as his savior entered the chamber. Hair the color of darkest shadow framed a very pale face before cascading down several inches below her shoulders. Eyes icy silver glittered beneath long lashes. Below the tiny, upturned nose, the full, crimson lips curved ever so slightly toward a smile.

Form matched face. The flowing, black gown that reached the floor had been cut open almost to her stomach, revealing far more of her nature than Jarric had been accustomed to viewing. A thin cloak clasped at her neck fluttered as if some wind had risen up around her. Each step she took accented a shape intended to draw the unwary male to her.

"You see?" she almost sang, smiling wide now. "You've nothing to fear from Zyn. . . ."

Jarric wanted desperately to believe that, but the smile had undone for him what the rest of Zyn's body had promised. Jarric had seen the long, pointed canines, much too long for a normal human.

He had been saved from the scevan by a vampire.

Chapter 10

A GREAT GUST OF WIND THREATENED TO rip the tent of Lord Baskillus from the ground despite how well it had been tethered. The Lizcanth leader cursed as he fought to keep charts from blowing off his table. Bad enough that the commands the dark one had given him had yet to be fulfilled without this sudden wind storm adding to his frustrations.

Cries from without stirred him from his ire. His warriors, not just those of his own race but the lesser ones as well, did not cry out for no apparent reason. All knew the penalty for disrupting the order of things. Something occurred outside, something to do with the wind—

"Where is he?" rumbled a voice. "Where is your lord?"

Baskillus hissed, for a brief moment contemplating hiding. He feared but one creature besides the dark one and now that great beast had come in search of him.

One of his officers stumbled in through the tent flaps, bowing and apologizing. "The dragon, my lord! Your presssence he wishesss, the dragon doesss!"

Steeling himself, the reptilian warlord nodded. "Come I."

He marched out pretending as if he had expected Azur's arrival all along, yet the first sight of the massive blue leviathan almost weakened his resolve. Then Lord Baskillus saw the ruby embedded in the great draconian's throat and his fear lessened. What a fool he had been to forget the ruby. Like the Lizcanth, Azur bowed to the dark one and, therefore, could cause him no harm.

"Here am I, dragon."

Huge eyes stared down at Baskillus, nearly battering the Lizcanth's confidence again. "Do you have him?"

"Have who?"

His apparent ignorance nearly drove the dragon furious. "I speak of the fire mage, little lizard! The fire mage! Do you have him?"

"No . . . and sssee I that you do not, alsssо!" he added when the leviathan looked prepared to berate him further. "The quessst, the dark one ssset upon you, too."

"Do not seek to humble me!" rumbled Azur. Nonetheless, his fury abated some. He could not deny his failure so far. Their mutual master would know of it the moment he contacted them. "He must be near! All of them must be near. . . ."

Some of them were nearer than others, but Baskillus had no intention of mentioning that to the dragon. If the Lizcanth could locate the greater prize before his draconian rival, then it would prove again to the dark one who was the most valuable of servants. When Lord Ganth's horde fell upon the rest of Delos, crushing it beneath his skeletal fist, Baskillus would reign as his supreme commander. Baskillus knew that the black wizard did not desire so much to rule as to control, two different things. He would leave the mundane matters to his second, and the reptilian warlord intended to be that second.

"I will have him, Lizcanth!" Azur thundered. "I will gnaw on his bones in the end!" His gaze turned skyward, as if Azur imagined the scene even now.

Baskillus wondered if the dragon meant the young human or their unliving master. The gargantuan creature had never hidden his bitterness over being forced to serve Ganth. That, in the Lizcanth's eyes, made him unreliable, once more proving that Baskillus remained the most true servant to the lich. He had willingly entered Ganth's service, although at the time Baskillus had not known about the ruby he would forever wear.

"Caught he will be," agreed the warlord, not necessarily meaning that Azur would be the one accomplishing the task.

"Hmmph!" Suddenly the vast wings of the leviathan spread, creating a new wind that nearly buffeted Baskillus to the ground. "He will, Lizcanth! He will!"

With no concern for the chaos he caused, the blue dragon rose up into the air, swiftly disappearing into the clouds. In his wake he left much confusion, the winds having tossed about loose supplies and a few hapless warriors.

Baskillus silently cursed as the dragon vanished. Some day, when Ganth controlled and he ruled, the dragon would become a liability. On that day, the Lizcanth would convince his master that but one thing could be done . . . and he hoped he would be a witness when the lich ended once and for all Azur's arrogance.

He started back to the tent, debating on where next to send trackers. Baskillus knew the general location in which the gargoyle had dropped the human. The fire mage could not have gotten that far away, not with Azur in the air, sniffing for traces of magic at all times and his own warriors hunting on the ground.

The ruby in his throat suddenly warmed, causing the Lizcanth to stiffen in astonishment and fear.

Baskillus . . . I would have words with you. . . .

The reptilian leader swallowed. He had hoped to have the human in hand before Ganth contacted him again. To the air, he whispered, "Yes, dark one."

He rushed inside the tent even as Ganth began to speak. It never served to show the warriors any sign of a commander's own fears and, at the moment, Baskillus felt very fearful, indeed.

Feryln surveyed his rescuers again. With the notable exception of Theron Kain, they were a disreputable lot. True, they looked better trained and kept than many mercenaries, but the mrem suspected that much of that could be due to the efforts of their leader.

He sat a little distance from them, rescued but not a part of their band. The band hid behind a tall rise dotted by a copse of trees, which shielded them well from prying eyes to the north. Kain and his men had gathered around a dirt map the lead reaver had drawn in the ground and the former knight seemed to be having some trouble convincing his group of the need to press on in a direction opposite that of Fuego.

"The young mage is the one we're seeking. We cannot go back without him, not if we want to be paid in full."

"We've already gone too far, man," a heavy, bearded reaver argued. "The contract said nothing about coming this far north! There are lizards everywhere!"

"Not to mention ogres and the like," grumbled another. "And they're all lookin' for this lad themselves. . . ."

"But he won't come out in the open for them. He'll want to find us, especially with the mrem here part of our group now. He traveled with the cat; that'll show him we're friendly."

"That's if we even find where he's hidin' himself," the grumbler returned.

"We have a contract." For Theron Kain, that ended the matter.

The other reavers were not so convinced, but they said nothing more for now. Feryln did not entirely trust them. More than one had cast a longing glance southward, as if debating running off. They had handled the floater well enough, not to mention two Lizcanth whom they had surprised, but one of their number also lay dead, victim of a second floater that had been wounded and, if it had not bled to death, might now be alerting the Lizcanth Baskillus of their presence. The uncertainty on that point remained one of the most significant reasons why Kain's party desired to go home. A dozen or so men, however well trained, could not face down the legions Ganth had gathered.

"I will go on alone," Feryln finally announced, tired of the bickering. So many monstrous hunters around meant that Baskillus, the Lizcanth warlord the gargoyle king blamed for the destruction of Feryln's village, might be in the vicinity. The thought of tearing the lizard's throat out had become, as time passed, more and more the mrem's goal, second only to finding his companions. If he could somehow accomplish both . . .

"And get yourself killed?" Theron Kain shook his head. "You know mountains, which gives you one advantage, but you've not fought enough battles. There are still too many mistakes to make, like forgetting to look up," he added pointedly. "Prasch forgot that, too, and he'd been fighting for some twenty years."

"I will not return to Fuego without the others." Nor without the Lizcanth's head, he added to himself.

Kain rubbed his broad chin with the flat of the dagger he had been using to draw the crude map. "We can't do anything about the other mrem. My contract calls for the safety or rescue of the mage Jarric, nothing else. You were fortunate enough to cross paths with us, cat, nothing more."

"Should've left 'im for the lizards," someone muttered.

Feryln's ears flattened, his claws extended, and he hissed in challenge. The man who had spoken began to reach for his blade, but Kain forced the sword back into the sheath. "Enough of that! We're on the same side here! The Lizcanth and their allies would flay any one of us, man or mrem! Remember that whenever you feel the urge to fight with one another!"

Feryln sheathed his claws again. "I am going after them."

The reaver captain studied him. "Them and maybe this Lizcanth lord you told us about? This Baskillus?"

"The gargoyle king said that Baskillus serves Ganth of the Black Flame and that, under the dark wizard's command, the Lizcanth lord has slaughtered village after village of my people, my own included."

"I see. What will you do if you find your friends first? Go with them or keep hunting Baskillus?"

Feryln had given that some consideration since his rescue. The longer he stayed near the vicinity of the Lizcanth, the more difficult it grew to imagine leaving without doing something. He had originally intended to return with Rowlen and Jarric to Fuego, but no longer. "I will stay behind. I will haunt the camp once I find it.

Eventually, I will find a time to slip past their sentries and kill the butchering lord."

"Then die gloriously yourself." Several chuckles rose from amongst the reavers and even Theron Kain wore a sardonic grin. "Very idealistic. Very suicidal. The first rule of a reaver is never agree to a battle that you have no good chance of winning."

"I am no reaver, though . . . nor have I ever been a knight."

His barb struck true. Kain's face paled, his eyes brooding. The other reavers grew silent. While they might argue with Kain, none in this group was foolish enough to challenge his honor so bluntly.

"No . . ." he finally replied. "you're not."

Feryln's ears flattened, this time out of shame. The human had saved his life. He did not deserve the mrem's bitter attitude. "My apologies."

"For what?" Theron rose. "It's settled then. We go north."

Feryln noted dismay among several of the reavers, but no one disagreed. Still, the young warrior wondered if the mercenary group would remain intact for long. The farther north they journeyed, the more likely that nerves would get the best of some.

If Theron Kain also thought this, it did not show. He had already started off, sword ready. The other reavers slowly followed and, after a moment's hesitation, so did Feryln.

For some time, the party saw no more signs of the forces of Ganth. This cheered Kain's men, but not the mrem, nor, surprisingly, the reaver captain. Feryln feared that if the hunters had abandoned this part of the mountain, it might be because they had already found what they had been searching for, namely Jarric. Perhaps Kain also thought this, for the veteran warrior pushed on with more determination, sometimes pulling far ahead of his band.

Then one of the other mercenaries paused, listening. "I heard a call."

The others listened, two men immediately nodding. Before long, the rest had heard one sound or another. Faint sounds, but too many to ignore.

"An encampment," whispered Kain.

Nerves taut, the warriors cautiously continued, following the sounds to their source. Feryln spotted the first pair of sentries, two Lizcanth. Considering that the other creatures were supposed to be allies, this Lord Baskillus evidently trusted most of his operations only to his own kind.

Thoughts of the warlord being possibly so near sent a surge of adrenalin through the mrem. He started forward, intending to take the sentries himself, but the reaver captain took him by the shoulder, pulling Feryln back. Instead, Kain pointed to four men, sent them forward in two different directions. The rest of the party waited. Several minutes later, both Lizcanth fell, throats cut.

The rest of the party joined up with the assassins. Feryln felt no pity for the reptiles; they would have given no quarter to any of their victims. He only wished that he had been the one to strike them down.

Despite the sentries, it still took some time to reach the outer edge of the encampment. At first, the mrem could see little through the trees, some tents, moving figures, and much noise, but then Theron Kain led them to a higher site, where they could better survey what stood against them.

"Gods!" whispered one of Kain's men. "Where does it end?"

A good question and one which Feryln could not answer. Beyond them the encampment extended as far as the eye could see. There were tents everywhere, mostly with Lizcanth nearby. Score upon score of ogre shuffled through other regions, many of them so stirred up that they looked ready to fight one another. Now and then a floater or some other grotesque cousin of it drifted by, lizards and others giving way quickly to them. Toward the more distant regions, there moved creatures Feryln could not even identify, some of them so unnerving he quickly looked away.

Scevan by the score howled and yowled from pens. A Lizcanth officer marched past one pen, followed by misshapen, walking skeletons of different colors, animated dead brought to serve the cause of the lich. In a shadowed region, a vast group of pale humans sat huddled, staring at those around them with what looked like hunger. Something about them disturbed the mrem more than almost any of the other monstrous creatures below.

"Vampires," Kain muttered. "Ghouls, skeletons . . . there!" He pointed at a mound of earth, which suddenly shifted as if of its own accord, sprouting vaguely humanoid arms. It rose higher, developing crude legs as well. Two ogres in its path quickly darted aside, their eagerness for battle not sufficient to keep them from fleeing the greater monster. "A stone giant." The reaver captain went on to list other horrors, his tone one of detachment. He might as well have been describing how to polish a sword blade.

Feryln at last abandoned trying to identify the many servants Ganth had gathered, instead searching for some sign of his companions. How, though, would he be able to locate them among all this? In such a sea of evil, one human and one mrem could be easily lost . . . if they were still alive.

"That banner there," Kain suddenly added. "That'll be Lord Baskillus's tent, I'll wager."

The mrem's eyes immediately fixed upon the tent in question. Larger and wider than the rest, it stood surrounded by a full legion of Lizcanth warriors, the tallest of their kind that Feryln had thus far seen. The tent seemed like an island in the middle of the encampment, the area for several yards around it completely devoid of clutter or warriors. It said much for the power behind the Lizcanth lord that Baskillus himself earned such respect from the antagonistic creatures under his command.

The mrem extended his claws, his blood boiling. Here before him were the ones who had slaughtered his village. If he could not find his friends, then perhaps he could yet strike a blow for not just his village, but for all those threatened by Ganth's horde.

"Baskillus," he whispered, unmindful of what his companions might think. "Baskillus." Feryln studied the distance between himself and the great tent. So many stood in his path and yet the feline warrior still thought about reaching the sanctum of the murderous Lizcanth. One swift slash of his claws; Feryln only needed time for that. Even if he died afterward, torn apart by reptilian talons or gutted by blades, then Feryln could die in peace knowing that this Lord Baskillus had preceded him. For Herrick, for so many others, he would gladly risk it.

"Easy, mrem," Kain whispered, noticing his growing edginess. "No one's going down there just yet."

"No one's going down there at all," one of his men suddenly snapped.

"Aye, it'd be more than suicide to enter that place!"

"They won't just kill us, they'll eat us beforehand!"

Kain glared at the men. "Stop that racket!"

They would not be quieted, though. The vast, overwhelming encampment had proved to be the last straw. The men were brave, Feryln could not deny that, and perhaps if only a legion of Lizcanth represented resistance they would have pressed on, but only one who had gone mad would consider entering such a hellish place. Feryln did not deny his own demons and, it seemed Theron Kain might have them, too, but these others desired to live to spend whatever gold they had . . . and one could not blame them.

Kain tried his best to regain control, but even the former knight could not compete against the horrific view below. One of the reavers finally backed away, daring his captain to run him through.

"I've had it! I'm for the south! If Fuego's not close enough, I'll take Astra or somewhere else!"

"Wait up, Yurl! I'll be goin' with ya!" Before Kain could stop them, all but three of his men had defected to the second group and those last three looked uncertain at best.

The reaver captain studied his mutinous crew. "All right. I don't blame the lot of you for turning back. Go south, then, with my blessings, but go directly to Fuego." He reached into a pouch, pulled out some scraps of paper which he handed to one of the three loyal fighters. "Restyn. Take these to Castlana Dumarcus, majordomo of Master Prymias of the Ruby Eye. Tell her everything about this situation you can remember." Theron Kain glanced at each of his men. "Tell her I sent you all back, knowing one could do what needs to be done better. She'll see you're all paid."

The mutineers looked embarrassed, but Feryln noticed that none of them volunteered to stay.

Kain waved them off. "Go! Now! If they find those guards missing, it'll be harder on the lot of you!"

The reavers, even those who had volunteered to stay, started off toward the south. Feryln did not find himself saddened to see them go; two or a dozen, it made little difference against such a horde.

Not until the last had vanished in the distance did Kain turn his attention to the mrem. "Well, cat. It's us now."

"You should have gone with them." While Feryln admired the human's skill, Theron Kain had no reason to sacrifice himself. He would be able to spend no coin once dead. The mrem had no such concern. He expected to die, but only after freeing his friends or executing the savage warlord . . . or both, his ancestors willing.

"I've a contract to fulfill," the reaver remarked, once more studying the encampment. "Now, shall we see if we can note anything of significance?"

Unable to fathom the mind of the former knight, Feryln, too, turned his gaze to the vast army. Lord Baskillus's tent continued to act as a beacon to him, drawing his attention every time he decided to try to look elsewhere. If anyone might know where Rowlen and Jarric were, surely it had to be the Lizcanth commander. In the end, Feryln knew that he would have to enter the tent no matter what.

"Trackers returning," Kain commented. Feryln looked, saw that more than a dozen warriors, including ogres, were entering the encampment from the southwest. Six leashed scevan came with them, the beasts not at all pleased to be forced to return to this place.

Sight of the hunters gave Feryln some hope. If they were still sending out search parties, then perhaps at least one of the two might yet be free. It would perhaps make his task a little easier.

His view again shifted to the tent . . . only to catch a glimpse of a furred figure moving off from the Lizcanth lord's abode. Feryln's ears perked up, only to fall a moment later when he realized that the mrem could not be Rowlen. Yet, if not Rowlen, then who?

He said nothing to Kain, first wanting to see where the other mrem went. Two Lizcanth followed the stranger, whom Feryln assumed must be a prisoner. What use did Ganth or Baskillus have for mrem, though?

"Get down!" Kain abruptly whispered.

The reaver practically pushed Feryln's face in the dirt, but for what the stunned mrem soon saw had been good cause. Another search party came into view not far below them, three Lizcanth and a figure wrapped completely in a voluminous robe. Two of the lizards fought with barely controlled scevan on leashes. The third either protected or kept under guard the robed figure, Feryln could not tell which. The party slowly moved along, cutting a path that would lead them directly in front of the pair.

"Not a sound, mrem."

Feryln nodded, having needed no warning. He and Kain watched. These hunters moved with much more purpose than those the young warrior had encountered earlier. They could not have found the trail of the pair, but perhaps someone had already come to relieve the guards and found them missing. Kain had made certain that the two bodies would be difficult to find, commenting that missing sentries left more questions and created more delays than corpses did.

The lead Lizcanth suddenly reached up, tugging back the hood of the fourth member's robe.

Feryln gasped, almost rising. Kain barely got him to the ground before one of the scevan glanced their way. The lupine monster sniffed the air, then both heads turned away.

"Are you mad?"

Feryln shook him off. "It's Rowlen! Look! You met him when you first met me!"

"The mrem warrior?" Theron Kain peered over the edge, studying the robed mrem just long enough to make a clear identification. "Looks like your friend, all right. Looks like he's a prisoner, too. Pity. I thought he'd be the hardest for them to catch."

Taking a risk, Feryln again peeked. Rowlen did indeed stand just below them, a captive of the lizards. He had been beaten at some point in the recent past, but otherwise looked in one piece. Roughly-tied bandages wrapped around his chest. If there were other wounds, Feryln could not see them, the robe obscuring much. He wondered where Rowlen had found it. Regardless, it had evidently proven an insufficient disguise.

"I have to rescue him!"

Kain glared at the mrem. "You're as mad as my men think I am! He's their prisoner already and there's three of them, not forgetting that the scevan will attack you, too."

"If I wait, Rowlen will be in the camp and then the odds become nigh impossible!" Feryln would not be argued out of this. He had to save the older mrem. Kain looked ready to say more, but then Feryln recalled something else. "He might also know where Master Jarric is!"

"Jarric. . . ." Kain's eyes narrowed in thought. The mrem could see him calculating the odds versus the potential reward. If he brought back the mage alive and with the shard, Kain's reputation, not to mention his purse, would grow. "You've a good point there, mrem." The reaver captain again studied the party, which had slowly moved off to the east. "Only three. The scevan are cowards if you wound them quick in the face." He tightened his grip on his sword. "All right, mrem. Let's go."

With Kain in the lead, the pair cautiously descended to the rear of the hunters. The reaver sent Feryln farther north, to come around and catch the Lizcanth from that side. The human would catch them from the south. Much of their success would depend on surprise.

"Wait for me to attack," Kain commanded. "Don't do anything until I move."

That proved easier said than done for Feryln. The first few minutes did not bother him, but when time continued to pass and he had to pace the hunters and Rowlen, his patience grew thin. It did not help that the Lizcanth in the lead made threatening gestures with his weapon every now and then. Clearly, it would not take much for the lizard to kill the prisoner rather than take him back in.

Yet more time passed, critical time. Twice the search party crossed near areas perfect for an ambush and yet Feryln saw no sign of Kain. What delayed the reaver? Had he decided to follow the lead of his men and abandon the contract?

Feryln could wait no longer. The lead Lizcanth had brought the edge of his weapon extremely close to Rowlen's chest, informing the mrem at the same time how much he liked raw cat flesh. Feryln gripped his weapon, gauging the distance between himself and the nearest foe.

Moving in silence, he leapt at one of the Lizcanth in the rear.

The lizard did not notice him until too late. Feryln's blade bit into the scaled warrior's side, sending the tall reptile to his knees. The scevan pulled loose of its leash, smelling the nearby blood. Feryln feared that it would attack him, but instead it turned on the wounded Lizcanth, the scevan's loyalty to itself, not its handler.

The second Lizcanth released his scevan, then turned on Feryln with his whip. The lash stung the mrem hard on his sword arm, nearly making him drop his weapon. Feryln sought to catch the whip with his claws, but the reptile moved too fast.

As the Lizcanth pulled back his arm for another attack, the second scevan tried to charge under the mrem's blade. Feryln managed to strike one of the heads on the nose with the flat side, which sent the beast yowling. Unfortunately, now both remaining lizards harassed him, the leader swinging his clawed weapon back and forth with the skill of one long practiced.

"Fool of a mrem. . . ." the leader hissed, showing his teeth. "Fool of a mrem. Your head I will have. . . ."

"Rowlen!" Feryln called. "Why do you stand there?"

Indeed, even unguarded the older warrior had remained motionless. However, at the other mrem's call, he finally moved. Rowlen reached out, caught the lead Lizcanth by the the back of the throat, and threw him aside. The other lizard fell to his knees a moment later, stunned by a blow to the head from the former prisoner.

It happened so quickly that Feryln could only stand and watch. Rowlen, the robe still obscuring much of him, slipped past the two fallen reptiles to join his young companion.

"Your sword!" he growled. "Quick!"

Assuming he meant to capture or dispatch the pair, Feryln obeyed. Although it unnerved him to surrender the weapon, he knew that of the two of them Rowlen could make the best use of the sword.

The veteran warrior briefly examined the blade, then stared at Feryln. "Good. Much more simple."

Feryln's fur rose, though he could not say what disturbed him. He almost reached to take the sword back, but thought better of it.

Rowlen turned to the two Lizcanth. "Up, you fools! Can you do nothing correctly?"

The reptiles obeyed. The leader began to reach for his weapon.

"Rowlen! He's—" Feryln cut off, horrified. The robed figure had turned the tip of the sword toward his young friend. The eyes that stared at him did not blink.

"Signal the others," said a voice that was and was not Rowlen's. "Not the prize sought, but very close. Very close."

As one of the Lizcanth moved to obey, Rowlen undid the clasp of the robe, allowing it to drift to the ground. Feryln's eyes widened as he stared at Rowlen's throat, stared at the ruby embedded within.

"Gods, Rowlen! What has happened to you?"

"Simpering mrem," the voice coldly retorted. "Have you no intelligence at all? There is no Rowlen; there is but the shell." The tip toyed with Feryln's own throat. "And soon, you will be the same."

A horn sounded, one of the Lizcanth giving the signal. From the north, dozens of warriors, mostly reptiles but a few ogres and the like, emerged from the woods. Feryln had walked directly into a trap.

"Take the mrem to Lord Baskillus," Rowlen commanded, handing the sword to one of the original reptiles. "Do not maim him," the older warrior smiled, a shivering image. "I may need him as bait next. . . ."

The Lizcanth bound Feryln, then led him away. The young mrem struggled to understand all that had happened. Rowlen—or something that wore his form—had captured him for Baskillus. The image of the ruby in the other mrem's throat haunted Feryln. He recalled the question Jarric had asked of the gargoyle king. Ganth Kazarian, it seemed, had also been a fire mage—one surely with the knowledge of how to use rubies in a myriad number of ways, including this horrible spell. Ganth, if it had truly been him who had spoken through the other mrem, had altered Rowlen, destroyed the veteran warrior from within, and hinted that such a fate awaited Ferlyn as well.

Feryln silently cursed Baskillus and the dread Ganth for his fate, but, most of all, the captured mrem cursed the one who had truly betrayed him in the end, who had sealed his fate.

The treacherous reaver captain . . . Theron Kain.

Chapter 11

SO VERY NEAR, YET AGAIN NOT THE ONE he sought.

Seated upon his crumbling throne, Ganth peered again into the stygian flames he had summoned. The young mrem represented the other of the fire mage's companions, leaving only the spellcaster now. Ganth tried to take some measure of pleasure from this capture, but the knowledge that the true prize still lay beyond his grasp caused the fire within him to blaze in fury.

The Lizcanth had failed to find the mage Jarric. Azur, for all his vaunted power, had failed to find him. Even the shells through which the wizard himself searched had not delivered up the young fool.

His minions awaited the word, awaited the signal to march against Fuego. He had intended it to fall first, having believed that somewhere within lay either the ruby shard or an artifact equally powerful. With the discovery that he had been wrong, though, Ganth had delayed again and again. Once the shard became his, victory would be inevitable. No power in Fuego or the other cities would stand against him.

They will simply have to wait a little longer. . . . Fear of his power had, more than anything else, forged this uneasy alliance. Without him, the impudent Baskillus would find his forces at one another's throats in days. All knew the vast might of Ganth Kazarian . . . but none realized how far he had already stretched it.

Skeletal fingers stroked the scarf around his throat. When he made the pact with the Laria, he had not realized its limitations. He had been tricked, but he would fool the trickster. The ruby shard would save him, then give all to him.

Ganth passed one twisted hand over the flames, altering the image. Now he saw through the eyes of the dragon, although not with the control he had over the mrem. Azur had too strong of a will for that, even if in all things he had to obey the lich. Even now, the dark mage could sense the dragon knew of his presence and resented it.

He had caught Azur in the midst of tearing asunder the caverns of the gargoyles, but not one of the cursed creatures fluttered about, trying to protect it. Azur had taken too long in his futile search for this Jarric. The gargoyles had fled.

They continued to be thorns in his side. Of the few who had defied him, the gargoyles were the worst. Their wretched king had mocked his demands and now, it seemed, sought to keep the shard from him.

"I will have the shard and your head on my wall, gargoyle," Ganth swore. For now, though, it served no purpose for Azur to continue this devastation. Ganth passed a hand over the flames again, then, in his thoughts, called, *Azur! Azur! Hear me!*

I hear you . . . oh, Master. . . .

Cease this! The winged ones will suffer yet! For now, you must return to your first task . . . find the fire mage!

He could sense the leviathan's eagerness. *At last! I wondered how long I would have to rip away at this mountain before you came to your senses!*

Ganth broke the link, needing to hear no more of the blue dragon's prattling. Azur would put his supreme effort into the hunt now. Baskillus had hunters by the scores combing the mountain range. The lich himself had more than two dozen shells, most of them the hated mrem, doing his work. For now, they were useful, tricking their brethren into his hands and using their keen senses to hunt where the others failed.

He banished the black flames. "I will have you, Jarric of Fuego . . . and I will have my ruby shard!"

The lich's hands went up to smooth the tightly bound scarf. Eyes of fire searched around, seeing only the miserable Lizcanth and floaters who guarded his hall. Even the shadows, which could hide nothing from him, revealed not a trace of the one he sought. She should have been here, should have been at his side the moment he desired her presence.

Ganth turned on the nearest lizard, who cringed at so near a view of the lich's macabre face. "Where . . . is she? Where is my Zyn?"

* * *

Fleshless hands reached for Jarric from all directions, trying to throw him into a vast, black inferno. Just beyond his grasp, the ruby shard glistened and spoke, its voice too much like that of the gargoyle king.

"So sad, so said," mocked the voice. "What a waste of such potential! Aah, well, at least you'll fuel the fire."

Something suddenly lifted him above the clutching, skeletal hands. Jarric looked up to thank his benefactor, only to discover a huge bat with two human heads, both the same beautiful woman. The faces smiled, revealing canines ten feet long.

"Don't you worry, my sweet little man, little man, I'll save you!"

Twin mouths sought his throat. Jarric tried a spell which produced but a bouquet of daisies. He struggled, trying to avoid the teeth. At the last second, his robe tore, sending the mage plummeting.

The black blaze below turned into a pair of baleful eyes. Skeletal hands formed a net and voice from the grave said, "I have you now, Jarric. . . . You are mine forever and ever. . . ."

The mage screamed—

—and woke up in a sweat, having nearly toppled off the platform.

Gasping, the fire-tressed mage pushed himself away from the edge. He did not recall having dozed off, although from the feel of it he must have slept hours. Jarric had tried his best to stay awake, fearing both the scevan and the vampire, but exhaustion had finally set in.

She had offered him her aid, swearing that she did not want his blood and reminding him that she had saved him from the treachery of the guardian. Jarric had assumed, with some justification, that Zyn simply saved him in order to feast upon him later. Fortunately, she, too, had not climbed up the steps. No doubt, like the scevan, the vampire could not touch the artifact. That, and that alone, had been why he had allowed himself to drift off to slumber.

Where did she hide now, though? Jarric blinked, adjusting to the illumination of the platform. The guardian remained by the entrance as if never having moved, twin pairs of eyes watching the human very intently. However, Jarric could see nothing of Zyn. Had she left to feed? Perhaps now might be his chance to escape. As formidable as the guardian appeared, the odds would not be nearly so impossible as they would when the vampire returned.

He started to rise, found out too late that his leg still slept, and began to tumble. The scevan immediately leapt to its feet, but before Jarric could fall over the edge of the platform, pale, graceful hands caught him about the waist and pulled him back.

"You should always let the blood flow before you try moving, silly one."

Zyn had her arms around him. She had been standing behind him all the time, unhindered by the magic of the platform.

Struggling free, Jarric whirled to face the vampire. Why she had not fed on him while he slept, he did not know. Perhaps she enjoyed having her food watch helplessly while she drained him of his life. Whatever the reason, he swore he would not give in to her so readily, although as his eyes lingered over her body, Jarric knew that the battle would be a monumental one.

"Such active blood!" she commented wryly, full ruby lips pursing all too enticingly. "You should be more careful, though."

"What game are you playing at? Why wait until I woke up? You could've had me at any time!"

She stretched as if just waking herself, her every movement displaying her generous form to the fullest effect. Zyn inhaled, the thin garments straining to hold together. "I play no game, dear wizard, except the oldest one. . . ."

"You know what I mean!" Jarric forced himself to stare her in the eye, not all that unpleasant of an experience, either. Nowhere seemed safe to look.

Zyn tried her best to act innocent. Jarric almost, but not quite, believed her. "I've other ways of feeding, mortal, other desires as well. I want nothing from you that you wouldn't be happy to give me, I think."

Too near the truth. Jarric had to constantly struggle to remind himself that this creature would drain him of his life fluids, then leave his dry husk for the scevan. "I warn you! I'm a fire mage! I won't simply stand and be killed, not by you or the guardian!"

Now Zyn looked annoyed. She planted her hands against her hips, which only served to give Jarric yet more distractions. "I cannot speak for him, but I only want to help you!"

"Why?"

"Because you are handsome, you are powerful, and you are very, very much, vibrantly . . . alive."

Jarric had trouble believing any of her reasons save the last one. Still, he could not help drinking in some of her praise.

She saw his disbelief. Drawing herself together in as demure a pose as possible for one such as her, Zyn explained. "You and I are of different worlds, mortal, but that does not mean that sometimes those worlds do not cross. I have tasted—no, not in the manner in which you think—a little bit of life. There are times I'd be happier with so short a span as you have, if only to not be subject to other needs." She took a step forward, but when Jarric raised one hand in preparation of a spell, Zyn paused again. "Such desire drew me to one I thought personified life, one who would enable me to savor it without devouring it whole."

She stopped there, as if afraid to continue. The fire mage's curiosity got the better of him and at last he asked, "Who?"

"He is called Ganth Kazarian . . . Ganth of the Black Flame."

Ganth! Zyn had uttered the one name that could stir him from the alluring spell the vampire constantly cast. Jarric had come across one of the lich's concubines. He cursed his luck. Even now the dark wizard must be coming for him. Jarric glanced at the steps, then at the scevan. The guardian's tail wagged, both faces eager. The moment Jarric descended, the scevan would certainly attack him.

"You need not fear his coming!" she cried, realizing his horror. "Ganth does not know I come to this place! He never has!" She grew more subdued. "Sometimes, if I'm fortunate, he forgets me for weeks. Some may call the Laria a monster, but if there is one who now rivals it, it's Ganth."

"Ganth. . . ." Despite his anxiety, curiosity got the better of Jarric. "How . . . how did you come to know Ganth?"

"When he wore the mantle of life, few there were who were female who could resist him. Eyes burning with ambition, broad chin with a beard perfectly clipped, flowing locks of hair, regal nose . . . Ganth Kazarian could have any female he desired and yet he desired so very few. I was one of those few. His power made it impossible for me to snare him with my abilities; he commanded and I obeyed. I would have obeyed until the end of Delos if Ganth had not chosen a different path, one which he took because of that which I most envy in you."

Jarric felt less concern now, more interest and, although he would not yet admit it to himself, sympathy. He sensed that Zyn spoke the truth, at least to a point. "What do so you envy?"

"You age, mortal. I watched Ganth age and found it fascinating. He, though, found it horrid. Already he had made known to Fuego his ambitions and, in truth, he could have ruled then as well as any, I think. He grew desperate, for, even though a mage may live far longer than most mortals, still you die in the end. . . . I'm sorry if I bother you by saying that."

He waved off her apology, wanting to learn

more about Ganth. Any weakness, however small, that Zyn revealed might help the fire mage if he could escape from here. Also, while she remained busy talking, Jarric felt more secure about gazing at her without having to worry about her attacking.

She smiled, again setting his heart ablaze. "You're so sweet . . . and I don't even know your name. . . ."

"Jarric!" he blurted, forgetting suddenly to maintain his distance. More calmly, he repeated, "Jarric. Of House Gaius."

"And I'm simply Zyn." The vampire looked, of all things, wistful. "Ganth searched every record, every scroll, trying to find a way to extend his life. He learned of the legend of the ruby shard and determined, without fact, that some of those who feared him in Fuego kept it hidden for their own use."

Zyn went on to tell of the darker magics Ganth summoned, the creatures he commanded, all to gain access to his prize. There came the pact with the Laria, which served for a time to mollify the mage. For a while, he had even believed that what the sinister creature had given him would take the place of the shard . . . but it had not.

"In the end, he discovered that the Laria had played with him as he himself had played with others, forcing him into a pact that would serve only it in the end. Ganth had extended his life, but for only awhile."

Jarric wanted to hear more about the pact, what it entailed, but here Zyn drew the line. Not out of any concern for Ganth, but rather now because of the fear she had of him . . . or what remained of him. In the end, his ambition and the Laria's ploy forced the ancient fire mage to declare his personal war on Fuego. He might have won had his rivals not struck first. Zyn had been away, fulfilling a mission for the mortal she already feared more than admired, when Ebonyr had been attacked. The vampire had returned to find only ruins and the once mighty mage a blood-soaked corpse with its throat torn out. Zyn herself had entombed the corpse, following intricate measures Ganth himself had requested of her long before in preparation of such a dire event.

She had not known then that Ganth had planned for his own revival.

"But how?" Jarric demanded. "How did he manage such an act? Was it the Laria?"

Zyn simply stared at him, finally saying, "I cannot tell you, sweet, living Jarric. Should Ganth discover what I've already said, he would punish me. To tell you his secret . . ." The vampire actually shuddered. "I will not . . . I cannot say more."

Zyn continued to tremble, so much so that the mage actually took steps toward her before recalling what she was. She looked almost disappointed that he had not come to her, but said nothing.

Below them, Jarric suddenly heard growling. The guardian stood near the base of the platform, malevolent gazes fixed on the human. Jarric gave thanks that the beast could not touch the artifact.

"Made her sad, made Zyn sad!" snapped the first.

"Bad to make Zyn sad, bad to make Zyn sad!" snarled the second.

"It's . . . all right, my dear friend," the vampire soothed. "He didn't make me sad! I only fear the dark one, that's all!"

"Hate the dark one, hate the dark one!"

"Eat the dark one, eat the dark one!"

The ensorcelled scevan appeared very protective of Zyn. Clearly they had spent much time together.

Zyn read his expression. "I come here when I can. The guardian . . . is lonely and I enjoy the company."

Glancing down at the fangs that would have torn him to bloody ribbons, Jarric could not bring himself to sympathize much for the beast. "How did that come about?"

Some of her humor returned. "I'm a little older than I look, sweet Jarric . . . a little. I've had time to wander, time to search, and a vampire always likes to find a place where there's darkness, you know, even more than a human!"

So she had found this place while seeking refuge from the ever relentless light of the suns. Vampires suffered their own troubles in this world. Only when fully satiated did they have no difficulty with the burning suns. The longer they went without feeding, the harsher the effect. There were some scholars who claimed they were also affected differently by each orb, but beyond that, Jarric could recall none of what he had learned. As an apprentice, he had never imagined he would some day find himself in confrontation with a vampire . . . and so beguiling a one, at that.

Remember yourself! he chided. She could be at his throat in an instant, he a victim due to his own weak will.

"He wanted to eat me, the poor dear!" Zyn continued, apparently oblivious of his constant inner struggle. "He doesn't have to eat, but he can do it if he wants. Poor creature, he has so few distractions! Those nasty creatures left him trapped in one area, condemned to forever guard something they just left behind!" As Zyn talked, the scevan relaxed, sitting back on its haunches and letting its tongues hang out. The guardian's tail wagged back and forth. "Well, I soon showed the darling that he couldn't eat me and besides, wasn't it better to have someone to talk to from time to time?"

He tried to imagine the conversations the vampire and the scevan might have and failed. "So you talked with one another? That's all? As you just want to talk with me?"

The full lips smiled again. "If that's all you wish of me."

Jarric had learned all he would about Ganth from her. The mage still did not entirely trust Zyn, but at the moment his options were few. He did not know if the dragon still lurked nearby, but suspected that if it did not, other hunters might very well be in the vicinity. The sooner he could be away from here the better.

He eyed the portal. "Do you know how this works?"

"I only know that it takes one such as yourself to power it."

A mage? Maybe that had been where Jarric had gone wrong. He had assumed the artifact would simply work by stepping through it, never thinking that, like some devices, it would need to be set into motion by spellwork or a simple touch of power. Jarric turned to the marble frame, studying it while at the same time making certain that Zyn never stepped too near.

Runes of some sort marked the side edges, but nothing that the young mage could read. They seemed to run along the edges to the top. He touched one, felt a tiny bit of heat. Encouraged, Jarric pressed harder. The rune grew slightly warmer, but nothing else happened.

Below, the guardian laughed, the first head adding, "Stumbles in the dark, stumbles in the dark!"

He briefly glared at the beast, annoyed that it should know what he so desperately sought. Jarric ran his fingers over the other runes, felt each of the symbols warm. The frame began to hum.

His spirits rose. He ran his fingers over the symbols again, only to find them now cooling. So, one direction warm, one cool. One direction to make the artifact function, the other to put it to rest when not needed. Jarric ran his fingers over the symbols again, causing the doorway to hum once more.

Zyn clapped her ivory hands. "Oh, very good!"

Jarric felt his face flush under her encouragement. He forced his mind back to his efforts, though, determined to be away from this place, away from anywhere so near the sanctum of Ganth. However, try as he might, the fire mage could not discover the next step to making the portal function. Touching the runes at random did nothing. They simply remained warm unless he ran his fingers over them the wrong way, in which case they cooled again.

After several minutes, he had to admit that he had gotten no further. Jarric stepped back, so caught up in his failure that he failed to notice that Zyn had been standing next to him for much of the time.

"I wish I could read those," he muttered.

"They're older than me," the vampire added uselessly. "Ganth might have been able to decipher them. He knew much about times far past."

"I can hardly ask him." Jarric finally noticed their nearness and took a few steps to the side . . . but not without some regret.

Zyn seemed to take no notice of his slight. Instead, she turned and leaned down over the edge of the platform, staring at the guardian. "But someone here does know, isn't that correct? You know, don't you, my sweet little one?"

The guardian's tail wagged. The second head proudly replied, "Learned all by watching, learned all by watching! Never taught, never taught!"

Tearing himself from his view of Zyn, the wary spellcaster considered the guardian's remarks. So although the scevan's masters had never shown the beast how to control the doorway, it had watched and learned, likely because it had not had anything else to do. Somehow Jarric had to convince the creature to tell him what to do next.

Zyn descended the steps toward the scevan, her voice beguiling. "So clever, too! The masters probably never knew how clever you were, did they? They never saw how special you were. But I did. I saw immediately how special you are."

Both heads tilted. The tail wagged with more eagerness. Jarric suppressed a smile. The guardian, like many another male in the past, had grown absolutely smitten with the vampire. So beautiful . . . and so deadly, he reminded himself. She no doubt did this only to gain his trust, get under his guard. Even vampires had to be wary of mages. With the right spell, Jarric could leave nothing of her but a pile of pale ash.

Now Zyn scratched the twin heads behind the ears, sending the scevan into bliss. Jarric held his tongue, not wanting to disturb her efforts. If she could enthrall the guardian into telling them about the keys that controlled the portal, he would be grateful . . . to a point. He had no intention of falling prey to her charms, however abundant and well-placed they were.

"So very clever!" Zyn continued. "You know how to touch the runes, how to read them, too, don't you? Would you read them for me? Would you tell me which to touch, which to say?"

The second head pulled back, narrowed gaze twisting to the waiting mage. "Only want to know for him, only for him!"

It actually sounded jealous . . . of Jarric. He found that hard to believe, considering how actively he had avoided the vampire's wiles. Still, if it did resent his presence, the scevan could remove the problem by showing him the way home. With Jarric departed, things could return to the way the guardian preferred.

Of course, with Jarric dead, the results for the scevan would be the same . . . and the beast seemed to prefer that option more.

Caressing fingers took control of the second scevan head again. Leaning close, Zyn murmured, "He only wants to go home. He only wants to keep something from nasty Ganth! You remember what I've said about Ganth, don't you? You don't like Ganth, do you?"

"Not nice to Zyn, not nice to Zyn," both blissful heads muttered.

"He has something that'll hurt Ganth. . . ."

Jarric listened carefully. He had mentioned very little about himself to the vampire, but in the company of the lich she had clearly learned enough. Likely she had known everything about Jarric except his name by the time they met. How much more did she know, though? The worry enabled Jarric to strengthen his resolve again, which had begun to slip as he watched Zyn play the guardian for his sake.

"Hate Ganth, hate Ganth," the first head growled.

"Then if you tell Zyn how the portal works, Jarric will go home and you'll have tricked nasty Ganth! Won't that be clever?"

The scevan suddenly pulled away from her touch. The heads glanced at one another, seeming in conflict for a moment. One snapped at the other, who repeated the challenge. Jarric wondered if the guardian might fight itself, unable to come to a mutual decision.

At last, the scevan ceased its internal struggle and looked at Zyn again. The tail wagged, albeit much slower. "Will send him away for you, will send him away for you."

Something about the way they phrased their response made the fire mage pause, but the vampire appeared satisfied. She leaned down, pressing the animal's heads against her and hugging the scevan so tight that Jarric actually felt a twinge of jealousy. The guardian reveled in her embrace.

The moment Zyn pulled away, the scevan's gaze fixed on the human. Jarric could still see the hatred in its eyes. It did what it did only for the sake of the entrancing vampire. Jarric vowed to be on his guard.

"Have one key already, have one key already," the first remarked.

"Magic is key, magic is key," explained the second.

So by being a mage, he had already passed the first step. A normal human being would not have made the portal function, but then a normal human being probably would not have found himself in this situation.

The guardian slipped around Zyn, who headed back toward the steps. "Must read the runes, must read the runes."

Jarric looked at the symbols, still not recognizing one of them.

"Surely you can read them for him?" urged

Zyn, now back atop the platform. "You probably know them by heart?"

"Know them, know them," explained the first head. "But to be spoken and touched together, spoken and touched together."

"I have to say them while I touch the runes?" the human asked.

The scevan acknowledged this with a pair of nods.

"Tell me the words, then, and I'll be gone from here."

"Must do more, foolish one, must do more! Must look at the runners, must look at the runners!"

Runners? The spellcaster warily studied the marble frame and, after some searching, noticed a pair of runes on each upper corner that seemed to resemble some four-legged beast in flight. In the left corner, one ran to the side, the other down. On the opposite edge, the first again ran to the side, but the last flew skyward, not down.

"Touch the fourth, touch the third," the pair intoned.

With some hesitation, Jarric obeyed. As his fingers grazed the fourth runner, he gasped. The rune took on a faint glow. He touched the third with the same results.

"Now what?"

"Speak the words, touch the words, right to left, bottom to top."

Start from the bottom right and touch the words as he spoke them. Straightforward. Jarric nodded, putting his right hand over the first rune. "Tell me the words."

The guardian's voices altered then, becoming higher-pitched, more sing-song. Jarric almost forgot what he should be doing, fascinated. He suspected that the new voices closely resembled those of the guardian's masters.

Fascination changed to uneasiness as the litany began. The words the scevan spoke were not the ones that Jarric had expected to hear.

"Death . . . doom . . . dire . . . destruct . . . disease," the heads called. "Despair . . . dismay . . . destroy . . . depose."

The mage repeated the words after the scevan, touching each rune as he did. In the back of his mind, he wondered what had caused the elves or whoever the masters had been to choose such symbols for their portal. Did it have to do with the reason they fled Delos in the first place? He wanted to ask the scevan, but then a change in the artifact drew his attention.

The entire doorway gleamed now, but, more important, a haze formed in the opening, a haze that did not spread, but remain fixed exactly between the frame.

"With these words do you pass through," the guardian completed. The massive scevan stepped back, one head watching Zyn, the other Jarric.

The portal now blazed, the power emanating from it so great that the spellcaster could feel it through every fiber of his being. Jarric stared at the haze, more like a curtain now rather than simply fog. He suspected that if he parted that curtain and walked through, he would indeed find himself beyond these ruins.

"Not much time to wait, not much time to

wait!" the guardian called. "Will not work again for some time, for some time!"

"This'll take me to Fuego?"

"Will go where you should go," the second head replied, with a glance toward Zyn.

Jarric, too, turned to the vampire. She had done nothing to stop him from fleeing. He reached out to thank her. Zyn reached out in turn.

"Go now, go now!" the scevan roared.

Startled, the mage pulled his hand away just as their fingers brushed. He turned back to the portal, saw that the aura surrounding it had already faded slightly. How long before it might be able to function again, he could not say nor could he risk.

Bracing himself, Jarric threw himself toward the portal.

Behind him, the twin heads of the guardian burst out into wild laughter.

"No!" A feminine hand of remarkable strength whirled him about. Jarric lost his balance, falling backward into the portal. As he did, he saw the vampire leaping at him . . . hands outstretched and mouth open wide, the fangs gleaming in the blazing aura of the artifact.

She had tricked him after all. Zyn had bided her time, waiting until Jarric had been most off-guard . . . and now she had him.

Chapter 12

PRYMIAS OF THE RUBY EYE PEERED UP FROM his scrolls to find Castlana Dumarcus staring at him. Despite the many years he had suffered this habit of hers, it still made him jump slightly to discover the woman patiently waiting for his attention. Had she not been so efficient in her duties, the senior mage would have reprimanded his majordomo long ago, but this same skill had worked for him so well and he did not wish to stifle it.

"What is it, Castlana?"

"A word with you, Eminence?"

"Speak."

"Eminence, I've spent the past few days reading through every significant manuscript, scroll, and scrap in your vast collection. After that, I researched in the archives of the council—"

"I am failing to see any point to this so far, Castlana."

She gave him a perfunctory nod. The crooked little smile so often there failed to materialize, a rare sign hinting of great concern on her part.

"Forgive me, Eminence, I am coming to that. In the end, I searched every available avenue to me and the results were all the same. While I found some bits of information, most of what the Dismas ambassador has told you is not listed."

"Dismas? Menthusalan, you mean?" The mage sat up straight. "Castlana, in general you move immediately to the reasons for your reports, but this once you've got me completely lost. What is it that Menthusalan's told me that, I gather, he shouldn't have known?"

"It all concerns Ebonyr, Eminence. Ganth of the Black Flame, the ruby shard, all of it. Other than a few references to the dark one himself and one note stating the legend, there exists nothing in the records. Not near enough considering what he's said to you."

"Perhaps Menthusalan has records of his own."

"He stated that the information came from yours, but that could be true. Nonetheless . . ."

Prymias waited, but when Castlana did not continue, he finally urged, "Yes? Nonetheless what?"

"Nonetheless, I have a feeling I can't shake, Eminence, and it stirs whenever the mentor is involved in this."

"I see." The master mage considered this. When Castlana Dumarcus had such feelings, they generally proved to have merit. Yet, here she stood almost accusing both an ambassador and friend of . . . of something wrong. "What would you have of me, then?"

"Permission to go on."

"You generally don't ask that. I'd have assumed you were already in the process of arresting Menthusalan on suspicion of being suspicious." Her eyes widened ever so slightly. "A jest, Castlana, and a poor one." He thrummed the top of his desk with his fingers. "You know that in this case I cannot tell you to do what you have to."

"No, Eminence."

Prymias frowned. Did she or did she not understand him? "I could never tell you to proceed in whatever manner necessary, do you understand?"

She blinked. Just once. Of all those Prymias had known over the years, his majordomo blinked the least. He took the timing to mean that she did understand him.

"I want no mention of this in my presence ever again." The councillor reached for a scroll and pretended to peruse it. "You may go."

When he did not hear her depart, Prymias looked up. The uniformed woman had disappeared. He exhaled, wondering if perhaps the tales he had fostered over the years had some truth, that his majordomo had magical skills undetected. It would have explained much.

She's got a feeling about Menthusalan. . . . Troublesome. The mentor represented Dismas, who, too often, found fault with the rigid, conservative manner of the emperor of Fuego and his council. If something should go awry, if Castlana were forced to deal with Menthusalan in a permanent manner, Dismas might demand satisfaction from the fire mages.

Castlana would be discreet, though. She always had been and always would be. Menthusalan might be an ambassador and a friend, but first and foremost Prymias had to be concerned about Fuego. If his second deemed it necessary to go beyond the rules to satisfy her uneasy feeling, so be it.

Menthusalan, my friend, I almost pray for your sake that she finds herself wrong . . . if that is at all possible.

Feryln woke, a sense of nausea briefly sending his world spinning. He shook his head and tried to rise, only belatedly recalling the ropes binding his arms and legs. The mrem blinked, looked around.

Memories returned, memories of being dragged to the encampment, a thousand eager, hungry eyes watching his every misstep. They had brought him to a tent which seemed to serve for storing supplies, untied him long enough to feed him some repulsive green mixture with a small tail in it, then bound his limbs so tight that his muscles now screamed. After that, his captors abandoned him.

He had slept, somewhat, but for how long? *Too many hours,* Feryln guessed. Small wonder he hungered even for the foul mess the Lizcanth served. Did the army eat the same gruel? Amazing then that even the wizard Ganth could keep them loyal.

The tent flaps parted and two Lizcanth entered. Without a word, they pulled Feryln to his feet, then undid the ropes binding his legs. That done, they immediately pushed him forward, sending the weakened mrem to his knees.

"Up!" hissed the larger of the pair. "Sssee you will the Lord Bassskillusss now!"

Feryln fought to his feet, determined not to shame himself before the lizards. However, he swore that if he ever got loose, he would teach this pair proper respect.

The reptilian warriors tapped him with the flats of their weapons, urging him on. The scene outside the tent had not altered. Creatures by the scores milled around, waiting for orders, any orders. Lizcanth with whips kept some of the most impatient in line, but the mrem wondered just how long this alliance could stand. Ganth had to attack somewhere or even his vaunted power might not be enough to keep such a horde together.

It did not take long to reach the tent of Baskillus. Feryln recognized it from the banners at the top. The blood red one with the black inferno in the center could only be that of Ganth; the second, a green, tearing claw surrounded by white had to be the Lizcanth lord's personal standard. Feryln had hoped to enter it armed, ready to slay the unsuspecting Baskillus while the murderous warlord slumbered or leaned over his maps. Now . . . now the beaten warrior wondered how soon he would be joining those he had failed.

"Inssside, mrem!" The lizard punctuated the command with a kick to Feryln's backside, sending the mrem falling face down into the tent.

"Ssso," hissed a deeper voice. "Knowsss the mrem hisss proper place."

Snarling, Feryln managed a standing position. He thought of charging, but a swift glance at the guards warned him of the insanity of any such attempt.

"Fool of a mrem." The Lizcanth who spoke looked to be the largest of his kind that Feryln had ever met . . . or ever imagined. Lord Baskillus rose well over seven feet tall, with muscles and claws to match. Feryln could not completely disguise his sudden fear and that clearly pleased the reptilian warlord. "Ssso brave before, were you not? Not ssso brave now, though."

Fear gave way to rekindled fury. "Give me a weapon, meet me in combat, and you will see how brave, lizard!"

"Ha! Ssspirit ssstill! Makesss the blood warmer!" Lord Baskillus opened wide his jaws, the better for Feryln to see his teeth. "Makesss the meat sssweeter."

Feryln refused to give in to his fear again . . . and yet, when he finally noted who stood beside Baskillus, he could not help shaking a little. Rowlen, face emotionless, stared back at him as if not recognizing his young companion. Feryln wondered if the dark wizard who had possessed the veteran warrior had fled elsewhere, leaving behind only the husk. Somehow he found that even more frightening. Ganth Kazarian might next be looking to use Feryln's body.

As if reading the mrem's thoughts, Baskillus indicated Rowlen, pointing directly at the ruby buried impossibly deep. Then, to Feryln's shock, the Lizcanth raised his head up slightly, revealing that he, too, had a stone in his throat. This one looked smaller, and where Rowlen's glowed slightly, the ruby Baskillus wore did not.

"Ssserve I the great dark one, Ganth of the Black Flame! Ssso shall all ssserve, in one manner or another. One of the favored am I; one of the hated are you, mrem! The Lizcanth dessspissse you, but not ssso much asss the dark one." He laughed, a harsh sound like steam, then indicated Rowlen again. "For the few mrem who live, thisss their fate will be."

So it would be just as Feryln had feared. He wondered why they had not already done the foul deed. He was their helpless prisoner; what more did they require?

"A little longer, though, before your fate, mrem. Needsss you, the dark one doesss, but . . ." Baskillus held up a flattened belt pouch. ". . . not until for you there isss a ssstone."

He had been granted an unintentional reprieve because Baskillus had run out of the rubies Ganth used to control both his minions and his slaves. Relief flooded through Feryln, but he kept it masked. "What do you want of me now, then?"

The Lizcanth's answer eradicated completely that growing relief. "Quesssstioning."

Feryln knew exactly what that meant. The reptiles would torture him to find out what he knew about Jarric and the shard. They would keep him alive, but no doubt just enough to serve the lich.

The young warrior struggled, not willing to suffer so readily the Lizcanth's foul ministrations. His guards seized him, but, with his legs still lose, he managed to kick one to the ground.

The other grappled with him, claws digging into his arms enough to drawn blood. Desperate, Feryln tried to bite at the scaly creature's throat, but could not reach his target.

The guard struck him a vicious blow that sent him tumbling to the ground. Both guards then proceeded to kick at his sides, nearly rupturing Feryln's kidneys. Baskillus appeared uninterested in stopping them. Without meaning to, Feryln vaguely realized that he had instigated the beginning of his torture.

"Let him alone."

Although the new voice spoke with little emotion, it caused the Lizcanth to halt their trepidations. The guards scurried back, suddenly fearful. Even Baskillus bent low, abasing himself.

Feryln stared up at Rowlen. The other's countenance had changed, taking on once more a foul animation. The eyes of the older mrem burned and now the ruby fairly blazed with power.

Rowlen turned to Baskillus. "He will remain untouched, for now."

"Yesss, dark one!"

"He will be questioned, though." The possessed warrior stepped toward Feryln. "But by my methods."

The shell that had once been Rowlen raised its left hand. Against his will, Feryln rose to his feet, sides still aching from the harsh blows. He tried not to stare into those burning orbs, but the power within Rowlen would not let him do otherwise.

"Know me, mrem, as I know your kind much too well. Know that I am Ganth Kazarian, Ganth of the Black Flame, and no Lizcanth will hate you as much as I do. You exist only because I will use you to betray your friends and your kind. Now and forever, I am your master."

"Never mine!" snapped Feryln. "I will avenge my family, my village, and my friends! I swear it!"

Rowlen looked perversely pleased by his resistance. "You simply make it harder on yourself, mrem, and more entertaining for me."

The older mrem reached out and clutched Feryln's struggling head in his larger hand. Feryln's senses seemed to cloud. His surroundings took on a surreal quality, the Lizcanth and Rowlen madly distorted, their arms and legs stretching long, the heads blowing out of proportion.

Through the haze, he heard the voice that was and was not that of his companion. "You hear me. You cannot deny me. . . ."

Rowlen's already twisted form shifted. No longer did he resemble a mrem, but rather some elongated, horrifying human corpse clad in the tatters of a once-elegant golden robe. Only a thin layer of skin covered the corpse's face, and the nose and lips had long decayed away. A battered crown covered what once had been hair.

"You cannot deny me," the lipless ghoul repeated.

Feryln tried to pull away from the macabre sight, but his body would not obey him. The corpse drew him nearer, seeming to delight in his wild terror.

"You cannot forbid me any answer I demand, mrem."

He would gladly answer all questions if only to escape. Feryln could feel the touch of the grave where the ghoul's fingers came into contact with his fur, smell the decay in such close quarters.

"The fire mage, Jarric. He has the ruby shard, yes?"

"Yes! He does!" The mrem felt no shame, only relief that he had been able to answer the first question.

"There were no more in your party. Only you three."

Again he blurted out agreement.

"The gargoyles. Do you know where they brought this Jarric?"

For this he had to think, an eternity of time when so near to the living dead. At last, Feryln said, "Northeast of . . . of me! More east than north!"

"In the direction of my sanctum? The gargoyles would not take him that near. They might not be able to use the shard, but they would certainly keep it from my reach, knowing that I can!"

Feryln stood there, helpless. He had no more answer for his tormenter.

"This Jarric. He is a mage of renown? He can manipulate the shard?"

The mrem tried to shake his head. "He is young. This was to be his quest."

The macabre figure paused. Then, "Curious . . . but perhaps clever. They thought I might not take notice of a young fire mage on his quest . . . and might not have if the truth had not leaked out." Another pause. "Very well, mrem. Enough about the shard. It will be mine soon enough! You were recent to Fuego. I have delved into what remains of the mind of your friend, but you are fresh, better able to impress images seen at but a glance. You will now tell me all you know about the Fuego of this time. You will tell me everything, even that which you do not recall."

The corpse drew him close. Its mouth opened wide, wider, so wide that it could swallow the frantic mrem whole . . . which it did.

Feryln screamed.

When he woke, he lay sprawled on the ground in Baskillus's tent, arms and legs folded into a fetal position. Feryln remained that way for some time, too weary and too frightened to move. With each breath he recalled the sensation of feeling the thing from the grave burrowing through his mind, summoning those memories, however deep, that concerned even the most obscure information about modern Fuego. Shame began to overwhelm him, shame that he had surrendered so readily what few secrets he might have had.

Of course, Feryln realized now that the corpse had been the lich Ganth. If the reality even remotely matched his imagination, he could see why any would fear the dark one's power. Had it been so for Rowlen? No, Feryln suspected that the older mrem had suffered far worse. Feryln had not yet had his life ripped out and a parasitic ruby put in its place.

His hand went to his throat. He breathed a sigh of relief. Baskillus had evidently told the truth. Had they had one of Ganth's rubies available, Feryln would now be like Rowlen.

He tried at last to uncoil, discovering slowly that he had been left unbound. A shred of hope rose. Feryln started to roll over, then froze. Glaring at him were two hungry Lizcanth, possibly the same pair who had brought him to their leader.

They said nothing nor did they make a move toward him, save to brandish a weapon. Feryln understood the message: move false and he would suffer. Feeling too weak to fight, anyway, he rolled back over . . . to discover Rowlen standing in silence near the vast table on which Lord Baskillus evidently kept his battle charts.

At first he thought Rowlen stared intently at him, but then the younger mrem realized that Rowlen simply stared. As before, without Ganth to animate him, the warrior appeared to be nothing more than a puppet, a body for the evil lich to don when he needed it. The ruby glowed but faintly now, moving in rhythm with Rowlen's breathing. Had he not seen how Ganth used the body like a plaything, Feryln might have hoped that something remained of his friend. That hope, though, remained as minuscule as his own chances for freedom.

He sat there, pondering what, if anything he could do, when Lord Baskillus returned. The Lizcanth warlord looked very pleased, which did nothing to ease Feryln's misgivings.

"Awake you are, young mrem! Good, ssso

very good! Wondered the dark one did if he had delved too deep, dessstroyed what he ssstill desssiresss to ussse." The fearsome Lizcanth noticed his free hands. "Foolsss! Bind his wrisssts!"

The two guards lumbered over, quick to obey. Feryln did not struggle as they tied his hands behind him. What could he have done anyway? He barely had the strength to stand and each glance he made toward Rowlen only served to sap his will yet more. Feryln wished he could at least do something for the mrem warrior, at least give him an honorable death so Ganth could no longer use his body.

The guards made him stand straight, but even then the mrem had to look up to see the visage of the leader. Baskillus smiled, then stalked to the table. "Bring him nearer."

They dragged him to the table, made him look where Baskillus indicated. Feryln stared at a map of Delos, specifically the area surrounding Fuego. The detail impressed him; he would not have expected it of the Lizcanth. Then he gradually noticed new marks, new additions. Hill formations had been corrected, river directions altered. To the side of the larger map, a smaller, cruder one of the kingdom itself lay, with yet more corrections, including some notation of the strength of the defenses.

"Of excellent aid have been the pair of you mrem in preparing for the attack! Yesss, even you, mountain mrem! Grateful the dark one isss! With or without the mage and shard, invade Fuego he will before the week isss done!"

Feryln's wits, finally waking, enabled him to

slowly absorb what the Lizcanth meant. Through Rowlen and himself, Baskillus and Ganth had garnered much information about their intended target, so much that the black wizard had decided to send his horde on whether or not he had captured Jarric yet. Feryln choked back tears of frustration; instead of assassinating the butcher of his loved ones, he had quite possibly opened the way for Baskillus to slaughter the entire kingdom of Fuego. Surely now the ghosts of his family and friends would never forgive him.

The Lizcanth laughed at his obvious consternation. "March in two to four daysss we will, you with usss. Gloriousss battle, gloriousss ssslaughter! To you my gratitude!"

That many of his own would die did not appear to bother Baskillus. He believed, perhaps rightly so, that the power of his master would this time make victory inevitable.

They were interrupted by a smaller reptile, one who groveled in the presence of the huge lord. Baskillus ordered the puny creature forward with a single gesture. It crawled to him on its knees.

"Great one! The Yngling, the ogresss . . . they fight among themssselvesss again!"

Baskillus hissed, a sound so vile that Feryln, the guards, and, especially, the messenger backed away. The Lizcanth warlord glared at everyone as his fury mounted. "Insssufferable creaturesss! When Ganth massster of all isss, othersss he will not need! No more ogresss, no more Yngling, no more any but Lizcanth! Bind hisss legsss and leave him! Go nowhere the mrem will!"

It took but a moment for the guards to comply, one shoving Feryln to the floor when they were done. Unable to halt his fall, the mrem hit the rocky ground hard. His head shook, the pain not easing until long after Baskillus and the others had left.

Infighting among those Ganth had gathered. A small, likely temporary, victory. Fear of the lich certainly held the horde together. All Baskillus would likely need to do was remind them of the cost of failing to obey their master's dictates. Ganth would certainly be willing to sacrifice a few dozen ogres and the like to prove to the rest that he tolerated no dissension in the ranks. Ganth wanted Fuego almost as much as he wanted Jarric and the ruby shard. Whatever enmity existed between those who made up his infernal legions would not be allowed to keep him from making his dread desires a reality.

He rolled over, to once more find himself staring at Rowlen. The emptiness in those eyes tore at his soul. If he could do nothing for himself, Feryln still hoped that he could at least end Ganth's control of the other mrem's body. It would be some redemption for the young warrior, however minute.

"Feryln."

The beaten mrem stiffened, thinking at first that Rowlen had spoken. However, he quickly saw that the other had not moved. Feryln blinked, wondering if his own mind had reached its limits. Perhaps madness would save him from Rowlen's fate.

"Feryln."

The voice again, but now he noticed that it came from behind him. Feryln rolled over, facing that direction. At first he saw nothing, but gradually the mrem realized that something pushed against the outer side of the tent.

"Who—?"

A hand raised the bottom edge of the tent. A wary human face appeared. "Quiet! We don't have much time!"

Theron Kain. The mrem blinked, at first not sure whether to be grateful for the reaver's return or angry for his having abandoned him earlier. "I thought you decided to follow your friends, human."

A mocking smile briefly crossed the reaver's face as he crawled inside, weapon in hand. "Is that what you thought? I was tempted, but no, I realized too late that what we saw had to be some sort of trap, although I hadn't expected your friend there to be part of it."

As Kain moved to cut his bonds, Feryln explained, "It was the wizard Ganth, Kain. The ruby in Rowlen's throat allows Ganth to control the body like a puppet."

"Does it? Wonder what happens when you take it out?"

Feryln had not really considered that. Rowlen would die, he suspected, the hole in his throat too large and too deep. Still, perhaps it would at least sever the bond between the other mrem and the horrific lich.

"I tried to warn you, you young fool, but you never saw me. When they took you away, I watched, studied the encampment. I knew that as huge as it was, I could use that to my advantage. When soldiers, whatever race they are, are constantly tripping over one another, they aren't always keeping the closest watch on the rest of their surroundings. . . . There!" He had Feryln's arms free.

The mrem moved to undo his legs while Kain looked around. The reaver captain noticed the maps and began to study them. After a moment, he shook his head, reached for the ones Baskillus had shown Feryln earlier, and crumpled them up. The pieces he thrust into his belt pouch.

At last free, Feryln rose, searching for a weapon. Again his eyes alighted on Rowlen and he recalled Kain's question. Remove the stone and Rowlen would likely die . . . but, in all reality, he was probably dead already. At least, Feryln hoped that was the case.

Kain saw him moving toward the still figure. "What're you doing, mrem? We've got to be away from here now!"

"I have to free him, one way or another." He reached up, trying to steel himself before tearing the ruby out.

"There's a quicker way." The massive reaver stalked toward Rowlen, readying his blade. "Quieter, too. He might scream when you pull that thing free, mrem."

Feryln had not considered that. Yet, despite the sense of Kain's words, Feryln felt the sword insufficient. Only if the ruby were removed would the other mrem truly be at peace. He waved the reaver back. "I must do it this way. I will cover his mouth to block any cry."

"Then do it now!"

Nerves taut, Feryln placed one hand over Rowlen's mouth, the other over the ruby. The stone radiated heat, which startled him for a moment. He blinked, took a deep breath, then took hold of the edge of the stone. Feryln did not doubt that he had the strength to do this task, he only hoped he had the courage. If he hesitated any longer, Theron Kain would simply run Rowlen through, which, as Feryln saw it, did not necessarily mean that the warrior's soul would be free.

"Away from me!" Baskillus suddenly roared from somewhere close by.

"Damn!" Kain whispered, turning toward the tent entrance. "Too soon! Finish your friend now, mrem, while I give the warlord a proper greeting!" The reaver hurried to one side of the tent flaps, blade raised high. The human's countenance had grown pale, but Kain still looked ready to take on the Lizcanth.

Baskillus shouted at another underling, his voice clearly indicating that he neared the tent. Feryln forgot his own task as he stared at the flaps, waiting for the gigantic Lizcanth to step through.

The reptilian warlord paused just beyond the entrance, snapping again at someone who had obviously failed him. "Happen again it will not or on your head it will be! Undersssstood?"

"Yesss, great one!"

"Away, then!" The Lizcanth's huge, clawed hand reached in to move away the flap.

The reaver tensed. Feryln cursed under his breath, eyes still fixed on the oncoming warlord instead of his own task.

Another hand, a mrem hand, suddenly clutched Feryln by the throat, cutting off his air. The young mrem twisted around, stared into feline eyes with no life left in them.

Ganth had returned to Rowlen's body.

Chapter 13

JARRIC WOKE CRUMPLED IN A HEAP AND chilled to the bone. He opened his eyes, found himself staring at earth. Gasping, the fire mage slowly, carefully rolled himself onto his back, trying to assess the damage.

He looked up into the haunting face of Zyn, who knelt but inches from his side. Jarric shifted his gaze downward, trying to escape those entrancing eyes, only to discover that the vampire's flowing gown hid not nearly enough of her ample beauty. Every nerve on edge, Jarric pulled away from her, recalling how she had lunged at him just as he had attempted to depart. They must have both fallen through the portal and now she had come to finish him.

"Can't you see yet that you've nothing to fear from me, sweet Jarric?" She smiled, remembering not to open her mouth much as she did. "I could have taken you in your sleep, but search your throat and you'll find no mark, I promise you."

He grabbed at his neck, frantically searching for blood or the tell-tale holes of which the legends spoke. Despite the fact that he found neither, though, Jarric did not yet believe all Zyn had told him.

She saw his reluctance to accept her. "You should be all right, but I didn't dare move you. I'm so sorry, sweet Jarric! The guardian sought to betray you in the end and I tried to pull you back. I had no idea he would be so jealous of you."

"Jealous?" Jarric rubbed his head, recalling the scevan's laugh. "What did he do?"

"When he laughed, I realized that he'd decided to send you to other than your chosen destination. I feared for you, but when I tried to grab you, you foolishly thought I wanted your—wanted to harm you."

The cold continued to torment the mage. He instinctively began formulating a spell to create a campfire, but Zyn's suddenly shocked visage made him falter. "What is it?"

"Do you plan to cast a spell?"

"I'm cold. Freezing." Despite her thin garment and the substantial amounts of flesh exposed to the elements, the vampire appeared not at all affected by the chill. "If I don't, I might die."

"I'm sorry. I forgot about the cold . . . but you can't cast a spell! Not here."

"Why?"

"Look around you."

He did, not at first seeing what she meant. They had clearly been sent somewhere higher in the mountains. Here, the trees had thinned out and cliffs dominated. To the east, a mountain rose some distance with other, smaller ones looming beyond it. "I don't see any—"

What remained of a castle the color of bone stood perched on the side of the nearest mountain. Much of the left side of the once mighty edifice had been destroyed, either by fire or . . . or something greater, for even the peak itself had been scarred there. Five craggy spires still stood atop the massive ruins, creating the image of a battered and burnt crown. Jarric judged that once the ghostly castle had been even mightier, that a good third had been torn away by the terrible assault. Scorch marks still decorated some of the remaining sections. At least one of the towers hung precariously; it seemed a wonder that the fierce winds had not yet blown it free.

Near the devastated section, a huge balcony still perched, the left edge broken off. Far above, near the battlements, an inner wall had caved in, large fragments looking ready to plunge down the mountainside at any moment. No lights shone from the castle nor did the mage see any sign of life. Jarric might have thought the imposing citadel long, long abandoned, if not for the fact that he recognized this stone goliath by name.

"Ebonyr. . . ." he finally managed to utter, certain that it could be no other place.

"The guardian tried to send you as near as he could to Ebonyr." Zyn looked apologetic. "I suppose he thought that you and Ganth would fight, perhaps destroy one another. I knew he hated Ganth simply because of me, but I didn't think he despised you for the same reason."

The vampire had been the scevan's constant companion for who knew how many decades, perhaps centuries. The beast had seen her interest in the mage, feared that she would never return to the ancient realm if she remained infatuated with Jarric. In retrospect, Jarric could understand some of the foul beast's jealousy, but he now wished he had tried his spells on it after all. "How long have I been unconscious?"

"A few short hours. I've watched over you, kept you well, except for the cold." She moved nearer. "I could help you with that, too, if you'd let me."

He shivered, but not from the cold. What did a vampire feel like? If Zyn did not sense the cold, could it be because her body had no heat of its own? "No, I'll . . . I'll be fine. I just need some shelter. Something." Jarric stared her in the eye. "You know this region well, don't you?"

"Some parts, yes. Others, I never much paid mind to."

"Is there an empty building? A cave?"

She pursed her lips, something Jarric wished she would cease doing. It confused his already jumbled emotions. "I know of one place in particular, an old tunnel, but it will take a little time to reach. . . . Plus, you must be careful. Ganth has many servants and not all would like you as much as me."

"All right. Just give me a chance to rise." Bones creaked as the fire mage slowly managed to stand. He refused Zyn's offer to help him, in part fearing that he would enjoy it too much.

After several minutes of stretching cramped muscles, Jarric decided he could hope for no better from his battered, half-frozen body. He looked around, noting that while several hardy trees dotted the area, the landscape consisted mostly of treacherous slopes and rocky passages carved into the mountains by time. The area where he stood proved to be part of a lesser peak, one that melded into the giant upon which Ebonyr perched.

Not a promising place to find oneself. Jarric tried to think of a plan, but his mind would not function properly. He needed shelter for a time . . . and perhaps once he found it Jarric could yet risk the tiniest of spells. The fire mage found himself envying his mrem companions' abilities. They would have readily known how to create a brisk bonfire using but a few twigs and rocks, no doubt. He, city raised and mage taught, knew only tricks that now might garner him too much attention from the lich.

Thinking of the mrem, he wondered how they fared. Perhaps they had made their way back to Fuego and had even now warned Master Prymias of all that had happened. Jarric suspected that his sponsor did indeed know a bit more than he had told the younger mage, but still, if anyone could help Jarric, it was Master Prymias.

Yet, he could not rely on that. Jarric had been raised from birth with the notion that, if he did not fail miserably in the attempt, he would some day be a fire mage of the greatest caliber, a future leader of House Gaius. If he hoped to live up to that notion—and live at all—he had to try to fend for himself, however incredible the odds.

"Which way?"

"Come." Zyn offered a hand, but when Jarric did not take it, she pouted, then said, "Very well, I'll lead."

They started across the mountainous landscape, the human clutching himself close, the vampire moving lithely along the uneven and ever rising path. Jarric could not help admiring her form and movement, the ethereal gown fluttering about as if with a life of its own. Zyn seemed a part of the wind, a goddess of the mountains. Had he not known her for what she was, he could have easily lost himself to her.

The ground turned more treacherous. The fire mage had to take hold of rocks or lean against lone trees in order to maintain his balance. Even Zyn slowed a little. Twice in the distance they heard sounds which the vampire identified as sentinels. Jarric soon realized that Zyn purposely led him along a complex path because she sought to avoid the many guardians. It softened his emotions toward her, yet still he could not bring himself to even accept her physical help whenever he stumbled.

Then the vampire, whose own step seemed so perfect, slipped. Zyn grabbed for a branch, missed it, and fell back. Jarric reacted without thinking, catching her in his arms even though it sent him, too, to the ground. They ended up sprawled against a large rock, Zyn still held tight in his arms.

"My sweet Jarric! My sweet hero . . ." Before the spellcaster understood what had happened, Zyn began to kiss him. He discovered then that a vampire could be very, very warm.

Suddenly he recalled who—no, what—he held in his arms. Old fears stirred. Jarric wrenched himself away, trying to forget the sensation of her lips against his.

"Why do you still run from me, sweet Jarric? You must know by now that—"

Both her question and the response he would have struggled to give ended unfinished as a huge shadow passed overhead. Zyn stiffened, for the first time showing true fright. Jarric did not have to ask what could strike fear in a vampire, not when he recognized that shadow immediately. Only one creature of the air could blot out the light of a sun so well.

The blue dragon had returned.

He watched as the leviathan soared toward Ebonyr, a grim look on his draconian features. He did not seem at all pleased, no doubt because he had been seeking Jarric but not finding any trace. The dragon could never have followed the magic of the portal. That he flew toward Ebonyr surely verified that the creature served Ganth and now had to report his continued failure, which would please neither beast nor master much.

"Azur. . . ." he heard Zyn mutter.

"Azur?"

"The great blue. The most terrible of the dragons. You saw him now. It was his enslavement by Ganth that drew so many to my lord's banner, sweet Jarric. If Ganth could control such a gargantuan power, he surely could control all of Delos. So have many thought and with good reason!"

Jarric could see the horrible logic. He wondered why any wizard who could keep a huge dragon under rein would even need the ruby shard, however valuable to his kind. Ganth Kazarian appeared invincible.

Yet, however invincible the lich might be, Jarric realized that he could not simply surrender himself to Ganth. If he could still get the shard to Fuego, then surely the combined might of the fire mages there, concentrated through the artifact, would be enough to end Ganth's ambitions.

"How much . . . how much farther to the cave?"

"Not too much more, but if—he comes back!"

Jarric saw him, too. The draconian giant had banked and now headed back in the general direction of the pair. Had Azur smelled his presence? Did the dragon know exactly where he hid?

Zyn seized his hand. "Come! This way!"

Unmindful of the contact now, Jarric allowed her to lead him over rocks, around trees, and through narrow passes. As swift as they ran, however, the dragon flew much faster. Already it neared their original location, flying much closer to the ground. Azur sniffed as he moved along, reptilian eyes surveying everything.

"Behind here!" The vampire nearly threw the mage around a massive boulder, then pressed against him.

Slowly, Azur hunted along the land. While Jarric could not read the dragon's expression clearly from here, he thought that Azur seemed puzzled, as if not at all certain himself of what he did now. "He must be a bit confused," Jarric whispered. "He must not be sure what he smelled."

"Azur is tenacious, though," Zyn returned. "Dragons have much pride and Azur has more than most of his kind. He wouldn't want to return to Ganth unless absolutely certain."

They watched as the leviathan gradually moved westward, almost hovering over some areas. With each passing moment, Jarric breathed a little easier. Azur, it seemed, would pass them by.

Then the blue dragon suddenly arced back, this time heading directly toward them.

"He has the scent!" Zyn murmured. "Hurry!"

She darted out from their hiding place, leading him along the side of a ridge. Jarric glanced behind him, saw that although he still searched methodically, Azur nonetheless drew nearer and nearer. Only the landscape truly kept them from his view, but not for much longer at the rate the dragon flew.

"The cave is only a short distance ahead!" Zyn called.

But still much too far, thought Jarric, seeing Azur moving more swiftly.

His eyes on the blue, the mage did not see the trees through which the vampire had so delicately slipped. Jarric missed the trunks, but his left arm caught on the branches of one, his sleeve becoming snagged. He struggled with the sleeve, freeing it after several precious seconds.

Zyn seized his other arm. "Hurry! Only—"

Azur roared. "Ha! I see you, mage! I see you! You will not escape me this time!"

Tearing free of the vampire's grip, Jarric clutched his medallion, touching the ruby. He tried to think of a spell, any spell, that could at least delay the great beast. As he struggled mentally, his eye happened to fall on the area below Azur's terrifying jaws.

A ruby. The dragon had a ruby embedded in its throat. The stone glowed with some inner life.

Ganth had enslaved the greatest of the dragons . . . could this be how it had been done?

An idea formed in the hapless spellcaster's

mind. While he might not be so powerful a wizard as the lich, Jarric understood the properties and uses of the stone through which fire mages cast their spells. He also understood their detriments.

Muttering, Jarric kept his hand pressed against his own ruby while he stared directly at the other. For once in his life, he prayed that his tendency to pour too much into a spell might work for him.

Zyn tugged at him, nearly upsetting his concentration. "Dear Jarric! You must come—"

Azur's ruby flared bright.

The blue goliath roared, this time in utter agony.

The ruby's light continued to brighten, spreading across the landscape, showering even far-off Ebonyr when the dragon twisted and turned, trying to escape what he could not.

"What did you do?"

Jarric ignored Zyn's question. "The cave! Lead us there! Quick!"

She did not move at first, clearly startled that anyone other than Ganth could have struck the dragon such a blow. Her delay cost them, Jarric realized, for even as she finally turned, he heard Azur bellow. Fury, no longer pain, drove the dragon now.

"Wretched human! Wretched fire mage! I will crush you, eat you, tear your limbs from your body!"

Fierce winds pummeled them, throwing Jarric and Zyn against the rocky side of the ridge. Jarric tried to keep moving, but Azur flew too close. He could barely rise and the dust stirred up by the leviathan's expansive wings made it nearly impossible to see.

"I will swallow you whole, fire mage, and you will spend your last few moments of life being digested in my stomach, knowing agony greater than that which you dared force on me!"

Desperate, Jarric fumbled for the medallion, but his fingers seemed numb, unable to keep the ruby in his grip.

Zyn seized him, then, an act which caught the human completely unaware. Instead of trying to bring him to a place of refuge, though, the vampire threw him forward so that he landed on his knees almost directly before the dragon. "Hold, Azur! You cannot eat this one! You know Ganth's command! I claim this one, claim him so that he can be brought back to our lord!"

"Zyn!" The dragon paused in mid-flight, as perplexed in his own way by the vampire as Jarric. "I did not see you!"

"Obviously!" She stepped forward, used one hand to keep the mage on his knees. "You were going to eat him, Azur! You were going to eat him despite Ganth's will!"

"A moment of rashness, vampire! The mage hurt me!"

"And Ganth would've hurt you more if you'd not recalled yourself in time! What would he have done to you if you came back and reported you'd devoured the one he sought?"

Jarric managed to look up. Azur had a most uncertain expression now, one bordering on fear. "I would have remembered in time! I swear!"

"Perhaps, perhaps not! I think it better if I take

charge of this prisoner. Then you won't have to worry about losing control again."

At last Jarric thought he understood what the vampire intended. If Azur thought Jarric her prisoner, he would fly away. Then the pair could make their way to safety, the dragon discovering his mistake far too late to do anything about it.

"I will not lose control!" the leviathan rumbled. "I will see that he reaches Ganth relatively unharmed!"

Jarric did not like the sound of that, but fortunately, Zyn refused. "I am his, Azur. I am Ganth's and have been for very, very long. I've claimed this prisoner." In a gesture which unnerved Jarric but which he realized necessary, the vampire tore the medallion from him, showing that the human would be no trouble for her. "And Ganth wouldn't like it if you took him from me!"

The blue dragon looked ready to argue, then evidently thought better of it. He finally shook his massive head. "He is yours by right, Zyn, and I will not cross you . . . or Ganth . . . in this."

"I thought not."

"I will make my error up to you, though," the draconian giant suddenly added. "I will carry you and this cursed mage to Ganth myself!"

"There is no need!" Zyn responded, perhaps a little too quickly. "I need no help!"

Azur eyed her. "But, as you said, Ganth has sought this one! The sooner he is in the wizard's hands, the better for all of us! No, I must do this! Ganth would expect it!"

Jarric waited for Zyn to say something else,

but the vampire remained silent. To argue with Azur much longer might reveal that she had been aiding the human, not hunting him.

"You might be tempted to crush him," Zyn finally managed.

"Oh, I will be very gentle, Zyn! He will arrive in the most perfect condition so that Ganth may do with him as he pleases! Then, when he is done with this wretched one, Ganth has promised to give him back to me! Once that happens . . ." the leviathan chuckled, ". . . I will have more than enough time to teach this puny human what it means to hurt me!"

With that, Azur dropped down, reaching for both Jarric and Zyn. The dragon's paws were so large that he could have taken the pair up in one, but Azur chose to separate them. As the behemoth seized the mage, Jarric could not help struggling. Azur laughed, squeezing just tight enough to discourage any more displays of defiance.

"We will be there in a few minutes!" he roared, leaping into the air.

As the wind rushed against Jarric's face, he twisted enough to see the vampire. Zyn, though, looked only toward Ebonyr. Once more the mage wondered if she had played him for a fool all this time. Had Zyn decided that her chances would be better if she returned to the fold?

Azur flew with blinding speed. Ebonyr shifted from a distant ruin to a tall, imposing ghost that refused to die. Great faults in the bone-colored stone materialized, faults which again made it surprising that Ebonyr still existed at all. Perhaps the castle would have crumbled long ago save for the machinations of its master. Jarric could sense the powers of magic at work within. Ganth had likely employed his skills in order to bring his citadel back to some use. Of course, to one who could cheat death, recreating part of the castle surely would be a small matter. He wondered why the lich had not gone on and finished reconstruction of his dread domain. What had Zyn told him of Ganth Kazarian? Something about being tricked and only a limited time remaining? Perhaps he would understand better once he confronted the other fire mage.

Jarric realized what he had just thought and shook. He had no actual desire to confront Ganth. Such an encounter could end only one way, with Jarric the lich's to do with as he would.

The dragon flew over Ebonyr, barely missing the tallest of those towers remaining. Jarric might have admired the ancient edifice's design and size more, but not when he knew what power had caused it to be built. He wished the ancient mages who had fought Ganth Kazarian had been more thorough in their task. They should have leveled the vast citadel completely, leaving no traces to remind anyone of its ever having existed. In part because of them, Jarric and Fuego would suffer.

At last, Azur alighted on the immense balcony, almost a second structure unto its own. As the human had thought, a good portion of the balcony had been sheared away and while the part on which the behemoth landed held, it groaned under the immense weight. Jarric almost wished that it would collapse.

"Ganth!" the mighty blue rumbled to the dark chamber beyond the balcony. "Where is he? Ganth! Your prize awaits you, oh, Master!"

He lowered his front paws, releasing first Zyn, then, with less delicacy, Jarric. The vampire immediately took the mage by the shoulder, which happened to save him from Azur's prodding talon.

From within came a voice reminiscent of the creaking gate of a mausoleum or tomb. Had not Zyn been holding him tight, he might have tried to run regardless of his chances. "I come in my own time, Azur. Never presume again. I deal in many matters and if you must wait, then so be it!"

"I only thought you wanted to see this puny human," the leviathan returned with some petulance. "You've pestered me about him for so long!"

"And I do. Good to see that you have him at last. I'd begun to wonder about your loyalty."

"You know my loyalty, mage. You know it well."

"So I do." A pause. "Very well. Show me now this Jarric who has so long eluded so many."

"I have him here, sweet Ganth," the vampire purred.

"Zyn, my loyal Zyn, I'd wondered what became of you." A figure detached itself from the darkness within the castle. A thick, dark cloud overhead Ebonyr thundered, as if paying homage to the evil that walked.

Nothing could have prepared Jarric for the sight of Ganth Kazarian. The black mage should not have lived. He wore little, if any, flesh, had only a dry covering of skin in most places. No nose remained. Skeletal fingers opened as the walking corpse neared Zyn and Jarric. One bent hand caressed the cheek of the vampire, who smiled as it happened but shivered when Ganth could not see her reaction.

The smell of the grave hung around the monstrous visage, little more than a skull wrapped in the wasted shell of life. Jarric could not long look into the lich's eyes, for he could feel as well as see the darkness within those burning fires. Below Ganth's horrible features was a thick scarf wound very tightly around his throat. Perhaps, Jarric found himself musing, *to keep his head from falling off.* It amazed him that any part of the lich could remain intact with so little to hold the corpse together.

"You . . . are Jarric of House Gaius." He did not wait for the human to continue. "Jarric of Fuego . . . dear, lovely, cursed, treacherous Fuego." Ganth of the Black Flames took a step back, turning to Azur. "You redeem yourself, dragon!"

"Much credit must go to Zyn," the dragon admitted.

"Zyn, yes. . . ." He turned to the vampire. "Zyn, who remained loyal to me even after death. I had wondered where you have been these last couple days, dear Zyn! I thought perhaps . . . that you had grown distant. . . ."

"Never, sweet Ganth! How could you even think—"

The dark one's gaze switched back to Jarric, studying long his face. "Yes . . . how could I think that?"

Jarric sensed the suspicions. Ganth knew what he had become and he saw how young and alive the fire mage before him was.

"Well?" thundered Azur. "You have your spellcaster, Ganth! Take the shard from him so that I can feed on one of you!"

"The shard . . . yes . . ." The flames grew stronger. "At last, an end to this! Give me the artifact and your death will be swift, Jarric of Fuego!"

"I don't have it." A flimsy lie, but Jarric swore he would defy this abomination to the very end. He could do little else.

"Spare me your weak tricks." Ganth stroked the scarf over his throat. "I will have my shard!"

Jarric could not move. He could barely even breathe or blink. Ganth raised his other hand, taloned fingers outstretched.

"Show me . . ." the lich murmured. "Show me. . . ."

Every fiber tingled. Jarric wanted to tear himself away, at least keep from having to stare into the pits of dark flame that were black Ganth's eyes.

"Show me . . ." the fearsome lord of Ebonyr repeated yet again. "I command it!"

The gold-enshrouded lich began to shake. Jarric heard a gasp from Zyn, a rumble of curiosity from Azur.

"Something amiss, oh, Master?"

"Silence!" Ganth Kazarian rubbed the area of his throat again. Jarric slumped but managed not to collapse. The monstrous figure looked first at Zyn, then at the dragon, as if trying to decide something. Both the vampire and the leviathan cringed ever so slightly under the inhuman glare.

"Sweet Ganth, is there—"

"If one here seeks to play me for the fool," he interrupted, again glaring at each. "they should know the penalty." Ganth reached toward his throat.

"Wait!" roared Azur. "What do you insinuate? I have obeyed you to the letter, wizard, however much I might prefer to munch on your bones! I have done nothing!"

"And you know how I've stood by you, my darling Ganth."

"Then where is my shard?" the furious lich demanded. "He does not have it on him! Where is it?"

Jarric clamped his hand against his side, instinctively seeking the pouch in which he had stored the artifact—only to discover that the pouch no longer hung there.

Chapter 14

FERYLN STRUGGLED IN ROWLEN'S DEATHLY grip, but could not free his throat. He waited for the wizard who possessed the other mrem's form to call out a warning, but Rowlen continued to stare blankly ahead, as if not even noticing that he slowly choked his younger companion. The ruby in his throat glowed very faintly.

As consciousness slipped from him, Feryln acted in desperation. Heedless of whether or not Baskillus would hear, he ripped the ruby from Rowlen's throat.

The mrem warrior's eyes widened and he gasped. Blood trickled from the opening and Rowlen's grip slackened. The eyes fluttered closed, then opened again, looking directly ahead. Coughing, Feryln pulled away, the bloody gem still clutched in his hand.

At that moment, the Lizcanth warlord entered. Baskillus registered the sight of the two mrem, opened his mouth to shout, but froze a breath later, the tip of Theron Kain's sword resting against his throat.

"A single sound wrong and this goes through to the hilt," the reaver captain warned.

For all his size and savageness, Lord Baskillus did not prove reckless. He nodded very slightly, raising his hands where his captor could see them.

Still watching Baskillus, Kain whispered, "Are you all right, mrem?"

Feryln coughed once more before finally able to answer, "I am."

He glanced up at Rowlen. The other mrem still wore a look of shock on his face and although the gaping hole still dripped with his life fluids, he did not fall, not even slump forward. Feryln at last realized that Ganth had not been within, that some vestigial spell of the wizard's must have caused the body to try to strangle the young warrior.

Pushing the Lizcanth farther into the tent, the human at last had the opportunity to see what had happened. His expression, grim already, somehow managed to be more so. "Your friend is dead even if he doesn't know it yet, mrem. You've done what you can for him, now we've got to see about getting out of here."

"Die here you will," Baskillus hissed quietly.

Kain pressed the point of the sword just enough to silence the reptile. "First, last, and only chance, lizard. Your next word, unless I ask it of you, will be your last."

Feryln leaned near his friend. "Rowlen? Can you hear me?"

The unblinking eyes continued to look ahead.

"Give it up, mrem! He's gone to us! Do something useful and help me with this one!"

It unnerved Feryln to leave Rowlen standing as he was, but nothing more could be done for the veteran warrior. As Kain had indicated, Rowlen was dead. The body simply did not know that yet, although it could only be a matter of minutes, possibly even seconds. He swore that when time allowed, he would mourn Rowlen as he had those of his village.

Using the very ropes with which the Lizcanth had bound Feryln, the pair set to work on Baskillus. Under the reaver's guidance, the mrem strapped their captive's arms behind him, so tight that Baskillus once even grunted in pain. After a moment's consideration, Kain also had Feryln bind the reptilian warlord's snout shut, just in case. This last made Baskillus furious, but with the human's blade so near, the Lizcanth dared not protest.

"What about his legs?" Feryln asked, eyes drifting toward Rowlen. The other mrem still stood as if alive, but now blood dripped to his chest. The sight horrified Feryln, yet he could not bring himself to do any more for his friend. The younger mrem eyed the captive, his hatred for the butcher rising. He considered the ropes in his hands, thinking about how tight he could wrap them around the captive warlord's throat.

Kain took the ropes from Feryln, perhaps suspecting his sudden interest in Baskillus's neck. "We leave the lizard's legs free, mrem. How else will he be able to come with us? I've no ambition to carry him out of here."

"Take him with us?" Feryln had not even considered such an option. "How can we hope to do that? It will be difficult enough for you and I to escape!"

The reaver grunted. "I know that, mrem, but the warlord here is also our best chance. They wouldn't dare harm a scale on his ugly head. If we can get out of the encampment, I can find us places where even those scevan they have for tracking won't be able to pick up our—" Kain suddenly stilled. "Do you hear something?"

Feryln had already learned that of all humans, only Theron Kain appeared to have ears superior to mrem. Try as he might, he could not hear anything and, after several seconds, Feryln shook his head. Kain frowned, stepping nearer to the tent entrance. After another moment, he, too, shook his head.

"Wishful thinking, I suppose. I kept trying to think of some diversion, something that would keep our friends out there occupied, but I'd have needed an army for—there! You hear that?"

This time Feryln heard it. Anyone could have heard the horn now blaring. It repeated over and over, others joining in. Shouts rose up from around the tent. Voices began giving commands.

"What is happening?" the mrem whispered.

"If I didn't know better, I'd swear . . . I'd swear that our warlord's dear horde is under attack!"

At this, Baskillus struggled with his bonds. Theron Kain quickly struck the Lizcanth on the back of his head with the flat of the blade. As hard as the reptile's skin and skull were, the blow still managed to stun him. With a muffled groan, Baskillus fell to his knees.

"Who would dare attack so massive a force as this?"

The reaver shook his head. "Can't be Fuego! They wouldn't have had the time to march here, not even with the aid of every fire mage in the kingdom!" Brow furrowed, Kain slipped to the entrance. Using the tip of his blade, he pushed aside one of the flaps just enough to peer out. "Interesting. . . ."

Feryln forgot both Rowlen and Baskillus. "What is?"

"Seems your friends the gargoyles have come back, mrem, and in good force!"

He ran to join the reaver, glancing out. Sure enough, gargoyles filled the sky. They ranged in size, some of them no more than half as tall as Feryln, others nearly as great as their shadowy monarch. The mrem tried to locate the gargoyle king, but, of course, that proved impossible.

"This could be the break we need," Theron Kain remarked. "All we have to—"

From behind them came a muted but savage growl. Baskillus had risen and the immense Lizcanth had snapped most of the ropes holding his arms. He twisted around to face the two, breathing heavily but hardly weary from his attempt.

Feryln leapt at him, hoping to throw the reptile to the ground before Baskillus managed to remove the ropes keeping him from calling out. However, the Lizcanth warlord managed to free his hands and met his mrem adversary head on. Feryln found himself at a distinct disadvantage;

not only did Baskillus tower over him, but he stood nearly twice as wide.

"Move away from him, mrem!" Kain urged. "Let me take him!"

Feryln could not have obliged even had he so desired. Lord Baskillus turned both himself and the mrem around, assuring that the young warrior remained between him and the more experienced human at all times. Feryln felt fortunate that he at least kept the Lizcanth too occupied to remove the makeshift muzzle. Despite the intensity of the struggle, Baskillus could still not call out.

"My lord!" another reptile called. "My lord! The gargoyles, they attack!"

A shorter Lizcanth flew through the tent flaps, stopping dead when he noted the pair struggling. With a hiss, he pulled free a sword and started toward Feryln and Baskillus, only to be met by Kain, who nearly severed his hand with the first stroke.

The reaver in combat with the officer, Feryln had to rely on his own abilities . . . and, unfortunately, against Baskillus he found them wanting. The Lizcanth slowly stretched the mrem's arms apart, clearly with the intention of eventually breaking them. He would be able to do it, too, if Feryln had judged the warlord's phenomenal strength accurately. It seemed, too, that nothing, especially not Feryln, would be able to stop him.

Theron Kain dispatched the Lizcanth officer, but before he could even remove his blade from his foe's chest, a second reptile came in search of the first. This one leaped at the human, already armed with one of the wicked claw weapons. He shouted a warning, but the noise level beyond the tent had already grown to chaotic levels, drowning out the lizard.

Kain backed away, the Lizcanth's weapon giving the scaly warrior a much greater reach than the tall reaver. Feryln, meanwhile, fell to one knee, forced there by Baskillus's weight alone. The warlord wore a triumphant expression. One hand slipped free, caught Feryln by the throat. The mrem gasped, then tried to reach for the ruby in the Lizcanth's own throat. Tearing the stone from Rowlen had ended that threat; perhaps if he could do the same to Baskillus, the warlord, too, would die.

However, with Baskillus the ruby not only had the protection of depth, it also had scales crowded against it, further shielding the stone from Feryln's desperate attempt. The Lizcanth knew that, too—a muffled laugh escaping his bound jaws. He squeezed tighter, certain to finish off the foolish mrem in but a few seconds.

Furred hands with strong claws suddenly flung themselves around Baskillus's neck. The Lizcanth released his victim as a strong arm pulled his head back. Released from death, Feryln fell back, unable to do anything more but try to breathe. The world swam and for a moment he could make out nothing. Then, when his vision at last cleared, the mrem saw who had saved him.

Impossibly alive, Rowlen struggled to maintain his hold on the warlord's throat. The mrem warrior braced himself on the Lizcanth's back, pushing with his knee and giving himself more leverage. Baskillus hissed, first trying to grab at his attacker, then attempting to shake him off.

"Go . . . Fer—" Rowlen managed, each word forced out.

Someone seized Feryln from behind, he started to struggle, but then heard Kain's voice near his ear.

"Easy, mrem! Come on! This is our one chance!" The reaver, blood splattered over him, started to drag his companion to the back of the tent.

"I cannot . . . leave Rowlen!"

"You'd better! There's more of the reptiles coming!"

True to his warning, a pair of lizards burst through the tent, their warlord's prolonged absence having at last come to their attention. The reaver used Feryln's weakness and shock to his advantage, practically throwing the young mrem under the side of the tent, then following him.

The guards rushed not toward them but rather Baskillus, who clearly risked an imminent broken neck. Rowlen had a literal death grip on the Lizcanth lord, the mrem warrior's eyes already glazing. As Kain pushed him through, Feryln thought he already saw the life gone from his companion. Rowlen had pushed himself beyond all Feryln could have ever imagined, his final sacrifice perhaps saving the pair.

Outside the tent, the mercenary brooked no hesitation from Feryln. "This way! Keep low! They'll be after us in a minute!"

Perhaps they would be, but not many. As they

darted from spot to spot, Feryln watched the skies. The gargoyles were everywhere, diving and flying. Some carried weapons, others large boulders and the like which they rained down upon Ganth's horrific legions. The timing of the attack still impressed the mrem, almost as if the gargoyle king had planned it because of Feryln's and Kain's presence. An absurd notion, though. For what reasons would the leathery monarch of the caverns bother with them? Jarric, perhaps, but hardly a reaver and a mrem.

They reached the edge of the encampment surprisingly unhindered, but Feryln soon understood why. The Lizcanth seemed the organizers, the most dedicated of Ganth's minions. When the gargoyles had attacked, the swiftest ones to react had been the reptiles and many of them had been forced to organize the others. Left to their own devices, the ogre and kobold guards proved insufficient to their tasks, leaving great gaps in the perimeter.

Into the woods the pair ran. Kain led him along a staggered trail, possibly designed to confuse any trackers. The reaver paused only once, to rearrange the papers he had stolen from Baskillus. Feryln had forgotten the charts and felt grateful that the human had managed to salvage them. Baskillus and Ganth might recall some of the information, but certainly not all of it.

The sounds of battle continued as they moved deeper southeast. Kain had not wanted to go that direction, preferring a straighter, much more southern route to Fuego, but the landscape fought against them. They had also run across traces of at least one band of scouts or hunters who might still be in the area.

Now and then a gargoyle fluttered past. At one point, both paused, hiding behind tree trunks as two gargoyles and three of the multi-limbed floaters struggled in the air. One gargoyle managed to cut through the thick hide of a tentacled monstrosity, but the second perished, caught between the strangling appendages of the other pair. The remaining gargoyle fled back in the direction of the encampment, the two floaters following.

The twisted body of the winged creature lay not far from where they had to pass. Feryln eyed the dead gargoyle, pitying it in death. Mrem and gargoyles fought when they met, but now those same enemies battled creatures much more foul. How much damage the aerial ones would inflict, Feryln did not know, but that damage would come with its own cost, a cost his own people had already paid. He extended his claws, wishing he knew whether Rowlen had at least finished the dread Baskillus before himself dying.

On and on they ran, Feryln amazed at the human's endurance. Kain dodged around thick trees, avoided huge rocks that suddenly seemed to pop up before the pair, and adjusted for gaps in the uneven ground, all without even slowing. Feryln had not thought much of the potential of humans when he first met them, but in many ways they had surprised him, especially the spellcaster. City-raised, Jarric had proven himself as determined as any mountain mrem. However, Feryln hoped that the mage's determination had not led to his death. As for Kain, he would have impressed any of the mrem's people, not only with his skills, but with his sense of honor that clearly ran beyond the limits of his pay. Theron Kain might claim himself no longer to be a knight, but from what Feryln had gleaned, the reaver stood among the most dedicated, possibly even more dedicated than the paladins.

At last, Feryln had to beg for a rest. Kain gave in grudgingly, eyes constantly shifting back along their path.

"Can't stay here long, mrem! One way or another, they'll be on our trail before very long."

"Do you think . . . do you think Lord Baskillus is dead?" As Feryln gulped air, he noticed that the reaver barely seemed to be breathing hard.

"Maybe. Your friend surprised me, mrem. Somehow he pulled himself out of wherever that stone sent him and did what he could. Wouldn't surprise me if he took the lizard lord with him, but we can't relax even if that proves the case. Baskillus's officers will have known about the charts; his successor will want them."

"What do you plan to do with them?"

The reaver captain looked uneasy. "I've been debating that for some time, mrem. It would be good if these made it back to Fuego; not only would they warn the city about possible shortcomings, but someone made notes about the horde's strength as well. Could be some use to the defenders." He shrugged. "At the very least, if I can just keep them out of the lizards' claws, it'll put them at more of a disadvantage when they attack the city."

"Do you plan to give up on Master Jarric, then?"

"I never implied that!" snapped Kain. A little more subdued, he added, "I said I'm still debating the best course of action."

He started to say more, but then twin howls cut through the silence of the forest. Kain and Feryln looked back. They could not see the beasts who had made the noise, but both knew what it meant. From what they had seen of the encampment, the odds that many loose scevan remained in this area were minuscule. If any of the twin-headed beasts had picked up their trail, then it had been because someone had urged the scevan to the task.

"Trackers, already!" Kain muttered. "Someone's very eager to find the charts, us, or both! If Baskillus is dead, he's got himself one excellent successor! I'd have bet we still had at least another hour before they could've even organized themselves for a hunt."

Without another word, the mercenary started running again. Feryln took a deep breath, then hurried after.

Another set of howls cut through his nerves, this time nearer. The hunters were closing in on them . . . and much swifter than Feryln liked. He doubted that he could run much longer, even with the brief rest. Soon . . . soon they might have to turn and fight.

Soon they might die.

Yet again Feryln heard a sound, this one a shout that set him on edge and nearly caused him to stumble into Kain. It had been a Lizcanth voice and, while unintelligible across so great a distance, the young mrem had thought he recognized it. Yes, soon they might very well die if Feryln had heard true.

The voice had sounded like Lord Baskillus.

Ganth would have his skin. Ganth would literally peel the Lizcanth's armored hide from his living body, unmindful of the screams, perhaps even reveling in them.

"Hurry, you plodding foolsss!" he screamed, outpacing all but the scevan and their handlers. A hundred warriors, nearly all of them Lizcanth but a few hastily conscripted ogres and two floaters, followed behind Lord Baskillus, trying to keep up with the giant warlord's great steps. If he could have, the reptilian commander would have left them all behind, hunting down the foul mrem and the deadly human by himself. They had brought shame down upon him, shame that the dark one would punish unless Baskillus personally redeemed himself by leading the hunt. His officers could manage the horde now that the gargoyles had been repulsed. He needed to be here, to be the one to make the capture.

He thanked the eternal sunlight that the black wizard had not yet contacted him. Whatever held Ganth's attention, Baskillus hoped it would continue to do so for quite some time, even days. Baskillus dared not confront his master until he had the mrem, the human, and the precious maps in his claws again.

The human Baskillus would slowly tear limb from limb, Lizcanth healers keeping the captive alive for as long as possible. The mrem he could not slay for now, although a few strong bruises would assuage some of the Lizcanth lord's frustration. Once Ganth finished with that one, though, Baskillus intended to request him returned. He would dine on the cat, savoring every bloody bite.

Tail slashing at the tree trunks as he passed, the warlord peered through the woods, seeking some sign, even a glimpse of the prey. In one hand he carried a huge, twin-bladed ax and in the other, a long sword only one as strong as Baskillus could wield. This time, he intended to be well armed. Memories of the human's sword and, later, the mrem's arm, continued to haunt him. He would not be caught off guard again.

It still disturbed him that the other mrem had lived long enough to nearly choke him to death. Baskillus's throat still hurt and despite his determination and endurance, the Lizcanth lord's breath occasionally came out in gasps, all that due to the dead mrem. He had not even had the decency to let Baskillus or the guards skewer him before he died of his other wounds. Only the gaping hole where the ruby had once been buried had eventually saved the warlord, the same gaping wound that marked how the mrem had been able to attack him in the first place.

The bloody ruby the feline Rowlen had worn now rested in a pouch at Baskillus's side, destined to be used on the other cursed mrem. Baskillus had never tried using the same ruby twice; the matter had never arisen. However, he expected that the power of Ganth remained sufficient to utilize the stone again. If not, the Lizcanth would batter the mrem unconscious with the flat of his ax and drag the limp body back to his tent.

One of the scevan suddenly twisted to the right, picking up a strong scent. The others followed. Baskillus looked on with eagerness. He had chosen from the best of the beasts, wanting no mistakes, no distractions. The prey would not escape him.

If only he could get his warriors to keep pace, though. . . .

"My lord!" one of the handlers hissed with enthusiasm. "Look there! Look there!"

A figure, barely glimpsed. Perhaps only a trick of the mind, but doubtful. Baskillus summoned the floaters. "Ssseize, but do not kill! Command it I do!"

The bizarre creatures drifted off, rapidly outpacing even the eager warlord. Soon he would have his prisoner and the maps back. Baskillus contemplated sparing the human, too, in case he carried more vital information about Fuego, but bloodlust almost immediately pushed that idea away. It would be troublesome enough for the warlord to keep his head when capturing the mrem. Baskillus needed to vent his fury and the human would serve just perfect for that. Ganth certainly could not blame him if the one prey chose to fight back, which the Lizcanth felt certain the man would do. Baskillus would just be defending himself when he slowly tore his adversary to bloody pieces.

A squeal caused him to stop short. One of the

floaters flew back, its path erratic, the creature spraying life fluids everywhere. Three of its tentacles had been severed near the main body and a dagger hilt projected from the center of the mass. The warriors watched, even Baskillus was fascinated, as the dying floater at last collided with a tree, collapsing into an odorous heap.

The second floater did not follow after the first, but already the Lizcanth suspected that it, too, lay dead, possibly with a twin of this dagger buried deep. A loss to his forces, but Baskillus would have risked a hundred of the tentacled horrors if it meant he captured the mrem and the human. Unfortunately, the gargoyles' assault had kept the rest of the floaters and their ilk too busy and scattered. Baskillus had been forced to act with haste if he hoped to catch the pair.

Still, the floaters would have delayed and tired the two yet more. Baskillus sniffed the air, catching a brief scent. While his nose might not be as sensitive as that of a scevan, he thought he smelled mrem blood, which meant at least one had fresh injuries.

"Mine you are," he hissed, picking up his pace. Now the warlord no longer cared whether the rest could keep up. The handlers and the scevan would keep pace with him; they would be sufficient. Perhaps he would even let the lupine horrors tear the human apart. Now there would be good sport.

Again a figure flashed in sight. The human warrior, stumbling as if hurt! Baskillus smiled. Yes, he would do that, even if he risked the mrem, too. His blood lust had gotten the best of him. The Lizcanth wanted to see their torn bodies scattered over the mountain. Nothing would please him more.

"Releassse them!" he commanded. "The ssscent they have! Releassse them now!"

His minions obeyed. Five scevan rushed off directly after the distant human. Lord Baskillus laughed, eyes bright. He pushed himself harder, wanting to be there for the screams, both those of the human and the foul mrem.

As for the possibility of Ganth's ire, the warlord would make some excuse. He had done it before . . . especially when it came to slaughtering mrem.

Chapter 15

GANTH HAD NO NEED FOR HER NOW, HAVING at last decided for himself that Zyn remained loyal. For that the vampire had been grateful, even if what he had decided was no longer true. Zyn knew that among those who had chosen to join the wizard's cause were many of her kind, the possibility of so many helpless humans an enticing prospect, but she had lived around the mortals too much, especially in the years prior to the destruction of Ebonyr. For all that they could be prey, they could be fascinating as well. Ganth himself had given her a temporary replacement for the human blood she craved had assisted her in being able to observe them close up without desiring their lives.

Zyn had learned so much, in fact, that she rarely took the blood of humans any more. Sometimes there were moments when she could not resist the call, but more often than not she preyed on animals of any sort or even forced herself to drink the sluggish blood of Lizcanth or the foul soup flowing through the ogres' veins. Ganth knew nothing about her conversion, but if he had, Zyn realized that he would have eyed her with more than a little suspicion. A vampire who could not bring herself to seek her normal prey might lack the will in other matters, most notably obeying the commands of the one who had once been her lover and now remained purely her master.

At the moment, Zyn disobeyed many of Ganth's current commands, foremost the one he had given but a short time ago. He had wanted her to remain nearby, should his questioning of the mortal require her in some way. Since she could serve no purpose during such a time, Zyn had suspected that Ganth wanted to erase any possible interests she might have by showing her Jarric bending to his will.

While she had at first toyed with Jarric because he had been a mage, his freshness, then his determination, had soon attracted her more than Zyn had expected. If she could never be a part of his existence, Zyn could at least see to it that he did not fall victim to Ganth. To do that, however, she had to be willing to completely betray her former lover . . . which was why the vampire haunted the forest beyond Ebonyr now, searching for the shard. She would retrieve it, but for Jarric, not for Ganth. The vampire had witnessed just enough of the mortal's skills to suspect that, with the shard, he could end Ganth's reign forever.

If not, both she and Jarric would suffer the most terrible of punishments her former lover could devise.

Twice already Zyn had searched the landscape between the castle and the area where they had first materialized. Still nothing. She wondered if Azur had lied after all; the dragon did not desire Ganth to gain any more power. Surely he of all creatures would have reason to keep the shard from his master. Yet, even the blue leviathan greatly respected the lich's might. Azur had no desire to feel Ganth's wrath, probably not even for something so precious as this shard. No, the dragon had likely not hidden the artifact. That meant that it lay lost somewhere, perhaps never to be found for another thousand years.

Zyn glanced back at Ebonyr, knowing already how long it had been since Ganth had begun the questioning. The knowledge proved enough to send the vampire hunting again, this time with even more urgency.

He could not scream again. He had no strength to scream again.

Jarric screamed.

"Again. . . ." came the lich's graveyard voice. "Tell me again that you do not know where you left it."

Jarric hung, suspended by invisible shackles that left him spread-eagled in the air. He floated in the center of the largest of Ganth's dungeons, a dubious honor at best. He had been here for several hours now, most of them in the company of the black wizard.

Only a disturbing black fire ball illuminated the cell, revealing in its awful light the moss-encrusted walls, the moist stone floor, and, in one far corner, the remains of some animal long dead. No windows existed save for the tiny one in the door, which accounted for the dungeon smelling of decay and death even after so many years of disuse.

The young fire mage gasped air. His throat burned, his head throbbed. Outwardly, little so far had changed. Someone just arriving might have thought that Ganth had only begun his tortures, but in truth, Jarric had suffered for hours, almost from the moment he had been transported here. Ganth preferred spells that wracked from within, using his magic like that of a mentor.

"I . . . don't . . . don't . . ." Jarric managed.

Ganth of the Black Flame tilted his head, waiting. When Jarric did not continue, the lich calmly said, "I almost believe you . . . which makes matters all the more terrible for you, Jarric of Fuego."

The young mage flew backward across the cell, colliding hard with the wall behind him. Jarric cried out as his back threatened to shatter under the force, nearly losing consciousness. The invisible bonds sealed his wrists and ankles to the stone, keeping him in a hanging position just an inch or two above the floor. Jarric did not look up, hoping that Ganth might think him beyond questioning for now.

The lich glided forward, undeterred by the attempt of his young counterpart. A twisted, bony hand reached up, tugging on Jarric's hair in order to force the prisoner to look. Jarric did his best to keep from looking away even though the flames within the eye sockets unnerved him greatly.

"If you do not know where my shard is, then you haven't much use left, Jarric of Fuego. Then, I only need consider what to do with your remains." Ganth let Jarric's head drop. "And Azur hungers."

The black wizard went to the door of the cell, turning back at the entrance to stare at his prisoner. Jarric lifted his head up just enough to stare with some defiance back at Ganth. The lich, though, simply chuckled, then departed. A Lizcanth bolted the door shut, not that they had anything to fear from the imprisoned spellcaster. Without his medallion with the ruby, which Zyn had turned over to her master, Jarric could do very little. In fact, he had to admit he could do nothing at all except wait for whatever fate Ganth chose for him.

What had happened to the shard? The last time that Jarric had paid it any mind had been in the ruins. Had it been knocked free of his belt just before he had fallen through the portal? He almost believed that, in which case the guardian must truly be laughing at him now.

Perhaps it had not been left there. Perhaps Azur had it. That appeared to be a more likely scenario. Azur had no love for the one he called master and if the dragon could secrete the shard in some place where Ganth would never find it, the leviathan would have won a victory of sorts against the lich.

"Azur," he whispered. Yes, the dragon probably had it, the same dragon who would eat him when at last Ganth tired of asking questions that had no answers.

Pain wracked Jarric's head again. He closed his eyes, trying to rest. At the moment he knew not what else to do. Ganth had in his hands the key to Jarric's own power, the ruby so valuable to any fire mage, and without that all of the young spellcaster's education meant nothing. No mage could cast a spell without a stone, not even—

Not even Ganth? Despite his pain and weariness, Jarric frowned. Where did the dark one carry his ruby? Jarric had seen no medallion, no stone in Ganth's hand. How could Ganth cast even the smallest spell without a ruby?

He kept his eyes shut tight, letting his body recoup while he pondered the secrets of the lich. At some point, Jarric discovered that he must have drifted off, for suddenly he realized that someone called quietly to him from the door.

"Mage . . . Jarric . . . please wake . . ."

Zyn. She peered at him, her beautiful face framed by the tiny window. He wondered what she wanted, his muddled mind uncertain as to whether he had decided her to be an ally or an enemy. In the end, Jarric chose simply to stare, waiting for her to make the move.

She did, slipping into the cell without a sound. The guards had conveniently disappeared and for a moment he wondered if she had killed them. For all her appearance of gentleness, Jarric could not forget that she retained the strength inherent in all vampires, the same strength with which she had kept him on his knees when Azur had discovered them.

"What . . ." He could barely speak. "What . . ."

"Drink. Quickly!"

She thrust a small water sack to his mouth, from which the mage greedily drank. The cool liquid coursing down his throat woke him more, enabling Jarric's mind to begin to work in a more normal manner. Now he wondered why Zyn had come, what she hoped to accomplish with this mysterious visit. Did Ganth know? Had he hoped that Zyn could uncover what his torture had not?

Satiated, Jarric indicated that she could pull the nearly empty sack away. He started to ask her the purpose for her visit, but suddenly Zyn's mouth pressed against his, silencing him for a very long time. Jarric could not and, in fact, had no desire, to resist. If she toyed with him for Ganth, it would not change his overall fate and at least it would leave him with something to savor.

"I prayed he would not play with you long, sweet Jarric, but Ganth was always thorough! I'm so sorry!"

"Why are you here?"

"For you, of course!" She briefly glanced behind her. "The guards will do my will for a short time and recall nothing later."

His hopes rose slightly even though for the most part he still believed her to be loyal to the lich. "You're going to free me?"

She looked downcast. "I dare not! I . . . forgive me, dear Jarric! If I try to break the magical bonds Ganth's fashioned, he'll surely know it immediately!"

Jarric grimaced. "Then what can you do for me?"

Her hand pressed against his side. "I can give you this."

He looked down, his eyes widening. In her palm she held the ruby shard. Jarric almost said so out loud, but Zyn put a finger against his lips, silencing him. As he watched, she slipped it into one of the voluminous pockets of his robe.

"Why the pocket? Why not place it in my hand so that I can use it to cast a spell immediately?" the puzzled spellcaster finally whispered.

"If you hold it now and try to cast a spell, Ganth will sense it and surely come before you can free yourself. I know this. However, later they will surely unbind you before you are dealt with. Since for now Ganth is convinced that you don't have it, he'll not search again. Use it then as you will . . . but use it."

"You could've given it to him, Zyn."

She nodded, unable, for the moment, to look at him. "And once I might have."

Before he could say more, she turned and kissed him. Again, contrary to legend, Jarric found nothing chilly about the vampire's lips.

Without another word, Zyn slipped away, not even looking back as she left the cell.

Jarric watched the door for some time, hoping for her return. Zyn did not come back, although the guards did. The two Lizcanth returned to their positions without a word or a glance to indicate that they recalled anything odd about their recent behavior.

The power to defeat Ganth lay in his pocket. With the shard, Jarric felt certain that even he could bring the lich's reign to an absolute end. He cursed himself for not having used it sooner, his awe and lack of experience keeping him from even touching it. Master Prymias, whom Jarric had begun to wish now hung in his place, would not have hesitated to utilize the artifact despite not knowing its full capabilities and the dangers inherent.

They will surely unbind you before you are dealt with, Zyn had said. Without a stone, Ganth considered him less than useless. All the younger mage would need would be a few seconds' opportunity. Then he could confront Ganth.

That he might still die did occur to Jarric, but, compared with the earlier choice, he found himself willing to take the risk. The thought of trying to escape to Fuego he rejected almost immediately. There would never be a better opportunity for anyone to destroy the lich before he pushed on with his war.

I have to do it! There's no one else. . . . Jarric exhaled, thinking about Zyn again. She still risked herself; Ganth would wonder how Jarric had come to retrieve the shard since he had spent all his time in this cell. The black wizard already suspected her attraction to the human. It would not take much for him to turn on the beautiful vampire. None of her powers would save Zyn then. For her sake as well as everyone else's, Jarric could not falter.

He shut his eyes, this time determined to get as much rest as possible. Every fiber of his being ached, but Jarric tried to ignore the pain. He had to keep his mind fully on the task at hand . . . or he would only be the first of many to die in the days ahead.

Ganth stared into the black flames, seeing Fuego in all its present glory. The kingdom had grown since he had known it, grown fat and careless. After he conquered it, Ganth would change all that, shape the ruins and what remained of the inhabitants into a kingdom such as not had been witnessed on Delos since before the fall of technology.

Those mages he could not bend to his control would be publicly executed, of course, as would most of the other survivors. Only a select few with the potential to be his magical legion would survive. Under his control, they would aid his horde in sweeping over the rest of Delos . . . and from there even the Laria would prove no terrible threat.

But I must have the shard! Already he had to move with care, preserve his power for what he required, not what he desired. With the shard and the dark spells he knew, the lich could later expand his power, but, for now, caution might be required. Of late, he had not kept in contact with Baskillus for that very reason. The Lizcanth warlord knew his task and so far had performed it well, although with the unexpected discovery of the young spellcaster, the two mrem that had been captured had become expendable. Ganth desired to waste no more power on their ilk. He had enough of the cursed cat people under his will, enough to enable him to trick other villages into lowering their defenses.

Of the mrem, nothing would remain in the end but their bones. The lich uneasily stroked the scarf, correcting himself. *No, not even the bones would remain.*

He still recalled the surprise, the realization that his throat had been torn out. Ganth still saw the mrem who had done it, a warrior with fur much like that of the younger cat who had accompanied Jarric of Fuego. He wished he had ordered Baskillus simply to kill the mrem immediately and be done with it. Although Ganth would not admit it to himself, Feryln's vague resemblance to a long dead warrior unnerved the lich, made him fear for his throat again.

The mrem could be dealt with later, though. Ganth dismissed the flames, rising and moving to the balcony. Below, he could see his servants, Lizcanth, skeletons, ghouls, ogres, and more, pouring across the mountain landscape, tracing back the route Azur had taken. In the distance he could even see the blue giant circling endlessly around the region. Azur had protested his part in this search, claiming there were those on the ground more worthy of it, but a simple touch of pain had changed the dragon's mind.

There would come a time when the dragon would have to be removed. Another, much younger dragon could be used in his place, one trained earlier to be subservient. Azur spoke too often of his taste for fire mages, any fire mage.

The dragon suddenly banked, turning toward Ebonyr. Ganth would have frowned had he the lips. He had ordered the dragon not to return without the shard. Ganth touched the scarf gently, but decided to wait to hear what the leviathan had to say before he invoked punishment.

It took but moments for Azur to cover the distance. He landed on the balcony eyeing the lich with caution. By now, even the stubborn dragon had to know what he risked.

"Hail, oh, Master!"

"I . . . presume you do not have the shard."

"No," rumbled the beast with the slightest wariness. "No, and I do not think it out there at all!"

If Azur had wanted to choose the worst news to report, he could not have chosen better. Ganth stroked the scarf around his throat. "Why do you say that? It must be there!"

"Look there!" Azur indicated the legions scouring the landscape. "They have searched for the third time and still they find nothing! Even ogres should be able to find a pouch or a crystalline shard after so thorough a hunt! Either it was never there or someone found it before this lot began!"

"Someone?"

The blue leviathan blinked, looking around. "I have not seen Zyn of late! Does she also search?"

Ganth understood the insinuation but did not react to it. He had his own thoughts concerning his dear Zyn, many of them dark. "She's no concern of yours, dragon. Your only concern has to do with finding the shard."

"It is not out there."

"Search anyway."

Azur hissed, but bowed his head. "Yes, oh, Master!"

The lich stepped back as the draconian giant stretched his tremendous wings and took to the air once more. Ganth did not move until Azur had become a tiny dot once more perpetually circling the mountains surrounding Ebonyr. Then Ganth slowly turned, already aware that another stood not far behind him.

"You hear my thoughts," the black wizard commented, "or you heard Azur's booming voice."

"Dear Ganth, when have I paid any attention to the mutterings of that arrogant, lazy lizard?" Zyn approached him, every movement that had once enticed the fire mage now seeming to mock his dread existence.

When she drew near enough, he suddenly cupped her chin in his hand, noting the slight flinching when he touched her. "And where have you been, my adoring Zyn? I commanded that you stay near in case I required you."

"But you didn't and I grew so bored! You know how I am, dear Ganth! I must move, I must fly. . . ."

Ganth squeezed her chin harder. "And did you fly beyond the walls of Ebonyr? Did you fly below . . . where the others search, futilely, it seems, for the shard?"

"I've been out, yes, Ganth," she looked down. "But you know that I must feed."

He released her chin. "So you must. Perhaps

I should let you feed on the young mage. I might enjoy watching that."

"I fed well. I won't need to again for some time."

"How unfortunate." Ganth came around behind her and put his hands on her pale shoulders, noting the tension in her body. He knew that she feared him, as nearly every creature feared him, but that Zyn, who once had gladly done his bidding, now could scarcely bear his touch further fueled the black flames within. "I have neglected you, my darling Zyn. I've pushed with other matters so long and so hard, you've had nothing but your thoughts with which to occupy yourself."

She amazed him by actually putting a hand on his own. "I've understood, dear Ganth! You must do this. You said so yourself!"

"Yes . . . I must. The Laria's pact comes near to its end and with it . . . me. The shard will prevent that and Fuego, loyal, conniving Fuego, who turned on me, will be razed for its crimes! My army will cover all of Delos, forcing creatures of light and darkness both to bow to my desires . . . and you will be at my side, my darling Zyn."

"Where else would I be?"

"Yes." He squeezed, eliciting from her a sudden gasp. "Where would you be? Nowhere without me, Zyn. I could not accept otherwise. Not at all."

She remained silent and at last the lich released her, stepping back into the darkness of his hall. Zyn remained out on the balcony, perhaps thinking it better for her if she left Ganth to his thoughts. Had she known some of those thoughts, the vampire might have trembled.

Zyn would bear watching, Ganth decided. Azur might have been trying to foist off some of the blame for the shard's loss, but he had raised points which the wizard could not ignore. Had she been outside earlier, hunting with a better knowledge of where the shard might be? Possible. Foolish, but possible. In the end, Ganth always discovered the truth.

In the end, he always dealt with those who betrayed him . . . as Fuego would soon learn.

Chapter 16

NO ONE SAW CASTLANA DUMARCUS AS she approached the sanctum of the mentor, Menthusalan. No one saw her because Castlana desired that and when Castlana desired something, it generally came about. This visit, though, might be one of the great, rare exceptions.

She had gathered what information she could, but the trail had ended. All that remained for her had been Menthusalan himself. Outwardly, he revealed nothing that suggested something amiss, yet the majordomo felt the truth could only be learned from him . . . even if she had to force it from his lips.

She had chosen the hours when those of Delos generally slept, deciding that the fewer she needed to deal with, the better. The locks meant nothing to her, nor did the lesser spells protecting the entrances. Castlana had trained long and hard to be foremost in her work.

A short time later, she stood before the door to the chambers of Menthusalan himself. He might be awake; he might be asleep. Whichever the case, Castlana Dumarcus did not care. The crimson-tressed officer touched the tiny, enchanted dagger at her belt. She would end this tonight, no matter what it entailed.

In silence, Castlana opened the door.

"Do come in, my dear woman."

She froze in the doorway. Menthusalan sat in a chair at the other end of the chamber, book spread across his lap. If he had been reading, his eyesight had to be excellent, for the single light in the room stood several feet from him. The shadows caused by the dim light seemed to gather around the mentor in a most unnatural manner.

Castlana immediately surveyed the room, looking for any possible threat besides the man himself. Even more orderly and meticulously cared for than the chambers of her master, Menthusalan's abode met with her approval. Every book, every scroll, had been cataloged and shelved accordingly, the same also done with the jarred items in the case on the right side of the room. Castlana's eyes briefly alighted on the artifacts atop that case, but almost immediately she dismissed them as nothing to fear.

Other than the padded chair in which the mentor sat and the small table upon which she suspected he performed some of his spells, the immaculate chamber held little more despite its fairly large expanse. Only the much too deep shadows disturbed the majordomo, seeming to move as they did even when the light did not flicker. However, they did not bother her so much as Menthusalan himself, who appeared to have been waiting for her arrival.

"I do not bite, Castlana Dumarcus," he finally added, smiling in a manner that hinted otherwise.

Annoyed at her brief show of uncertainty, she entered, keeping one hand casually by the dagger. The door shut of its own accord, but Castlana had long grown used to such tricks from mages. All that interested her was Menthusalan and what he had in mind. The mentor watched her as she neared, but trying to read his eyes proved impossible. In the shadows, they appeared to be little more than black pits.

"Please be seated."

"I'll stand."

"As you like." Menthusalan steepled his fingers. Castlana's brow furrowed. His manner reminded her little of the man she knew. While Menthusalan had spoken little to her over the years, she had observed him well enough to know him inside and out. What sat before her might have looked on the outside like the mentor, but inside . . .

"Aah, my dear Castlana! Always the loyal shadow, the protector of the master! Deadly and beauteous, a creature of the darkness! I would make you my mate were it at all possible!"

His words jarred her, so incongruous were they to the situation. "You compliment me, but I must decline."

He chuckled, another very contrary response. The shadows played around his face. "Does Master Prymias of the Ruby Eye know that you are a mentor, dear Castlana?"

Castlana's hand grazed the dagger . . . and stopped there. Try as she might, she could not grasp the handle. Her fingers, her entire hand, felt numb.

"Now I would surely not reveal such to your master! How could I . . . aah . . . without making him wonder just how I knew!" The slim mentor put aside his book and rose, gazing down at her. He reached out, touched her cheek with one finger. "Yes, a lovely killing spirit! Would that there were more like you! That fool Ganth . . . now there's one to understand only slaughter, not the hunt, not the game! Not like us, dear Castlana, eh?"

She should have pulled away, would have pulled away except that she could not. Her entire body resisted her commands. She had expected to possibly face Menthusalan's might, but—but the man had no stone in sight, no chain around his neck indicating some medallion. How could he be casting spells then?

"Mentors only come from Dismas. That's what they say, do they not? That's like saying gargoyles only live in caves, you see. Totally inaccurate. They may live in cliff sides or in old ruins . . . many delightful places! Mentors, too, can develop anywhere, especially in secret."

That he knew so much about her frightened the officer. She had always kept her secrets well hidden. No one could have known. Even her parents had not known of her secret interest in the power of mentors or how, after failing with fire magic, she had discovered an aptitude for something else. As with everything she had done,

Castlana Dumarcus had entrusted her training to herself, enabling her to achieve heights the more rigidly-taught mages would never have tried.

"And all you would need is a stone, a pearl . . . hidden ever from sight." Menthusalan let his hand drift below her neck to the center of her rib cage, index finger tracing the path all the way down. It paused exactly where she knew it would pause. "Hidden here?"

His nail looked well-trimmed and short and yet it cut through jacket and blouse with little effort. Menthusalan used the finger to move aside the material, revealing what lay beneath . . . a single perfect pearl bound to Castlana, always in touch with her skin. She had learned how to use the pearl so, leaving her hands free. Castlana Dumarcus also knew how to cast her spells in perfect silence, something it took many mages years to learn. No one she had come across could cast spells quite the way she could, making Castlana justifiably proud of herself . . . until now.

"Yes, so very clever." Menthusalan walked slowly around her. "As would be expected of you."

More and more as she listened to him, Castlana neared a conclusion. She did not want to believe it, but Menthusalan's contrary manner, his contrary actions, all pointed to it.

"Who are you?" the majordomo blurted. "Who are you inside of this man?"

From behind her came an unearthly chuckle. "As I said, so very, very clever! Perhaps I should reconsider making you my mate! The others are such dullards, not a quick mind among the lot! You, you are the only one worthy of me."

He came around to the front again, very close now. Castlana could feel his breath on her face, but although she tried her best, still she could not see through the shadows obscuring Menthusalan's eyes. "And do you plan to kill me?"

"Kill you?" he chuckled again. "I? So trusted an ally? I've worked so hard, so long, to make you and yours see the danger, see the threat, of Ganth Kazarian and you think I'd kill you? If it served my purpose, yes, but I think you an understanding sort of female! I think you'd rather see the lich defeated, preferably burnt to little tiny ashes!" The face of the mentor smiled again. "I do so love a good fire . . . it's so cleansing!"

Menthusalan stepped back to the chair, seating himself. He waved one hand in Castlana's direction and suddenly she could move once more. The majordomo did not reach for the dagger, knowing the folly of such a move against the power within the mentor.

"You will leave this chamber, leave this building, Castlana Dumarcus. You will report none of this. Your search ended with nothing to prove. If Menthusalan, dear Menthusalan, has been acting strangely, it is merely because of the strain."

"Why should I do that?"

"Because if you interfere at this juncture, we may all bow to Ganth . . . before he cuts off our heads. Events are in motion, as they say, and if young Jarric and the mrem follow their paths, we may yet see the end of Ebonyr." He shook his head. "If only your precious mages had been more thorough the first time!"

Oddly, despite her fears concerning that which possessed the mentor, Castlana found herself believing his words. She had never distrusted her feelings before and even now she could not. Still, Castlana could not help asking, "This plan . . . is it necessary to sacrifice Jarric and the others? I've men who—"

"Man, really. The honor of reavers has fallen to a new low. The rest should be here very soon; we watch over them. They have information. One still follows, last seen with a young mrem."

The mrem had to be Feryln . . . did that mean Rowlen had died? Pity. She had admired that mrem for his sense of duty. One man followed. That had to be Theron Kain. Only he would be mad enough to go on when others would turn back.

"As for your suggestion . . ." The dark pits seemed to grow darker. "If it meant the end of Ganth, would you be willing to accept it?"

"Yes." That she did not hesitate to respond did not surprise Castlana. She liked Jarric and found him an attractive young man, but if it kept Fuego standing, she would sacrifice him a thousand times. He would certainly understand that, she thought, what with Prymias being his sponsor.

Menthusalan's chuckle echoed through the chamber, an eerie sound that seemed to have wings. For some reason, wings struck Castlana Dumarcus as an apt symbol for that which possessed the mentor. "Oh, yes, female, you and I would do well together. . . ."

"The sacrifice would be a necessity," she snapped, disconcerted by his talk of a union of some sort. "I would even sacrifice myself, if necessary."

"I will do my best to see that such a travesty doesn't come to pass, dear Castlana." Menthusalan leaned back and retrieved the book. "We will not speak again, Castlana Dumarcus, whether win or lose. Once you leave this chamber, the choice is yours whether or not to pursue your investigation."

She considered carefully. If the officer were any judge of character—and she had always been so far—then although Castlana could not necessarily trust the possessor in all things, she could trust him when he indicated he wanted the dark wizard eliminated as much as she did.

"All right. I won't say anything . . . not unless I deem it necessary."

"I would have you no other way, dear Castlana, no other way! I will miss you, believe me, I will miss you! You are the most entertaining of your kind."

The door behind her flung itself open, this time disconcerting the majordomo. Castlana slowly backed through the doorway, eyes never straying from the shadowed figure in the chair. Another question still bothered her, though, and she finally asked, "You brought up the legend of the ruby shard to Menthusalan, then Prymias, didn't you?"

"The answer is an obvious one."

"But the risk! If Jarric doesn't keep the shard from Ganth Kazarian, we're all lost!"

Menthusalan shook his head. He motioned with one hand and the door began closing, forcing Castlana back into the hall.

"No," she heard him say as the door shut. "We may win."

We may win. . . . Castlana stood before the mentor's chambers, unwilling at first to move. She wanted to go back inside, demand to know more, but doubted that her demands would be met. Possibly she would even be met by Menthusalan's uncomprehending stare, the force that had possessed him gone.

Disgruntled, the majordomo finally turned and fled the building, as before, no one seeing her. Tonight had taught her many things, the least of which had been that even she had to beware becoming too confident in her abilities. There were always those who could teach her otherwise.

We may win. Even he who had made use of the mentor's body and held her frozen in place had not promised certain victory, only the hope that, if his mysterious plan involving Jarric and the ruby shard succeeded, it might put an end to Black Ganth. Yet that bothered her most of all . . . for how could giving the dark wizard what he so long had sought after save Delos from his madness?

Castlana did not know if she wanted to find out.

The scevan had been set loose, the beasts howling as they closed in on the pair. Feryln glanced back, saw the first of the twin-headed monsters just over the last ridge. A few more minutes, and they would be upon him and Theron Kain. Feryln wondered if he would even have the strength with which to fight them. It grew tempting just to fall to the ground and simply let the scevan tear his limp body apart. At least then he could rest.

Rest forever, you coward! Feryln could not believe that even for a moment he had considered such an act. Better to die with a weapon in his hand than give his life over so readily to those who had murdered his loved ones. Yet, if he did hope to take at least one foe with him, the mrem knew that he had to stop soon and prepare himself.

Beside him, Kain spoke, echoing his thoughts. "We're being outrun, mrem! Better to take a stand. Maybe . . . maybe if we kill the beasts quick enough, we can stall their masters."

The reaver captain slowed as he talked, turning at last to face their pursuers. He dropped his sword, both hands coming up with daggers. Kain tossed them up once, catching each at the tip of the blade. The reaver studied the approaching scevan, then, with astonishing speed, threw the two daggers as hard as he could.

A scevan fell, the hilt of one blade sticking out of its chest just below where the two necks met. A second stumbled, tried to rise, then fell on its side, still breathing but no longer a threat.

Kain pulled two more daggers from his belt. Feryln looked, saw that they were the human's last. "You may need those later."

"We'll be dead later."

The mercenary waited longer this time before throwing and at first Feryln thought that one of the daggers had gone well beyond its mark. The other had flown true, cutting down one of the remaining beasts, yet the last flew farther, seemingly toward the trees. Then, at the last moment, a Lizcanth, one of the handlers, ran into sight, whip raised high. He appeared just in time for the dagger to sink into his throat.

The reptilian warrior sank to the ground with a hiss.

Perhaps recognizing the threat Theron Kain represented, the sole remaining scevan leaped instead at the mrem, jaws open, fangs bared. Feryln wasted no time, sweeping his blade along in a great arc that the monster could not avoid. The sword cut through the nose of one head and buried itself in the muzzle of the other.

The scevan landed in a heap at Feryln's side. Before it could rise, he plunged his sword into its torso. The beast shuddered once, then stilled.

Kain stood facing the first of the pursuers, another handler. Somehow, in addition to his sword, the mercenary had managed to gather a large rock, which he suddenly flung at the unsuspecting reptile. The rock bounced off the leathery hide, but it startled the Lizcanth, which had been what Kain wanted. He charged forward, taking on the reptile before the latter could recover.

Feryln confronted a less savory foe, a toothsome ogre with a club as long as the mrem's arm. Although slower than him, the ogre swung the club with abandon, threatening to kill Feryln simply by accident, if nothing else. Try as he might, he could not get under the ogre's lengthy guard and as precious seconds passed, Feryln grew more and more separated from his companion.

Shaggy hair covered most of the ogre's porcine face, but the anxious mrem could see the savage eyes, hungry for mayhem. The ogre continued its sweeping swings, pushing Feryln back.

Feryln's back collided with a huge tree, stunning him. The ogre grinned, closing in. Swift or not, the mrem could not avoid the blow this time. Feryln tried to lunge, hoping at least to wound the towering attacker before he battered his tinier adversary to an unrecognizable pulp.

The ogre grunted. To the mrem's surprise, his savage foe suddenly dropped the club in midswing, leaving himself open to Feryln's counterattack. Yet, before Feryln could strike, the ogre teetered forward, collapsing toward him. The confused warrior leaped aside just in time as the shaggy giant fell against the tree, cracking the trunk.

"Mine you are," hissed an all too familiar figure. "No one elssse'sss are you!"

Initially blocked from Feryln's sight by the ogre, Lord Baskillus now filled the mrem's view. In one hand he held a twin-bladed ax, in the other a long sword from which the ogre's life fluids still dripped. The eyes of the warlord burned with blood lust that would clearly not abate until Feryln lay dead at his feet, the various parts of his body no doubt spread over some distance.

The mrem dodged a strike from the ax that nearly severed the trunk of a tree twice as thick as Feryln. He tried a lunge at the Lizcanth, but Baskillus defended with the sword, almost knocking his furred opponent's weapon free. The reptilian warrior forced Feryln to quickly retreat even more, Baskillus's ability to handle both weapons with independence putting the mrem at an even greater disadvantage than he had had against the ogre.

"Dead you will be! Cut into a hundred bloody piecesss you will be, cat!"

A massive floater materialized from the branches, its leathery tentacles reaching for Feryln. However, Baskillus waved it away, hissing in fury. The floater swiftly ascended, clearly not eager to earn the vicious lizard's wrath.

Using the floater's distraction, Feryln attempted an attack. He managed to slip below Baskillus's guard, but the tip of his blade only grazed the scaly hide, not even piercing it. Nonetheless, the Lizcanth backed up a step, giving the weary mrem momentary breathing space.

Far beyond, Feryln could just make out Theron Kain staving off attacks by two other reptiles. A kobold lay dead at the reaver's feet, but others from Ganth's infernal legions rapidly approached, most of them heading toward Kain. The huge mercenary did not seem to care, though. He fought with an almost detached air, possibly knowing he would die but intending that with him would come a host of foes.

Kain's steadfast attitude touched Feryln. If he, too, had to die here, then he would do his best to make certain that Baskillus joined him. It would be some vengeance for the raids the Lizcanth had commanded, some vengeance for the mrem's family and friends.

His abrupt change of heart caught the warlord by surprise. Moving with renewed fury, Feryln actually forced the much taller reptile back several paces. Some of the bloodlust faded from the eyes of Baskillus as he realized that this foe would not simply bare his throat for the Lizcanth to chop. Baskillus altered his style, acknowledging that warrior fought warrior. In some ways it seemed to Feryln that the shift actually pleased the warlord more, possibly because it would make his inevitable victory that much better to savor.

Feryln dodged the ax again, purposely adjusting his stance so that by missing, Baskillus would bury one head deep in an old tree. The miss forced the reptile to slow as he pulled his weapon free, enabling the mrem to move in and, for the first time, prick the skin.

Baskillus glanced down at the minute wound on his chest. Only a few frail drops of blood dripped out. The Lizcanth laughed, saluting Feryln with his sword. "Excellent! Well ssstruck, mrem! Firssst blood to you, but lassst blood mine will be!"

"You have taken enough blood, Baskillus! It is time you gave some in return!"

"Yoursss I will give, furred one, yoursss I will give!"

The Lizcanth thrust, almost skewering Feryln's head with the blade. The mrem ducked, then rolled away. So powerful, Baskillus needed only one good strike to finish his foe while Feryln wondered if a dozen wounds would be able to slow the reptilian warlord.

Again Baskillus forced him back, sending them far from the other combatants. Feryln still heard cries, which meant that somehow Theron Kain had managed to stay alive so far. Feryln wished that he had half the human's adaptability to battle. Despite his determination, he could see that Baskillus slowly gained advantage. The young mrem's strength had already begun to flag again. More and more he gave up ground simply to catch his breath. Meanwhile, nothing seemed to slow the Lizcanth. Feryln had pictured this fight in his head a thousand times since first hearing the reptile's name from the gargoyle king, but never in his imagination had he seen himself in such desperate straits. He prayed to his family, hoping that they would give him the strength to go on, but ever it was Baskillus who pressed the advantage.

Suddenly, a third, unexpected, force struck at Feryln. At first he thought that some other Lizcanth had come up from behind the warlord and attacked with a whip, but then Feryln realized that the whip had actually been Lord Baskillus's tail. The mrem cursed, now having to fend off three possible attacks. His own tail, while flexible, hardly compared to the long, scaly weapon of his foe. In battle it only served as yet another target, one that the blade of Baskillus had already nearly removed twice.

"Tire you do," Baskillus uttered. "Drop your

weaponsss and quick I will make it, mrem . . . a better fate than that the dark one would grant."

"I will not stop until you are dead."

The warlord laughed. "Impudent feline! Lassst blood mine will be, told you I have!"

He raised the ax high, clearly intent on bringing it directly down on the mrem's skull. However, as the ax fell, something large and hard struck the Lizcanth's huge hand, causing Baskillus to lose his grip on the weapon. The deadly ax went flying into the trees some distance away.

Baskillus hissed and turned, wary of a second attacker. Feryln, too stunned to take advantage, also looked.

Theron Kain, at least half a dozen dead foes lying near him, slumped to his knees. Blood covered much of his face and chest. One arm still clutched his sword, but the other, the one which had thrown with such accuracy the projectile, reached down to cover a gaping wound in his stomach.

Suddenly a grotesquely huge kobold, mouth open in a toothy caricature of a human smile, came up from behind and, before Feryln could shout a warning, smashed the reaver in the back of the head. Kain fell, somehow rolling onto his back. The grinning kobold ceased grinning as the human's sword, propped against Kain's body, went through the oncoming monster's stomach.

The kobold collapsed next to the mercenary, who had not lived long enough to watch his last foe strike the earth.

Baskillus hissed, Feryln's only warning as the reptile's blade came within inches of his throat. "Near the end isss for you asss well, mrem!

Sssurrender and die ssswift you will, not ssslow like your friend!"

Theron Kain's death had galvanized Feryln, though. Twice now he had been saved from the warlord by those who had sacrificed themselves. No more. Even if he died here, Feryln would not let anyone else perish at Baskillus's hand.

The ax no longer a threat, he found himself better able to compensate against the sword and tail. Now at last, Baskillus, too, showed signs of exhaustion. The long hunt had taken some toll on the Lizcanth and clearly he had not expected his smaller adversary to last so long.

Again and again, their blades clanged against one another. Their battle drew them away from where Kain had died, drew them away even from the bulk of Baskillus's party. There existed for neither anything but the other. The Lizcanth would have Feryln's head or he would have Baskillus's. Nothing else mattered.

The landscape grew more treacherous, rising behind the mrem. Although it meant that he had the higher position, Feryln also could not see where he had to step, the result being that when the warlord took a thrust at him, the mrem warrior dodged to the left, a dreadful mistake. His foot went into a small gully, stealing his balance.

Still clutching his sword, Feryln tumbled to the ground, rolling past Baskillus. The towering Lizcanth did not turn immediately, forced to catch his breath, but Feryln could not halt his descent. Only when he landed against a small, dead tree did the mrem manage to orient himself. However, by then Baskillus stood above him.

"Lassst blood mine!" he repeated.

Reacting instinctively, Feryln thrust.

The tip of his sword sank through the scaled hide a good two to three inches. Baskillus gaped, his long, toothy jaws opening wide in a silent hiss as the pain sank in. He pulled himself free of the blade, attempting to regroup. Feryln charged him, fending off the Lizcanth's own weapon. The massive reptile tried to claw the mrem in the face, but Feryln easily dodged the clumsy assault, coming in again.

Baskillus's tail wrapped around his legs, nearly throwing Feryln to the ground. The warlord brought his sword toward the mrem's throat in an awkward but still lethal stroke.

Feryln deflected the blade, then used Baskillus's own tail to propel himself toward the Lizcanth. As he collided with the warlord, Feryln used both hands to thrust upward as hard as he could.

The upper half of the blade went into Baskillus's throat.

The Lizcanth shuddered, dropping his weapon in the process. The tail went mad, tossing Feryln aside. The weary mrem landed hard on the ground, his breath knocked out of him.

Baskillus gasped once. Hands feebly clawed at the sword still embedded in his throat. The Lizcanth fell to his knees. His gaze fixed on Feryln, just rising.

"As you said, Lord Baskillus, the last blood of the battle was yours after all."

Hatred briefly burned in the reptilian warlord's eyes . . . then they dulled, the life vanishing from them.

Baskillus collapsed.

Sheer will drove Feryln on. Some distance beyond, he could see several of the warlord's minions, each of them standing stunned. None had expected Baskillus to lose; such a thing had been unthinkable.

Not wanting to be unarmed when sense returned to them, Feryln rolled the large corpse over and struggled with his sword. He would have taken Baskillus's own weapon if only he could have lifted the lengthy blade. Feryln doubted that he would escape, but the young mrem hoped that perhaps his victory would make the others leery of being the first to attack.

That did not prove to be the case. He had not even retrieved his sword when the first of the Lizcanth started for him, a savage gleam in the reptile's eyes. That sparked the rest. Feryln cursed, pulling harder, but the blade would not come free.

Tentacles wrapped around his arms, some also seeking his throat.

In his exhaustion, Feryln had forgotten the floater that Baskillus had sent away. Now the creature intended to do what its master could not.

Feryln managed to fend away the tentacles trying for his throat, but instead they moved to his waist and legs. Slowly but surely, the bizarre creature lifted the mrem into the air, no doubt intent on finishing its task where Feryln could not run. However, Feryln twisted, tearing free of some tentacles, and managed to get one hand on the hilt of his weapon. For a few moments, a peculiar tug of war took place, but then the sword slipped free of Baskillus's corpse and mrem and floater flew high into the sky.

Tangled in the multitude of tentacles, he could not strike clearly. At the same time, though, his constant twisting caused much consternation for the floater, resulting in several of the tentacles becoming wrapped around one another. Feryln took advantage, further confusing the mass of leathery appendages.

Perhaps fear or some other emotion that a floater could experience drove the macabre beast higher and higher. Feryln glanced down, saw that the warriors and their dead leader were now no more than dots on the landscape. A bit farther to one side he thought he could make out Theron Kain. Belatedly he realized that Kain still carried with him the maps and charts, but, other than Baskillus, none of the warriors probably knew that. Ignorance might very well work for Kain in the end; Baskillus's soldiers might leave the maps with the body.

On and on the floater darted, ofttimes changing direction suddenly, as if now trying to shake Feryln's weapon loose from his grip. The mrem refused to surrender it despite a lack of room to swing. He had managed to cut off a lesser tentacle with it, but no more. Now, though, a new fear struck him. If he did kill the monster, surely Feryln would then plummet to his death. Yet, if he did not kill the floater, what would happen to him?

Perhaps the floater pondered similar questions, assuming it had something like the brain of a mrem or human with which to ponder at all.

Perhaps it knew that if it tried too hard too shake him off, Feryln would somehow kill it, knowing he would be dead either way.

The stalemate continued for several minutes, the floater ever moving on at speeds which stunned the mrem. The higher mountains rose around them and briefly Feryln wondered if the creature intended to batter him against the side of one. The monster grew more and more subdued the faster they flew. It could not carry the mrem forever and so if it could not also readily kill Feryln, what was left for it? What could it hope to do?

The floater shifted direction again, briefly causing Feryln to turn. Out of the corner of his eye the warrior glimpsed a structure of some sort. He tried to twist back into position, but could not because of sudden activity by the thing that carried him. Suddenly the floater had found the need to try to snare him again. What could have stirred it to renewed action? What had Feryln seen?

A tentacle caught the wrist of his sword arm. Feryln tried to pull free and in the process he twisted around again, getting this time a steady look at the structure, now much nearer.

The mountain mrem's ears flattened and a hiss escaped him. Now he understood why the macabre creature had brought him here. Ahead lay a castle, long ruined by some titanic strike. Only one such ghostly citadel existed in the mountains as far as he knew.

The floater had brought him to Ebonyr.

Chapter 17

GANTH STIRRED FROM A DREAM. SINCE HIS revival he no longer slept, but on a rare occasion when he emptied his thoughts, images of the past overwhelmed him, giving a brief respite to the existence his cursed rivals of Fuego had unknowingly bestowed upon him. If not for their treachery, he would never have died. Ganth would have conquered Delos, put order to the world at last. At his side would have been his adoring Zyn, not lost to Ganth as she was now because with life he would have retained the face and form that had won her.

In his dream, he had momentarily lived that time again, reveling in flesh and form, not death and the grave. In that dream he had watched as his knights knelt in honor of him, his acolytes bowing their heads. The world had been his for the taking.

It still would be, even if he had to destroy everything to gain it.

A sense of unease touched the lich as he sought what had broken his reverie. Some contact . . . or rather the loss of it . . . had stirred him. Ganth opened his hand, summoned the black flame. An image appeared, the encampment. Something about the encampment.

He would need a more personal look. The one mrem still stood in Baskillus's tent; that would be the one to use. If the Lizcanth was also there, Ganth could question him, too.

Dismissing the flames, Ganth touched the scarf. By rights, his mind should have transferred immediately to the waiting shell . . . but no shell awaited. Not even a spark remained in the ruby; no hint of life.

Someone had killed the mrem.

Although he despised them, intended all to be slaughtered when his war began in earnest, Ganth still required these few. If Baskillus had dared kill the creature, then the Lizcanth had better have a very, very good reason.

Touching his throat again, he called, "Baskillus! Baskillus! Your master summons! Hear me!"

Now the lich shuddered. The same sense of emptiness he had felt when trying to locate the mrem shell in the warlord's tent touched him now.

"Impossible. . . ." The robed wizard tried again. "Baskillus! Speak with me!"

Nothing. The warlord's link, one of the strongest Ganth had formed, no longer existed.

Someone had also slain the Lizcanth lord.

The reptiles were prone to fighting for position, but all knew that Baskillus had been the dark one's chosen, that none dared defy the warlord unless they wished to defy Ganth as well.

There were few foolish enough to attempt that course of action.

Yet . . . someone had slain Baskillus.

An attack? The gargoyles? Fuego? Could . . . could the Laria be ready to betray him again? Ganth still had time remaining, but the Laria loved to trick those who made pacts with it. He had to know and know quickly. All his plans were about to come to fruition even without the shard he needed so badly.

Ganth Kazarian turned on the hapless Lizcanth guards trying to make themselves as unseen as possible near the doorways. "You! All of you! I am not to be disturbed for any reason! Do you understand?"

They quickly nodded, fearful to even speak in his presence.

Satisfied that they would obey his command to the letter, the black wizard returned to his throne. Other shells, mostly mrem, remained to him, scattered over different regions. He would find the nearest to Baskillus's last known location and discover the truth. Someone had dared strike against him and Ganth did not forgive such arrogance. He would find out the truth . . . and someone would die for it.

Feryln had underestimated the floater's intelligence. Either because of its own choice or that of its master, the monstrosity had brought him within sight of Ganth's sanctum. Feryln doubted that the lich would receive him with kindness, especially if Ganth had already discovered

Baskillus's death and the cause of it, namely the mrem.

What could he do? Feryln had to think quickly, for already the shattered castle filled most of his view. In a few more minutes, he would be on its very steps, but not in the manner in which he desired. Feryln suspected that somewhere within he would find Jarric, but the mrem wanted to enter his own way, without the lich's knowledge . . . if that were possible.

He had but one choice. Trying not to think of what it would be like to fall from so terrible a height, Feryln started to pull himself up. His movements immediately caused a reaction by the floater, which attempted to tangle his limbs again and strip the warrior of his sword. Three tentacles wrapped around the blade, tugging hard.

Feryln released his grip and while the floater tried to compensate for the sudden and contrary action, the mrem extended the claws on his now empty hand and slashed the underside of the beast.

It felt like trying to cut through thick tree bark, but determination more than anything else enabled Feryln's claws to penetrate the hard, leathery hide. The floater made no sound, but its movement grew jerky. Monster and mrem dropped several hundred feet, giving Feryln a brief, if numbing, look at much too close a cliffside. Some sort of brackish fluid dripped from the creature, splattering Feryln, but he dared not give in. Again he slashed, making certain not to cut too deep, but deep enough.

Rocking, the tentacled horror drifted to the

side, away from Ebonyr. Feryln tugged on some of the tentacles and found he could actually force the wounded beast to drift in a more suitable direction. Some of the limbs again sought his throat, but Feryln slashed one, driving the rest back. How much longer the floater would take his abuse he could not say. Feryln needed to get closer to Ebonyr's mountainside if he hoped to survive.

Below, he suddenly sighted several figures carefully wending their way through the rocky landscape. They appeared to be intent on some search, but moved too slowly to be chasing someone. Feryln frowned, wondering what they could be doing, and while he grew distracted, the floater at last chose to attack in earnest.

The intensity with which it struck amazed him. He had thought the wounds he had dealt had weakened it into submission, but now Feryln saw that the floater had played with him. Suddenly the tentacles bristled with energy, darting everywhere to snare his legs, arms, and, of course, his throat. In the midst of his struggle, Feryln also noticed that they now drew near the mountainside at much too swift a rate. He wondered if perhaps the floater had decided his unwanted passenger no longer worth the risk and intended to fling him against the rocky earth.

Snarling, Feryln bit into the nearest tentacle, severing it with sharp mrem teeth. The floater shook, some of the remaining limbs loosening their grip. Finding one hand free enough, Feryln tore at the underside of the creature again, this time attempting a killing blow.

Again, brackish fluids splattered him. The floater dipped, twisted sideways. This time the young mrem knew his adversary attempted no trick; the floater had been badly wounded and could hardly stay in the air.

Faster and faster Feryln flew toward the mountainside. He gritted his teeth, hoping that he would not shatter every bone in his body when they struck. The floater appeared not to care if it perished. Possibly it did not even know what it did any more.

Desperate, the mrem tugged on some of the rear tentacles. To his relief, he caused the floater to turn upward, slowing its descent some. Feryln prayed it would be enough.

They bounced against the rocky, slanting landscape, the floater at last losing hold of him. Feryln released his own grip, frantically trying to dig into the hard earth before he slid too far. The monster tumbled down, tentacles making only a token attempt to stop its descent. It would be dead before it hit the bottom.

Screaming with effort, Feryln buried his claws in the harsh surface. One claw snapped, another twisted, nearly breaking his finger. He slowed, but still did not stop. One hand came loose, but the mrem buried the claws in deep again. He wished that he had disposed of the boots so that he could have used his feet as well; the footwear slid hopelessly against the smooth rock.

Just a few feet from the end of a precipice, Feryln came to a halt.

The frantic mrem peered down. Past the edge, the landscape dropped several hundred feet, ending in a craggy, rock-strewn region where slides of the past had clearly deposited their efforts. Feryln hoped that nothing above him remained loose; a few falling rocks might be enough to send him plummeting into the abyss. Two large trees, their trunks battered in half, lay as mute testimony to the strength of recent avalanches.

Despite the danger, Feryln remained where he was for several minutes, trying to recoup strength. It amazed him that he could go on at all, but the ghosts of his friends and family, now including Rowlen and Theron Kain, would not let him rest. Perhaps he could still save Jarric at least . . . or die trying.

Slowly, cautiously, Feryln finally began his ascent, mostly still relying on his hands. Well above him stood Ebonyr. So far, it seemed that no one had seen him arrive or, if they had, they must have assumed he had fallen to his death, something he still might do. The path ahead promised little relief until the very top.

As Feryln climbed, he felt as if each of his claws threatened to rip out of his fingers. On his right hand he had only three good nails, which made it difficult when he had to rely on that side. The extra effort placed on his left hand soon caused those digits to throb as well. In addition, those areas where the struggling mrem could get some sort of hold invariably showered him with loose dirt and stone, sometimes nearly blinding him.

Suddenly a shadow covered the mountainside.

Feryln pressed against the rock, peering from one eye.

The great blue dragon that had attacked the gargoyles soared past, evidently intent on entry into Ebonyr.

The mrem warrior swore quietly. If the leviathan had noticed him, Feryln could do nothing but wait to die. He took a deep breath and watched the sky. The winged leviathan did not reappear. After an eternity, Feryln finally began to relax. The dragon had not seen him. The knowledge encouraged him. His hands still throbbed, but now at least he had some hope that he would indeed be successful in reaching the top.

A short while later, an overhang blocked his path. Feryln had tried to ignore it earlier, hoping he could find a handhold that would enable him to go around it, but, unfortunately, the only route appeared to demand he climb over. The mrem hissed bitterly, not at all happy to hang onto the underside even for a few moments. Nevertheless, Feryln pulled himself up, praying that his last glimpse of the world would not be upside-down.

There were some footholds, at least to start. The mrem struggled, stretching just enough so he could reach the outer edge of the lip. Trying not to look down, he pulled himself toward it, hoping to locate another foothold at the same time.

He found nothing. Suddenly Feryln hung by his claws, the nearest ground more than a thousand feet below. Urged on by anxiety if nothing else, Feryln pulled himself up. His muscles shrieked, but he dared not stop now, not until he got on top of the overhang.

When at last he had done so, the mrem nearly collapsed with his legs still dangling over the edge. A final effort enabled Feryln to safely rest without fear of rolling off. The overhang proved much larger than he had supposed, stretching into the mountainside. In fact, once Feryln had recovered enough to look, he discovered that what he had first thought a simple ledge now turned out to be the mouth of a narrow cave.

Rising slowly, the mrem staggered over to the entrance, peering inside. He saw no sign that anything inhabited it. Investigating further, Feryln discovered that the cave became wider as one entered. He stumbled inside, falling against one wall the moment he assured himself that nothing flying outside would be able to see him. Then, exhaling, the mrem slid to a sitting position and rested.

The next thing Feryln knew, the sunlight creeping into the cave had changed color, going from red to green. He leapt to his feet, regretting the act a moment later when aching muscles nearly made him collapse. Feryln carefully stretched, trying to calculate how long he had slept. Many hours, unfortunately. He hoped nothing had happened to Jarric in the meantime . . . assuming that the mage had been brought to Ebonyr in the first place.

One fortunate thing, clearly no one suspected his presence, else he would have been captured long before now. Feryln looked around, decided to see where the cave ended. Perhaps it led to some secret entrance to the citadel.

However, he soon found that cave extended only a few minutes' walk beyond where he had slept. The mrem did find some small lizards, which he forced himself to prepare as best he could. While not the most appetizing meal he had ever devoured, at least Feryln had found sustenance. His strength slowly returning, the mrem knew that he now had to return to the outside if he hoped to gain entrance to Ganth's castle.

Below, scores of Lizcanth, ogres, and others continued to search for something. Feryln again pondered their hunt, but, unable to come up with a reason for it, he gave thanks that the activity would keep so many of the lich's minions looking at the ground, not the mountainside.

Renewed, Feryln made swifter progress than during the first portion of the climb. It helped that the distance he had to cover amounted to no more than half the previous trek. The mrem's spirits rose as he sighted the top edge. A few minutes more and he would attain his first goal.

A torrent of wind rose up, nearly tearing Feryln from the rocks. He flattened against the mountain, trying to see what had nearly flung him to his death.

As he suspected, the blue dragon had flown by again.

The great leviathan soared along the mountain range, eyes trained earthward. Like the rest of Ganth's servants, it appeared to be intensely interested in something lost on the ground. Curiously, Feryln thought he read an expression of extreme impatience on the draconian giant's face. Perhaps the blue believed his power wasted on this task, what with so many other searchers nearer the landscape.

On and on the dragon soared, eventually banking. His path took him well south of Feryln's position, but the young warrior, recalling tales of the terrible creature's senses of smell and sight, still flattened himself as much as possible against the rock. So near the top, he did not want the behemoth to notice him now.

The dragon vanished behind a pair of tall peaks. Feryln exhaled, then pushed on even harder. As swift as the dragon had shown itself to be, the mrem wanted to be at the top before it made another circle.

And then at last he pulled himself over the top. Seeing no threat, the weary mrem paused long enough to catch his breath, then carefully stood. The ruined castle stood some distance away, seemingly deserted. However, Feryln soon spotted the first of the guards, a pair of surly ogres not at all pleased with their task. The mrem slipped behind some rocks, watching the savage monsters as they stalked past and belatedly realized that if he had been but a few minutes slower they would have been upon him the moment he reached the top.

Feryln flexed his claws, his only weapons now. Somewhere he hoped to gain a sword, but for now he had to prepare to defend himself as his ancestors had done. Gingerly, the mrem warrior slipped closer to Ebonyr, darting to whatever rocks or protection he could find. At any moment, he expected to find himself facing a legion of skeletons or some other horror conjured up by the lich, but Ganth's citadel remained remarkably deserted save for the few guards.

The immense castle stood like a wounded but still dangerous sentinel, overshadowing in some ways even the mountain on which it perched. This near, Feryln could see the scars in the high walls, the faded yet still intricate reliefs, mostly majestic animals, that lined the battlements like guardians. Along with such decor, shriveled plants, all that remained of a sculpted garden, hinted that once Ebonyr had been a place of beauty as well as evil.

He tried to wend his way toward the ruined part of the structure, thinking that among so much wreckage he might not be seen as he entered. Feryln still did not know whether Jarric had actually been brought to Ebonyr, but it seemed logical. Besides, he had nowhere else to turn at this point. If the mrem found that the mage had never been brought here, then Feryln's next step would be to try to put an end to the black wizard, even if it meant fighting magic with tooth and claw.

Near his goal, Feryln suddenly leaped back, seeking quickly the shelter of a wall. But a breath later, more than a dozen Lizcanth stomped past, each armed with either swords, axes, the clawed weapons, or some combination. The mrem grimaced, recalling his earlier curiosity concerning Ebonyr's so scant defenders. Apparently he had only been fortunate. If this patrol proved an example, Ganth's citadel had more than sufficient protection. Feryln would have to move with greater stealth and cunning if he even hoped to gain entrance, much less find Jarric.

The last of the reptilian guards vanished from sight. The mrem slipped back around, hoping to reach the damaged side before any others appeared. He wondered why Ganth had not completely rebuilt his citadel, then thought that perhaps the lich had left the building ruined simply to hide the fact that he had been gathering his forces all this time. Perhaps once his horde swept down over Fuego, the dark one intended to force his beaten enemies to build him an even grander sanctum.

Whatever the reason, the ancient damage afforded Feryln an opportunity he could not pass up. As the mrem came around, catching his first glimpse of the devastated side, he grew encouraged. The entire west wing of the vast edifice had been torn asunder, the crumbled stone walls still lying in heaps throughout the region. A veritable forest of rocky remains thrust up, giving Feryln a hundred different places to hide. Here and there an occasional object, part of a small watchtower or even a rusted shield, thrust up above the otherwise unidentifiable rubble.

He started forward, then quickly leaped to the side, hiding behind a bit of wall still standing. From among the rubble stepped a towering, nearly black Lizcanth, the largest and most ferocious Feryln had seen other than Baskillus. The reptile wielded a pair of axes that the dead warlord would have found a heavy burden and with them in hand the sentry marched through the ruins, peering here and there.

Feryln shifted position, ducking behind what might once have been a mosaic floor but now served well as a shield. He should have expected that someone would be guarding the area. Not for the first time the mrem wished that he had not had to abandon his sword, but such wishes would not bring the weapon back. The best he could hope would be that the Lizcanth would move on, enabling Feryln to slip past him.

It seemed the guard might do just that. Lower and lower the reptilian warrior descended, pausing here and there to look behind some of the larger fragments. Gradually he went past the level where Feryln hid, fortunately concentrating more on the opposing side. The mrem waited until some distance lay between the guard and himself, then began to climb.

The ground proved less stable than it appeared, Feryln more than once nearly losing his footing. Each time he looked behind him, but fortunately the Lizcanth never noticed. Ahead of the mrem, a dark, gaping hole shaped almost like a mouth awaited. Feryln tried not to think what such an image might portend, especially in the domain of Ganth. He had no choice but to enter.

Then a second Lizcanth appeared just over the edge. Smaller than the first, the reptile still stood taller than Feryln and came armed with a sword, too. He did not notice the mrem, instead intent on seeking something to his right, perhaps mistakenly believing his predecessor had gone that direction. Unfortunately, Feryln could go no farther without confronting the lizard. The mrem's ears flattened as he gauged the distance between himself and his foe. He would only have one opportunity; if he failed to catch the Lizcanth by surprise, the reptilian warrior would give the alarm.

Slowly the guard stepped toward the right, turning his back toward Feryln.

The mrem jumped.

Perhaps the Lizcanth heard something, for he turned toward his attacker. Feryln cursed, throwing himself on top of the sentry. The Lizcanth opened his mouth to give warning, but Feryln clamped it shut. The pair fell to the ground, the mrem struggling to remain on top.

Talons raked Feryln's legs, yet he did not cry out. He kicked the sword away, then, steeling himself, buried the claws of one hand directly into the Lizcanth's throat.

With a slight gurgle, the guard died.

Gasping, Feryln released his hold on the lizard's snout. He looked down the debris field, fearing that the other guard might have heard, but the massive Lizcanth did not reappear. The mrem made immediate use of his good luck, dragging the body out of sight just in case the other sentry chose to return unexpectedly. Feryln then retrieved the Lizcanth sword which, while slightly awkward in the design of the hilt due to differences in the reptiles' hands, would serve him well enough.

Encouraged, Feryln entered Ebonyr. As he moved through it, though, he could not help admiring its past majesty; Ganth Kazarian's castle had surely once provided a grand spectacle. Vestiges of color yet remained on the walls where once lengthy murals had been painted. Most of the images that he could make out concerned a bearded human, glorious in his power, who seemed to be the friend and savior of everyone else in the paintings. In one mural, the imposing figure even held what had to be a representation of the three suns and Delos. After some consideration, Feryln assumed the bearded human to be Ganth. It said much for the overwhelming pride of the wizard that he would have such images in his own citadel. Clearly Ganth had always envisioned himself as the only one who knew how Delos should be governed.

The shadows made it hard to see clearly in some areas even after his eyes adjusted. His foot kicked a round object that rolled a few feet, making a slight clatter. Feryln froze, waiting for some reaction, but no one came to investigate. He looked at the object, saw to his horror that he had kicked a helmet still containing the skull of its wearer. One of those who had followed Ganth during his first campaign, no doubt. Feryln wondered how many more lay dead here, decayed victims of the wizard's ambition. Not so many as would die if the lich renewed his quest, though, with or without the ruby shard.

He came across several other skeletons, mostly partial, often gnawed. Rats scurried out of sight as he passed, the only victors in this madness. Most of the long-dead the mrem ignored, although a few caused him to pause. Some mrem had perished here, he discovered, no doubt part of the force that had entered after the devastation. That so many of his people had perished here showed how much they, too, had sought the end of Ganth's terror.

Their ghosts joined the others that haunted him. For these distant brethren as well as the rest, Feryln knew that he had to go on. Someone had to stop this insanity.

A figure stirred among the rubble. Feryln quickly hid, hoping he had not yet been seen. The figure moved slowly, methodically. The mrem heard the clank of armor.

A knight with a crested helm marched by, but not one as Feryln had seen in Fuego. The armor hung lose, looked very rusted, and some pieces were missing. A crest, a blazing black inferno, spread across the breast plate. The sword the knight wielded had been chipped and brown stains covered it.

Through the broken visor, a foul, yellowish skull peered out.

Feryln held his breath, not wanting to give himself away. The horrific knight marched on almost laboriously, looking left and right. Feryln wondered if he had been one of those who had died during the destruction, then been summoned back somehow by the lich.

The knight passed beyond his hiding place. Feryln emitted a slight sigh of relief . . . which caused the macabre warrior to halt.

Slowly the skeletal knight turned, moving back toward the mrem's position. Feryln held still, sword ready. The knight paused before where he stood, then slowly started around the other side.

Unwilling to wait any longer, Feryln jumped out, swinging for the head.

The knight turned, parrying the first strike. It thrust at the feline's midsection, nearly catching Feryln off guard. The mrem fended off a second thrust, countering with one of his own that simply clanged off the breastplate. How did one stop a skeleton? Feryln looked over his monstrous foe; there had to be a weakness.

The knight slashed at him, forcing Feryln back. Part of the visor swung in front of the fleshless face and the skeleton reached up to tear it away from its empty eyes as if it still needed the blank sockets to see. A notion formed in the mrem's mind. He prayed it would work; nothing else he had thought of would do much to slow the unliving warrior.

When next the knight thrust, Feryln deflected the blade down. As he did, the mrem reached out and batted the helmet, causing it to turn. Half blind, the knight faltered, reaching for the helmet in order to right it. Moving quick, Feryln brought his blade up, aiming for the neck.

Helm and head flew from the skeleton's body, coming to land several feet to the side.

Even headless, the skeleton took a feeble swing. Somewhat daunted by its persistence, Feryln leaped back. The body stepped forward, but to his left. Carefully the mrem moved around it, noting that the body continued on. It took two steps, three, then fell to one knee, still swinging. The headless knight managed another kneeling step, then collapsed. The sword arm continued to make feeble strikes at the floor.

Shuddering, the weary warrior quickly left his macabre opponent behind, also avoiding the head . . . just in case. Feryln listened closely as he hurried through the ruins, though, waiting for some call, some sound of running feet. No one had come to check on the noise. Perhaps, he finally decided, the rest of the guards were outside or down below, engrossed in the search.

Despite his luck so far, he entered the next room with much trepidation. The deeper Feryln got into Ebonyr, the more the risk. Surely there had to be guards stationed elsewhere. As for Ganth, perhaps he had ventured outside to coordinate the mysterious hunt. With so many at work, the prize had to be of great value to him. The lich would want to make certain that his servants searched everywhere, no matter how unlikely.

If so, perhaps Feryln might be able to rescue Jarric without the lich discovering what had happened until they were both long gone from Ebonyr.

The next room proved to be a great hall, possibly where Ganth had held his audiences. Marble columns had once held up the ceiling from each of the room's six corners, but only those on the far end remained intact. Feryln marveled that the side of the room from which he had entered actually retained a ceiling at all, so cracked or broken were the nearest columns. A tattered banner with a primitive version of the black flame design Feryln had noticed over the tent of Baskillus hung near the ruined doorway, a relic of the last battle.

From what little Feryln could discern, the hall had seen little, if any, use since its devastation. Ganth, he decided, had to have his sanctum below, possibly near where the cells would be. Rowlen had taught him something of castles and their basic design and so far that knowledge had proved invaluable. Feryln gave thanks to the shade of the veteran warrior, knowing that if he managed to save the mage it would be due in great part to the older mrem.

He stepped deeper into the once magnificent hall, noting where long ago great chandeliers had hung, where once statues had stood. More than two hundred people could have stood in this chamber and still left room for a legion of guards lining each wall. At the head of the room, a massive throne, now crumbling, stood upon a dais. Here Ganth would have sat, acknowledging the loyalty of his minions.

Thinking of Ganth, Feryln gripped his sword tighter. He had so far been astonishingly fortunate, but how long could his luck continue? Somewhere nearby there had to be steps leading down to the dungeons; he had to find them and find them quick.

A raspy chuckle broke the silence.

"Most amusing. When Azur informed me that a mrem had been crawling up my mountain, I knew it could only be one in particular, a most dangerous cat who has much to answer for. . . ."

Feryln whirled. The throne no longer stood unoccupied. The same fearsome ghoul who had haunted his mind in the warlord's tent now sat there, fleshless fingers steepled in judgment.

With a cry, Feryln charged the throne . . . or tried to do so. He stopped after only a step, unable to move at all.

"Much to answer for." Ganth stroked his throat, which Feryln noted was tightly wrapped with a scarf.

The mrem's insides suddenly felt as if they tried desperately to gnaw their way out of his body. Feryln screamed and dropped his sword. The pain kept increasing, forcing him to the floor.

"While you've been a bit amusing, so carefully stalking into my domain, the time for humor is at an end." Again Ganth touched his throat and again pain, this time akin to spikes being pounded through Feryln's brain.

"Kill . . . kill me and be . . . be done with it!"

"When I am satisfied, mrem, something which will take me very, very long. Your kind has been a thorn to me, feline, and you threaten to be the worst of all! For a Lizcanth, Baskillus served well and now I must decide upon a new warlord from the fools left. I now also wonder if perhaps you might know something concerning the whereabouts of my shard . . . knowledge which I found your mage friend to be sorely lacking, much to his regret."

Feryln struggled to his feet. The pain had abated but its after effects left him drawn. "I . . . know nothing . . . about the shard you seek!"

The eyes that were flames blazed. Ganth appeared to smile grimly, although it might also have simply been the shadows playing off the fleshless skull. "I will see the truth of that, mrem." He reached up to touch his throat, which Feryln had come to realize meant for the warrior new agonies. "I could never avenge myself against the mrem who slashed my throat, but perhaps I'll take some measure of satisfaction by imagining you him."

Ganth's fingers grazed his throat . . . and once more Feryln screamed.

Chapter 18

JARRIC HEARD THE SCREAMS EVEN FROM the dungeon where Ganth had left him. He wondered what poor soul had garnered the lich's wrath and felt some guilt that it relieved him that he had not been the one chosen to suffer this time. The mage could well imagine what Ganth did now, imagine too well.

Despite Zyn's words, no one had come to release him from his bonds. As time passed, Jarric saw the many holes in her plan. Desperation had made him believe her words, but now he knew he had to think of some other plan . . . only what? What could Jarric do imprisoned as he was? Zyn had presumed too much, thinking that simply by giving him the shard Jarric could save them. He understood her fear of Ganth, suspecting that betrayal meant a worse fate for her than what he had already suffered.

There had to be something he could do with the shard so close. While it did not exactly touch him, it pressed against the cloth which in turn pressed against his side. Could he still cast some sort of spell because of that? He recalled during his lessons hearing that more experienced mages could perform spells in manners impossible for younger, newly accepted ones such as himself. Perhaps with the impetus of torture and death staring him in the eye, Jarric could do as the senior mages did. He could try.

The fire mage concentrated on the pocket which held the artifact, trying to focus through it the way he would have the ruby on his medallion. A mage had to make his mind one with the stone, link to it. Jarric imagined the shard, saw its every facet, its soft color. The shard would magnify his spell, make it stronger than any he could have performed with a normal ruby. He had used the one in his medallion to affect the stone in the dragon's throat and look how powerful that spell had become. With the artifact, Jarric might have actually been able to destroy the blue leviathan . . . and even Ganth.

Suddenly Jarric felt a warmth in his pocket, the ruby shard reacting. Encouraged, he focused his will as best he could, trying to blot out all outside sounds and sights. Even the screams faded, although that might have been because the lich had finished with his victim.

A pinkish glow emanated from his pocket. The heat within grew more intense.

Someone came to the cell door, shattering Jarric's concentration. The heat faded and the glow vanished. The fire mage looked up to see a pair of Lizcanth guards opening the door.

The pair approached Jarric quickly. One held a pair of the clawed weapons, the other a small pouch. When they neared, the one with the pouch reached in, removing a small ruby. Jarric eyed the stone with interest, but knew he could do nothing with it at the moment. Even if he managed to affect it simply by concentrating, the guards would have plenty of time to cut him down.

The reptile touched the stone to his ankles . . . and the invisible bonds released Jarric's legs. A moment later, the guard did the same for his wrists, not bothering to catch the human when he nearly fell.

"Come you will," the one with the stone grunted. He put the ruby back into the pouch, then retrieved one of the weapons from his companion.

"I need some time. My legs are numb. I might not be able to walk otherwise." As he spoke, his hand slid near the pocket. If he had but a few seconds of actual contact with the artifact—

The second guard prodded him with his weapon. "Walk you will . . . now."

Frustrated, Jarric obeyed. He still had some hope, though. If his hands remained free the entire time, he might just be able to—"

"Wait!" hissed the first guard.

To Jarric's further dismay, the reptilian warrior produced a pair of cuffs which he used to secure the mage's hands behind him. With the guards keeping an eye on his every move, Jarric did not dare attempt to touch the shard even with his mind, such a try requiring too much time and concentration. He tried not to lose hope, but unless a miracle happened, he would soon die,

Fuego perhaps soon to follow, if Ganth found the shard on his corpse.

The lich awaited him in his hall. Ganth stood staring into the darkness, possibly envisioning his future victories. Jarric blinked when he saw Zyn sitting on the dais next to the black wizard's throne. She did not look at him, pretended he did not even exist.

Forcing his gaze away, Jarric met with another surprise. Huddled in a corner, face drawn and eyes weary, lay Feryln. The fire mage had not expected to see either of his companions again and certainly had not wanted to under such dire circumstances. His hopes, already low, managed to sink further yet. He had at least thought Feryln had escaped Ganth's grasp.

"Master Jarric," Ganth rasped. "I believe you might know this mrem. I believe he might've been a traveling companion of yours."

"You know that; why pretend any uncertainty?" Jarric's outward boldness surprised even himself.

"Spirit still. I thought I'd rectified that. No matter, you won't exist long enough to annoy me." The lich turned so that he could see both mrem and human. "Unless you've something to give me?"

For just a breath, Jarric wondered whether Zyn had admitted to her master that she had given the human the artifact Ganth so much desired. Then he realized that the lich's question had been in part rhetorical. Ganth no longer believed Jarric had any notion as to where the ruby shard had ended up.

If I can at least die without him knowing the truth,

then Fuego might have some slim chance. . . . A pity he could do nothing for Feryln, though. "I've nothing."

He thought he saw Zyn tense when he replied, but Jarric dared not look in her direction much. Doing so would not only endanger the vampire, but also possibly give the lich some hint that the shard lay only yards from him.

"Nothing. . . ." The skeletal figure glided toward him, right hand outstretched. Ganth caught Jarric by the throat, squeezing just enough to make the young spellcaster gasp. "Nothing, indeed. How very true. I thought for a time that perhaps I might have a use for you, that perhaps you might serve me as Baskillus and others did, but too much your very presence reminds me of what has once more slipped through my grasp!" He released Jarric and turned back, heading for the great balcony. "Bring both."

The two Lizcanth pushed Jarric forward. From the shadows emerged several more guards, all of them reptiles. Ganth might have gathered many monsters for his horde, but he seemed to have definite preference for the Lizcanth. Two of them pulled Feryln to his feet, nearly dragging the battered mrem along.

Chill mountain winds swept over the open balcony, making Jarric shiver. He wondered if the lich intended to throw him over the edge, watching his fragile body splatter on the rocks far below. Jarric swallowed, trying to steady himself for the inevitable. At least he might keep the shard from Ganth. Perhaps the great fall would even shatter it, forever foiling the dark wizard.

At the edge of the balcony, Ganth paused. Stroking his cloth-enshrouded throat, he called out, "Azur! Azur! I command you!"

Azur. Jarric wanted to back away, but the guards held him in place. Why did Ganth now summon the fearsome giant?

Only the wind responded first, howling louder as the lich stared out at the mountains. Then, a roar echoed through the chain, a roar that grew louder. In the distance, a huge form appeared on the horizon, a form that grew larger and larger with each passing second.

The speed with which the blue dragon flew astounded Jarric again. In but a minute, perhaps two, the sinister leviathan covered a distance that would have taken a man at least two days. Azur soared high above, circling Ebonyr once before beginning to descend. Ganth stepped back, giving the behemoth ample room.

"I come, Ganth, as I always do . . . as I always must!" The hatred the dragon had for his master shone clear, but the lich stood unperturbed. "What would you have of me now? I have flown over this region a hundred times this day and still I do not find your trinket! If you have no better task for me, then at least allow me some time to return to my lair, for—"

"Cease your prattle, Azur," Ganth quietly admonished, "or I may decide you unworthy of the reward I give you."

A hint of avarice touched the dragon's expression. "Reward? Something of . . . gold, perhaps?"

"Nothing so trivial. I've decided, my scaled

friend, to present you with what you've yearned for so long . . . the life of this fire mage."

Now Jarric did struggle, although to no avail. Zyn gasped, then quickly pretended she had not. Even weary Feryln tried to tug free of his captors, albeit with the same lack of success as had Jarric.

"Indeed?" Azur's great head swung down to investigate the prize. He sniffed the air and exhaled appreciatively, sending a moist gust of wind toward Jarric and his guards. "He is mine? I may eat him?"

"You may do it here if you like." From the tone of Ganth's voice, he would have found such a spectacle quite entertaining.

Azur raised his head, snorting in disdain. "Whatever you think of me, Ganth, I prefer my meals private, not as some court fanfare. I would rather take this morsel to one of the mountains, there to savor every bite. . . ."

Jarric paled, yet somehow he stayed on his feet. Visions of the dragon gnawing off one limb after another coursed through his mind. Now he wished that the lich had thrown him over the edge of the balcony. Being dashed against the mountainside had to be a less horrible fate than this.

Ganth turned, eyes of flame looking over his mortal counterpart. "Do what what you wish. I've no further use for this one."

"At last!" Azur roared. "Finally!"

The guards threw Jarric forward, then retreated in order to ensure that they did not accidentally share his fate. Jarric struggled with his bonds, but with no hope.

The dragon reached out, scooping up his prey with one mighty paw. The mage twisted around, trying to breathe. Azur sniffed him once more, then glanced at Feryln. "And what of that one?"

"Perhaps later. I may deal with him myself."

"Then I will go feed now . . . with your permission."

Ganth nodded. Azur spread his wings wide and leaped off the balcony. Jarric and the leviathan plunged a terrifying distance before the dragon suddenly swooped up and away from Ebonyr.

The dragon's paw continued to threaten to crush the life from Jarric. He struggled upward, trying to better position himself while at the same time straining to come up with a way, some slim chance, of escaping the beast's jaws.

"You would do well to cease squirming, meal," the dragon rumbled. "You only make your last few moments tiresome."

"You don't have to eat me, you know!"

"But I want to! I have yearned to eat you since I was sent to hunt you. I have a fondness for fire mages . . . as delicacies. You taste . . . warmer."

"Then why not eat Ganth? Why suffer his commands?"

Azur laughed. "You think I would not if I could, meal? As gristly as he is, I would eat the great Ganth of the Black Flame first if not for this!"

The leviathan indicated the ruby in his throat.

Even now it glowed as none of the others had. Azur could not even bring himself to touch it.

"Tricked I was, meal! Tricked by that cursed wizard! I slept atop my hoard, sleeping many mortal years as my kind often does. I thought my lair secure, my own devices wary enough, but the foul lich slipped past everything, worked his magic even while I slumbered. By the time I discovered what had happened, the ruby had sealed itself to me and I found that I could not disobey." Draconian orbs stared hard at the human. "You have felt the ire of Ganth, meal. Would you like to feel it again?"

Jarric shook his head. If Azur had suffered anything akin to what he had, Jarric understood the dragon's fear of crossing the lich. And yet . . .

"You defy him each time you talk, though! His control can't be complete!"

"Complete enough, meal! Words mean little to Ganth, although even I must choose them with care at times. Do you think I have not strained to overcome his magic? Three times did I believe I nearly had him and three times did he punish me with pain such as even a dragon fears to sense again! Would that I could devour him, but I prefer life without agony and that is all I would gain from such an effort. Now be still! We approach!"

Ahead stood one of the tallest mountains in the region. Jarric could just barely make out a cavern mouth in the side. The fire mage sweated despite the chill air. A few more minutes and Azur would dine upon him.

Shaken as he was, Jarric knew he now could never use the shard by thought alone. If only his hands were free. After what he had been able to do against the dragon with only his small ruby, Jarric could have readily defeated the beast with the shard. Then, the mage could have returned to Ebonyr, confronting Ganth and—

A plan formed, a desperate plan but his only hope.

Azur alighted before the cavern mouth, a far wider, higher opening than it had first appeared. Jarric had expected to see bones scattered all about and refuse lying in random piles, but Azur proved to be a most fastidious dragon. Rubble that had clearly been knocked loose by the leviathan's great form lay carefully piled in a corner. The human saw a few odds and ends, but most were neatly put to the side . . . save for the high mound of jewels, gold, and treasures at the rear of the cavern.

"You admire my hoard, meal? Not so great a mound as the one in my true lair. Yet another demand by Ganth; he will not permit me to return to my true home until Fuego is no more . . . and I do not trust that he will let me go even then!"

"You can't trust him at all, can you?"

"Do you think I even try?" Azur looked up to the ceiling, bitter. "Humans are a most devious race, saying one thing but meaning a hundred others. Ganth is worse than most, a terribly treacherous creature!"

Jarric saw his opening. "And, as you said, you

would eat him at first chance if you could do so. . . ."

"I have already remarked upon that to no good end. Now ready yourself, meal! I have yearned for this for some time."

Praying silently, the mage shouted, "But what if you could devour Ganth? What if you could be free of him?"

The blue dragon stared at him, maw open. Azur clamped his mouth shut, puzzling over the morsel in his paw. "Why do you persist? Accept your lot and be eaten!"

"Would you trade anything to be able to devour Ganth, end his control over you? Please! Just answer me that!"

"Very well. A few more moments will not matter. Yes! A thousand times, yes! I would trade this hoard and even the other if only for the opportunity to nibble what scraps of skin remain upon the foul lich! Does that satisfy you, meal? May I eat you in peace now?"

Trying to look powerful, Jarric announced. "I can help you gain that opportunity!"

Azur eyed him . . . then burst out laughing. "You? You can help me overcome Ganth? Ganth of the Black Flame? How delightful to have some entertainment with my food!"

"I know where the shard is!"

Silence. The dragon ceased his thundering laugh. The eyes narrowed, studying Jarric again. Then, "Tell me. Tell me where it is."

"It won't do you any good! Only a fire mage can wield it!"

"Such as yourself? I think this an act of desperation, and you may trust my judgment, for I have seen desperation on a thousand faces."

"It's the truth!" Jarric stopped for breath, the dragon having squeezed a bit tighter. "I know where the shard is and I can use it just as he would! I have the power! You remember how I used the ruby in my medallion against you—"

"Oh, I remember that all too well! None but Ganth had hurt me so much in . . . in . . ." At last the blue leviathan gazed at him with interest. "Yes, you hurt me, too. You, of all mages!"

"With the shard I could've done much more."

"I understand that, mage! What, though, do you propose to do with it? Why should I not fear that you would use it on me, too?"

"Because Ganth is more a danger to everyone at the moment," Jarric quickly replied. "Because without you I won't even be able to reach him before he realizes I'm alive! You . . . you would have to distract Ganth for a moment so that I could come close enough to destroy him!"

"You ask for much, mage!"

"To destroy Ganth requires much, Azur, but it can be done if we work together."

The scaled behemoth snorted. "You presume so many things, mage! You presume I would risk agony on the chance that you might be able to defeat Ganth. He is powerful, even I will ever admit that."

Jarric stared briefly at the ruby. "You came close to overcoming his will . . . at least, that's what I thought you meant."

"Close, but never close enough!"

"If Ganth could at least be weakened by my

attack, do you think you might be able to overwhelm the hold he has on you?"

He had Azur where he wanted him. The blue dragon cocked his head, seriously considering the question. What might have been a faint smile formed on his draconian countenance.

"I dream of freedom always, do you understand that? Each hour I rage against his power, but each hour it holds true, yet he does not control me as he does the others, either the puppets whose forms he uses or the sycophants like the Lizcanth Baskillus. To be free . . ." Azur mused, ". . . and once free, to pick the bones of that cursed wizard!"

"We can do it together."

"And you have this shard? You know where it is?"

Jarric tried to look confident. "Release me, free my hands, and I'll show you."

Azur nodded, "If you speak the truth, we work together until the lich's end. If not, I will devour you little by little, ensuring that you stay alive as long as possible, mage!"

The dragon lowered his prey to the ground, releasing him. Jarric swallowed mountains of air, for the first time since Ebonyr feeling his lungs expand to their fullest. Azur indicated that he should turn around, which the fire mage did, trying not to think about the huge talons directly behind him. He heard and felt a long scraping sound, one that coursed through his nerves.

"You are free."

Jarric gratefully stretched his arms. With astonishing precision, Azur had cut through the bonds at the wrists, leaving not even so much as a scratch on the human's arms. He tried not to imagine what the behemoth would do to him if he failed. Jarric could trust Azur only so far. If somehow they managed to defeat Ganth, the young spellcaster would have to beware of treachery on the blue dragon's part. Azur might desire dessert after dining on the lich.

"Well, mage? Where is the shard?"

"Here," Jarric replied with false confidence. It occurred to him only now that during the flight the shard might have slipped out of his pocket. Fortunately, the moment he slipped his fingers in, he felt the crystalline artifact. It seemed to warm to his touch. Jarric clutched the shard tight, pulling it free with a flourish. "Here is the key to defeating Black Ganth!"

Azur pulled back his head, actually inhaling in fear. He had clearly not forgotten the pain which Jarric had caused him and now that same mage held an artifact that could multiply the effect, possibly even kill the dragon. "You had it on you?"

"Yes, but my hands were bound, otherwise I would've used it before."

"But surely Ganth searched you! I know him to be no fool, however much hatred I have for him."

He would not risk Zyn's secret. "Yes, he searched me."

"But did not find it. You surprise me, mage, surprise me very much!" Azur nodded. "Yes, I think that this alliance will benefit . . . but we must be wary. The slightest mistake and Ganth will make both our ends so very painful."

"I have no intention of failing."

Azur laughed. "No, you do not. Good, for neither do I." The dragon stretched his wings. "Come, then, my compatriot, my comrade. We must discuss some final details before we attack."

The fire mage nodded, wondering how he would deal with his ally should their mad plan succeed. Jarric knew at the same time that Azur must be pondering the same thing.

Of course, neither would have to worry about the other if they failed. Ganth would see to that.

He stared down at the golden pool, shadowy eyes fixed upon the sight within.

Suddenly, the color of the pool changed briefly, turning from gold to red to gold again. Had he blinked, he would have missed it.

"The shard," he whispered. "He touches the shard again. It will be soon. . . ."

The gargoyle king turned to summon his warriors.

Chapter 19

ZYN SHIVERED, UNABLE TO STOP HERSELF despite the risk her reaction presented. If Ganth noticed, he might wonder why she so regretted Jarric's terrible death . . . and the vampire doubted she would be able to lie again. Up to the point when Azur had flown off with Jarric she had thought the human would somehow turn events around, forcing the dragon to release him, then destroying Ganth.

She felt nothing for Ganth but horror. All vestiges of care had faded at last, Jarric's death the final straw. Zyn only wished that she could do something, but of all of them the vampire knew the wizard best, knew the terrible power he wielded. She also knew his few weaknesses, but could think of no method by which to capitalize on them.

To her right, the mrem snarled futilely at Ganth. The lich appeared not to notice, his attention on the mountains toward which Azur had flown. Did he imagine the dragon devouring poor Jarric? Did Ganth savor the images?

I failed Jarric, she realized. Zyn had been too cowardly, too tentative. If she had acted to free him there and then, he might have had a chance. Forever bound as he had been, the mage had not had any hope of defending his life. Now both he and the shard were Azur's, which still meant some possibility that Ganth would win the artifact in the end. Surely the dragon would do his best to curry his master's favor.

There had to bé something she could do, something. Yet, when the raven-tressed vampire looked around, she could think of nothing. Only the mrem seemed to still defy Ganth, but what could he do?

Then Zyn recalled how her one-time lover had initially perished, how he still shook now and then when the memory caught him unaware. If she acted, Ganth would certainly recognize her treachery, but the mrem just might have the chance to repeat history. Zyn could only hope.

She moved silently over to the cat and guards, who looked at her with some measure of the fear they reserved for their master. Hideous though the reptiles might be, they were nonetheless susceptible to her powers. She stared at the two nearest the mrem, commanding with her eyes that they step away. For a moment they held their places, then first one and at last the other moved back. Two others nearby also fell to her spell.

The mrem did not react at first, thinking his guards directly behind him. Zyn slipped to his side, whispering, "A mrem once tore his throat out, did you know that? Hence the scarf. It protects what remains, protects what keeps him alive. You might think about that."

He stiffened, clearly estimating the distance. Zyn pursed her lips. If he waited much longer, she could not promise that the guards would not stir.

The mrem's ears flattened. Zyn quickly flowed from his vicinity.

The feline warrior pounced. His leap took him a much greater distance than the vampire would have expected. He cleared the space between himself and Ganth with little trouble, perhaps urged on by what the wizard had already done to him.

"What—?" Ganth began, turning too slowly. Zyn's hopes rose. He had been so caught up in Jarric's death that only now he sensed something amiss.

"Murderer!" the mrem roared. He slashed with his right hand, sharp claws readily tearing away at the fabric of the scarf.

Ganth Kazarian screamed, no doubt remembering his death. The tattered fragments of the scarf fell away, revealing the gaping hole where the lich's throat had been . . . and the impossibly huge ruby, larger than an egg, glowing within.

To his credit, the mrem did not hesitate. His left hand came up, clawed at the very spot where the stone lay.

Ganth's hand moved swifter. Already recovered from his initial shock, he caught the mrem's attack, twisted the arm back so much that his adversary roared with pain. The lich reached forward, seizing the other by the throat.

Belatedly, the guards started forward again, but Ganth waved them back. His burning orbs stared into the very soul of the mrem.

"You dare? You dare?" The skeletal figure raised his attacker by the neck, causing him to choke. Ganth let the mrem fall to the floor, then, cupping his hands together, he created a ball of flame. Not yet finished, the fire mage took the ball in both hands, stretching it out, shaping it into a crude, blazing sword. The edges of the flame were tinged in black.

Zyn backed away, trying not to look conspicuous, but Ganth immediately glanced her way. "You go nowhere, my dear Zyn! As incompetent as these fools are—," He indicated the cringing Lizcanth. "—they would know better than to allow this one so much free rein . . . unless someone had convinced them otherwise!"

"But my darling Ganth—"

Flaming sword in one hand, the lich gestured toward Zyn with the other. "Come to me, my love."

Her body moved of its own volition, walking with jerking motions toward him. Zyn understood how a vampire's victim sometimes felt, knowing what waited at the end of the terrible journey. She could do nothing but stare into sockets that now held only the dark flames that had long ago burned away Ganth's soul.

When she stood within his reach, he pulled her to him, caressing her cheek with bony fingers that scratched her skin. The blade of the fire sword he placed much too near her hair, as if

Ganth were tempted to simply burn away Zyn's treachery.

"Zyn, Zyn, sweet, dear Zyn . . . how I knew your betrayal would come soon! I so repulse you now, do I? You, a creature feeding on the life forces of others? I am a monster . . . but what are you, Zyn? Did you think that the young mage would accept you, would gladly take you in his arms without fear that you would drink his blood at the same time? I gave you the greatest semblance of life you could hope for, made you my lady before my court, and this is what you choose instead?" Ganth thrust his hand in her face, pushing the vampire to the floor. "I find you pitiful."

"You've become a worse monster than me," she managed. "I should've never followed you!"

"Have no fear," he replied, hefting his creation. "Neither you nor this abominable mrem will have long to suffer your mistakes!" The ruby flared each time Ganth spoke. "It is the least I can do for you!"

Again the ruby blazed. Zyn recalled the massive stone, recalled the day when the still-living Ganth had shown it to her, made her swear that upon his death, by whatever cause, she would bury him with it upon his body. She knew that as a fire mage the ruby meant power for him and that such a huge stone surely enabled Ganth to perform miraculous spells, but little had Zyn known of his pact with the Laria. The ruby had been the key to that, a promise of life after death . . . or rather what had become a parody of life.

Yet now the ruby, for all its greatness, revealed cracks throughout. The more Ganth utilized it, and he did so even by existing, the more it cracked. The Laria had set a limit that the wizard had not noted; when the stone at last broke, Ganth Kazarian would truly die, his soul the Laria's forever. Yet, Zyn thought that perhaps the creature with whom Ganth had made the deal would also be disappointed, for surely, as she had noted before, no soul could remain in this shell. There existed only darkness, darkness as even a vampire could not comprehend.

The mrem had failed to dislodge the ruby. Now they both would perish and Ganth would go on, more determined than ever to bring Delos under his heel so that he might use its resources to extend his existence further. Perhaps the shard had been lost, the shard that would have been the ultimate replacement for his own stone, but somewhere, likely in Fuego, the lich would find another ruby like his own. In the process, though, he would sacrifice servants and enemies searching for it, even those who thought themselves his favored.

Jarric, sweet Jarric, if only you had survived! With the shard, surely he could have struck Ganth down.

"You, Zyn, I think will be first." From his tone, Zyn imagined a grim smile on the face that had once entranced her with its own magic. "It's the least I can do for one who served me so well for so very long."

As he readied the blade, from without rumbled a voice, "Hail, oh, Master! I must speak with you!"

Azur? As Ganth turned toward the newcomer, the vampire tried to flee, but neither her body nor her abilities functioned. The black wizard had once again proven his superiority by stealing her power. Zyn could not move from the floor.

Azur's great form filled the sky as he descended onto the balcony. Zyn eyed the dragon with both fear and hatred. How quickly he had disposed of Jarric of Fuego. Did he now come to request the mrem . . . and her, too?

"Finished so soon?" Ganth said, echoing her thoughts. "I had no idea you were so hungry!"

"I would eat you, too, if only you would let me!" the behemoth returned. "Do consider it. . . ."

"What is it you want, Azur?"

"I spoke with the young mage before dining upon him!" Azur chuckled. "How eloquent they become when faced with me!" He smiled revealing row upon row of jagged teeth.

"So you played with your supper," the unliving mage commented. "Of what interest is that to me?"

Azur had finally noticed that Zyn lay on the floor. It took no time at all for the dragon to recognize the facts. "Have I interrupted a quarrel between lovers?" His gaze shifted to Ganth's unconcealed ruby. "A very lively quarrel at that!"

"You requested to speak with me, Azur! Be quick about it and then be gone from here!"

"As you like! Although if you should have a spare morsel from one of these two—" The blue dragon ceased upon noticing Ganth slowly turning the flaming sword toward him. "Forgive me! I wander somewhat! As I said, I spoke with my dinner and he said some things I thought you might have some interest in hearing!"

"Of what interest would the fool's last words be to me?"

"Well, he did mention something about this shard you so desire."

Ganth took a sudden step forward. "The shard? You have it?"

Azur snorted. "I said no such thing! I said that he spoke of the shard, tried to bargain with me—" One of the blue leviathan's paws reached up and almost touched the gem embedded in the scaly throat. "—but, unlike some here, I know better who the master is!"

The lich grew impatient. "Did he tell you where it was, then? I find that hard to believe! I discovered nothing from him!"

"Yes, well . . . he had cast this spell on himself, to make him forget. . . ."

Listening, Zyn could not help but wonder why Azur did not simply tell Ganth what he knew. The dragon rambled, something he rarely did. He almost seemed to be waiting, but for what the vampire did not know. Perhaps the dragon hoped to bargain for his freedom in return for the shard, which he must have taken from Jarric as the human died. However, if Azur thought to deal with the lich, he would be sadly mistaken. After the Laria, Ganth distrusted any who sought something from him. Unless the dragon told his master what Ganth wanted to know and told him soon, Azur would face his wrath, not his gratitude.

"A spell . . . to make him forget he knew where the shard was?" Ganth cocked his head. "I would've found such a spell! What sort of drivel are you telling me, Azur? For the last time, do you know where the shard is? Tell me or suffer for your weak jest!"

The dragon hissed. "You think I would jest with you? I know how much you want the shard and so I, your loyal servant, have done my best to bring the two of you together, I assure you!" Azur suddenly glanced over the lich's head. "Why, as a matter of fact, I do believe that it is behind you even as we speak, Ganth!"

The lich opened his mouth to reply, no doubt with the intention of telling the dragon what torture he would now suffer for his intolerable manner, when someone called out from near the throne, "Ganth! Surrender now!"

Zyn could not look back, but both she and the mrem immediately recognized the one who threatened the master of Ebonyr. The vampire thought the name, but it was the mrem who spoke it out loud.

"Jarric!"

Trying to hide his fear, Jarric took the dragon's cue. "Ganth! Surrender now!"

Azur had insisted that he should immediately attack, sparing no time for offers, yet the red-haired mage refused, having still some sense of honor. He doubted that Ganth would listen, but if by some quirk of fate the lich would indeed capitulate, it would save Jarric from having to dare spells which should be beyond him. Besides, there were two others here that he wanted to save and at present they lay on the floor between the two spellcasters.

The moment Jarric spoke, the blue dragon reacted . . . but not as had been planned. Azur leaped into the air, flying off as fast as he could. Jarric gaped as the gargantuan figure dwindled from sight. The behemoth had chosen to let the mages battle it out, possibly thinking Ganth would still be weak enough to allow Azur to overcome his will should Jarric fail.

The confidence, or lack thereof, the dragon had in him did little for Jarric's resolve, but he had committed himself and nothing could be done.

"A day of treacheries," the lich rasped. The flaming sword vanished from his hand. "From two who should know better than any the cost of such folly." He turned to completely face Jarric and for the first time the latter saw the great ruby buried in Ganth's throat. "Azur will face his own punishment soon enough, but you, young mage, may save yourself further torture by handing me the shard now."

Jarric could not believe the wizard's audacity, expecting the fire mage to give up the one item he could use against his foe. He took a deep breath, tried to look more fearsome than he felt. "I won't ask again, Ganth Kazarian!"

"Neither will I." The hooded ghoul pointed.

Jarric raised the ruby shard, calling upon the strongest spell he knew, a storm of fire that should have struck Ganth full, reducing the lich to cinders. The shard warmed in his hand, a good sign at first, but then the heat increased rapidly, reaching a point where the fire mage could not stand to hold the artifact any longer.

Fingers seared, Jarric dropped the shard.

Ganth's eyes literally blazed and the hand he had pointed at his adversary completely opened, as if he sought to catch the artifact from where he stood. To Jarric's dismay, the shard ceased falling . . . then flew toward the skeletal figure. It landed gently in Ganth's palm, the lich cautiously holding it.

"As inept as you are foolish, Jarric of Fuego." Skeletal fingers snapped.

A burst of flame sent the hapless mage flying against the far wall. Jarric struck with such force he felt certain that he had broken his back. He slid to the floor, unable to rise and surprised that he even remained conscious.

Four Lizcanth scurried over, seizing Jarric and dragging him back to Ganth. The fearsome master of Ebonyr looked down at him, fleshless face mocking. "If you are Fuego's hope, then its day of doom has been long overdue. . . ."

Ganth raised the ruby shard high so that the guards could see it. The Lizcanth hissed in both fear and admiration, knowing that the lich's victory meant victory for them. Jarric watched the black wizard's moment of triumph wondering how he could have failed so miserably. Azur had been correct; he never should have offered Ganth a chance to surrender. In the space of a few seconds Jarric had lost the war for Fuego even before the hordes of Ganth had been unleashed against the city. What could his home do against the lich now that he wielded the shard?

"So long . . . so very long," Ganth whispered. He glanced down again at the fire mage. "Did you not understand that you could never keep me from the shard? That its fate and mine have been intertwined for centuries? Ever since I discovered its legends, knew of its existence, I knew that it would come to me! The wait has been longer than it should have been, perhaps longer because I made the mistake of thinking that Fuego hid my prize, but now we are together! Now at last I need not fear the Laria!"

He laughed, a sound which, with the howling wind that coursed through Ebonyr, sent chills through all, even the loyal guards.

Calming at last, Ganth showed Jarric the ruby in his throat. "You see this, fool? You see the cracks? Centuries past, power such as you could only dream of was stored within, creating a reservoir from which I've drawn. Over time, I added to that power, but although the ruby would absorb it, the transfer took its toll just as each use also did. Faults developed, faults the cursed Laria knew would occur. It promised me power beyond death, but never added that there would be a limit to the time! Now, though, I have the one object that can truly replace the stone, forever free me from the constraints of death and life!"

The ruby in Ganth's throat throbbed with each word. Jarric stared at it. Both beautiful and frightful, the great stone shone like a beacon. He could sense the power within, power so great that Jarric felt like a fool indeed for having even dared confront the one who wielded it.

"I will be whole again," the lich commented, no longer looking directly at anyone. He raised the shard close to admire it, his fiery orbs creating macabre shadows through the crystal. "Whole—"

Ganth paused, pulling the shard nearer. Jarric watched him, wondering at the sudden shift in the hooded figure's mood. The lich acted as if uncertain about something.

"No . . ." Ganth at last muttered. "A trick of the eyes, nothing else." He looked at the three prisoners. "You shall be granted one last honor before I deal with you. You shall witness as I transfer the power from the stone to the shard, witness the beginning of my true glory!"

He had the guards drag Jarric and the others to the side, then stepped to the center of the great hall. In one hand he held the shard, with the other Ganth pointed at the floor before him.

Ebonyr shook. The mountain rumbled. The Lizcanth hissed in consternation but held their ground.

"What does he do?" Feryln asked Jarric.

The mage shrugged. Ganth had centuries of arcane knowledge at his fingertips. For all Jarric knew, the lich intended to summon the Laria itself. It certainly would not have surprised him at this point.

The stone floor burst open, great tongues of stygian flame rose high in the chamber. Jarric had never seen fire so dark, so soulless. It well suited the macabre spellcaster. Ganth raised his free hand higher, the flames following suit. They rose to the ceiling, licking at the stone yet burning nothing, so completely did Ganth have them under his control. Jarric tried to peer through the ruined floor in order to see the source, but gave up. What he could see did not look like one of the lower sections of the castle, but rather a bottomless pit that should rightly not exist. The fire simply began in emptiness.

Ganth muttered words, some of which Jarric recognized, many others of which meant as much to him as they did to the guards. The lich held the shard near the flames, then brought it back again. The shard gleamed from within, but not nearly so much as the ruby in Ganth's throat.

"Traskelet!" he roared. Then, reaching to his throat, Ganth tore the cracked ruby free, holding both artifacts high now.

"How does he still live?" Feryln muttered. "I thought the stone the only reason!"

"He still maintains a hold on the stone," Jarric replied, guessing more than knowing. "I suppose that if he dropped it, then he'd die."

"Would that we could reach him. . . ."

Jarric's desire, too. Here Ganth stood at his most vulnerable and they could do nothing but watch. The lich muttered several more words, then carefully placed the shard in the hole where once the ruby had lain. The crystalline artifact flashed as he did this, then the bone and brittle skin suddenly folded in, covering the edges and dampening the glow.

"Too late," Zyn whispered. "Now it is all too late."

Jarric could only agree with her. With the shard now in place, all Ganth had to do next would be to transfer the rest of the power stored within the ruby to it. Then, he would be as before . . . or even better, for the shard carried with it more potential than any stone, no matter how great in size.

"Ny zelaz!" the lich finished. Although Ganth had no need to breathe, his form shook as if he gasped from excitement. One finger gingerly touched the enclosed shard. Ganth stepped back from the flames, which dampened, sinking into the stone floor. The fragments blown loose by the fire's emergence rolled back into place. Before the very eyes of the captives, all trace vanished, the floor again looking as undisturbed as it had for the past several centuries.

"Is there nothing we can do?" the mrem asked. "There must be! We cannot let this creature—" He cut off as a zealous guard prodded him with a weapon.

All that remained now would be the transfer. From what little Jarric knew of such things, it should take Ganth but a few scant moments. Could he devise some distraction before that happened? The exhausted mage struggled hard, but nothing came to mind. Yet, something had to be done—

The lich raised the ruby high, muttering again. Three times he held it up, then, with much expectation, he lowered it to his throat, gently touching it to the shard . . .

. . . And immediately pulled it away again.

"No!" Ganth roared. "No! Not so close! It cannot be!"

He groped for the shard, trying to tear it from his throat. Zyn and Feryln looked to Jarric for some explanation, but he had none to give. Everything appeared to have gone as the lich desired . . . why now did he struggle as if fearing for his very life? Why did he now seek to dislodge the artifact?

The shard would not come free. Still gripping the ruby, Ganth whirled on Jarric. "You! You dared to trick me!"

Flames suddenly burst all around the young mage. His guards hissed, quickly abandoning their hold. Jarric tried to smother the fire, but the magical flames resisted all efforts. Through his pain he realized that they did not actually consume him, only inflicted agony.

"Clever little apprentice! Did you think I would not notice in time? I wondered about the texture, wondered about the aura, but only when the ruby touched it did the truth come to light!" Ganth's orbs blazed stronger and as they did, so too did the flames around Jarric increase in intensity.

"You will suffer long, Jarric of Fuego, suffer until you either die from the pain . . . or tell me where the real shard lies hidden!"

Chapter 20

MASTER PRYMIAS OF THE RUBY EYE CURSED as he passed his hands over the flaming sphere. Try as he might, he could not penetrate the haze now surrounding Ebonyr, a haze that hid momentous events of some sort. Even the most ignorant apprentice could at least sense the powers coming into play there, but only he and a handful of others would have any idea as to the monumental proportions of those powers.

The shard. It has to be the shard. The shard that should not have existed had fallen into the decayed claws of Black Ganth, along with Jarric, no doubt. Prymias had no manner by which to verify this, but he could hazard a good guess, almost as good as Castlana Dumarcus—

Where was she, in fact? He had summoned her several minutes before and it was not like the woman to be late. In fact, Prymias could not think of a single incident when his majordomo had arrived late. Where could she be now?

"Eminence?"

He jolted. His aide stood by the doorway, acting as if she had been there for some time. "Castlana! How long have you been there?"

She did not answer his question, instead asking, "You wished something of me, Eminence?"

The senior mage chose to ignore her impertinence, the present matter far too pressing. "Something is happening in Ebonyr!"

"Indeed?" Castlana returned, taking the announcement with far too much calm as far as Prymias was concerned.

He eyed her. She had been very quiet of late and her investigation had ground to a halt for no good reason that he could see. Prymias wondered what had happened. He had been certain that she would confront Menthusalan, but neither gave any indication that such a meeting had ever taken place. The one time Prymias had asked her about it, Castlana had indicated that she had learned all she could and that she would inform him if any other items of interest arose.

"Do you have any conjectures?" he finally asked, "Anything of relevance to the fact that magic of great proportions is taking place over Ebonyr?"

The majordomo looked lost in thought for a time before replying. "No, Eminence, nothing to add." Castlana hesitated, something unusual for her. "But if I may make a suggestion, one based on substance . . ."

He frowned. "Do so."

"Let it follow its course and then see what happens."

Prymias blinked, wondering if he had heard her right. *Do nothing? Take no step toward prepar-*

ing for a possible magical onslaught or trying to interfere with the spellwork? The councillor tapped his fingers on his desk, studying the handsome woman standing at attention before him. He detected no spell around her, no compulsions. As far as he knew she had made the remark of her own free will, utilizing judgment that had served him well throughout the past. Now, though, Castlana wanted him to almost ignore the fact that Ebonyr had at last stirred, that Ganth of the Black Flame performed magic that might possibly presage the end of Fuego and the human race.

"Let it follow its course, eh?"

She nodded. "My opinion, Eminence."

"You've considered the consequences."

"Yes."

"Have you . . . have you spoken with Menthusalan on this subject or one related to it?"

Castlana stared straight ahead, but for the briefest of moments the edge of her lips curled ever so slightly upward. "I can promise you that I have not spoke with Menthusalan himself on any subject related to this, Eminence."

Something in the inflection of her words made him wonder, but Castlana had never lied to him . . . which did not mean she did not omit truths now and then.

Prymias glared at the haze in the fire ball. "Very well. We shall do as you suggest . . . but, Castlana?"

"Yes, Eminence?"

"If you're wrong, I won't punish you. There

won't be a need, for, if things go awry, I doubt that there'll even be a Fuego left standing."

Castlana Dumarcus nodded calmly. "Understood, Eminence."

The mage shuddered. She did understand . . . and that made him all the more wary concerning what she knew.

Feryln struggled with his captors, trying to reach Ganth. He cared little about the shard, false or real, only about Jarric, who had fallen to his knees in agony. The mrem had lost his family, seen first Rowlen, then Theron Kain die, and he could take no more.

The two Lizcanth who held him had never bothered to bind his arms, but they still kept tight rein. Feryln knew that if he tried to simply pull himself forward, he would manage but a few inches before the reptiles pulled him back. However, distracted as they were by what their master did, the warrior wondered whether another ploy, desperate at best, might work. He had to try something, for soon Ganth would tire of torturing Jarric and start killing him . . . slowly.

Even despite his pain, the human still showed courage. "I don't—" Jarric gasped. "I don't . . . know where the true shard is, but I'd never . . . tell you, anyway!"

The lich clutched the ruby tighter. "Then we have nothing more to discuss, do we?"

Jarric screamed louder.

The vampire Zyn, who had already shown herself to be Feryln's ally and someone clearly attracted to Jarric, pulled free of her own guards. "Stop this, Ganth!"

The lizards keeping watch over her moved belatedly, clearly uncertain about holding their former mistress prisoner despite her obvious betrayal. However, the vampire moved quickly, dodging their arms and throwing herself at the dark wizard.

Still keeping the magical flames burning, Ganth swept her away with his other hand. "Have no fear, dear Zyn, you will not be neglected!"

With Ganth preoccupied, Feryln acted. Instead of pulling forward, he threw his weight back. Caught by surprise, the guards tumbled back with him. The mrem immediately shifted direction, pulling free and leaping for the throat of the lich.

Feryln let loose with a war cry, a yowl that his people knew set even the Lizcanth's nerves on end.

Startled, Ganth turned and belatedly tried to defend himself with a spell, but Feryln moved swifter. Claws dug again at the undying wizard's throat, the mrem gritting his teeth as the claws tore through decayed skin and petrified bone. He had failed once; this time Feryln would strike clean. More important, he would strike not only at the throat, but, as Ganth found out too late, the hand that held the ruby as well.

As the lich reached uselessly for the claws tearing at the false shard, the mrem struck a blow against his other wrist, forcing Ganth's hand to open.

"NO!" The horrific spellcaster tried to snatch

the ruby back before it hit the floor, but Feryln pulled Ganth's arm up, ensuring that nothing would save the stone.

The ruby fell to the floor, followed closely by the shard. Yet, where the false artifact shattered abruptly into what seemed dozens of tiny round rubies, the great stone only chipped. That chip, however, released a fount of energy that caught Feryln in the eyes, blinding him.

Fleshless fingers caught the stunned mrem by neck, throwing Feryln to the hard floor. Still unable to see properly, he could not defend himself when someone kicked him hard in the head.

From beyond the bright haze of his eyes, the raspy voice of Ganth taunted him. "Insufferable mrem! Did you think I would simply collapse in a heap of bones without the ruby in my grasp? Some magic remains in me as well, fool! I am Ganth Kazarian! I am power!"

Struggling to see, Feryln made out a murky form that had to be the lich. Ganth moved a bit unsteadily, as if being separated from his precious ruby had begun to have some affect on him, but he nonetheless moved well enough to reach the stone while Feryln still struggled to stand.

Reptilian hands seized the mrem, pulling him back. As his vision cleared, Feryln saw Ganth anxiously inspecting the ruby.

"Cracks . . . more cracks . . . too many cracks . . ." the lich hissed. "The power leaks free." He clamped the ruby between decaying hands. Ganth seemed not to see anyone or anything but the gem. "But it can be sealed again . . . for a time! Fuego, though, in Fuego there will be a suitable replacement, one to last until I find the true shard! Yes . . . Fuego will fall. My armies will march the moment I've sealed the new cracks. . . . I still have more than enough time. . . ."

Ganth Kazarian turned briefly to his prisoners. "You will be the first to die once I am whole again, a matter of moments! The false shard, the damage to the ruby, all but delays! Through my hand, I can use the stone to repair itself well enough . . . then you and Fuego and, if necessary, the rest of Delos will be swept away!"

He held out the ruby and began muttering in the same arcane language the mrem had heard earlier. The stone took on a pale glow, which quickly intensified. Had Ganth been able to smile, Feryln felt certain that he would have, for almost immediately a transformation began to take place. The cracks pulled together, started to seal. One vanished completely, then another.

Feryln let his head slump. Twice now he had tried, and twice now he had failed. Everything he had done had been for nothing. *Forgive me, my family, my friends,* he begged the ghosts. *I have failed you, failed all of Delos!*

Jarric, too, felt as if he had failed Delos time and time again. He had experienced a surge of hope when Feryln had leapt at Ganth, using the dark one's fear of mrem to his advantage, but now that chance had passed unfulfilled. As for the shard, that it had proved a clever fraud both dismayed and relieved him. He could never have beaten Ganth with it, he saw, but neither could Ganth use it against Fuego. Unfortunately, the lich still had the original ruby, which, while weakened, would soon be once again whole enough for its master to wield.

Weakened? He stared at the ruby, watching another crack seal itself. Ganth might be able to hold the stone together, but just how much of its power had he lost? How much had leaked away? Enough for—

"Azur!" he shouted, not knowing whether or not the dragon remained within earshot. "Azur! This is your only hope!"

"Sssilence!" one of the Lizcanth ordered, striking him on the side of the head. Ganth, meanwhile, paid no mind, concentrating wholly on repairing his precious stone.

And then a wind that nearly tore everyone save the lich from the floor swept through Ebonyr, a wind with wings and a mocking laugh that resounded in the ruined halls and corridors.

Azur, the great blue, descended onto the balcony, draconian maw stretched into a satisfied grin. "No need to shout, little morsel! No need at all! I merely had another matter pressing!"

At last Ganth tore himself from his task, turning on the leviathan. "Azur . . . you need not have come back so soon for your punishment." He held up the stone. "But if you like, dragon, I'll be more than happy to teach you the cost of betrayal, just as these will learn when I'm done with you."

The stone blazed in the lich's bony hand, blazed . . . and had no effect whatsoever on Azur.

The scaly behemoth laughed again, then stretched

his neck so that Ganth and the others could look at it. Where the ruby had once been embedded in the dragon's throat, there existed now only a slight, red wound, barely a scratch for one such as Azur.

"Your trinket lies down at the bottom of the valley below us, oh, great Ganth! Thanks to the interference of these little mortals and the damage to your stone, I was at last able to overcome your control! I no longer serve your petty schemes, your delusions of grandeur! I am once again Azur, mightiest of the blue dragons, mightiest of all creatures!" He abruptly lowered his head, nearly putting it on a level with that of the black wizard. "And I am still hungry for the bones of a fire mage. . . ."

He reached for Ganth.

"Insolent beast!" roared the monstrous mage. Ganth thrust the stone out, muttering.

Gigantic fingers of onyx flame reached out and seized the dragon. Azur roared as the fingers singed his scales, burned through his leathery hide, yet the blue leviathan pressed on, his own great paw but a few yards from his tormentor. Azur fought through the flames, snarling, forcing Ganth in turn to back away several steps.

"You have taught me too well with your past punishments, oh, glorious Ganth," Azur rumbled. "I fear I have become much inured to pain, especially now that I know you are at last within my grasp!"

The lich, though, did not seem at all disturbed. Ganth's horrific orbs blazed hotter. "I have only begun to teach you pain, my traitorous lizard."

He muttered again and a rain of fiery imps landed upon the leviathan, tearing at his scales with hands of fire. Startled, the blue dragon roared, then twisted, trying to shake the imps free.

Jarric saw the danger first, the sweeping tail racing toward them. "Look out!"

He threw himself toward Zyn, taking her with him as he rolled away. Jarric caught a glimpse of Feryln trying to pull free from his guards, but then the dragon's tail filled the mage's view.

A Lizcanth screamed; crushed, Jarric suspected. He and Zyn continued to tumble, at last coming to rest against the dais where Ganth's throne stood. The vampire seemed disinclined to untangle herself from him, but Jarric forced himself free, looking up quickly to see if they were still in danger from the tail.

Not the tail, no, but Ganth's spell had begun to spill over, fiery imps leaping everywhere. Two had already clamped onto one of the guards, who tried to shake them off but to no avail. Unlike the dragon, who appeared to have some immunity to them, the luckless Lizcanth had already begun to burn terribly. Other imps leaped about, seeking something, someone, to attack.

Several landed near the throne.

Jarric reached for his medallion, only to recall that he no longer had it. He had nearly resigned himself to his fate when he noticed several small rubies strewn about. They were some of those that had formed the false shard, rubies with just enough magic imbued in them to fool an inexperienced spellcaster into thinking that he had found a legendary artifact.

Small as they were, though, these were still rubies. Jarric reached for the nearest, pulling his hand back just as one of the imps leaped for it. They had only basic humanoid forms with no faces, but their primitive limbs ended in jagged claws of fire that had already proved themselves quite effective once they had a hold on their victim.

This one had Jarric in mind.

Even knowing that, the battered and weary Jarric could not wait. Taking a deep breath, he threw himself at the scattered stones. Immediately the imp fell upon his back, joined quickly by another. Jarric grimaced, already feeling the magical heat, but he managed to seize three of the rubies. One had a long crack in it and another proved too small to be effective, leaving a last one that at best could be called adequate. To the fire mage, though, the stone seemed the most precious of treasures.

Flames licking at his back, Jarric muttered a spell.

The imps on top of him faded, puffs of smoke the only traces remaining. He rolled over in time to see Zyn caught by others, the vampire trying to ward them off. Again Jarric muttered and again the imps he stared at were doused.

Beyond him, the creatures continued to wreak havoc on all save their creator. To Jarric's horror, Azur had backed away, the hundreds of imps crawling over his form tearing through the scales, leaving scorched flesh wherever they touched. Ganth strode forward, clearly aware of his advantage and savoring the agony he caused the great blue. He cared not that most of his guards had either fled or been consumed by these same imps. Only Feryln remained, struggling with one Lizcanth who refused to leave in the face of disaster.

"Jarric!" Zyn seized his arm, once more revealing the astonishing strength of a vampire. "Come with me! We can flee from here while Ganth is distracted!"

"No!" Too soon it would be over unless something turned the tide. "I can't leave this as it stands! Not while Ganth wins!"

Against the lich's power, he doubted he alone could prevail, but Jarric hoped that all he needed to do would be to create a reprieve. The rest would be up to Azur.

He eyed the black wizard and cast the spell, a variation of Ganth's own darker one. Instantly a swarm of insects formed around the lich's head, but they were not the bees that Jarric had used in the village. These were instead tiny, flaming mites that darted in constantly, trying to sting the hooded figure. True, Ganth had no flesh of which to speak, but these magical pests would be able to hurt him if they managed to penetrate his defenses.

Few did. With a simple wave of his hand, Ganth dismissed many of them. However, the ones who did slip past his guard performed as Jarric had hoped. Some scurried back and forth before the lich's face, others sought entrance into his robe. The result of all of this proved to be what the young mage had intended; Ganth grew distracted, furious at the mites.

His own spell faltered, no longer fed by his will. Azur regained ground, threw off the weakened imps, then, obviously realizing how fleeting might be his advantage, reached again for his former master.

The dragon scooped up Ganth, stone and all.

"I should separate each bone from your gaunt body, oh, most glorious Ganth, but this one time I will make quick of a meal, savoring instead the fact that I will not have to hear your grating voice giving insipid and ill-advised orders ever again!"

"Release me!" snapped the lich. "Release me or you will suffer more yet, Azur!"

The dragon laughed, shaking Ganth Kazarian like a rag doll. "I shall release you, oh, precious lord, directly into my gullet!"

Still shaking the lich about, Azur raised him up high, intending to swallow the wizard whole.

Nearly pressed against the ceiling, Ganth lost his grip on the great ruby.

Jarric gaped. "No!" He pulled Zyn toward him, heading in the only direction open to them . . . that of the shattered balcony.

They had only made a few steps toward it when the lich's prized stone struck the hard floor, this time shattering into a thousand fragments. A titanic burst of power in the form of a raging black inferno rose from the fragments, centuries of stored magic unleashed at once. It spread as quick as thought, devouring whatever it touched.

So near the center, Ganth and Azur were enveloped before either understood what happened. The black flames shot up and where one second dragon and lich had been locked in combat, the next both had ceased to exist. No cries, no ashes, the magic had consumed them completely.

Jarric might have cheered, but those same sorcerous flames continued to spread unabated. He pulled Zyn outside, only realizing at the last that they had nowhere to go after that. Behind them, bleeding and weary but otherwise whole, the mrem Feryln looked beyond the edge of the broken balcony.

"Too far down . . . not enough time to climb under!"

The human doubted that he could have done as the mrem suggested, anyway, lacking as he did Feryln's incredible climbing skills. Jarric looked at Zyn. "You can get away from here, can't you?"

"I could . . . but I could not safely carry you so far and so I will stay—"

"There's no need for you to be here, too!" He looked back, watching as the inferno fed on the very stone of Ebonyr. What the mages of the past had left, Ganth's own power was destroying. He only wished that they could have watched it from a much more distant venue.

Feryln hissed, ears bending back. The mrem pointed skyward. "Look there!"

They did, Jarric at first glimpsing nothing, but then seeing tiny shapes that resembled a flock of birds. However, as they moved swiftly toward

Ebonyr, the figures grew more massive, revealing also arms and legs.

Gargoyles.

Jarric wondered whether they had come to finish the task that Ganth had begun, but as the first few dove toward them, he saw that they intended to seize the trio, not kill them there. He looked at the inferno and prayed they would hurry, for as the black flames ate away at the castle, the balcony began to creak. Its support had been all but eaten away and already the structure tilted dangerously.

One gargoyle snagged Feryln, lifting the unprotesting mrem high. Another reached for Jarric.

The balcony gave way.

Both he and Zyn slid toward the rail. The vampire seized him by the arm, crying, "I have you, Jarric!"

Perhaps so, but it did not prevent the both of them from continuing to slide toward the immense drop. Then, two huge gargoyles maneuvered in front of him, pulling the fire mage from Zyn's grasp. Another flew past them, rushing, Jarric hoped, for the vampire.

The balcony of Ganth's citadel tumbled down the mountainside, an immense rain of death for those of the lich's minions still at work far below, oblivious up to this point of the dire events taking place in Ebonyr. Jarric felt little sympathy for them, knowing what had happened to so many of Feryln's people. Instead he twisted his head around as much as possible, trying to get a last, long look at Ebonyr.

Not much survived now of the vast sanctum of the lich. One of the few remaining spires collapsed as the fire ate at its base, crashing first onto the battlements, then plunging down the side of the mountain, a second titanic avalanche descending upon the dark wizard's doomed minions. The rest of Ganth Kazarian's stone edifice burned like tinder in the black flames. The intensity of the inferno had died somewhat, but little more than ash and a few scorched wall fragments would be all that remained once the magic faded away.

Fuego, all of Delos, had been saved from Ganth's proposed reign of terror, but, as Jarric turned his gaze from the castle to the monstrous creature carrying the human so effortlessly, he wondered what fate awaited him.

Chapter 21

"YOUR EMINENCE?"

Prymias wiped his brow, which had sweated more than he could ever recall. The senior mage felt positively dehydrated, no great surprise. Maintaining a watch on the haze surrounding the spellwork at Ebonyr had been exhausting . . . even before sensing the tremendous burst of power that had erupted but minutes ago.

"It's . . . it's over . . . Castlana. It's over."

A rare look of relief crossed her features and the handsome woman asked, "Eminence, is there absolutely—"

Prymias felt a tingling. Someone sought his attention. He waved his majordomo to silence, then created a fire ball. A breath later, the face of Menthusalan formed within. Prymias took a surreptitious glance at his aide, but Castlana did not appear at all taken aback by Menthusalan's appearance. He frowned, but put aside his curiosity as the mentor spoke.

"My friend," the slim figure whispered. He,

too, wore a sheen of sweat. "My friend, did you feel that?"

"I imagine every mage in the Four Cities felt it to some degree, those of us more sensitive getting the brunt of it. It was Ebonyr, Menthusalan."

"Ebonyr. . . . What happened?"

The councillor grunted. "Specifically, we may never know. Generally, some great spell or outpouring of magic seems to have engulfed Black Ganth's citadel. A haze covered it before, but as far as I was able to discern a moment before you contacted me, nothing remains but a few fragments."

"Then . . . Ganth is no more?"

"Who can say?" Again, Prymias glanced cautiously at his majordomo. Something in her eye made him answer, "But I would guess that perhaps the shard didn't work for him as he supposed and he and all within Ebonyr were engulfed by his folly. We'll watch for a time, of course, yet I don't think much could remain."

"Over. . . ." Menthusalan looked very relieved. "Yes, I think it must be over. Do you know, my friend, after I sensed the outpouring of magic, a great weight lifted off my shoulders. I felt as if I were my own self again . . . a strange way to put it, I admit, but that is the way it was."

My own self. . . . Prymias made a mental note to ponder that choice of words, considering Castlana's mysterious attitude. In the meantime, he had other matters to consider. "We'll watch what little remains of Ebonyr, as I said, but I think both of us will sleep much better this evening. Wouldn't you agree, Menthusalan?"

"I certainly will. The first time in some days." The mentor sighed. "Goodbye, my friend."

Prymias nodded, dismissing the sphere the moment Menthusalan vanished. He looked up at Castlana Dumarcus who, as usual, waited in patience. "You agree with what I told him? That the shard must've backfired on Ganth somehow destroying him?"

"It seems the most reasonable answer, Eminence."

"I thought it would." He drummed his desk with his fingers. "Curious about that shard. I still wonder how it came to light at so perfect a time."

"Eminence?"

"Yes, Castlana?"

"What about Jarric?"

"Aah, yes. . . ." Prymias shifted his immense bulk, staring off for a moment. "A pity. I must assume that he died sacrificing himself for the effort. Yes, he and the two mrem perished as heroes. I like that. We'll give it a few more days, then began to hint of what happened. Jarric will become immortal, a champion of House Gaius and Fuego, who brought about the end of a terror that would have engulfed our fair land! What do you think of that?"

"I would rather he had lived, Eminence."

"I suppose I would, too," Prymias returned offhandedly, "but since he didn't, we'll just have to make the best of it for his sake, yes?"

The officer nodded. "As you say, eminence . . ."

"As I say." With Ganth gone, his legions would be leaderless. The council would also keep an eye on them, but Prymias suspected that only the black one's power had kept them melded together as a fighting unit. Yes, the horde would disintegrate. All in all, the councillor thought that things had worked out rather well, even in terms of Jarric. While he would miss the lad, so much more could sometimes be done with a dead hero as opposed to a live one.

Of course, he would be the first to want Jarric to come marching through the gates of the city, but naturally that would never happen. . . .

The gargoyles carried them for some distance, flying not to the mountain caverns where they had first brought Jarric, Rowlen, and Feryln, but rather farther south, nearer to the region where the mage had first found the false shard. The cave, tucked into a hillside, was not as impressive as the gargoyles' original home, but simply knowing what lurked within made the mage shiver in expectation.

Hundreds of the creatures perched in cramp quarters, clinging to every outcropping available. Jarric ignored them all, though, sighting the one dark-eyed goliath awaiting them toward the rear of the cave. Before the gargoyle king lay a tiny golden pool identical to the previous one, a pool whose light intensified as the mage neared it.

"My dear, dear friend, so good of you to come." The gargoyle extended one thick, leathery paw with claws longer and sharper than Feryln's. When Jarric made no attempt to take it, the king chuckled. "Aaah, but is that any manner in which to greet one who has only had your best interests at heart?"

Jarric stared at the black pits that were the gargoyle king's eyes, so similar and yet so different from the dark flames of Ganth. The flight had lasted long enough that he had come to some conclusions, none of which eased his troubled mind. He straightened, tried to look calm. "You created the false shard, didn't you?"

"I?" The winged giant looked aghast, so much so that his manner only served to verify Jarric's beliefs. The gargoyle king had a tendency for theatrics that would have put him in good stead with many a stage actor in Fuego. "How could you possibly think such a thing?"

"The constant timing, your decision to let us go with the shard. The direction your servants brought us after our talk. The skill it would've required to disguise the rubies as something else . . ."

Another chuckle escaped the beaked creature. "So very clever, my dear Jarric of Fuego! So very clever!"

"I think you were the scholar, too—"

"And I thought I played him so well. . . . Yes, mage, I did indeed create the false shard which you so ably placed in the hands of the lich."

Feryln snarled, but Jarric waved him to silence. "Why?"

The gargoyle's brow furrowed. "Oh, I was quite honest with you, human. Delos under the sway of Ganth Kazarian? My kind would fare no better than humans or mrem in such a world. Now, Delos under my sway . . ." He saw Jarric's hardening expression and laughed. "But that for another day! We should celebrate! The false shard did as I hoped, putting an end to the dark one in a much more spectacular, more entertaining fashion!"

"It didn't exactly do that." Jarric quickly related the events in Ebonyr, emphasizing the false shard's near failure. As he finished, the dark pits grew darker. The gargoyle king hissed.

"So . . . not quite as I planned . . . more a near miss, eh?" He suddenly brightened. "But in the end, it all did come together, did it not? The plan still succeeded!"

The fire mage could not believe the creature's carefree attitude. "By luck! Ganth nearly had us all several times!"

"Luck is a form of magic, young Jarric, and some of us wield it in great amounts. You, especially, it seems. It will be interesting to see your future."

"My future? You're letting us go?"

Here the gargoyle looked shocked. "Why, did you think I intended to do away with you, my dear Jarric? You, my good friend, my so excellent pawn? Perhaps another day, perhaps another year, but certainly not now! You and yours have this day done my kingdom a service and at only the cost of a mountain home and a few careless knaves who should have flown swifter. Of course, you will be free to go."

Feryln dared speak. "Are we not forgetting those gathered under the dark one's banner? Are we not forgetting that they might go on without either him or even Baskillus?"

The gargoyle cocked his head. "Have I been remiss, mountain mrem? Have I forgotten to mention?"

"Mention what?" the mrem hissed. He clearly trusted the gargoyle less than Jarric did.

Their monstrous host clasped both clawed hands together. "Such are allies, never trusting beneath the surface, always nursing old hates behind the mask!" Again he laughed, something which had begun to get on the fire mage's nerves. "With no Ganth, without even the illustrious Lord Baskillus, did you think this alliance of darkness would stand together?"

"What's happened?" Jarric interrupted.

"Such a fine display of chaos as I have not seen in decades! Ogres against kobolds, kobolds against vampires—your pardon, my delicate rose—and everyone against the unfortunate Lizcanth, who may not be seen in great numbers for some years to come after this. Those who wore the rubies, those like Baskillus or the mrem whose bodies the lich wore, they all perished when their master did . . . and for the latter I so grieve, of course," he quickly added, seeing Feryln's dismayed expression. "They were already dead, mrem, know that. Now, as to Ganth's minions again, left to their own devices, we see this wondrous horde fragmenting, falling upon itself . . . such a pity, such a pity. . . ." Despite the last words, the gargoyle king smiled.

"Such a pity," Jarric added. "Although it opens up so many horizons for those who watched and waited."

"Why, so it does! So it does."

The mage's eyes narrowed. "Tell me this . . . is there truly a ruby shard?"

"The legends say so," the leathery monarch remarked flatly. "And if you believe legends . . ." He would say no more, suddenly snapping his fingers. Three winged monstrosities nearly as large as the gargoyle king himself fluttered down from the cave ceiling, taking their places behind each of the trio. "I trust you will not mind being set down a short distance from the gates of your fair kingdom."

Jarric shook his head. "No . . . and thank you."

"I thank you . . . but do not assume that when next we meet, Jarric of Fuego, we will meet as allies. . . ." The beak twisted into a toothy grin. "You may find one day that you will have wished that Ganth had won instead!"

Before the fire mage could reply, the gargoyles in the rear seized the three by the waists and lifted them into the air. Jarric had one last glimpse of the winged monarch, who sat silent, dark eyes brooding. He doubted that he would ever completely understand the creature, who seemed friend and foe mixed. Should the day come when the gargoyle king did indeed become a threat to Fuego, Jarric hoped that he would not have to face him.

Despite many misgivings, the winged monarch proved true to his word, his minions dropping the three off just a short distance from the edge of Fuego's border. The forested area provided a safe place for the gargoyles to land without anyone seeing either them or their passengers. The moment they had accomplished their mission, the bat-winged creatures flew off without another word nor even a backward glance, leaving the human, the mrem, and the vampire to decide their own fates.

"Must you go to Fuego?" Zyn whispered, somehow having moved near him while he watched the gargoyles vanish. She pressed against his side. "I could take you to so many more interesting places, do so many more interesting things with you."

As enticing and, at the same time, unnerving as her offer might have been, Jarric knew that he had to return to Fuego, if only to report what had happened to Master Prymias . . . and possibly demand some explanations in return. Still, Jarric could not and did not want to forget the vampire. "I've got to go back. I want to go back. They can't deny me my place among them, not now. I deserve that much. After that—I won't try to forget you, Zyn."

She twisted around in front of him, smiling. "You won't be able to human." Zyn crushed her lips against his, then when Jarric could no longer breathe, she pulled back, adding, "You won't ever be able to forget me, as I won't ever forget you."

The vampire pulled away, vanishing into the forest in the twinkling of an eye.

Jarric sighed, knowing that he would see her again because he had to do so. When he gave his report, the young spellcaster would omit her part in the entire quest; Master Prymias would just not understand.

Turning, he faced Fuego, the city from which he had departed not that long ago. He was not the same Jarric who had left there but a few short weeks ago. Master Prymias, Castlana Dumarcus, and the others were in for several surprises. . . .

With Feryln beside him, the fire mage marched off to his destiny.

Feryln, too, marched off to his own destiny. Although some of the monsters who had slaughtered his village might still live, those responsible for their rampage had been dealt with, in some small part due to his efforts. The memories of all those who had died would never truly leave him, but now at least he had some sense of peace. Baskillus lay dead. Ganth of the Black Flame had perished almost at his own hand, his obsession his downfall.

Some day, Feryln would return to the mountains, at least for a time. Fuego, though, for all its faults, had become his home, the place he understood best now. More importantly, the mrem warrior realized that Fuego gave him the best vantage point from which to work to save Delos once and for all from the Lizcanth, the ogres, all the monsters terrorizing it—even one day, perhaps, the Laria.

A dream likely never fulfilled but one worthy of pursuing. It did not mean that Feryln could not create for himself a normal life as well, though. Rowlen had helped him become part of a new clan and there were those, such as Alevi or Pureesha, with whom Feryln might want to share some of that life. Time would see.

Time. They might have that now. The black flames that had threatened to engulf humans and mrem alike had been extinguished, its master consumed by it. Delos still had a future . . . and Feryln would be part of it.